THE WAGES OF KIN

THE CANNON FIRE PLOT
BOOK ONE

C.J. CAUGHMAN

EISCEN NORTH
EISCEN SOUTH
FREE ISLANDS
Sever
Elona
Barucca
Acko
Prospier
Onuh
Leeze
Tyver
Lassau
Ria
Swayos
ECROSIS

THE WEST

Tearing Sea
NORTHWOOD
Alterborn
CRIMSON LEAFLAND
ROSEFELL
Port Randolph
VESTER
BRICKFORD
DRYBURN
RUSTLING
Fort Pierce
RENZONIA
Copper Road
Port Spryte
PENNWAY
Fort Centre
Windless Isle
LEIGHTON
Grand Road
Conah Road
Terkhill Road
BLUEMORE
Molten Bay
Molten City
SWIFTWATER
AXELFORD
West Road
Leyfield
ROGUEWAVE
HELMBUROUGH
BEAKER
Beaker Gulf
Vexington
Whitefin Bay
Capital
Grand Harbour
Emper Delta
Sea Bridge
REDRAINN
Mount Caldera
CASTE VALLEY
AUTERA
Rainforest
RUNKOR VALLEY
RUNKOR PLATEAU
OKAMARA DESERT

THE EAST

PRAISE FOR C.J. CAUGHMAN

In *The Wages of Kin*, **C.J.** Caughman masterfully weaves an engrossing narrative set against the backdrop of a family torn apart amidst political turmoil.

— LITERARY TITAN

An easy and fun read, with lovely descriptions and great development of scenes and characters!

— PROFESSIONAL READER

Such an exciting read!

— READER/EDITOR

CONTENTS

One — 1
The Father

Two — 16
The Widow I

Three — 24
Sharkeyes I

Four — 38
The Champion I

Five — 49
The Coward Boy I

Six — 58
The Widow II

Seven — 68
The Silent One I

Eight — 73
The Aidman I

Nine — 83
The Coward Boy II

Ten — 93
Sharkeyes II

Eleven — 99
The Widow III

Twelve — 105
The Champion II

Thirteen — 118
The Aidman II

Fourteen — 125
The Silent One II

Fifteen — 130
Sharkeyes III

Sixteen — 136
The Coward Boy III

Seventeen — 149
The Pirate King I

Eighteen — 159
The Champion III

Nineteen   166
The Aidman III

Twenty   174
The Widow IV

Twenty-One   177
The Silent One III

Twenty-Two   189
Sharkeyes IV

Twenty-Three   197
The Former IV

Twenty-Four   205
The Aidman IV

Twenty-Five   215
The Silent One IV

Twenty-Six   221
The Widow V

Twenty-Seven   230
The Coward Boy V

Twenty-Eight   241
Sharkeyes V

Twenty-Nine   249
The Former V

Thirty   257
The Aidman V

Thirty-One   265
The Silent One V

Thirty-Two   275
The Widow VI

Thirty-Three   290
Sharkeyes VI

Thirty-Four   301
The Coward Boy VI

Thirty-Five   310
The Pirate King II

Thirty-Six   314
The Coward Boy VII

Thirty-Seven   328
The Former VI

Thirty-Eight   332
The Aidman VI

Thirty-Nine   335
The Former VII

Forty   337
The Aidman VII

Forty-One   340
The Former VIII

Forty-Two   351
The Silent One VI

Forty-Three   361
Red Sand I

Forty-Four   370
Sharkeyes VII

Forty-Five   384
The Widow VIII

About the Author   395
To the reader   397

Cover Illustration by Youness Elh

Map by Bmr Williams

Formatting by Brady Moller

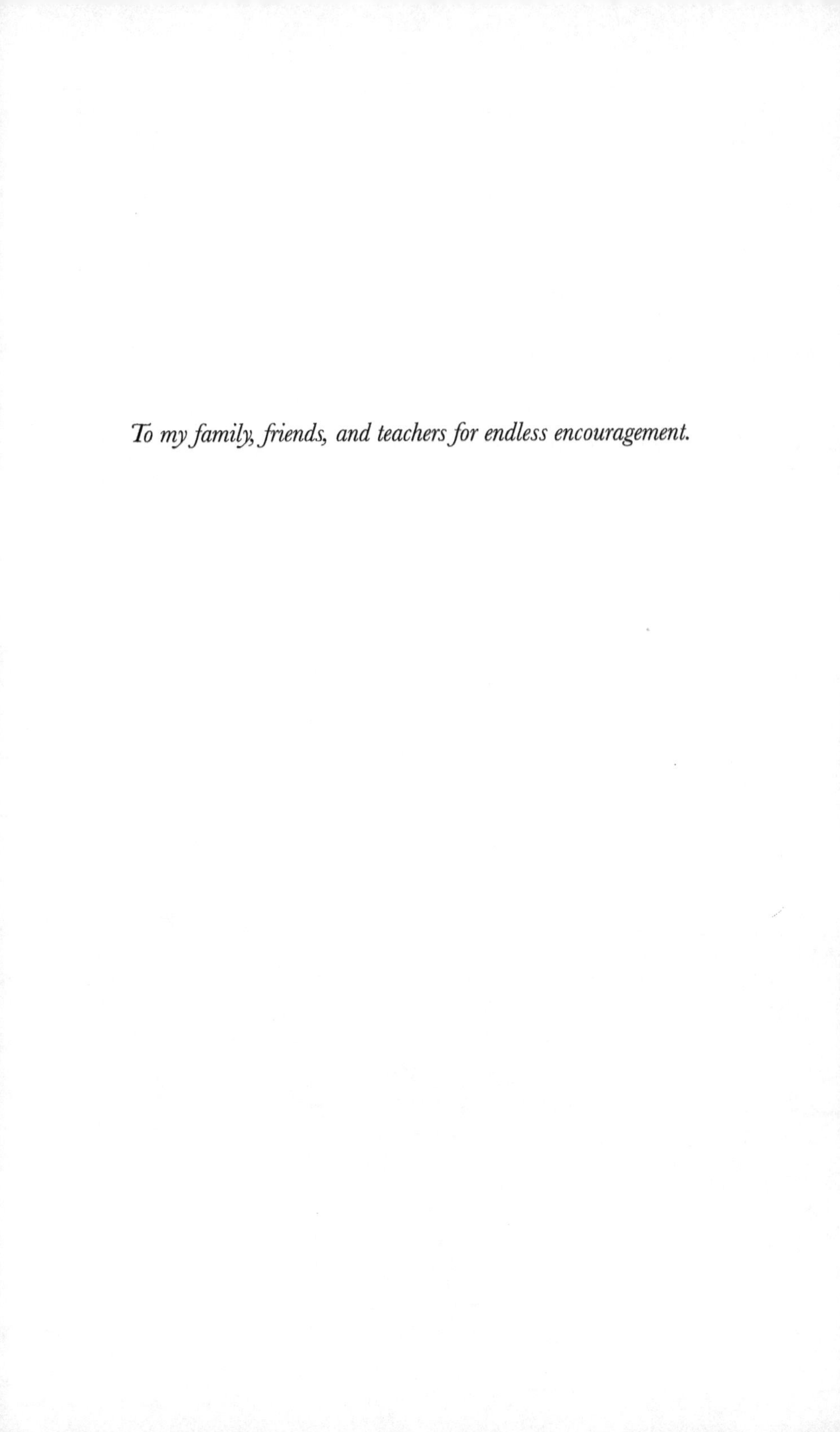

To my family, friends, and teachers for endless encouragement.

ONE

THE FATHER

Mathias Battier stared upon the bleak horizon line beyond the rocky waters of the Alexandric Sea. The waves soared towards him, and droplets of salt water spattered him in the face as his boots sunk into the sand. His captain's coat slapped against the back of his thighs, buttons fought the high winds, ensuring his pristine attire enveloped him.

I suppose this weather is appropriate for what is to come.

Lost in contemplation for the mission ahead, a few flashes of lightning burst behind violet clouds to the northeast. Thunder sounded, sending a steady reverberation that shook the beach. It was then two small arms wrapped around his knee. He saw a familiar, dark-haired boy staring at him with big eyes. He smiled and hoisted his one-year-old boy, Xavier, into his arms.

"Don't be afraid, son. Don't be afraid," he said, stroking his head.

Xavier pulled away to look at him, yet the fear remained in his eyes as the thunder roared. Mathias took his tricorn hat tucked under his arm and placed it on his son's head, which it swallowed, and muffled laughter emerged from beneath it.

They proceeded to play a short game of peek-a-boo until Xavier's fear of the distant storm subsided.

The coos of an infant shifted his attention behind him. His wife, still as beautiful as when they first met, approached without shoes, wearing a white gown that contrasted her deeply tanned skin. No one in their province of Roguewave shared her complexion. This place was not her home. Adelaide was a former member of the Trezbe Clan in the southern continent. Their marriage had brought on a litany of consequences and unwanted attention, especially to a man of his station. They both did their best not to place their energy or concern into the social ramifications.

"We've come to see off Grand Captain Mathias Battier," she said with a sarcastic smirk and broken Worldly.

He embraced her and his second son, Caldwell, in this beach tradition they established when she joined him in his homeland. Before every mission, they would spend time on this beach enjoying one another's company before a long voyage.

"You come bearing gifts, I see," he said.

She placed Caldwell in his other arm, and had the blessing of holding both boys. Both of them shared a similar skin tone to their mother, so the uninitiated would question his fatherhood to them in these parts.

"You two going to take it easy on your mother while I'm gone?" he asked the two of them, and they responded with blank stares.

"They better, or you're taking them with you on the next mission."

He smiled. "That's fair enough."

Xavier dropped all his weight backward out of his father's embrace, dangling his head laterally, and Mathias lifted his knee for leverage to return him upright. "Easy, son."

"What's more difficult, wrangling a pair of babies or a large crew of sailors?" Adelaide asked.

"Well, in my experience, many sailors behave like babies. At least these two can't talk back yet."

She stepped closer to him and shared in the embrace. "You don't give yourself enough credit. I've seen the way those men look to you. They'd rather plunge themselves into the sea before they disappointed you."

He smiled and took a moment to reflect on her words. "Thank you, my love."

He kissed her, holding his lips to hers until Xavier asserted himself into the display of affection by lightly slapping the side of his face for attention. They chuckled at one another as they pulled away.

"Here, I'll take this one," she said, grasping Xavier by the waist, still wearing Mathias' hat. His excitement of being held by his mother was palpable, and he bounced in her arms, laughing over and over.

"Mother's boy."

Adelaide smacked Mathias on the arm. "There's nothing wrong with that."

He cocked his head. "I suppose you're right," he said with a wink. "I'm surprised he can't fit into that hat yet with the size of his head."

"How dare you speak about my son like that? He'll grow into it."

"Well, sounds like you agree with me either way."

She shook her head but couldn't fight the smile as she removed the hat and examined him. "Let's just say that I don't disagree." She spun the hat in her hand and held the front of it to set it back on Mathias' head. "For now, it fits his father. Noble Captain Mathias Battier, who keeps us safe from the scum of the sea."

He went quiet and stared at his two boys as the smile fell from his face. He could be convinced that hours went by in that moment of being lost in thought.

"What is it, my love?" she asked.

He snapped to attention but was too proud to utter any level of concern.

"It's the mission, isn't it? This one's different."

His lack of a response was enough to give her the answer she sought. He pulled Caldwell in closer and kissed him on the forehead, who had fallen completely asleep. All military operations were classified. However, that didn't stop leaks and rumors from spreading like wildfire. Especially details of naval missions in coastal colonies.

"So, it's true? You're going after Marstellar Lockett?"

His gaze met hers, and he replied with the subtlest nod. Captain Marstellar Lockett was the active leader of the Pirate Rebellion against the country, and his reputation was legendary, to say the least. His command over the sea and his ships rivaled the best the Unified Provinces could offer.

"Why are they just sending you?" Adelaide asked. Then, the wind shifted cold as it rushed by them. Baby Caldwell tremored from the chill. Mathias tucked him in tighter to provide warmth. "Why not a fleet to assure victory?"

It was a valid question he didn't entirely know the answer to, but he had an idea. "Perhaps I'm the most expendable Grand Captain now." He didn't want to utter those words but had to offer her something. He respected her too much to give her an unsatisfactory answer. Plus, she would sniff it out if it wasn't genuine.

She nodded, taking in his response. The government and most everyone that didn't know the Battiers on a personal level turned their nose up at their marriage to one another. Since then, Mathias' military advancement had gone stagnant, and their reputation had been tarnished. The fact that he brought a foreign woman from one of the warring clans to their homeland didn't sit right with the elites, including his father, Earl of Pennex, Miles Battier. However, not a day passed where he regretted his decision.

She touched his cheek and rubbed her thumb along his

auburn beard. "If that's the case, when Captain Lockett's ship comes into range, send him to the bottom of the sea."

Mathias pursued a treasure galleon that flew an emerald flag with seventeen gold stars of varying sizes representing each of the Unified Provinces, the most powerful empire the world had ever known. The empire he once proudly claimed to belong. The ship was stocked with supplies and resources from the southern clans residing in Autera. If he had been in command of his Grand Ship, the *Abyss*, this fight would be over before it began.

However, on this occasion, he couldn't captain such a vessel. On this day, he was captaining a hunter called the *Tipper*. The men sailing under him were not loyal countrymen tasked with obeying his every command in service of the Unified Provinces and the Assembly. No, in secret, he was captain of the pirates. On this day, Mathias Battier would reveal himself to the "enemy" as betraying his country.

To his left, another ship, a frigate called the *Reaper*, was captained by the notorious pirate leader, Marstellar Lockett, leader of the active and Third Pirate Rebellion. At a distance, Mathias looked upon the criminal with whom he had begun to form a unique kinship and bond and nodded. Lockett, in his long black coat, returned a smile before he started shouting commands at his crew.

Mathias followed suit. "Raise the black!" he commanded.

One of the pirates pulled the rope along the mast to raise their proud black flag, which whipped in the wind as it ascended. Both pirate vessels shared the same flag of Captain Lockett's making. It was an X with four symbols in all the spaces: a flintlock on the left, a scythe on the right, a fist at the top, and a compass at the bottom. Mathias was unsure of the symbolism behind the pirate captain's flag design, but more pressing matters filled his mind.

"Continue up the starboard side! Prepare to take fire from the stern chasers!" Mathias commanded the pirates.

Prior to setting sail, Captain Lockett had ordered his men to obey Mathias's every command, and whatever he desired of them was law. The pirates crewed their stations as efficiently as the sailors in the Unified Provincial Navy, if not better. They obeyed every order that Mathias barked from the quarterdeck with haste.

The ship he was pursuing was called the *Whirlwind*. It was a most trusted galleon that had seen a colossal amount of goods carried in and out of its hull over a long career. The *Tipper* and the *Reaper* angled away from each other to approach the galleon from both sides.

Mathias' warning proved correct. The *Whirlwind's* back stern chasers fired upon them. Their pursuit vessels made themselves wider targets as they began their break, revealing their broadsides. Luckily for the pirate captains, only two guns made up the *Whirlwind* chasers.

The first shot whistled between the foremast and mainmast. "Steady!" he commanded. "Mr. Blondie! Ready the guns on the port side!"

The gun master, Jimmy Blondie, wasted no time. "You heard 'em! Load the guns! Prepare to engage!"

The *Whirlwind* kept onward to stay ahead of the pirate vessels. Mathias and Lockett's prediction of the ship and its captain's reaction proved true.

"Are they going to surrender, Captain?" the quartermaster, John Rob, asked.

Mr. Rob was one of Marstellar Lockett's most trusted men. He was gigantic in stature with massive forearms, big enough to wield his broadaxe as part of the vanguard efficiently.

"Doubtful," Mathias told him. "We are right on him. He

would've surrendered by now. The importance of their cargo is paramount to the Assembly; they won't go down without a fight." Mathias took a break from his spyglass to look back at John Rob. "Is your vanguard ready?"

His voice was the rumble of thunder signaling a storm. "Captain Battier, I don't know how you soft-handed ship boys do it on a provincial ship, but on a pirate vessel, the vanguard is always ready."

Mathias left it at that and returned his focus to the *Whirlwind*. A follow-up stern shot flew through the air and impacted the railing on the forecastle at the front of the ship.

"Steady!" Mathias said once more. "Open the gun ports!"

"Open the gun ports!" Mr. Blondie repeated to the gun crew.

The flaps that concealed the cannons flipped open, and the barrels rolled out, sticking out of the ship like quills on a colossal hedgehog.

The *Reaper's* starboard cannons opened as well, mirroring the *Tipper*. Both ships were nearly in position to put the *Whirlwind* into an angled crossfire at its stern.

"He's going to have to make a decision," Mathias said to himself.

"Beg your pardon, Captain?" John Rob asked.

"Moments away from an onslaught on both sides, their ship has kept full sail ahead."

"Do you know the *Whirlwind* captain?"

Mathias knew him well. They had studied in the prestigious military academy in the Capital Province, Helmburough. "Yes. Captain Lawrence. Smart man but overthinks and is prone to indecisiveness. Today's not the day for that, John Rob."

His quartermaster gave an amused nod.

"At the last minute, he will most likely choose a side to drop anchor and exchange broadside cannons with one of us. He'll have to take a chance to repel boarders and fight hand to hand with whatever ship remains on the opposite side."

"He's running out of time to make that maneuver, Captain," John Rob pointed out.

"Right, you are." Mathias closed his spyglass, placed his hand on the railing, and yelled, "Fire!"

The twenty-three cannons exploded in a rolling pattern, with the front cannons first, following down the line to the back. This was done so there would not be too much stress on the ship and knock them out of alignment. It was a protocol Mathias had failed to go over with the gun crew before setting sail, and the thought didn't occur to him until the sound of those deafening explosions sang beneath him. The fact that everything went right told him that gun master Blondie was good at his job, for every shot found its mark on the stern while the *Reaper's* volley destroyed the rudder.

Captain Lawrence's primary means of rotating the ship was no longer accessible.

"Maintain fire!" Mathias commanded.

The shots ripped through the back of the *Whirlwind.* The concentrated attack on the stern was proving useful. The maneuver would be ineffective with only one ship, but two were perfect.

The gallery was also destroyed, and Captain Lawrence no longer had his own quarters to enjoy as it fell into the blue waters of the Aster Sea. The poop deck fell from its perch and dangled off the back of the ship with faltering support. Some of the *Whirlwind's* crew attempted to escape the fall but failed, accompanying the splintered wood that fell into the water.

It's too late for him to do anything now.

"Level us out! Prepare to board!" Mathias said. "Mr. Blondie, don't stop firing until we straighten out. We don't want to risk hitting the *Reaper!*"

"Aye, Captain!"

The *Tipper* straightened, and the last round of cannon fire ceased. Both pirate vessels approached on either side of the *Whirlwind*.

The pirates began to mobilize to the ship's port side with pistols and grappling hooks.

"John Rob, get me a grappling hook as well," Mathias commanded.

The quartermaster was already descending the steps to join the vanguard when he turned to face Mathias. "You're going over with the first wave?"

"Aye, I can't go on hearing all about your fighting prowess and not see for myself," Mathias explained.

John Rob smiled. "Aye, very well, Captain."

Moments later, John Rob returned with the captain's grappling hook. Mathias was outfitted with his sword strapped to his back, which was uncommon for sailors and pirates, but he found he had more mobility when that was the case. Two pistols were tucked into his belt, and a tre-axe, gifted to him by his father-in-law, leader of the Trezbe clan, was strapped to his thigh.

"I want ten men providing cover fire!" Mathias told John Rob.

"Ten? Is that excessive, Captain?" he replied respectfully.

"Not if it keeps us from getting shot. Put them in pairs behind cover. Your best marksmen."

"Aye, Captain."

The *Whirlwind* cast a shadow over the crew as they crept beside it. It was quiet from the opposition. That didn't put Mathias at ease.

"Put your backs into these throws, lads!" Mathias told them, for it was at least another ten feet up from the side of the *Tipper*. "Pop smoke over the top! Grenades through the gun ports!" were his final instructions before yelling, "Now!"

And his crew followed directions exactly as he instructed. Around thirty men began boarding the *Whirlwind*. They tossed their hooks over and found purchase on the galleon's railing.

Greencoat soldiers took firing positions to shoot at the oncoming vanguard, but Mathias' marksmen were ready. The first several enemy soldiers didn't have time to set their sights before a hail of gunfire found them.

John Rob was the first one to commence the climb. Mathias threw his hook, and it clanked on the deck from above. He gave it a few tugs, and it proved stable enough to ascend. Once his vanguard passed the gunports, they threw the grenades into the interior of the *Whirlwind.* Multiple explosions shook the sides of the ship, and smoke filtered outward. If men were on the gun deck, they would most likely be in pieces now.

They all reached the top and took their positions to go over. Mathias was the first one to commit, in an attempt to further earn the pirates' respect. That way, they would consider saving his life should the occasion arise, and he could return to his wife and sons.

His boots hit the deck, and he met many provincial sailors still mobilizing and preparing for battle. Had it not been for their disorganized and claustrophobic state, this fight might have been an uphill battle, nearly impossible to overcome due to the size of the crew. The pirate vanguard followed behind him, and on the opposite side of the galleon, emerging from the other side, was Captain Lockett, eager and ready for a scrap.

How could Captain Lawrence have failed this miserably? Mathias asked himself.

Instead of an organized resistance, scattered troops engaged the pirates. Mathias knew victory was pending.

Mathias fired his pistol at the first soldier, charging at him with a sword waving over his head. The shot found its mark, center mass, and the overzealous greencoat dropped at Mathias' feet.

He had no time to reflect on the ramifications of his actions. For he just took the life of a fellow countryman in the act of his revolution. He tossed the gun, unsheathed his sword and tre-axe, and pushed any attempt at contemplation away.

The axe worked efficiently at trapping swords and bayoneted rifles for counters. And for the first dozen soldiers Mathias came across, he used a version of the same move to kill whoever was unlucky enough to cross swords with him. *Trap. Control. Counter. Attack.*

John Rob proved himself to be the kind of warrior any crew would want at their side. Men ran at him, and he repelled them with his massive frame and broad axe. Soldiers went airborne as they bounced off his body. He even grappled some greencoats and threw them over the side of the ship.

Captain Lockett had a different style. He wasn't a large man with brooding prowess, but his effectiveness when cutting men down was equivalent to his quartermaster. He moved like a serpent through the enemy soldiers. Lockett's twin swords found the enemy before they could even get their guards up. The more blood caking his visage, the more the efficiency of his melee skills increased.

Mathias stopped amid battle to evaluate the carnage, and the guilt grew. The pirates overwhelmed the soldiers. His treason was definitive and undeniable.

The clattering of steel on deck sounded all around him, snapping him out of his guilt-ridden trance.

The crew of the *Whirlwind* had surrendered. All the greencoats dropped to their knees and raised their hands.

"Hold!" Captain Lockett ordered. The fighting ceased. "Confine them to the gun deck!"

The provincial sailors were put in irons and placed in rows on the deck below. The pirates kept them at gunpoint from the main deck above. The *Whirlwind* crew sustained heavy casualties, while the pirates on both ships suffered only a handful. Mathias cleaned his blade and axe and heard the whispers from below.

"That's Captain Battier," he heard a soldier say.

However, the word "traitor" stung his ears and soul the most.

"How does it feel?" Captain Lockett asked at his back.

He turned. "Beg your pardon?"

Lockett placed his hand on Mathias' shoulder. "How does it feel to be a pirate?"

"I'm not sold that I am," Mathias replied.

Lockett cocked his head to the side. "Well, you conspired with pirates to capture a Unified Provincial vessel. And if I'm not mistaken, you were just wiping greencoat blood from that fancy axe of yours. So, you might not be sold, Captain Battier, but I am."

At this point, Mathias' denial remained, but he was coming to the realization that Captain Lockett was correct.

"Captain?" John Rob said, approaching from the deck below.

And both Lockett and Mathias replied, "Yes?"

John Rob stammered for a moment, navigating who to address, but went with the safe bet and eyed Lockett. Mathias was satisfied that it took the quartermaster a moment to consider it.

"Go on, John Rob," Captain Lockett prodded.

"There's no sign of Captain Lawrence anywhere."

Mathias and Lockett exchanged a look.

"Perhaps he was in the captain's quarters when our broadsides tore the stern to pieces?" John Rob continued.

"No, he wouldn't be in there during combat. He would be on the deck giving the crew commands," Mathias said.

Lockett agreed. "Get one of the *Whirlwind* crew up here."

"Yes, Captain."

"Has the hold been searched yet?" Mathias asked.

"No, Captain."

"Take at least ten men to search it immediately," Mathias commanded.

John Rob looked to Lockett for assurance on obeying Mathias.

"You heard the captain," Lockett replied as John Rob left to accomplish his captains' tasks.

Moments later, John Rob returned with a sweaty, bloody, and bruised greencoat, looking as if the battle had taken everything out of him.

"Where is Captain Lawrence?" Lockett asked. The soldier was exhausted and still catching his breath. "Now's not the time for silence, son."

"We, the crew, found his command hazardous," the soldier said.

"Aye, but that doesn't answer my question, does it?" Lockett replied.

The soldier adjusted the tight irons around his wrist, panting. "We mutinied during your pursuit. We bound his hands, strapped chain shot around both of his ankles and threw him overboard."

Mathias shook his head. *That would explain their weak and unorganized defense.*

"Perhaps if you would've put that chain shot to better use and spared your captain in the heat of battle, your ship wouldn't have been captured in mere minutes." Lockett nodded to his crew. "Put him back with the others."

John Rob dragged the sailor away with little resistance.

"What a mess," Lockett muttered to Mathias.

"Truly. Everything went our way on this day."

Lockett laughed. "Don't get used to that feeling in a pirate's life, my friend."

Pirate's life? Friend? Mathias left those alone.

One of the pirate crew members searching the hold returned to the main deck in a rush. "Captain! Captain! Come with haste!"

The pirate rushed down the stairs, and Mathias and Lockett followed. They hurried through the dark bowels of the ship to the cargo hold door. The pirate opened the door for the two captains and revealed what the *Whirlwind* carried. The galleon was known for its space and carrying capacity. However, having an idea of what resided in the hull and seeing it with their own eyes was something else entirely.

Around two hundred people, mostly men, were seated and chained to the floor.

"Slaves?" Lockett asked with wide eyes. It seemed a rarity that the pirate captain was troubled, but there was no mistaking that he was indeed horrified. "You said we were recapturing stolen supplies from the southern clans. Not the southern clans themselves."

Mathias said nothing. Classified rumors of the *Whirlwind's* cargo led him to this outcome in the first place.

"Very well." Lockett moved on quickly. "Slavery is illegal, is it not? What would they be doing with this lot?"

Mathias didn't answer. His attention was on the clan people who appeared worse for wear. They were tired, malnourished, and likely hadn't seen the light in days. "Remove those chains," Mathias commanded.

The pirates looked to Captain Lockett again, awaiting his orders instead of Mathias'.

"*Now!*" Lockett roared at them.

"Escort them to the main deck and get them food and water immediately," Mathias added.

Lockett offered him a torch that stuck out from the beams. "I imagine your Aelic has improved over the years."

Aelic was the common language spoken by all seven warring clans in Autera. Mathias spoke the language well, as his wife was a former woman of the Trezbe Clan.

He approached one of the imprisoned clan folks not yet freed from his irons, a man with copper skin and a hardened face. He was a warrior, Mathias could tell, but then again, they all were. "What clan are you a part of?"

"Cindah."

"What's your name?"

The Cindah man's sensitive eyes fluttered from the torch flame. "Embero," he said.

"How did they capture you?"

"They arrived at night and held their guns to our women and children's heads. We were outnumbered and forced onto their ship," Embero said, turning his gaze away, indicating he was still grieving all that had transpired.

"Don't despair, Embero. I'm going to return you and your people home."

Lockett chimed in with friendly sarcasm, telling Mathias, "Don't let them forget that it was the bloody pirates that saved them, Captain Battier."

TWO

THE WIDOW I

They began at dawn to prepare for the funeral. The afternoon sun had finally broken through, with a subtle heat attempting to counter the foul chill of the day. Adelaide Battier led her five children every step of the way. Many times, she had made this walk from the eastern chapel to the Garden of Graves. However, this time, it was a solemn stroll of denial.

The guards said they found her husband Mathias in his study, his head planted atop mountains of scrolls and ancient text, hard at work translating documents for the Seabird Library. Coroner Ullman informed her it was most likely that his heart gave out, but he still wasn't certain. No matter the reasoning he gave Adelaide, she refused to believe him. She couldn't accept the reality of her husband being gone, not like this, not so soon.

She looked upon the body of her dear Mathias, which had gone pale as he lifelessly rested in the casket. To her, he was still as handsome as the day he arrived in her homeland so many years ago.

He was dressed in royal emerald, the same colors he wore as a naval commander, except this funeral robe was much more pristine and polished than any of the military attire he donned during active service.

The incense coming from the priest's ceremonial staff rose high into the sky as he prayed. Her children – Xavier, Caldwell, Avery, and Isla – stood firm and held together as best they could. Eddison, her youngest, a boy of thirteen, was on his knees, weeping. Adelaide wanted to join him, but she could not bring herself to. Instead, she fought the tears under her widow's veil. She felt those judgmental eyes staring at her, as if she were the one who killed her husband. *All foreigners are guilty here.*

Xavier pulled his youngest brother up to his feet by his collar. He showed no emotion as the quick jerk on the back of Eddison's shirt choked him. Avery glared at Xavier with her near-black eyes. Other kids in the province who were afraid of her called her Sharkeyes because those eyes showed no mercy to whoever picked on her younger siblings.

The sun illuminated all the colors of the garden. The blues, yellows, and reds never shined brighter amongst the tangled vines and green grasses. Adelaide would sit in the garden during the day with her children and have picnics or read her husband's letters that he sent to her while he was off at sea. Both of those she did in silence out of respect for the ones no longer amongst them. *It's too beautiful a place to have a funeral.*

On the platform behind the priest was Archcrane Vallei Junson, one of the seventeen clerics who represents the capital in their respective province. Vallei oversaw the Roguewave Province, which was not famous for housing the Battier family but more for being the poorest. But perhaps its main claim to fame was that it was home to one of the thirteen wonders of the world: Colwerth Prison.

Vallei's freshly trimmed beard was all grey. Still, he looked younger than fifty-five. He had bright blue eyes that flickered through the smoke, and he seemed not at all a man who desired to be here. Instead, he looked as if this was an unavoidable obligation. *What a miserable and foul man,* Adelaide thought to herself.

If it were any other captain's wake, there would be hundreds of people in attendance, and every member of the Navy would stand at attention, asking if Adelaide or her children needed anything. But ever since Mathias married a *southern beast* from one of the seven warring clans eighteen years ago, his title and prestige meant very little.

The funeral was performed in the clerical tongue. Adelaide couldn't make out much of what was being spoken or sung about her late husband, but her children could understand all of it since they were born and educated in this land. Every child from every province must learn multiple languages.

The priest eventually used Worldly to address everyone. He raised his arms above his head. "I now ask for the young men of Grand Captain Mathias Battier to join me in putting his body to eternal rest and his soul to life once more."

Xavier and Caldwell grabbed Eddison and walked him up the steps onto the funeral platform alongside volunteer guards.

"Who here assists this man into his eternity?" Junson asked.

"His three sons," Xavier said. Adelaide felt the rift deep in her soul grow wider when she heard her eighteen-year-old son's deep voice crack like he was a boy again.

The three of them grabbed a rod that went underneath the casket. The Roguewave guards did the same on the other side. The boys took a firm hold. Caldwell put his hand on Eddison's shoulder. "Make sure your feet are under you and you have a good grip on the pole," she heard her son whisper.

When they lifted, the planks were removed from underneath the casket, and they lowered their father into the ground. The grave keepers would wait until the ceremony was over to pile the dirt on him.

~

The walk back from the Garden of Graves was almost harder than the walk to it. She didn't cry. *I've had my time for tears. Now it's time to be strong for our children.* She gripped Isla's and Eddison's hands tightly. They looked up at her, but she kept her gaze forward, for if she were to look down at this moment, to see her children, who all reminded her of Mathias, she might lose it.

It was nearly a mile trek back to their living quarters. No one paid them any mind, even in their funeral attire. Shops were open for business, and wagons were still dangerously rumbling down the stone road. One almost clipped Xavier as the driver whipped his horse to hurry along. Her eldest cursed at the man. On any other day, she would scold him for his harsh words, but if there was a day she would forgive him for it, she guessed it would be today.

"Mother?" Eddison said.

"Yes?"

"Can I go into Mey's Bakery really quick?"

Eddison always had a tinge of nervousness in his voice. It was only amplified on this day after seeing his father buried six feet underground.

"You're thinking of pies right now? How is that possible?" Xavier demanded.

Avery wouldn't stand for it. "Leave him alone, you sourmope."

"Sourmope? Are you an idiot?"

"The two of you will not do this today. Understand me?" Adelaide didn't want to listen to them argue once more. She drove her thumb and middle finger into her temples until it hurt. Of the five children, they were the only two that just couldn't seem to coexist. "Yes, you may go," she told Eddison. "Avery, go with him."

Avery put her arm around her younger brother. "Let's go, Eddie."

Caldwell and Isla remained close by her side and silent. Isla was always quiet, but that was not by choice. She lost the ability to hear when she was five and struck with a severe fever that many believed would claim her life.

The streets were alive. Around midday, the fish markets had opened, and seemingly everyone was purchasing the fresh catch of the day. Roguewave was on the northeastern coast, and despite the freezing waters, it was home to molten crab, one of the redeeming qualities of their province. Adelaide never had any food from the sea until she moved here – there wasn't a lot of fish in the desert.

"Caldwell, get us some fresh crab for dinner tonight." She handed him six copper coins.

"Yes, Mother," he said. He hesitated for a moment. "After dinner, is it all right if I go back to the academy? I have to study for my hands-on aid exam for Thursday."

"Do you have to do that today?"

Caldwell thought about it the way he thought about everything: thoroughly. "Please?"

She saw the emotion in his eyes, believing it to be an attempt to not think about his father's death. "Yes, you can."

"Thank you."

Caldwell then advanced into the crowd of people gathered around the fish markets. Adelaide, Isla, and Xavier turned down the next street that led to the Seventh Quarter, where their home resided. It wasn't far until they came to the dead end of small homes stacked on top of one another. Theirs was on the third of the four floors. The courtyard in front of them had a large stone fountain with fresh water spewing high into the air.

She heard the pitter-patter of swift feet from above. Adelaide knew what that meant. Hustling down the narrow stairway was Isla's dog, Leo. Mathias had given her the hound as a gift after capturing a pirate vessel on open waters.

He had short and curly hair with a salt and pepper colored coat and massive paws. He could stand on his hind legs, put his paws on Adelaide's shoulders, and lick her in the face. Not something she particularly enjoyed, but Isla certainly did.

Leo leaped and licked Isla in the face. She didn't show emotion often, but when she did, it usually involved her loyal companion. "Can I take him for a walk?" she signed. "He needs it."

He needs it, or you need it? Adelaide thought. "Don't be gone long. I'll have dinner ready early," Adelaide signed back.

Leo was so big Isla could practically ride him around Roguewave. Luckily for the hound's sake, she kept his hips intact and avoided doing so.

It was just Adelaide and Xavier now. He didn't say much. He rarely did. There wasn't many that were quieter than Isla, but half the time her eldest came close.

"How are you?" she asked taking a seat on the edge of the courtyard fountain.

"I'm fine, Mother."

"Are you? It's all right if you aren't."

Of her children, Xavier was the only one she looked at as an adult. Life was difficult for both of them when he was first born. She had just turned seventeen when she gave birth to him. She had been a young bride with a young child alone in a foreign land while her husband was off at sea.

"I promise," he said stroking his beard that made him appear more mature than he already was.

"He loved you very much." She watched as Xavier reached his hand out and let the water from the fountain fall on his palm.

"I know." He took his wet palm and rubbed his shaved head. "What about you? Are you all right?"

She couldn't help but laugh, all the while realizing it wasn't an appropriate response. "Well, son, I'm miserable... but if I weren't, there'd be something wrong with me."

A rare smile crept across his face. He didn't do it often, but when he did, Xavier looked like Mathias the most. "I suppose you're right."

She put her hands on his face. His jaw was like stone even through his thick black beard. "We have to look after each other now. You have to look after your brothers and sisters... even if you don't want to. I don't know what's ahead of us, but we'll do it as a family. Understand?"

All he gave was a nod, and that was enough for her.

The sound of marching came from the main street. Adelaide and Xavier turned their heads to see around fifty greencoat soldiers passing. Their bayonets were high in the air as they stepped in unison.

"What's that for?" Adelaide asked.

Xavier straightened his spine and lowered his brow. "They're not in any hurry. Must be patrolling the area. Keeping the peace?"

"With fifty rifles? Let's call it peace," she murmured.

As the soldiers disappeared around the brick corner of the bank, Avery and Eddison emerged behind them almost simultaneously. Eddison was using both hands to carry something, and the smile on his face said he was proud of it. He stopped right in front of Adelaide. Flour was in his curly brown hair as he hoisted up a pastry.

"I got you a white apple pie, Mother. Mey baked it herself, and Renold picked the apples fresh from his tree behind their shop." The pie was golden brown, the sugar nearly glazed over the top, and heat still radiated from it.

"You got this for me?" she asked. Much like the pie, Eddison was afflicted with the curse of being sweet. While Avery was known as Sharkeyes, Eddison went by a different title: Coward Boy. A name the family wasn't fond of, especially

Xavier. The harsh nickname didn't seem to affect him as badly as it did the rest of them, however.

"Do you like it?" he asked with those round eyes.

"I love it." Adelaide put her arm around Eddison, and they all started up the stairs. The dark day was finished with a subtle flash of redeeming light. She tried her best to enjoy the moment of kindness, but something in her wouldn't allow it. She figured it was about her husband, who was now gone forever, but it wasn't.

No, this was a sensation. Her life and her children's lives were changing drastically. Mathias' death and this mobilization of troops heightened her sense of awareness. She would not accept the manner of her husband's death. Perhaps the coroner's report was correct, but this was a place unkind to clan folk sympathizers, especially those in positions of power. She needed to dig further to find a concrete verdict, knowing full well that the answers may terrify her and possibly change her life.

But first, she'd have a slice of pie.

THREE

SHARKEYES I

At midday, Avery ran along the Greenmore River that flowed west. She threw a small branch into the water before she began and attempted to keep pace with it as the swift current swept it away. Every day her goal was to improve and run farther than the day before. This was a ritual Avery had been doing for weeks since her father's passing. She had goals to follow in his footsteps and become a Grand Captain to travel the high seas, subduing pirates and enemies of the Unified Provinces, an accomplishment achieved by an elite few.

The title of Grand Captain was given to those who captained the Grand Ships. These galleons were so large they required nearly a thousand crew members to man. Years of construction went into vessels that size. That was why the Unified Provinces had only sailed five of them. Avery had dreams of captaining the *Hydra*, the first of the Grand Ships to be built a few decades ago. Today it was captained by Alistair Cross, arguably the most respected commander in not only the Navy but the entire military. They said the pirates feared him more than a tempest.

She descended a steep hill and gained speed. Once the

ground leveled out at the bottom, she passed the orange and black markers on the trees that told her she had crossed over into Swiftwater Province. Her mother didn't like her being outside of Roguewave, but what her mother didn't know wouldn't hurt her. She justified it by knowing Xavier got to leave and travel to every province to train and duel other boys his age. *Why can't I?*

Avery passed a pile of stones she stacked yesterday that marked her stopping point. She looked to the river to see if she was keeping up with the stick, but it wasn't there. Her eyes scanned the water. *There's no way it's that far ahead of me.*

Avery looked behind her to see if the stick was trailing. However, as her focus shifted away from what was in front of her, her foot dipped into a hole, and her knee buckled. Her stability vanished, and her momentum propelled her forward.

She tumbled hard onto the ground and rotated several times even in an attempt to stop herself. She dug her elbow into the riverside and continued to slide on her back. Sharp and jagged rocks scraped across her back, managing to cut through her shirt.

Avery lay there with dust flying over her head, aware that some of those rocks were embedded in her skin as the isolated areas pulsated with pain.

Well, that hurt.

The first thing she checked was her ankle. While it had already swelled, she believed she had avoided any major injury. She traveled up towards her knee and didn't feel like there was anything off, but she didn't know for sure.

Perhaps Caldwell can look at this.

Avery stood. Her ankle and knee didn't seem to be an issue as far as she could tell. She looked back at the stacked stones. *I got farther than I did yesterday, at least.*

She adjusted the sheathed knife on her belt that ran behind her back and slid it to her hip. The light touch of her shirt grazing her back sent sparks of pain lancing through her bones. The journey back home was going to be more grueling than normal.

The sound of the roaring river softened, and it was almost like she was deep in a cave. She knew what was happening.

Avery, help! her little brother's voice, Eddison cried out inside her head.

Where are you? she replied within her thoughts.

Avery cut through the woods. *If Mother knew he was out here alone, she would be furious.* She jumped over large patches of sinking sand and ducked under low-hanging branches. Her ankle was stable, her knee the same, but she'd be lying if she told anyone they weren't hurting. The hitch in her stride was subtle, and even though no one was watching, she attempted to play it off. Her back was burning, and warm blood spots were most likely staining her shirt. The forest was so dense that the sun could barely shine through, but she could see the trees begin to clear just ahead. *I'm not far.*

As she got closer, she heard a familiar voice outside her mind. She emerged from the woods and saw Eddie being ambushed by three boys around her age, maybe older.

His books were scattered across the ground, and a small wooden board accompanied by little stone pieces littered the forest floor. Those were parts of the board game her little brother loved to play so much, Board Battalion. His clothes were torn to shreds.

"Hard to believe you're Xavier Battier's little brother, coward!" one of the boys said as he backhanded Eddison across the face. The other two held him upright. "I would think your brothers would make you tough... or your dead father, perhaps."

He went for a punch.

"Hey!" Avery yelled, unafraid, standing like a stone pillar. "I wouldn't hit him again."

The one hitting Eddison turned. Quien Lowlend, son of Dex Lowlend, Commander of Molten Fort that overlooked Molten Bay. Neither father nor son had an upstanding reputation. It was often rumored that Dex abandoned his post and his men. Her mother's reasoning was that his job meant very little because there was nothing significant to guard in Roguewave anymore.

"Avery?" Quien said. "You just happened to be in the area? That's convenient for your little brother here... if you'd kindly run along. We're teaching him something your other brothers and father seemed to forget."

The mention of her father got her blood boiling. *He may be right about my brothers not looking after Eddison, but not Father.*

Eddison's face was bruised, and he appeared to be dead weight to the boys holding him. Avery walked up to Quien, who met her halfway with a pompous smile. Once she got close, she cracked him in the jaw as hard as she could, and he dropped.

Stunned by the blow, it took him a few moments to get back up. He swung back at her, but she ducked to the side, and Avery hit him again in the stomach. She didn't stop there, following up with a hammer fist to the back of his head that sent him face-first to the ground.

The other boys she didn't recognize dropped Eddison upon witnessing their ringleader go down. They charged her, and the first one got to her quickly. He ducked his head as he went for a takedown. She rolled with him as he tackled her. She yelled in pain, but it wasn't from anything he did – it was from her beat-up back hitting the ground.

She used their momentum to roll on top of him, using her pain to motivate her. She sent a couple hard blows right into his nose. He covered his face, went to his stomach, and pleaded for mercy. She stood, forgetting about the third attacker, which angered her more than anything.

He grabbed her from behind. His grip was tight across her chest. Avery tried to wiggle out, but his squeeze only tightened as she spit through her clenched teeth.

Avery dipped her head forward and threw it back. The boy's cheek cracked against the back of her head. He cried out in agony. As soon as his grip loosened a little, she flared her elbows out, turned, and kneed him in the spot where boys never wanted to be struck.

He folded, holding both his face and his private parts, leaving his exposed and unguarded stomach. She dropped to one knee and drove a punch into his torso, and the air left him on impact.

He wheezed in pain as he attempted to catch his breath. All he could do was wave her away. "No… more… please."

Guilt for the boys' pain did not enter her mind. Anyone who would bring harm to her family, especially her little brother, would not have the luxury of her pity. The only thing that crossed her mind was, *I wonder if I dispatched them better than Xavier or Caldwell would have?*

Eddison lay on his back in defeat, still covering his head. Avery looked down at her red knuckles. Her hands shook with adrenaline. She did her best to mask her post-fight jitters as she approached her little brother. *I'm not going to be able to hide that from Mother.*

"Are you okay, Eddie?" she asked.

"My face hurts," he muttered.

The boys rolling on the ground behind her continued to cough and whimper.

"I think that's from the punches, little brother. On the bright side, it probably doesn't hurt as bad as Quien's right now." She chuckled, giving Eddison a hand to his feet. *Oh, Eddie.* Avery grabbed his shoulders and centered him. "Can you walk?"

"Maybe, I don't know." His voice was shaky, as well as innocent. She held his head with both of her hands and looked into his blue eyes that only he carried from their father. "Don't tell Xavier or Caldwell, please... or Isla... or Mother. I guess no one."

Avery just smiled at him. "I won't have to tell them. Your face will tell them everything." She let go of him and backed away. "Shoulders back, chin up like we talked about."

Eddison looked awkward trying to appear confident. It was almost like he was wearing an outfit that didn't fit him properly. *What are we going to do with you, Eddie?*

"I'll see you soon, Sharkeyes," Quien said, limping away with labored breath. His weak voice didn't strike any fear in her, for his threat seemed hollow.

"How many do you see of me now? Double? Triple?" she replied.

Her brother's swollen face looked up at her with a grin. Avery smiled back and wrapped her arm around him. He reciprocated and slung his arm around her lower back. The adrenaline rush was short-lived as the pain returned. Eddie's soft touch nearly brought her to her knees.

"Are you all right?" he asked.

She rubbed his greasy and curly hair that all the boys his age seemed to have. "I'm fine," she said with a fake smile. An unpleasant odor that surfaced helped her forget as she walked next to him. "You need to bathe, Eddie."

"What? Why?"

"Because you smell horrible," she said.

"Is it that awful?" he asked.

"Awful adjacent."

~

A steady breeze through the trees and the smell of salt told her they were getting close to home. There was a rock her siblings often paid a visit to up ahead, a boulder that at its base was black but got lighter, almost white towards the top. Her father called it the monochrome rock. As far as Avery knew, it was the only one in the entire forest, maybe the world. Her father had never seen another of its like either. Avery believed him to be the man who had knowledge about everything. Whenever she had a question about the world, whether it be about sea creatures that occupied the northwestern waters of the Harpoon Sea or the legend of Captain Pointer's Gold, he had the answer. History, geography, myths on land and sea, her father knew it all.

I miss you.

"Avery?" Eddison asked softly, his eyes staring at the ground.

"Yes?"

"If you couldn't hear me… if we couldn't talk the way we can... they would've beat me to a pulp."

"Maybe. That doesn't matter now, though," she said sternly. "You haven't told anybody, right?"

"No."

"Promise?"

Eddison sighed. "Yes, Avery."

"Good."

"Why can't we tell Mother?"

Avery walked closer to the rock and leaned against it, pressing her hand to the chalky grey center. "I don't know... Only you and I can communicate like this. Doesn't seem right for anyone else to know. The moment someone else knows, it's not our secret anymore." Eddison smirked and continued to look down at the ground. "You agree?"

"Yeah, I guess so."

There was a rustling of leaves behind them. Avery turned her head to see her little sister, Isla, and her dog, Leo, emerge from the trees. Almost everyone had confused the two of them with one another once or twice, even their own parents. The only thing that delineated them from one another was their size. Avery was just a bigger version.

Avery often wondered if her sister was happy. Even before their father's death, Isla had had to navigate being deaf, something most people didn't have to deal with or understand. Many kids their age in Roguewave avoided Isla like she was infected with some disease. It made Avery just as furious as the bullying inflicted upon Eddison. Mother always said, "They're wary of her 'cause she's different, that's all. Sadly, that's all."

Isla gave a subtle wave. Her face turned pale once she saw Eddison's bruises. She ran to him and gingerly touched his face, feeling his lumps and caressing him as their mother would. Leo's large head pushed under her arms and began licking Eddison's face.

"What happened?" Isla signed, looking to Avery for a reply.

"Quien Lowlend and a couple of his friends beat on him."

"Did you fight back?"

Eddison shook his head. "Avery did for me."

"You were there?"

Avery hesitated for a moment. "Got there just in time before things got terrible." Even though Isla was younger, she had no problem admitting that her sister was smarter than her. So, trying to deceive or fool Isla in any way would be suspect, so she didn't. She might not be able to hear well, but her sense of detecting lies almost made up for it. "What are you doing out here by yourself, Isla?"

"She was going to meet me here to play Board Battalion," Eddie said.

"Well, you might have to play at the house from now on," Avery said.

"Not if I'm with either of you."

Isla stood upright. "We can't be with you forever," she

signed to him. "Sooner or later, you may have to fight for yourself… or run faster."

Eddie's big blue eyes turned to Avery, and she couldn't bear to look at him. Her sister was right. However, she was willing to lie and tell him she would always be there for him no matter what, knowing that might be an empty promise.

"Let's head home," Avery said.

"Xavier's not going to like it when he sees me," Eddie muttered.

"He's not going to like it because of how it makes him look. Don't worry about him," Avery assured him.

"That's hard to do," Eddison said.

Isla's concerned look never faded. She put her hand on Avery's shoulder and turned her around. "You're bleeding," she signed.

Avery tried to forget the pain, thinking that would help. Her younger siblings stared at her. "Luckily, we have an aidman in the family." She chuckled. Eddison and Isla didn't find it as funny. "Oh, come on, if anything, we're giving Caldwell more practice."

The claustrophobia in the markets was paralyzing from the endless waves of people crammed together, fighting for the fresh catch of the day fished from Molten Bay. Even now, at this hour so close to nightfall, the northeastern market's main commodity always remained molten crab. Avery didn't have the love for the local crab like the rest of her family. She took after her mother, for she enjoyed red meat much more.

This time of year, the midsummer sun was unrelenting. No clouds provided intermittent shelter from the heat. Avery weaved effortlessly in and out of the crowd because she wasn't afraid to nudge slow movers out of her path. Eddison, Isla, and Leo followed close behind, keeping up as best they could.

Isla was much more polite, though, letting the crowd move her like a plank of wood in the open ocean. Avery felt sorry for Leo and his thick fur. *Surely, he's burning up.* Drool dripped from his tongue onto the stone. It didn't seem to bother him, though. He looked happier than any of the miserable people in Roguewave.

To Avery, it seemed that Roguewave had always been a miserable place. However, her father once assured her that wasn't the case. He used to say that long ago, before he met their mother, Roguewave was the main province of the east. And before he set sail for Autera, many years ago, his ship launched from Molten Bay, and he saw commerce flourishing. Her father told her everything changed when the East Flame Tower fell. As one of the manmade wonders of the world, it was the epicenter for trade, banking, and business on the east coast. Her father would never talk about what happened that day, for he watched the tower collapse. In school, they were taught that it was pirates, led by Captain Marstellar Lockett, who secretly stockpiled gunpowder at the base of the tower and set it ablaze.

Once, when Avery was feeling confident, she asked her father if he saw or fought any pirates that day. She remembered how his face shifted into a serious and stoic gaze, and he replied, "Avery, the events surrounding that day keep me wide-eyed and awake at night. One day, I hope to fully comprehend it all and talk to you about it, but until then, I'm sorry, I cannot indulge you."

"Fresh molten crab! Fresh molten crab! Fresh molten crab!" a fisherman yelled ahead of them as he pitched his tent.

Avery stopped. "Is this molten crab fresh?"

The scowl he gave her said he wasn't amused by her sarcasm, but she found it hilarious.

"Shouldn't you be in your studies?" the fisherman replied.

"Shouldn't you still be fishing?"

"We've caught enough already."

"And I've studied enough already." Avery smiled at him.

He turned away and ignored her. He began yelling once more about his molten crab and how fresh it was.

Ahead was another tent that made Avery uneasy. Incense escaped from under its canvas, small vials of liquids in every color were on display, and animal bones dangled from the ceiling on strings. Under it all was a woman sitting alone at a small table with frizzy blonde hair draped over her face. She sat there quiet and unmoving. Avery wondered if she was asleep, but she wasn't going to stay and find out.

Once they passed the tent and the feeling left her, she heard a deep feminine voice call out, "Sharkeyes."

Avery turned back. She saw Eddison turn back as well. The woman in the tent looked at her, and a smile crept across her face. Avery decided to ignore her and motioned for her brother and sister to leave.

"If you walk away, you won't receive the gift I have for you," the woman said.

"I'm not interested," Avery replied.

"Of course, you are." The woman sat up straight in her chair. "Come, I would never harm you, girl." Isla looked at her, wondering what was going on with this odd encounter. The strange woman turned her head to Eddison and Isla. "Nor you two." Eddie's face went white, and Avery stepped in front of him. "I could never bring harm to the Battier children."

"Are you a witch?" Avery asked.

The woman laughed, and she displayed her yellow and brown teeth. "Am I that frightening, girl?"

"You don't frighten me," Avery assured her.

"I don't imagine so. With a name like Sharkeyes, I doubt much scares you at all." She looked to Eddison. "This one, however, wants nothing more than this little exchange to end."

Eddie stood petrified. *She's right about that.*

"What do you have for me?" Avery asked, irritated.

The smile from the woman never faded. "What's your real name?"

Avery hesitated. "Avery—Avery Battier."

"Do you believe in magic, Avery Battier?"

She thought of magicians who traveled from province to province, performing their tricks and illusions throughout the land. But her mother assured her that was all they were, tricks and illusions, not magic.

"No," Avery said sternly.

"Good, because magic doesn't exist here anyway," the witch said.

"Doesn't exist *here*? You're saying it exists somewhere else?"

Eddison stepped forward, "Avery, can we go, please?"

"No need to live up to your nickname in my presence, Coward Boy. You can receive my gift too, should you be brave enough." The witch addressed them both now. "Your father was a captain, was he not?"

"Grand Captain," Avery corrected.

"Did he ever tell you the things he witnessed during his voyages?"

"He was a loyal countryman who dismantled pirates."

The woman shook her head, seemingly unsatisfied. "What a shame your father kept so much from you."

Avery scrunched her face. "Don't insult my father!"

"My apologies, Avery, I would never mean to insult Grand Captain Mathias Battier." The woman removed her necklace and, at its center, dangled a foggy stone. "I sense a wanting of a journey in you. Perhaps a desire to travel to new lands and witness the wonders this world has to offer." She extended her arm and the necklace to Avery. "Should you make that journey, you should be shielded from its darkness."

Avery didn't accept her gift. "This rock will protect me from what, exactly?"

"Dark magic that dwells in other lands."

"I can protect myself without the help of an ugly stone, thanks." Avery turned to her brother and sister to leave the marketplace.

"To refuse a gift, especially one such as this, could bring further misfortune to your family, Avery. Don't be foolish. Throw it in the bay after you accept it if you must. But accept it nonetheless."

Avery hesitated once again, but she stepped to the woman and took the necklace. "Am I supposed to thank you?"

"Not today. But perhaps in the future, the urge to thank me will come to whoever wears this and witnesses its glow."

Avery didn't know what she meant by that. However, at this point, she was ready to be done with this interaction as much as Eddison. She took one last look at the woman with the yellow smile and walked away, hoping to never see her again.

They exited the market and watched the sun begin to descend, cooling the scorching day. Fishing boats were crammed together in the bay as fishermen unloaded supplies after a long day's work.

Isla kept her distance, admiring the ocean breeze while patting Leo's head the entire way. She lived in her own world, partly due to circumstances, but she also enjoyed her alone time.

Avery looked out upon the open ocean, and she thought about the journey that the woman hinted at her taking one day, secretly hoping she was right. The idea of the necklace shielding her from the darkness was lost on her; the voyage across the world was not. She breathed in the air coming off the bay and exhaled desire. A desire to be free and have no limitations. The thought alone made her smile.

"Are you all right, Avery?" her little brother asked.

"I'm great." Avery reached in her pocket and put the necklace around Eddison's neck. "I don't believe her, but if that strange woman is correct, you'll need this more than I do." She chuckled as Eddison looked down at the stone resting on his chest.

"Thank you."

Avery smiled. "You can thank me if it works."

FOUR

THE CHAMPION I

The dueling pits radiated a heat so unpleasant that many of Xavier's fellow training partners sat off to the side in an attempt to cool down. The sun turned the sandpit into an oven. Not unlike one Mey would use to bake her famous pies. On this day, boots were a necessity, even during the wrestling drills. Otherwise, there would be a lot of young soldiers tap dancing to avoid blisters on their feet.

Xavier made sure he stayed in the pit, no matter how hot it got. Lieutenant Chiesa had advised him to take a break, but he refused. *There's a reason I'm better. I won't get out when everyone else does.* He had been the Unified Provinces' all-around dueling champion for two years straight. He was 48-0 and closing in on the record for most wins ever. The current record was held by Jameson "Red Sand" Roke. His nickname originated from the fact that he almost always left his opponent bleeding in the sand, even with wooden swords. He had fifty-two straight wins before he was called to sea to combat the Third Pirate Rebellion. Jameson sailed as quartermaster under the command of his father.

Xavier did his best to not place people on a pedestal. He thought it weak to prop someone up like that. Even a man like

38

Jameson, whom Xavier met on several occasions as a boy when he came over to the Battier house for dinner. He remembered him being very kind and not at all a man that appeared to live up to his vicious reputation.

They moved on to sword training, Xavier's favorite of the three disciplines. The other two were hand-to-hand and wrestling. While he enjoyed them as well, he felt it more practical to train with swords because, in real combat, a sword would more likely be used. Gun training was a separate discipline that was not learned until boys were sixteen. However, Xavier's father had shown him and his younger brothers the way around a flintlock rifle long before that.

The wooden swords made a cracking sound when they collided, and Xavier loved it. One of his primary goals was to break his dueling partner's sword. Over the years, he had been responsible for the deaths of almost a hundred practice swords, so many that Lieutenant Chiesa had to instruct him to "ease up" on his swings—advice he never really considered.

Xavier's brother, Caldwell, was one of the boys taking a break from the pit. They hovered around the well, pulling water up in a bucket and dumping it on themselves. *There's not going to be a bucket of water to lean on during a real battle.*

In the pit with him was Emil Muse. He wasn't the best fighter, but he was one of the few boys in Roguewave that could give Xavier a hint of challenge.

"Caldwell, when you get done taking a bath over there, back in the pit against your brother!" Lieutenant Chiesa called out. Xavier's younger brother shook his head. "Don't give me that, or I'll tell him not to take it easy on you."

Caldwell was a good fighter, but Xavier knew his passion for it was fleeting. He was only here because he had to be. His head was often elsewhere, thinking about his studies. Xavier didn't know much about his siblings and had no shame about it because he didn't dwell on the thought.

Chiesa's eyes returned to Xavier and Emil in the pit. "You two, begin."

The two of them faced each other and tightened their grip on their swords. *It's hot,* Xavier thought to himself. He saw beads of sweat dripping from Emil's forehead and spill onto the sand. *But it doesn't matter. It doesn't affect me like the rest of them. They're not as strong. They will cave long before I even consider it.*

Emil sprinted forward. His first swing was from his strong side. Like most attacks against him, Xavier saw it coming from miles away. He parried the initial barrage effortlessly.

He could see Emil's growing frustration. *The fatigue is going to get to him.* Emil's attacks became slower and slower with each swing. Eventually, Xavier didn't have to use his sword to block. He merely dodged to improve his reflexes and movement.

After countless thrusts and swings, Emil dropped his sword in the sand and put his hands on his knees. "Yield," he said, out of breath.

You won't be able to yield in a real battle, either. My father couldn't have yielded at war, neither could Red Sand Roke nor Alistair Cross, and neither can Xavier Battier.

"He's yielded. That doesn't mean you've beaten him, Xavier," Chiesa reminded.

Xavier knew what his lieutenant was saying. Xavier stuck his left foot in the sand and lifted his right knee to his chest. In one swift instant, he push-kicked Emil off his feet and out of the sandpit entirely.

His brother gave him a blank expression of dissatisfaction that the group shared.

"You don't like that, Caldwell? Get in there and do something about it!" Chiesa yelled.

His brother stepped into the pit with his sword in hand.

Despite his status, Xavier had a very minimal number of friends. And the number only got smaller after his father died, as he pushed everyone away from him. Caldwell, however, had many, and Emil was arguably the closest of the bunch.

Friends aren't going to make me better.

They both bent their knees and leaned forward, waiting on Chiesa's command. The shadow from Caldwell's brow shrouded the whites of his eyes.

"Begin."

Caldwell didn't follow his friend's footsteps. He avoided the initial blitz in a foolish attempt to get Xavier by surprise.

Smart, brother.

They both stepped to the right, circling each other like two alpha wolves. *Let's see how he handles it.* Xavier burst forward, coming down from the sky with his first strike. Caldwell blocked it and circled to the left to set up a quick counter.

Xavier identified it and spun into his brother's body so he couldn't generate any force on the swing. A hard push impacted his back, and his head whipped.

By the time he turned around, Caldwell was setting up another swing. Xavier ducked under it and smacked his younger brother in the leg. The blow sent Caldwell to his knees.

That was quick.

"Do you yield already, Caldwell?" Chiesa asked.

His brother was on all fours, his hands planted in the sand.

Xavier stood over top of him. "Come on, brother, get up. That's not it."

Caldwell postured up and came to life once more. Xavier was not expecting the quick and powerful punch that struck directly in the stomach. For a moment, the air was taken from him, and it was difficult to breathe. Caldwell got to his feet and went after him, following up with a few more punches that Xavier managed to block.

"Swords only, you two," Lieutenant Chiesa said casually.

Xavier was furious that Caldwell managed to take him down, even if he was compromised. Xavier caught his lost breath and took hold of his brother. Caldwell continued to fight even through the grapple. Xavier rolled him over and rained down open palm strikes that slapped so loud it was equivalent to pistol fire.

It was then he felt his arms and waist grabbed by two of his brother's friends. They peeled him away. *He never yielded,* Xavier thought. He quit fighting and put his hands in the air.

"I'm done, I'm done," Xavier said.

The two boys that pulled him away were Maynard and Fili. Both were from the Eighth Quarter, directly across the street from where the Battiers lived in the Seventh. Maynard had big forearms that he inherited as well as earned from his father, Lyle Middle, who was the finest blacksmith in Roguewave. Fili was an orphan who spent most of his days assisting his foster father, Lieutenant Chiesa.

Everyone settled.

Maynard and Fili let go, and Xavier turned his back on Caldwell, who finally sat upright. He spat bloody saliva onto the sand.

"You feel better now? Did you get all your anger out?" Caldwell yelled.

No.

~

Xavier walked home alone. He doubted his brother wanted to spend any more time with him today. *One day he'll thank me for not taking it easy. An aidman doesn't avoid battles or war. He's right there with them, and he must fight alongside soldiers just as competently.*

The daylight was leaving Molten Bay, and the markets were quiet. Most of those who littered the streets now were peasants waiting for scraps of either unsold or expiring food from vendors.

"Please, young man, do you have any spare coin?" The man was thin yet had loose skin around his arms. His eyes were sunk in, and looked to be on the verge of death. "I haven't —"

"No, I'm sorry," he said coldly.

There were many more like that man, especially in Roguewave. On his short walk home, he laid eyes on about fifty homeless people, all just trying to get fed.

A sound that he knew quite well up ahead—marching. Xavier jogged over the bridge, and on the other side, he saw around five hundred greencoats of Helmburough marching towards the fort. *There are more soldiers every single day.* Unfortunately for Xavier, he didn't gossip with anyone, so he was always the last to find out about things, even about military issues.

To his left, he noticed a beat of clanking metal stop. Lyle Middle walked out of his blacksmithing shop to observe the marching and raised his eyebrows to meet Xavier. "Ah, Xavier, how are you today, son?"

"I'm fine, Mr. Middle."

Lyle's eyes returned to the soldiers. "Heard you and your brother had a good scrap earlier," Lyle said.

"How did you already know about that?"

As soon as he asked, Maynard walked out of the shop, putting on his smithing apron.

That's how. "You must've told him seconds ago," Xavier said to Maynard.

"It was the only thing I've told him about my day so far," the boy said with a grin. His eyes turned to the soldiers. "Can you believe all this, Xavier?"

"What's that?"

"Caldwell didn't tell you?"

"We don't exchange a lot of words."

"You exchange a lot of punches from the sounds of it," Lyle muttered.

Maynard got closer. "Xavier, the *Hydra* is sailing for Molten Bay right now."

The Hydra? The flagship of the Unified Provinces? Grand Commander Alistair Cross is coming here?

Xavier fought to maintain his stoicism. "Why?"

"Haven't heard much. Some say it's for naval recruiting along the coastline. Others say it's just so Grand Commander Cross can eat some molten crab. Although, I highly doubt the latter."

"That doesn't explain all the greencoats mobilizing and arming the fort," Xavier pointed out.

"Whatever the Assembly wants to keep from us, they will," Lyle said while slamming down hard on a red-hot horseshoe. "Goodnight, Xavier. Maynard, hurry. We have to finish up."

The Assembly was an oligarchy of very few members that ruled the Unified Provinces. All of them resided in the capital province of Helmburough on the western coast of Renera.

"If they're coming for fresh recruits, I think I'm going to go ahead and join," Maynard said with a determined look in his eyes. It was a good option for the more ordinary Academy enrollees to do so if their studies weren't proficient.

Xavier walked away. "You do that. You'll be doing grunt work and swabbing the deck for years without a degree."

Maynard scoffed. "Well, some of us aren't destined for greatness, Champion."

"If you really believe that, then you're right."

Loser.

~

Xavier walked down the main thoroughfare leading into the Seventh Quarter. Ahead, he saw his youngest brother Eddison playing alone by the courtyard fountain. *He's playing that bloody game again. If he spent his time training with me, he wouldn't be known as Coward Boy. I'd make sure of that.*

"Are you playing alone?" Xavier asked.

Eddison jumped upon hearing his voice. His little brother never raised his head. "Uh, yes... yes, I'm playing alone."

Xavier knew something was off. "Where are Avery and Isla?"

"H-Helping Mother with dinner." Eddison's eyes were glued to the game board.

"Look at me," Xavier said sternly. Eddison's head raised and revealed his bruised and swollen face. Xavier's nostrils flared. "Who did that?"

Eddison didn't answer.

"Who. Did. That?" he asked again.

"Quien Lowlend and his friends."

"Did you fight back?"

Eddison dropped his head again.

Coward Boy lives up to his name once again. Not anymore. "Tomorrow, you are going to come with me to the pits, and we are going to train day after day until people respect you— until you have respect for yourself. You will no longer be so comfortable being a coward. I don't care if you claim to be injured; you will fight through it."

All boys in the Unified Provinces must begin mandatory combat training at thirteen with their local lieutenants at their provincial academies. Eddison was supposed to start months ago but suffered a foot injury that left him sidelined and behind on his training. There were whispers that he staged the injury himself, hence how he acquired his nickname. Xavier paid no attention or care to them at first, but now, he was beginning to wonder if there was any validity to them.

"But Xavier—"

"No. Enough. You don't have a say in the matter. You won't insult our father and sink our family name lower now that he's gone." Xavier stormed past him up the stairs.

When he opened the door to his family home, he smelled the crab cooking in the pot. *Every night it's crab.* He liked molten crab; he would just prefer to have something else for dinner from time to time. His sisters were preparing their undersized table for the meal. Xavier waved to his sister Isla, the only sibling that didn't constantly grind his nerves.

Everything was cramped, and the aesthetic of brown and grey seemed to place them back in time a hundred years. There were only three bedrooms in the compact living arrangements. So, the boys shared a room, and the girls shared a room.

Xavier often wondered why his father had to sacrifice so much. Being a Grand Captain was one of the highest honors in the world, and yet his father was forced to give up his title, royalties, respect, and monitor the eastern waters where little transpired. *All because he married our mother.* Xavier has questioned it for eighteen years and still came back with nothing.

His mother looked over the boiling pot before she turned to him. "How was your day, son?"

Xavier cut to the chase. "I'm taking Eddison with me tomorrow to train with Lieutenant Chiesa. If he's actually hurt, we'll deal with it, but he's not going to walk around beaten and afraid anymore."

The rising steam danced past her face. "Very well."

He wasn't expecting that direct response. *It was that easy?*

"Remember, your little brother is not a fighter. If he doesn't want to be like you, you don't have to beat him down every day to try and make it so. He doesn't need to be a champion."

"Fair enough."

His sister Avery was staring daggers at him. "Maybe if you were a brother to him at all, he wouldn't be so afraid around you."

Xavier looked at his sister's red and freshly scabbed knuckles. "Afraid of me? He's thirteen, Avery. It's not like he's five. He can't just play all day and have his older sister come save him when someone pushes him around."

"You could've trained him a long time ago, but all you care about is yourself. Only reason you're helping now is because of the reflection on you!"

Correct.

"Enough, you two!" their mother yelled. "Avery, plate the table. Xavier, go wash up."

Again, her orders were direct, the way Xavier liked them. He went to make his way to the room, but a flash of white caught his eye. A letter rested under the open slot in the alcove by the entryway.

"Is this from today?" he asked his mother.

When his mother turned around, her eyes widened. "I guess so. It wasn't with the mail I received earlier." The letter had an emerald band with the Assembly's wax seal at the center.

He looked back to see the curious eyes of Avery and Isla on him. He broke the wax seal and pulled a large gold coin from the letter.

Champion Xavier Battier,

The time has come for a challenger's right to fight for your coveted title. Leave for Helmburough at once, for the duel shall take place in two weeks. As always, travel, lodging, and food will be provided.

As a native of Helmburough, your opponent, Declan Cross, is eager and ready. He hopes you arrive at your best.

Per usual, bring this letter and coin to your harbor master so you can set sail. We will wait for your arrival.

Sincerely,

Benjah Kearse of the Assembly.

A long and drawn-out exhale left Xavier's nostrils.

"Xavier?" his mother asked. He stepped to her and gave her the letter.

"I'll leave first thing in the morning," he said.

"You've never had a duel at such short notice."

"No, I haven't. Perhaps they are taking advantage of the fact that I'm always ready. I'll prove I am." He began to walk to his bedroom.

"Declan Cross? As in, Alistair Cross' son?" Avery asked.

He clenched his jaw and looked to his wide-eyed sisters. "I believe so."

"Is he a good fighter?" Isla signed.

"Guess I'll find out. 'Good' won't be enough for him to beat me."

FIVE

THE COWARD BOY I

All the ships resting in the harbor rubbed shoulders amid the violent tides. The skies had turned dark, and flashes of yellow light pulsed behind the indigo overcast. Eddie stood at the top of Pointer's Hill, which overlooked the bay from the south. His eyes widened in wonderment as he saw a ship approaching off the coastline to the southeast, the *Hydra*.

The flag ship's mainsail was so large it looked like a welcome rug to the home of a god. Perhaps one of the many gods his mother once worshiped in Autera, or the one god the nomad colonies called the Creator.

A streak of lightning burst from behind the Grand Ship that broke into countless jagged lines like a river delta. Many people believed Alistair Cross was seven feet tall and had two blunderbusses dangling from his broad hips. Eddie knew that wasn't true, though – his father and brother told him as much when he came to them about the rumors. Other kids his age chose not to believe him when he relayed that information. They wanted to live with the image of Giant Grand Commander Cross, and he didn't fault them.

One thing was certain: there was no denying Alistair Cross' power. He was one of the five leaders of the Assembly, the governing body of the Unified Provinces, and one of the most well-known names in the world. Cross' main duties were commanding the military and acting as leading strategist behind rebellions, attacks, or any acts of war.

Thoughts of battles and the potential for bloodshed made Eddie uneasy – at least, real battles. He enjoyed the world he made up in his mind far more than the one he was living. Nothing terrible ever happened to him in his imagination. No, in his mind, he was the best board battalion player in all the provinces and made his living traveling the lands facing off against the very best, and fear never crippled him.

Another crash of thunder snapped him from his daydream. He removed a spyglass from the bag that mostly housed his game board and accompanying pieces. He stared through the small tube, and his view of the ship, though dark, was much improved. It sailed closer, and he could see the small dark squares littered across the *Hydra's* broadside that housed around five hundred cannons. *One blast from those guns might as well be a lightning strike.* The harsh sea did not shake it, as if the water itself was powerless.

But his father always said, "When it desires, the sea will eventually claim every ship. No ship sails forever." Eddison knew his father to be very smart. But looking upon a ship of this size, he had his doubts.

Light drops of rain tapped his head, and he knew his time atop this hill was coming to an end. *This might be the last place I should be right now with that storm coming.*

It had been two days since his eldest brother Xavier left for his duel in Helmburough. Eddie was always timid around Xavier because he got the feeling his brother didn't like him very much. Avery always assured him he shouldn't feel bad because Xavier didn't care for anybody other than himself. Eddie knew that was just her valiant attempt at making him feel better, but it helped. If he was honest, he loved and envied his brother. Xavier was a great fighter who had no fear. Those were a pair of things he desperately wanted for himself but was too scared to pursue.

He walked alone through the Garden of Graves, keeping his head low in the enclosed area. His spine remained stiff and chilled as the thousands of headstones stared at him. The pending storm wasn't helping matters. Outside of his family, not many people frequented the garden, and he understood why. It was a stone maze of death.

He avoided walking directly past the headstones, including his father's, by creeping along the track on the outer edges. Vines crawled every inch of the walls, but the rainbow of flowers managed to shine through the dour day. He passed through a dark and narrow corridor beneath a stone archway. The abundant plant life on the ceiling made the space even tighter. He always scurried through as quickly as possible for fear that the plants would come to life and consume him.

The corridor led into a smaller, squared-off area that housed the resting places of former governors of Roguewave. Big stone tablets were their headstones, and they stood taller and broader than he was.

In one of the corners behind the hedges was a small table with two chairs. Eddie often came here to practice and play his games with his sisters when they were willing. However, most of the time, he ended up playing alone. Isla's mind, as usual, would be off somewhere else entirely. Avery would get bored after a short game and want to go off on one of her endless adventures.

Eddison laid the board on the table and emptied the small wooden pieces that were in the shapes of assorted ships. Originally, they had been little figurine men, but Eddie crafted ships from a plank of wood because he liked the idea of a sea battle modification. Everything was custom-built so that he could play with more pieces and have longer games. However, that meant he had to carry around a much larger board, but that didn't bother him.

The thin, foldable gaming platform was covered in small circles. Each player could arrange their pieces in whatever formation they wanted, but they had to be careful because each of the twenty-two pieces only moved a specific way. The object of the game was to capture all the opponent's ships or take out the commanding piece – in Eddie's version, that was the Grand Ship.

After he arranged both sides the way he wanted, he began moving his ships. He played the commander of both fleets and did his best to outdo his previous moves. He worried about what others might think of him when he played alone. But if he was honest, he rather enjoyed playing by himself.

He sat for around an hour, moving pieces and getting lost in the battle of his own making, before he heard a distant clash of thunder. What followed was the tapping of boots and the subtle clanking of metal, accompanied by a pair of low male voices.

"For security measures, that's why," a man was saying, closer now. "I plan on sailing back to Helmburough in no more than two weeks."

"Is there something we should be worried about?" the other man said.

A deep and confident chuckle came the first man that Eddison heard. "There's a thousand guns on my ship alone, Governor. No, you shouldn't be worried about anything."

He heard their voices grow louder as they entered the narrow corridor. *They're coming this way.* The sound of the heavy boots stopped. Eddison turned his head and looked wide-eyed at Governor Tytus, standing there in a white coat with gold trimming.

He was a plump man who was sweating profusely despite the cool day. His head tilted upon spotting Eddison in the corner, and his chin tripled underneath. "The governor's sector of the gardens are off-limits, boy," he said authoritatively.

Eddie honestly didn't know that this section was off-limits. If he had, he would've never have gone down that darkened corridor so many times.

He could see the governor concentrate a little harder. "You look familiar, boy. Who are you?"

"Uh, Ed-Ed-Eddison Battier, Mr. Governor, sir."

The man standing next to him in a royal emerald coat cocked his head upon hearing Eddison say his name. "Mr. Governor, sir?" the man said. "What a title you have, Tytus."

"Grand Commander Cross, I apologize for this intrusion," Tytus growled. *That's him? Alistair Cross?* "Eddison should find another place to play his games."

"It's quite all right." Alistair Cross raised his hand. "I knew this one's father." That much information was about the extent of what Eddie knew of Commander Cross. His father didn't speak much of his time in the Navy. "Your father was a great man."

"Th-Thank you, Grand Commander."

"I don't mean it as much of a compliment." Eddie didn't know what he meant by that. Cross looked to Governor Tytus, who stared at the ground after the comment. "Are you playing board battalion, Eddison?"

"Yes."

Alistair began walking around the bushes closer to Eddie.

Tytus cleared his throat. "Should we continue our conversation, Grand Commander?"

"I believe our conversation has run its course, Tytus." Alistair slid into the chair opposite Eddison. "You can go now. I'd like to play a game with young Battier here."

Eddison's arms couldn't move from the tension.

Governor Tytus wiped the sweat from his forehead. "Very well, then." The fattest man with the fattest wallet in

Roguewave waddled away with his chin high, but tail tucked firmly between his legs.

Alistair settled in his chair. Eddie was too timid to look him in the eyes. "I didn't mean to intrude on your conversation, Commander Cross."

"Grand. Grand Commander Cross. We must not forget that."

"I-I'm sorry."

"Regardless, you being here saved me from a prolonged conversation with the most irritating man I've ever met."

"Oh."

Eddison finally looked up. The Grand Commander had sharp eyes as blue as the sea he ruled over. He was around his late fifties yet had the appearance of a man twenty years younger. His black hair curled at his ears, and the skin under his eyebrows was meaty and red. His jawline glistened from a recent shave. Most officers in the provincial military were to abide by a certain grooming standard, but Eddie didn't remember the exact particulars.

Alistair scanned the board. He picked up the Grand Ship figurine that was painted black and examined it. "I have my own board battalion table set up in my captain's quarters on the *Hydra.* However, this isn't a standard version, I see... What is this?"

"Uh, no, sir, this is m-my own edition."

A smile crept up on one side of the commander's mouth. "Your own edition?" he asked while toying with the piece in his hands. "Well, young Battier, explain, and let's get started."

Grand Commander Cross is about to play me in my own version of board battalion...

"It's the same game. The board is just bigger, and the pieces are ships instead of soldiers."

"It's a naval battle edition?" His smile grew more prominent. "Did you make all the figurines yourself?"

"Yes, Grand Commander."

"Well, I already prefer your version, Eddison."

Eddie forced a smile. He could feel the area around his neck becoming tired from tension. He tried to breathe slowly and calm down. *Don't be scared. Don't be afraid. He's actually very kind so far. Don't be afraid.*

"I tried to get my son to play this and keep his mind sharp." He rotated the pieces and placed them in a manner that was to his liking. Then, he wiped his hands and fiddled his fingers. "However, he had little interest."

"M-My brothers and sisters don't really like playing with me either."

"Is that right? That's a shame," Cross said as his gaze never broke away. "However, I'd be willing to bet that you're smarter than all of them, aren't you?"

Eddison was at a loss for words. "All my siblings are v-very smart, Grand Commander Cross."

"Good. That's what you should say... even if you successfully dodged my question." He took a long pause and remained unshakably still. "What's your academic ranking for your age group?"

Eddison rubbed his leg and replied, "First."

"There it is." Alistair leaned forward. His head cast a shadow over his fleet. He spoke in Aelic, the language of the warring clans on the southern continent of Autera – his mother's native tongue. "Are you proficient in other languages as well?"

"Yes, sir," he replied in Aelic.

"Ah, I see some of your mother's influence."

Eddison wondered if it was appropriate to speak the language of the southern clans, but Aelic was the first one that came to his mind. *Father traveled the world, but he rarely spoke about the people he came across on his voyages. All he told us was how lucky we are, and we shouldn't take our place in the world for granted, even if we do live in Roguewave.*

He crossed his legs, leaned back in his chair, and removed

a pristine wooden box from his inner coat pocket. Inside was a tobacco pipe that he began the process of smoking. "Perhaps you should be educated in Helmburough. Our academy is much more prestigious than Roguewave's. It could allow you more opportunities once you're older."

"I don't like being away from my family. We're really close."

"Are you?" Cross pressed.

Eddie hesitated. "Well, my eldest brother is a great fighter, and he travels, so I don't really see him as much as my other siblings." *I may be talking too much,* he thought to himself. "I think my brother is dueling your son soon."

"They are."

"Are you going to be there to watch the duel?"

"No," Cross replied plainly. "I have more important matters to attend to than a silly duel between two boys attempting to disguise themselves as men." All Eddison gleaned from that statement was that he had insulted Xavier and his own son. "If either of them knew what was good for them, they wouldn't be wasting their time fighting in a sandpit and aim their focus towards their studies." Alistair pointed to Eddison's bruised eyes, which had now gone a shade of blue. "You're not a fighter, are you?"

"I wish I was."

"Eddison, I've spent my entire life around soldiers, and the ones that truly loved to fight for the sake of fighting were all morons. And more often than not, their time in this world was a lot shorter."

Eddie rubbed his damp palms on his pant legs. "Forgive me, Com—Grand Commander, but you're a fighter. The stories say you're one of the greatest to ever live. My father didn't even deny that."

"Perhaps they're true, perhaps not. The fact is, I'm still able to sit across from you today because of one thing and one thing only: I, more than anybody, will find a way to win. The honor of fighting and defending one's country is undeniable. But to put yourself in a position to win the fight or a battle before it even begins is another phenomenon entirely. Thinking outside of the ordinary to achieve something is a gift that most don't have."

Eddison thought about what those words meant as best he could.

Cross pointed his lit pipe at the board upon taking a puff. "Look at what you've done here. You've improved upon an already great game. My guess is you're very good at it as well, right? It's because you know how to win it. Let me tell you, Eddison, when the day comes where you find a way to apply that mind of yours to other things, that is the day your life will change forever."

A crash of thunder made Eddie jump.

Alistair's chuckle was unsettling. "Well, young Battier, before we start, I should tell you that there are nearly a thousand men on my crew, and not one has managed to claim a victory over me in this game. So, shall we begin?"

SIX

THE WIDOW II

Adelaide washed her children's clothes in the communal cleaning buckets along the riverbank. The water had risen, and the current flowed faster from the recent rainfall. Her youngest daughter Isla used this time of chores to practice her archery skills on a nearby tree. Since this was a weekly occurrence, her proficiency with a bow had grown to an expert level. It would have made the washing go faster if her daughter would lend a hand, but it was important for Isla to have this catharsis. She was always quiet, but after the death of Mathias, she had become near emotionless.

Leo rested at her feet until it was time to retrieve arrows. All Isla had to do was give him a nod when she was ready, and Leo would pull the arrows from the tree with his mouth.

If only I could get Leo to help with the washing as well.

Nearly a hundred buckets lined the riverside. This was considered the washing hour, but today, that was not the case. There were only around six buckets occupied, and the women using them couldn't be spaced farther away from Adelaide. *After all these years I've lived here, and still, some of these women are frightened of me.*

Adelaide felt fortunate to have five children keeping her

company and her mind busy. She often pondered the horror she would be living without them. Those thoughts had increased tenfold since her love passed.

Outside of her children, Adelaide mostly stayed to herself in an attempt to ease the stress of the domesticated shrews of Roguewave. But after this long, she wondered if it had the opposite effect. *If these women only knew who I used to be, their caution against me would be justified.*

She pressed hard against the washboard to remove the dirt and bloodstains from the shirt Eddison was beaten in. He had confessed that he spent the evening playing his game with Grand Commander Alistair Cross, a man whose gaze she hadn't trusted when they crossed paths so long ago. Adelaide's attempt to get any valuable information from her naive son about Cross' demeanor and intentions in Roguewave fell by the wayside. All he said was that Cross was different than he thought and better at board battalion than anyone he had played against. While that was interesting information, it wasn't the type she was attempting to pry out of him. He was the smartest boy she'd ever known, but he was still a boy.

Adelaide wiped the sweat from her brow and watched the tight grouping of arrows Isla was slamming into the tree. Her technique was flawless. *Mathias instructed her well. Not the way I was taught, but the only thing that matters is the arrow finding its mark.* Girls in the Unified Provinces were not allowed formal combat training. Their curriculum mostly consisted of managing the house and support jobs. Something neither her nor her daughters had an interest in.

The thought reminded her. "Leo!" she yelled. "Attention!" The curly-haired dog stood up and yanked on Isla's belt with his teeth. Isla turned her head. "Time for you to go see Livian," Adelaide signed.

Doctors from every province tried their best to fix her loss of hearing. Mathias even pulled rank and got the finest doctor from the Capital to look at her, but not even he could do anything for her. Educating her had been difficult. Most of it was done in Molten City by a language specialist, Livian Emerson. Aside from her, nearly every other professor informed Adelaide and her late husband they "couldn't spend the majority of their time devoted to a single student." But anyone who spent five minutes with Isla would want to do anything for her.

Livian was a wonderful woman that invented every hand signal and sign for their family to communicate with Isla.

Isla nodded and went to retrieve the arrows and place them back in her quiver. She flung the bow around her back, and then her hound barked deep and low, signaling his desire for a run. Isla obliged, and all Adelaide got was a quick wave before they both ran off into the thick foliage. *Looks like they're taking the long way.*

Before Adelaide turned back around, she heard, "Is this one taken?"

It had been so long since anyone approached her for conversation. The woman was not kempt by any stretch of the imagination. Her hair was tied back, and the bottom of her dress was worn and dirty from dragging along the ground. Adelaide was always very aware of her surroundings and the people in them. But she was confident she had never seen this woman before.

"No," Adelaide said. "It's all yours."

The crooked-faced woman gave her a comforting smile. "I apologize if I'm intruding, but it's so boring doing this alone. The prospect of company is nice."

"Sure." *This woman is going to talk me to death. I know it.* "I don't know if I'm considered great company these days."

"Don't be so hard on yourself. Us widows must stick together." The woman began submerging her clothes in the soapy bucket.

Widow?

Adelaide said nothing. She didn't have to.

"My Willam died just over ten years ago. He was a casualty of the rebellion," the woman continued.

Adelaide cleared her throat. "Which one?"

"The Pirate Rebellion… the third one."

"I'm sorry. Those... rebellions were nasty affairs. My husband used to tell me all about them."

"They were." The smile still remained on the woman's face. "He was a good man, my husband. I miss him every day. I still cry about him being gone. Never feel bad for missing him, and don't fight the emotions. In an odd way, it's how we keep their memory alive."

"I can't help but fight..." Adelaide snapped. "Forgive me. You know my name, but I don't believe I know yours."

"Oh, I'm sorry, my manners are rubbish." The woman wiped her hand on her dress which had yellowed from the sun. "I'm Naomi, Naomi Cobb." She extended her hand, and Adelaide shook it. "Pleasure to finally meet you."

"Finally?"

Naomi's smile faded ever so slightly before forcing itself back to its welcoming position. "I've been wanting to talk to you for a while now since I heard about your husband's passing. No one should have to go through something like this alone."

Adelaide corrected her. "I'm not alone. I have my children."

Naomi's comforting energy completely shifted. "Yes, but how long until they are taken from you as well?"

Adelaide stopped scrubbing. Soap slid down her forearms. "Beg your pardon?" she asked, and Naomi replied with nothing.

All she gave was an angle-eyed look of intensity emphasized by the reddish bags under her eyes.

Adelaide cleared her throat. "What provincial flag did your husband sail under?"

"He sailed under the flag of your late husband's cause."

Naomi's statement gave Adelaide pause. She had no idea what she meant. "My husband's ship was called the *Abyss*. Your husband sailed on the *Abyss?*"

"I'm not talking about his ship, Adelaide. I'm talking about your husband's plot to bring down the Assembly. The corrupt power that lords over all of us with violence and oppression with no repercussions."

This woman is mad, was the first thing Adelaide thought. "Excuse me?"

"My husband fought alongside the pirates under Mathias Battier's secret plot to bring justice and prosperity to the world. A plot that involved destroying the men of the Assembly and their self-made system that only allows them to prosper. His mission was to collapse it all into the sea."

"You are making daft and dangerous accusations about my husband that are not true. I will not allow it to continue." The sounds of the rushing water only grew as a silence built between them. Adelaide wrung the wet blouse and chucked it aside.

"You best believe it, Adelaide. Do you know what's been done to your people since you left? The warring clans in Autera are now in chains, working as slaves, living off one sparse meal a day. Your family and culture are dying off, and no one is doing anything about it because we are being lied to."

"My family is in chains?"

"Yes. Your father, your mother, and your sister... I promise, Adelaide, I'm telling you the truth. The Assembly must be stopped. I spent five years in Colwerth Prison, living in the dark. My child was taken from me because of Willam's opposition to them. I hate the repercussions of his actions, but I hold no ill will toward him. I couldn't see it at the time, but what he was doing was right." She dropped her head and closed her eyes. "Like I said, I spent five years in the dark. And when you spend so long in the dark, you learn to see clearly at some point. I know with all my heart that Mathias Battier's Cannon Fire Plot was right."

Cannon Fire Plot?

Adelaide's hands shook. She didn't know what to do with this stranger of a woman who somehow knew more about her late husband than she did.

It's a lie. Lies from a madwoman. Mathias was always open and honest with her about everything.

"So, you're saying my husband was some type of... what? Revolutionary?"

"No, Adelaide. Mathias Battier *was* the revolution."

She disregarded the clothes altogether and abruptly faced her, "You seem to know a lot about my husband and his dealings. I'm having trouble believing that something of this magnitude could be kept from me."

Naomi went quite smug. "You're right, only a highly intelligent and cunning individual could pull off such a thing. Surely that wasn't Mathias." Adelaide hated the sarcasm in her voice. "Listen, I don't mean to antagonize you in any way. My intentions here are the opposite, I assure you. I was sent here to help and deliver a message."

"What message?"

Naomi took a deep breath as she looked up and down the river. She leaned in close. "You must get you and your children out of Roguewave and as far away from the reaches of the Assembly as possible. They've gotten to your husband already. We believe they're coming for the rest of the Battiers next."

There were so many questions running through her mind. However, her mouth couldn't grasp a single one to get out first. Much like her nervous son, she stumbled over her words. "Y-You think they killed my husband?"

"We *know* they did. The coroner that did your husband's autopsy lied and was most likely paid off by the Assembly. Mathias' heart giving out was highly unlikely. He must've been poisoned after they finally figured him out." Naomi looked around once more. "I have to go. Find a spice trader named Leven Parke in the harbor."

"Find him for what?"

"To help save your family's life." Naomi stood to her feet, leaving her clothes behind. "Stay safe. Mathias' attack against the Assembly starts tonight."

"Attack? My husband is dead! Who's going to execute this plan?

The smile on Naomi's face returned. "Marstellar Lockett."

The name struck a deep nerve. It did with everyone. Captain Lockett was the Master and Commander of the Pirate Rebellion who famously captured Tyver Island and set fire to twenty Helmburough trade ships fully loaded with noble silk and sugar, two of the Capital's favorite commodities. The stories say he was the closest entity to taking down the Unified Navy until he was beaten by Alistair Cross in the Aster Sea.

That was where Adelaide questioned Naomi, because common knowledge said that Captain Lockett was hanged on the deck of the *Hydra* after his defeat.

Naomi finally turned and walked away, vanishing into the trees like a gust of wind.

Adelaide walked the busy harbor with the markets buzzing behind her. She had grown immune to the aroma of molten crab as her mind raced with endless thoughts from all the information the stranger unloaded.

She made her way down the steps onto the jetty, where the small ships bumped into one another while the larger vessels were at anchor in the bay. At the bottom of the steps, a manifest rested on a podium. The harbor master, not thirty feet away, argued with a merchant about a docking fee. The dispute was loud, and after only moments of eavesdropping, she found out that the harsh exchange was only over a single coin.

Time was of the essence to peek at the manifest and look for the name of the spice merchant, Leven Parke. She flipped through the massive ledger. The book was filled with all the information of ships that had sailed in and out of the bay this past year. She stopped when she saw his name, as well as his docking bay number and the supplies he was carrying in his cargo hold.

The wind continued to brush by Adelaide, and a familiar smell entered her nostrils. She walked farther down the dock until she reached the very end.

There was a cog at anchor. The smell Adelaide remembered amplified as her nose hairs twitched. Adelaide lifted her dress and walked on the narrow, uneven plank onto the small ship. The goods it had been carrying must have already been unloaded because it was sparse on deck. She decided she might have better luck down below. Adelaide descended the short staircase. There was rustling and the sound of moving crates. She turned her head to see a man hoisting a wooden box on top of another one.

"Hello?" Adelaide asked.

The man turned his greasy bald head to face her. He had a thick black beard that grew to his chest, and he was built like a tree stump. "May I help you, my lady?" he said in a deep voice while scooping coins into a pouch.

"I'm looking for a man named Leven Parke."

His facial expression never altered. "You Adelaide?"

"Yes."

The man nodded. "Anything smell familiar?"

"I smelled the Cindah spice as soon as I stepped on the dock."

He reached his hand into an open barrel. The man closed

in on Adelaide with a handful of red powder and offered it to her. She held out her hand, and he poured the spice into her open palm like an hourglass would drop sand. She brought it up to her nose and took a whiff. The sharp smell of spice burned so much she could feel it in the front of her skull. The aroma brought her so many memories of her childhood. Most of them consisted of feasts she used to share with her family and friends as a girl.

"Smell like home?" Leven asked.

"Yes, it does. You must have traveled a long way to acquire these if you got them from my homeland." Cindah spice was from the Cindah Clan, one of the smallest of the clans and ally to Adelaide's Trezbe Clan.

"That I did." His head dropped. "You wouldn't have liked what I saw either, Adelaide." His eyes met hers. "The Cindah were all gone, and the ones that remained were dead. The Assembly has successfully relocated them all to the Okamara Desert. The Trezbe is next."

Just like her conversation with Naomi, she didn't want to believe anything this man was saying. Her knees buckled a little, and she fell back to sit on the staircase. "Relocated? I don't understand. When did this happen? How is no one aware of this?"

"The Occupation of Autera that has been labeled in the papers as peaceful and good for everyone in the world is a lie. I saw it with my own two eyes. The Assembly wants the resources of your homeland, and they don't care if they kill every clan folk on the continent to get what they want."

She clutched her chest, and her heart beat faster. "How could they keep something like this a secret?"

"Because what they release in the papers is not absolute truth. It's *their* truth. Assembly Truth. It's all lies," Parke said. He continued to stack crate after crate, unloading and loading shipments the entire time. Adelaide followed him wherever he went as he went about his business to conceal truer intentions.

"This can't go on. If what you say is true, this can't go on."

He ushered into a quiet spot behind the cover of stacked crates. He then whispered, "I know. Your husband felt the same way. That's why he started supplying the rebellions shortly after witnessing it all."

Adelaide took a moment to gather her thoughts. "Why would he keep all this from me?"

"I can't answer that. It's possible no one can. You have to understand the level of secrecy he needed to make it as far as he did," Parke said. "The fact is you need to get your children so we can leave before nightfall."

"Before nightfall? That's too fast! All of my children aren't even here."

"I'm sorry we couldn't get to you sooner. It was Mathias who was planning your family's exodus from this place, and he never got to share the details with us. Regardless, it doesn't matter now. Things are going to get very dangerous tonight, and this might be the best opportunity you have to get out of Roguewave unscathed."

"And go where?" she threw open her arms. "You've already told me nothing good awaits me in my homeland!"

Leven leaned in close. "The Free Islands… I've also heard that new lands have been discovered to the West. Marstellar Locket will sail us to our new lives, Tarsa."

Tarsa. It meant "princess" — a title she abandoned long ago.

SEVEN
THE SILENT ONE I

The tiny flame flickered at the base of the dying wick. *Does everything that brings light into the world eventually snuffed?*

Isla was often lost in a web of endless thoughts that seemed to lack a beginning or an end. The ideas just appeared and disappeared in an endless cycle that never stopped.

At every waking moment, a foggy echo peppered her ears, mirroring the sound of an endless whistle.

A soft thud from a clap snapped her to attention. Her eyes were still locked on the melting candle until they eventually looked to Livian Emerson, her private speech and mannerisms professor.

Livian was shuffling around in her chair, for she was losing patience. But Isla wasn't going to miss seeing the fire go out. The wavering dance of orange and yellow had her transfixed. There was a calmness as well as a stimulating satisfaction that eased her mind.

Livian gathered a new candle. Before the fire died completely, Livian placed the new wick in the whimpering fire, and the new candle's life began. *Light will always find a way. Sounds like something Father would say.*

Her eyes turned to Livian, who was shaking her head at Isla with a smile. "Are you with me now?" she signed with crossed legs in her cushioned rocking chair.

"Yes, I'm sorry, Livian."

"That's all right, darling."

Livian's long brown hair curled and spiraled in every direction. She had pasty skin, and she often commented on how Roguewave's heat and humidity didn't agree with her. She was originally from the province of Northwood, where the rains fell almost daily, and lumber was more valuable than knowledge. Their academy tended to produce the strongest soldiers due to the boys learning how to swing an axe before walking, but they weren't the most scholarly and often finished last in academics.

There was probably not one person in the world that had done more for Isla and her family than Livian.

Isla remembered how Eddie learned so quickly. Even at eight years old, her mother and father would make him stay up past his bedtime to tutor them. Isla later found out they were rewarding his teachings with pies. If his ability to stay small and skinny hadn't been as great as it was, he'd be a little round boy. She didn't find out about Eddie's private tutoring sessions until two years later when he accidentally confessed while stuffing his face with said pies.

Livian showed Isla new signs she recently developed to add to her vocabulary while Leo slept at her feet the entire time. He would often wake himself up from his snoring. He had vivid dreams that made his eyelids quiver as he softly barked. Isla wondered if he was protecting her from evil while he slept or if he was merely chasing stray alley cats.

They were wrapping up their weekly lesson when Livian had a close-lipped smile come across her face. "I made something for you," she said while digging in her book bag under her chair. "Sadly, as you know, outside of your family, you will have trouble communicating with others. However, I think I found a way to make it a little easier for you," she signed.

Livian walked over to her and handed her a pocket-sized journal. Isla ran her hand across the leather cover and opened it to see the pages filled with illustrations of signs and descriptions of what they meant. It had everything from simple greetings to general statements that could be referenced if she were having trouble communicating with someone else.

Isla couldn't help but smile. She looked up at Livian, and involuntary tears of happiness spilled from her eyes. She jumped up and hugged her, squeezing her as tight as she could.

"Thank you," she signed repeatedly.

Livian was teary-eyed as well. "I started working on it the day we met. It's been a long journey, darling." A thump in Livian's belly caught her off guard. Isla looked up at her. "I suppose that should tell you I'm with child. Oliver is positive it's going to be a girl."

Isla opened her book and flipped through the pages until she found something she thought was appropriate. She stopped on the page that had the illustration of a "congratulations" sign. She turned the journal around and showed it to Livian, and they both chuckled.

Livian's husband was Oliver Emerson, but everyone around the bay just called him Doctor or Doc. He helped many citizens of all ages with ailments and oversaw the training of practicing aidmen like her brother Caldwell.

Doctor Emerson was the first man her father visited upon discovering Isla's condition. He felt terrible and near shame when he found there was nothing he could do to help. Little did he know that he and his wife would selflessly do more for the Battier family than anyone in the world.

Isla thought about Livian's child, and a stray thought

prompted a frown, and Livian took notice. "Hopefully, she doesn't turn out like me," Isla signed as she hung her head.

She felt the gentle hands of her professor lift her chin in the air, forcing their eyes to meet. "I could only dream of her being like you."

The smile slowly faded from Livian's face. She turned her head to the front door, and Isla heard the soft thumps of banging.

Someone is here, Isla thought. *Whoever it is, Livian doesn't seem to be expecting them.*

Shadows moved on the other side of the door. The wood pulsated from the repeated blows. Dust from the frame went airborne.

"The authorities are here for you," Livian signed.

Me?

Leo was now at attention. His ears, as well as the fur running down his spine, stood straight up. He was about to bark, but Isla instinctively put her hand down to stop him. Leo obeyed and awaited his master's command. "Why would they be here for me?"

"They aren't saying." Livian's eyes darted around the room. She took Isla's hand and pulled her up the staircase. At the top was a closet that Livian flung open. She fought through jackets and heavy coats to get to the wall behind them. Then, there was a shift of movement, and somehow, the wall opened like a door.

"Get in!" Livian signed.

It was a small crawl space that left Isla and Leo little room to move.

"Keep Leo quiet. Can you do that, Isla?"

She could see the fear on Livian's face. "Yes, ma'am."

"Don't come out until I open the door, okay?"

"Yes, ma'am."

Livian gave her a nod and a forced smile as she shut the hidden door.

Isla was in pitch-black. She couldn't remember ever clutching Leo so tight. She was never one to show fear, but she was petrified. *I didn't do anything wrong. Why would the greencoats be after me?*

Shuddering in the dark, seconds felt like minutes, and minutes felt like hours.

EIGHT

THE AIDMAN I

Caldwell finished setting the broken arm of a fisherman who sustained the injury harpooning a sword whale. It was a difficult task, to put it simply. There were rumors and sightings of sword whales in the Tearing Sea that were the size of a frigate. The name *sword whale* came from their sharp fins that cut through water, prey, and even ships with clean and deep slashes.

The fisherman said the rope attached to the spear caught around his arm and pinned it to the boat. After that, he felt a crack, and now, here he was. The man was around the middle of his life but appeared far older. His eyes had gone foggy, and his skin blistered from the sun. He was not pleased about breaking his arm, and he was more upset having a stick and sling attached over his "throwing shoulder."

"Ow long I pose to wear tis?" the man said with his jaw favoring the right side of his face.

"It's going to be a few months... Your name again?"

"Mine?"

Caldwell looked around the office with no one else around. "Yes, your name?"

"Mel," the fisherman said.

"Mel... what?"

The weathered man gave him a foggy glare, "Just Mel."

"Well, all right, then." Caldwell went to his narrow desk outfitted with a quill and ink and wrote Mel's name in his logbook. A practicing aidman must keep track of everyone he treated and provide full reports to the academy. The proper professors reviewed them and would check in on the treated patients sometime in the future to see how they did and how they were healing. Many folks didn't like taking their medical problems to aidmen because they were young and still in school, but it was a much cheaper option compared to going to a specialized doctor.

The exam room was a small and dingy place filled with a variety of old medical instruments dangling along the wooden walls. A significant upgrade of the academy facilities was in order, but this time, it seemed to be wishful thinking. Mel sat atop a withered table where old blood stains darkened the wood.

"Where do you live, Mel?"

"Live?"

"Are you having trouble hearing me?" Caldwell asked, mildly frustrated.

"I hear fine."

"Then, where do you live?"

"Boat," he replied.

"You live on your boat? What kind of boat?"

"Sloop."

"Okay, what's your sloop's name?"

"The *Fish*."

"The *Fish?* Hope it didn't take you long to come up with that name," Caldwell said with a hint of his sister Avery's sarcasm.

"Is you mocking me, boy?"

"Absolutely not, Mel of the *Fish*. Come back and see me if

you need anything adjusted. I'll be sure to help you in any way
I can."

Mel stood to his feet. "Ow am I pose to spear whales?"

"You're not going to for a while. And don't convince
yourself you're all better too soon and start chucking spears. If
your arm doesn't heal properly, you'll have to find a new
throwing motion or risk accidentally impaling one of your
crew members."

"Uh?" Mel said.

Caldwell put his hand on Mel's shoulder and ushered him
out the door. "Farewell, Mel. Hope it heals swiftly." He
returned to his log and finished writing down Mel's
address: *The Fish. A sloop.*

Surely the whales are smarter than he is.

Most of his time was spent in this small study above the
medical wing of Molten Bay Academy. Roguewave wasn't
known for its scholars and medical practitioners, but his father
always told him, "People who are great at something don't all
come from the same place. The good world is rich, and
potential lies everywhere." Caldwell tried to live by those
words. His brother was already the best duelist in the
world. *Can't I be great at something too?*

He touched his sternum, which still pained him from when
Xavier kicked him out of the sandpit days ago. Every time he
felt the pain, he reminded himself, *He's my brother and a good
person disguised as an ass.*

He leaned back in his chair to stretch out his sore and tender
body. He admired the collection of academic books that took up
a large portion of the wall. He had read all of them. Well,
almost all of them. There were a few that his youngest brother
Eddie got for him as a gift: *Dr. Poplinn's Guide to Exotic Plants and
Animals* and *A Traveler's Guide Through Botan Rainforest by Dr.
Poplinn.* Caldwell had scanned through them to appease his
brother's gift-giving mind but had little desire to commit to

them, for his academic books were more practical to devote time to and not casual reading. Besides, his brother wouldn't shut up about the rainforest anyway. He would go on for hours about spined tigers, insects as big as dogs and alley cats, plants that would alter body and cognitive chemistry, and even sightings of ancient water drakes. However, Caldwell's imagination was absent. Typically, he only believed what he could see for himself.

A knock at his door.

"You need something else, Mel?" he replied.

There was no response as the door swung open. "Who's Mel?" his best friend Emil said. Behind him walked Maynard and Fili. His trio of friends never left him alone for long.

"Mel is a fisherman who fishes whales aboard the *Fish*."

"What?" Fili said, rubbing his forehead.

"You heard me right."

Emil wasn't hearing anything. "Regardless, we're going to the commissary for lunch, so let's go," he said, as he wasn't satiated until he had eaten half of Roguewave.

"I'm not that hungry. Besides, I have to study for the next examinations."

"Carlie Domines and the other girls are up there right now!"

Caldwell closed his log before the ink had even dried. "On second thought, I could eat."

They walked along the academy campus that resided on the northern cliffs overlooking the bay. From here, Caldwell could see the harbor and the markets, and ever so slightly, farther to the south, he could see the sign for Mey's Bakery. The huge advertisement was the size of a fly from this vantage point. When he looked at it, he always thought of his little brother Eddie. *That place brings more joy to him as much as anything else in the world. Well, perhaps not more than his board game, but it's close.*

"Have you all heard any more reasons as to why the *Hydra* and Grand Commander Cross are here in Roguewave?" Fili asked.

"I hear there's a tropical storm building, and he's here to command it to go north so it doesn't hit us," Maynard joked as they trekked up the hill along the cliffside. The ocean breeze was a welcome after Caldwell spent his day in the humid medical room, and the crashing waves were decompressing ambiance.

Emil took it seriously. "Yeah, like the Assembly will care what happens to Roguewave."

"I don't know, seems like the capital needs us to make them look good," Maynard stated.

Emil scrunched his face. "How do you figure?"

"Well, you can't be the wealthiest province without there being a poorest province."

"You came up with that all by yourself?" Emil said sarcastically. "Are you dabbling in philosophy now?"

"I doubt that's considered philosophy," Caldwell added.

Maynard jumped in. "My cousin, who lives in Larwich of Axelford, went to the Helmburough Academy for some choir competition or something, and he told me the girl-to-boy ratio was at least seven-to-one."

"That should terrify you then, Maynard. That's just more girls to reject you," Emil said, chuckling before he even finished the statement. All three joined in the laughter.

They settled down. Caldwell took one last look over the bay. The sun directly above made all the water shimmer with specks of white. The wind whipped passed his face high on the cliff. "You have to admit, though, the view is something and can't be bought."

"Aye, it's something," Fili agreed.

"Not for long, though. Look northeast over here," Maynard said at the top of the cliff. Caldwell walked farther up the steps carved into the cliffside, and as the northeastern sky came to view, it was black. "Looks like there's another round of storms on the way. And all of you were laughing at me for my Commander Cross theory. I wouldn't be against an apology."

"Stranger things have occurred, I guess," Caldwell said, humoring his friend.

"They have?" Fili asked.

Caldwell shook his head. He took one final look over the bay and harbor. His eyes moved to the fort, and he noticed a small group of soldiers on horseback riding off in different directions at a hurried pace. *That's odd.*

"Caldwell," Emil said. "Let's head inside."

Potato and broccoli soup were on the menu. None of the boys were pleased about it, but then again, they weren't here for the food. There was an awkwardness in the air because there was hardly anyone in the commissary. There was Caldwell, his three friends, and a group of girls already eating at the middle table.

The space was large and used to feed around five hundred people at a time. The ceilings were high, and all four sides were open archways that led outside. In every direction he looked out, he could see only the sky, as if they were dining with ancient deities. Its beauty was tainted by harsh gusts of wind that often blew food and drinks everywhere.

They each grabbed a bowl and a spoon, and Lady Pamula filled them.

"How's the soup today, Lady Pamula?" Caldwell asked.

"Made it myself, so it's really good," she said.

She wasn't the best cook in the world, but she was a sweet older lady, and Caldwell could forgive her mediocre culinary skills.

"Where do we sit?" Emil asked.

"I don't know about you, but I'm going to try and sit next to girls," Caldwell said.

"You're just going to go sit by them?" Fili asked.

"Yeah."

"I'm with you, Battier," Emil said.

"Course you are."

Lady Pamula took Caldwell's bowl and began filling it. "Are you boys trying to court those fine young ladies over there?"

They all turned. "Why, yes, we are, Lady Pamula," Emil said, a little too confidently.

A big smile crossed her face. "Well, I overheard them talking, and long tall Carlie Domines has her eyes on you, Caldwell."

His cheeks flushed, and heat radiated off them.

Maynard smacked him on the shoulder.

"What did she say?" Caldwell asked.

"Oh, it's just girls talking. Perhaps you should go find out for yourself." Pamula gave him a wink, and she picked up her empty pot of soup and retreated to the kitchen.

"Let's give it a shot," Caldwell said.

He saw Fili squint and lower his head. He wasn't the most confident. Addressing girls was more nerve-wracking to him than the prospect of fighting pirates.

The boys made a beeline for the table, and the girls took notice of their approach.

"Mind if we sit with you?" Emil said with a chuckle to ease the tension.

The group of six girls all looked to one another with coy smiles. Carlie looked up to Caldwell with her big brown eyes. "Sure thing."

The girls grouped to one side of the table, and the boys sat opposite them.

"What are you ladies doing today?" Emil asked.

"We had our cooking class today," the short-haired blonde said.

I think her name is... Marsha... What is it... Marisha!

"So, if you're eating lunch here now, but you just came from cooking... I'm guessing whatever you made didn't turn out very well?" Caldwell said with a smile.

The girls' faces got red as they side-eyed one another.

"Let's just say, you won't want to sample anything we prepare anytime soon," Marisha said as the girls looked to one another, hunkered down, and giggled.

"I think you're overestimating our palates. If it's edible and free, you'll probably not hear any complaints from us," Maynard replied.

"Sure thing," Fili said quietly.

The laughter started to die, just as it became awkwardly quiet.

"We haven't seen Avery around much lately, Caldwell. Is she all right?" Carlie asked.

Caldwell swallowed a spoonful of potato soup and said, "My sister tends to do what she wants, and her wants don't in any way remotely involve studying for something."

Caldwell and Carlie shared a look across the table.

A crash of thunder roared overhead. The dark clouds from the northeast were upon them. They watched as the rain trickled down all sides of the commissary, gradually increasing in volume.

Behind them, accompanying the pending storm, was the neighing of horses. Riding them was a small group of five greencoats. *What's this?* The soldiers climbed down from their horses and marched to the table with fresh imprints of rain on their jackets.

"Caldwell Battier, we need you to come with us to the fort," the redheaded soldier demanded.

This had never happened to Caldwell before. Nor had he ever heard of greencoats retrieving someone like this.

The soldiers were only a couple of years older than he was, and he recognized their faces. A lot of greencoats consisted of men who went straight into active service of the Unified Provinces at the age of fifteen instead of continuing formal schooling.

"Am I under arrest for something?" Caldwell asked.

"I'm not going to ask again. Either get up and come with us willingly, or we'll force you." There was nothing but contempt in the soldier's eyes.

What did I do to this guy?

Caldwell was confident in his ability to best the man standing in front of him in combat. However, he didn't think he'd fare well against his flintlock pistol or blade.

Emil stood first. Caldwell, Maynard, and Fili followed. "Well, all we have are bowls and spoons, but I'm sure that's all we'll need against you well-armed, fine, strapping lads," Emil said.

Caldwell looked back at the girls, who were all pale with fear. He turned to his best friends, who were ready to challenge the authorities on his behalf. Their fists were clenched, and their knuckles white. He looked into the eyes of the greencoat that was attempting to take him into custody. Then it came to him.

"I know you," he said to the soldier. His face didn't show any emotion, "I thought you looked familiar. You're Ricky Meeks. My brother beat you in a local duel almost three years ago." Caldwell smiled. "If I remember correctly, his victory over you is the fastest in history... in any province." He watched as Ricky clenched his jaw. Any more pressure and his teeth might have shattered. *Yep, that's him.* "Now, how long do you think it will take me?"

A steady breeze cut through, and another crash of thunder slammed above the commissary roof. They stood there, locked in a trance, waiting for the other to make the first move. He saw the four other greencoats put their hands on their hilts. His friends didn't budge. They were willing and ready to back him, no matter how far it went.

Another moment passed. He thought about the situation and everyone around him.

"Fine," Caldwell said abruptly. "I'll come with you."

"What are you doing?" Emil asked.

"It'll be all right."

Ricky nodded to the other greencoats standing next to him. They put irons on Caldwell's wrists, grabbed him under his arms, and escorted him to the horses.

NINE
THE COWARD BOY II

Eddie saw the sky shift to dark through the lone kitchen window of the Battier home. He went for a closer look, and he could see the storm clouds churning above the bay. *Is it storming again?* A pulsating flash of light flared out from behind the clouds. A crash of thunder followed. *I guess so.*

Eddie didn't like storms. Like many things, they gave him an uneasy feeling. His sister Isla loved rain. She enjoyed standing out in the open and letting the water hit her face, no matter how hard it was coming down.

He walked back to the room that he shared with his brothers. But on his way, something caught the corner of his eye. There was a reflection on Avery's bed. He turned to see she had left her dagger behind, something she never did. He clutched it in his hand and focused. The sounds of rain and thunder above his head began to fade. All that remained was a soft echo.

Avery, you left your dagger on your bed, he said.

It took a moment. *Thanks for telling me. I've been searching for it in the grove for an hour now! I thought I dropped it!* Avery said.

The Hissing Grove? In Dryburn?

Yes.

Molten Bay was so massive that four provinces bordered it. The Battiers lived in the northernmost part of Roguewave in Molten City that touched close to the borders of Swiftwater Province and Dryburn Province. However, it was still an hour's hike to get to the Hissing Grove. The citizens of Dryburn tended to be a bit prickly, mostly due to their arid climate and untenable soil. "The Land of Calloused Dirt" was Dryburn's slogan. Each of the seventeen provinces had words that represented their landscape or what they were known for. "The Land Beneath the Waves" was Roguewave's. It was true that Roguewave's slogan was superior objectively, but there was still an undertone of melancholy as metaphorical waves crashed on top of them.

Mother doesn't like us being out that far by ourselves, especially in those woods.

It's only scary in name and in your mind, Eddie. I'm headed home now, so go ahead and lie for me if Mother asks where I've been.

I really don't want to.

Eddie...

Why stop now, I guess.

I love you, baby brother.

I love you too.

Thunder rolled, and the sounds of the physical world returned.

The main door opened behind him, and he saw his mother with wet hair sticking to her face. "Has Isla made it back yet? Where is Avery?" she asked frantically, ripping cabinets open and proceeding to throw food and clothes into luggage carriers.

"It's only me," he replied.

"Start packing clothes and anything else you think you'll need."

Eddison froze in place. "Is something wrong?"

She grabbed the back of his head. "You're just going to have to do what I say right now, okay?"

"Yes, ma'am."

"Go! Take what you need, Eddie!" his mother yelled.

He raced to his room but was halted by the dagger on resting on Avery's bed. He grabbed it for her and tossed it into his shoulder bag. His most precious board game poked out from under the dresser and after stuffing that in the main pouch, Eddie hardly had any room for essentials like the one's his mother had in mind. *It's essential to me…*

His mother slung open every door and slammed them shut. She hadn't stopped moving since arriving as he haphazardly stuffed some shirts and pants in between the tiny open spaces in his bag.

"Mother, where are we going?" His question was never answered as he was left in silence. "Mother?"

His mother was clearly off. She had taken off her dress and now wore brown pants and a white, loose-fitting shirt, like something Avery would sport. Then, unfurled a white coat, beautiful and pristine that went past her waist. It had aesthetics of an officer's coat yet had symbols of clannish culture. *Trezbe symbols?*

The coat would not be something easily commissioned in the provinces. *Father must have made that for her.*

However, that wasn't what caught him off guard the most. It was the pair of hand-axes dangling from both sides of her leather belt. His eyes grew even wider, and a cold chill raced down his spine when he witnessed her loading one of father's pistols. "Mother?"

"Eddie, you're going to have to be calm. Everything is going to be fine." She dusted off an old brown coat that was also his father's and flung it on in one swift motion. It fell just past her knees, successfully concealing all of her weapons, including the freshly loaded pistol in the inside pocket.

A loud series of bangs slammed on the front door, coinciding with the deafening thunder. "Open up! Molten City Guard!"

Greencoats?

He felt a motherly hand rake across his chest. She put her pointer finger to her mouth, telling him to be quiet. "Get your trunk," she signed.

"Open up! Molten City Guard!"

He put both of his hands through the loop to hoist the heavy trunk. The guards' voices faded for a moment.

Avery, please hurry home. There are guards here at the house, and Mother's got a gun!

This time his sister's reply was instant. *What are you talking about?*

Please hurry!

"Final warning! Open up!" the guards persisted.

He looked to his mother. "Out my bedroom window. Let's go!" she signed, to be discreet.

Eddie had a burst of adolescent adrenaline rushing through his veins that was quickly being counteracted by crippling panic. He tried to carry the trunk through the kitchen, believing he could make it, given the circumstances. However, the trunk hit the front of his knee just hard enough for him to go tumbling over the top of it and into the lower cabinet. *There is no way the guards didn't hear that.*

His thoughts were correct. A booming strike from a metal breacher sent the front door off its hinges. Three greencoats filtered into the dining room, stopping their exit.

"Adelaide Battier, your family is under arrest for suspected treason," one of the guards said, his wispy beard reaching his chest.

"This is a misunderstanding," Mother assured, shoulders back. "But we will come with you. Get up, Eddie."

We are going with them?

The second guard removed two pairs of irons from behind him and approached his mother. The three of them had lowered their rifles after his mother de-escalated the room.

Eddie was still on his back and felt his throbbing forehead where he struck the cabinet.

Then, cannon fire rumbled in the distance, and the guards took notice. They all turned and looked at one another. The low and repetitive sounds thundered and shook their home.

It's coming from the bay. That's the fort's guns.

Before the distracted guard slapped irons onto his mother's wrist, she grabbed the back of his head and slammed it into the countertop. The remaining two men did a double take after the hard blow. They went to grab her, but she was too quick. She kicked the next one off his feet into the wall. His back smacked hard, and he dropped his rifle. She ducked under a bayonet thrusting towards her, and she greeted the final guard with the butt of his companion's gun.

Eddie couldn't comprehend the speed and ferocity with which his mother moved. He never knew his mother could do such a thing. *Is everyone in my family a great fighter except me?*

His mother's warm hand clutched his wrist. His shoulder was nearly wrenched from its socket as she pulled him out the front door, stepping over unconscious guards along the way.

As they descended the steps, the cannon and gunfire grew nearer. His feet hit the level ground, and a massive crash shook the world. A cannonball tore through and smashed into the fountain ahead of them. Eddie's mother covered his head as the statue scattered into thousands of stone pieces. Rain pattered the courtyard and the remnants of the once-proud fountain in the middle of the Seventh Quarter.

A pair of greencoats watching over the courtyard was as confused about the situation as Eddie. "Halt!" one of them said with a shakiness to his voice. His mother stopped and let go of his hand. The blasts continued as she reached inside her coat. "Don't move!"

Her hand was frozen halfway to the pistol. The greencoats' rifles were both trained on them, and Eddie had never been more scared in his life.

The two guards cautiously stepped forward. "On your stomachs! Both of you!"

He followed his mother's lead as she dropped to one knee. Once Eddie knelt, another round of cannon fire blasted through the housing quarter. This time it wasn't just one but ten, destroying everything in the vicinity. Shrapnel and splintered wood dispersed in all directions. He looked back to the foundation of the eastern block of homes, and they were falling in on themselves.

A storm of dust covered them. It was impossible to see beyond a couple feet in any direction.

Avery, please hurry. Something's very wrong! Eddie's nerves and anxiety only grew once he was met with silence. *Avery?*

Nothing.

A tug on the back of his collar brought him to his feet. His mother coughed dust as she dragged him through the courtyard. "We have to get out of here!" she said to him.

The guards were nowhere to be found. From the look of it, they appeared to have been in the wrong spot at the wrong time because the trajectory of the cannon blast went right through where they once stood.

Adelaide dusted off one of the bayonets and gripped it tightly with her right hand while still holding Eddie's collar with her left.

The cannon fire became constant at that point. Anyone within miles of Molten Fort was unsafe. They spilled into the road, where Eddie's heart dropped. Mey's Bakery was in flames and collapsing. Another tug on his collar in the opposite direction choked him.

In the moments the fire ceased, he could hear the battle cries of men and the clattering of metal. The sounds grew louder as another round of cannon fire blew through the bank, sundering it in a matter of seconds. A piece of wood flew into his mother's side, and she screamed. She dropped and released the rifle in the process. She clutched the stake poking out of her.

"Mother!" Eddie cried.

He saw a look in her eyes that he had never seen before as if a new person was in front of him. Her knuckles went white as she roared and ripped the wood from her side.

With pain in her voice, she said, "We have to get to the harbor, Eddie." A loud grunt followed, and she stood to her feet on her own power, picking up the rifle once more.

The dust cleared just enough for him to see a force of thirty greencoats sprinting towards them down the thoroughfare. They were filthy, covered in dirt, gunpowder, dust, and blood.

Eddie heard shouts behind him. A group of fifty men with assorted weapons and clothing charged from the opposite end of the thoroughfare. None looked the same. They didn't have a uniform like the Unified Provinces Armed Forces. He saw a man who was near seven feet tall with a bald head, a skinny and pale man with one eye and a knife in his teeth, a dark-skinned man with a bow and arrow, and even a woman equipped with four swords dangling from her side with two already in hand. The only thing they all had in common was the black sash they had tied around their waists or forehead.

Pirates.

His mother yanked him away from the clash of swords, flesh, and bone, only feet away.

The rain rendered the gunpowder rifles useless. The pirates and the greencoats had no other course of action than a melee. The pirates quickly took the advantage in the fight. A few well-placed arrows found their mark from the dead-shot pirate. The goliath of a man used a boarding axe that broke many of the greencoats' swords. They attempted to try and surround him in the skirmish, but he could not be held down. The woman weaved in and out of the greencoat battalion, cutting them down like they were stationary targets made of hay.

"We have to move, Eddie!" Mother ordered.

The issue was that there was nowhere to go. A battle and the pile of rubble that used to be Mey's Bakery obstructed their escape.

They high-stepped over the debris of burning wood and broken glass. The wound on his mother's side seemed to not affect her anymore. The sensory overload of clanging swords, cannon fire, and heavy rainfall made Eddie's heart race. He looked ahead and could see the top of Molten Fort was completely covered in smoke from its endless barrage. Flashes of fire followed, zooming cannonballs emerging through the thick veil of white.

A battle cry froze Eddie. He turned his head in time to see a greencoat charging him and his mother. He wondered if he was being mistaken for a pirate or if they just wanted them both dead. His mother hurled the bayonet at the soldier like a spear that whipped him backward and dropped him.

She killed him.

Avery, where are you? he called out for his sister once more.

His mother nearly dragged him through the streets as they closed in on the harbor. The nightmare in the interior of Molten City was nothing compared to what was happening in the bay. *The Hydra* and the fort were engaged in an intense showdown against six tall ships cornering them near the shore. Smoke engulfed Molten Bay and claimed it as its own. Lightning struck just above his head.

"To the jetty, Eddie!" his mother yelled. His feet touched the dock, untouched by the surrounding battle. "Run to the very end!" She was slowing down on him. Her hand was permanently placed on her side as blood colored her fingers. He ran back to help her, nearly slipping on the wet platform. "Don't! I'll be fine. Go!" The intensity in her voice made him turn and not even look back.

At the far end of the jetty was an unmanned cog.

"Battier?" A bald man stepped off the ship. The trader reeked of something that made Eddie's nose hairs stiffen. It was an overwhelming smell of pepper, from what he could tell. "Where are the rest of your siblings? Your mother?"

"I-I'm the only one of my–"

Before he could even finish, his mother arrived behind him. Eddie saw the man's eyes go wide. "Tarsa, you're injured. Get on the ship!"

Tarsa?

"I can't. I have to go and get my other children," his mother turned to face the battle ahead of her, staring into the chaos of smoke and fire that left her unfazed.

"Adelaide, there isn't enough time. Those ships can only exchange fire with the *Hydra* and the fort for so long until they are put into the bottom of the bay!"

The guns fired in barrages. There was no estimate of how many cannonballs found their mark as his ears started ringing.

Adelaide grabbed Eddie's face. "Will you be brave for me?"

He didn't know what to say. "I-I don't –"

"Will you be brave for me, Eddison?" she asked.

He couldn't bring himself to say yes. All he could do was nod.

That seemed to be good enough for her. "This man is Leven Parke. You're going to stay with him until I return, and you're going to listen and follow whatever orders he gives you, understand?"

Again, all Eddie could do was nod. "Where are you going?" he asked with sadness in his voice.

"I'm going to get your brother and sisters." She leaned in and kissed him on his wet forehead. "I love you, Eddison. Family is all we have now."

His mother gripped both of her hand axes and fought through a limp as she ran back the way they came.

"Adelaide!" Leven stopped her. "You know what happens now, right?"

She stopped, but she didn't turn around. "Yes."

The cannon fire continued. Eddie watched his mother continue. *What happens now? We wait for her to return with Avery, Isla, and Caldwell.*

"Eddie, get on the *Dogtooth*," Leven said.

He didn't do what Leven told him, already disobeying his mother's orders.

Avery, please, you need to hurry!

With no response, he started crying like he had a hundred times before.

"Eddie, get on the ship," Leven said again.

It was almost as if he was in a state of paralysis. His body refused to move. He watched the fiery exchange between the ships, witnessing them tear each other apart. His imagination of a battle while playing was nothing compared to being in one.

"She can't hear me," Eddie said aloud.

Wide hands of the man he just met enveloped his shoulders. "We have to go, Battier. I'm sorry." A sudden thud jostled his head forward as his vision went black.

TEN

SHARKEYES II

Avery hadn't slowed her pace since her little brother's plea for help. *What the hell is going on?*

The trees in the Hissing Grove were spaced out well enough that Avery could run at full tilt without having to dodge low-hanging branches or the curling roots of the serpent trees.

This place was the subject of a lot of fear. Avery didn't find it scary, but rather peaceful. It was a place with a lot of false history and fairy tales. Her father warned her it was all nonsense to scare children from entering the grove. She tended to side with his logic above all others. Her father always told her never to lose her sense of adventure, for the ones content with being stationary were often left wanting.

Her back still pained from her tumble several days ago, but all that raced through Avery's mind were the awful things that could be happening to her mother and brother. Eddie was frightened by everything. However, this was different. His cries for help were never so perilous. Even when he was getting beaten by bullies, he never had the sheer terror in his voice as he did today.

Ahead, the trees grew closer, and the forest thickened. It was the natural border between provinces, informing her she had returned to Roguewave. The terrain became much more difficult to trek, but she made good time.

Every time she inhaled, she felt air trying to escape. Avery tried to think of the landmarks around her to give her motivation as if they were checkmarks to a brutal one-woman race. *I'll be at the river soon. Once I'm there, it's not far to the monochrome rock, then home.*

The sound of rushing water gave her the push she needed to fight the pending exhaustion. She didn't need to follow along the bank of the river to get herself home. As long as she could hear it, Avery knew what direction to go.

An unwelcome chill crawled up Avery's spine. Something had been wrong since the warning she had received from her brother, but this was different.

The monochrome rock that her father introduced their family to had changed. The boulder, in all its changing colors between black, white, and grey, had ceased. No, instead, the rock had turned almost lifeless. It looked like a massive chunk of blackened charcoal waiting to be set ablaze for a communal fire.

Avery ran her hand along the side, and a chalky black streak remained on her palm. She rubbed her fingers together. *What is this?*

In the distance, she heard booming echoes. It was like a herd of giant cattle running from a forest lion.

She took off once again, gaining speed.

Avery saw a flash out of the corner of her eye. There was a sharp and instant pain in her leg. At a full sprint, she crashed forward. She went face-first into the dirt and dead leaves as the bottom of her feet nearly touched the back of her head.

"I said you'd be seeing me again, didn't I?" a familiar voice said.

Her head was fuzzy. Avery rolled to her back and saw Quien Lowlend standing above her with a wooden baton. In a haze, she asked, "What's that sound… from the city?"

After she posed the question, she realized how strange it was to bypass the fact that she had been attacked by her brother's bully.

"What?" Quien said.

His head perked up. Avery planted her hands in the dirt and stood to her feet. Quien's focus shifted back to her. Avery's thigh was pulsing with pain.

Quien struck her again in the same spot, and she dropped to the ground. "That—that'll teach you not to try and fight me anymore," he said with fleeting confidence before running off into the forest.

While in the dirt, she dragged herself to the nearest tree. She was tired, bruised, and battered, but not ready to give up. Avery propped her back up against the tree and didn't even examine her leg. For if she were to acknowledge it, she would have to accept the reality of something being wrong, and she wasn't ready to do that at this time.

The skies above Roguewave were dark, and they brought torrential rain. The thunder rolled in, and she struggled to delineate nature's roar from the cannon fire.

A single raindrop hit the tip of her nose and ran down under her nostril. Avery looked beside her to see a branch on the ground. She grabbed it and used it to stand herself upright. She was too proud to let herself scream from the sharp pain. On her ascension, she nearly passed out from holding her breath and clenching her jaws. Black dots filled her vision, and it looked like gnats were flying all around her head.

Eddie.

～

She hobbled for almost an hour before she finally returned to Molten Bay.

The tree line stopped. When Avery emerged from the forest to look upon the bay, she was met with destruction. *Eddie?*

Smoke had risen towards the sky. It was so high it blocked out the sun. The Molten Fort's eastern wall had crumbled into the water below. The markets were ablaze, and Avery watched as vendors tried their hardest to save their merchandise.

The harbor took the brunt of the damage. There had been hundreds of ships in the bay of all shapes and sizes. Now, all that remained was scattered driftwood floating with the tide. The only vessel still afloat was the fortress on the water, the ship of all ships, the *Hydra*. Its sails were tattered, and the starboard side had taken a beating, but none could argue that it was still the most menacing sight on the ocean.

Avery limped through the smoke and debris down main street. Greencoats were either on the ground, not moving, or walking away, worse for wear, towards the fort. They moved like lifeless creatures who all shared a pale complexion and a wide-eyed stare at the ground.

The silence was eerie. Occasionally, part of a building would collapse and make noise, or there would be a random painful scream, but those were few and far between. Swords and rifles were scattered across the ground. *There had been a battle. Here?*

"Get him back to the fort! We'll get more out of him there!"

Rounding the corner, Avery saw two greencoats dragging a man under his arms. His hands were bound, and he had a black sash around his neck. His skin had been toasted from the sun, and he nearly shared the same complexion as Avery and her family. "On second thought, make sure he goes straight to Grand Commander Cross!"

The man didn't fight his capture. His face was emotionless. *Black attire?* Avery contemplated who he could potentially be. *No, surely not a pirate.*

The greencoat pushed Avery aside. "Out of the way, girl."

She was so distracted by the captive that the shove didn't seem to bother her. The man glanced up at her as they dragged him along. He looked around her mother's age, or possibly younger, with the sea having aged his body. He had bags under his eyes and looked on the verge of exhaustion. Avery guessed it was from whatever battle occurred here.

"My apologies, miss," the captive said after watching the greencoat push her away.

The soldier on his right side punched him across the face. "Quiet, bloody pirate!"

It is pirates.

~

A wave of sadness washed over her when she limped upon the sight of Mey's Bakery in ruins. *Eddie, I'm sorry,* she said to herself, knowing how much joy this place brought him. The tall sign that signaled everyone in Roguewave that fresh cakes and pies were to be found here was riddled with cannon and musket holes.

To her left, Avery saw a small band of greencoats sitting amongst the remains of the fountain in the center of the courtyard. Their heads bobbled as they seemed to be fighting off sleep. Avery approached them. They were heavily bandaged, but they were still covered in dirt and dried blood. She took one look at her home on the third floor and saw that the door was wide open.

The uncomfortable feeling of a rifle being shoved in her back made her stiffen up like a wooden plank.

"Don't move, Battier."

Other greencoats took notice and stood to their feet. They followed, aiming their guns at her.

"I didn't do anything!" she said.

The greencoat shoved his rifle into her spine, making her back arch. "You're under arrest to answer for treason."

ELEVEN
THE WIDOW III

Hours, maybe days, had passed. Time in the black cells of Colwerth Prison operated differently. Adelaide hadn't seen any semblance of light or hope in this wretched place. She found it interesting how something that was considered a wonder to this world could radiate so much pain and darkness.

Any memory of her capture evaded her. Her brain was a stack of puzzle pieces that were slow to come together.

The cell was a perfect stone cube with no windows. There was no furniture or comfort to be found. Peaceful sleep would be impossible. The floor wasn't smoothed over, so any way she laid down, jagged pieces of rock poked her body.

Adelaide's wound from the wooden debris still pained her. She wondered why the prison aidmen even patched her up only to throw her in a dark and unsanitary cell. She would never admit it, but a small part of her wouldn't protest the fatal outcome if something hadn't been done about her injury. She missed Mathias more than anything and wanted nothing more than to see his face once again in whatever afterlife she was allowed peace.

However, the burning desire to get back to her children and see them safe had taken control of her like a rabid disease. She felt guilty for sending Eddie off with a stranger. It made her sick to imagine how scared he must be feeling. *I left my boy in the custody of pirates. What kind of a mother am I? Where are they? Are they safe? Are they in the next cell over?*

As her mind pondered, the wall behind her opened, and she watched a pair of floating flames dance into the cell. Her eyes struggled to adjust, and a deep voice spoke before she could make out who it was.

"Adelaide Battier, would you like to inform me on just how instrumental you were in orchestrating the pirate raid?"

Once her eyes finally adjusted to the orange and red flame, she saw the rugged face of Grand Commander Alistair Cross with a torch in each hand.

"I wasn't," she replied.

"I think honesty would be a better choice for you to make today."

"I'll be honest when you and men like you return the favor to me and my family."

"So, you *are* lying to me?" he said.

She scoffed. "You'd like for it to be me, I'm sure. Then you'd have one of the plotting terrorists already in custody, and you could go ahead and add that to the lists of your accomplishments."

"I very well could," Alistair said as a thin shadow went down the middle of his face. He ran his palm across the crude stonework as he circled the room. "A foul place, isn't it? I believe in punishment, but the aesthetic here is dreadful. Not to mention, the foundation is rubbish. Those sadistic architects built this thing too close to the bloody ocean. It won't withstand the lapse of time."

"Does it have any plans of deteriorating in the next few hours?" Adelaide asked.

Alistair smiled, most likely exerting all his humor for the day. "You planning on escaping, Battier?"

Adelaide didn't respond.

"No one has escaped before, but I'd be interested to see how that goes for you." He stopped his rotation around the room and leaned against the wall. He exhaled and became lost in the torchlight for a while. Silence built between them. All that transpired was the creaking of the walls and water droplets hitting the floor. "How has it been raising five children on your own?"

She took her time responding, for she didn't know his intent. "I've done the best I could. I guess it's out of my control now. It's up to them to prove if me and my husband have done an adequate job or not."

"That it is. Being the wife of a Grand Captain is hard. My wives knew that struggle as well. The first two didn't enjoy my absence. The third one liked my absence a little too much." Alistair put his back to the wall and slid all the way down to the ground. "Perhaps I should've accompanied Mathias on the voyages south so many years ago to find a loyal woman such as yourself."

She couldn't tell in his flat tone if he was serious or not. "Perhaps you should've. Maybe he would've taught you some lessons in kindness and mercy."

"Kindness? Mercy? Sure, Mathias had both of those. Where is he now?" His demeanor shifted. He tucked his hands behind his back and stared down upon her like a gargoyle. "His heart gave out, so apparently, his own body had trouble living with those two things."

She hadn't felt this level of anger since she was a girl. "You're going to sit there and pretend like that's true?"

"That brave, brilliant, and balanced Captain Mathias Battier died in his study with one hand on a compass and the other on a map? Of course, Adelaide. Sounds like a death he'd choose for himself."

"About thirty to forty years too early, mind you."

"Who are we to question the arrival of death?" he said.

"The one left mourning his absence," Adelaide replied.

He exhaled a long, drawn-out sigh. The long pauses unsettled her stomach. "You know what? I'll level with you. This is all a lie."

"Excuse me?" Adelaide said as the chains yanked her back to her seated position on the filthy floor.

"We discovered his little plan. His act of terrorism. The only problem we're having is discovering what Mathias had planned for the long haul. Yes, he organized the pirate attack on Molten Bay, but why? What purpose did it serve?"

Adelaide didn't know if the question was rhetorical. "So, you did kill him?"

With no emotion, Alistair replied, "He had to die. That's it."

"What happens now? Are you going to tell the world of his treason?" Adelaide asked, fighting off tears.

"Not his treason… Yours. A Grand Captain betraying our country is not possible. It shall remain that way. But his foreign wife from the southern clans sure can."

Monsters.

"Xavier is still planning on going through with his duel against my son tomorrow. After that, he is forbidden to step foot in Roguewave or see you ever again. Caldwell is at Molten Fort and will await trial to see where his loyalties truly lie. He will also never see you again. Your eldest daughter Avery will be deported back to Autera to live amongst your former Trezbe Clan, never to return."

Her heart broke. She didn't breathe, and somehow, some way, the cell became darker. "You would do all this to my family, knowing I'm not guilty?"

The torch flames flickered next to him. "A few days ago, you were visited by someone while washing clothes in the river, a woman named Naomi Cobb, who has direct ties to the pirates."

"A woman who served her time here and was released. Is it a crime to talk with someone?"

"She admitted she was conspiring with the pirates once more as of yesterday morning. She also informed us of what she told you. Now, you might be an innocent bystander in this, but entertaining a conversation with such an individual is treason enough for the citizens of the Unified Provinces."

"Let's say my husband was challenging the Assembly." She sat up straight. "Tell me if I'm right, Grand Commander Cross. I'm assuming Mathias did this under your nose for a long time, and you didn't discover it until recently. When you did, you murdered him. Now you're trying to assure his legacy doesn't come back to haunt you."

Cross smiled. "I assure you the Assembly doesn't cower to a few kids and their foreign mother."

"Grand Captain Mathias Battier married me. By law, I am a citizen of this land, same as you, yet he was condemned for his decision. Perhaps that's one reason for his opposition against you."

Alistair stood to his feet and grabbed the torches off the ground. "Who would've thought a warring woman from one of the southern clans would be as sharp as you are."

"I learn quick. My husband proved to be outsmarting and outmaneuvering you for years. Maybe you'll find I'm capable of doing the same."

"That would be something," he said, rolling her eyes away from his gaze. "Your two youngest are unaccounted for, and they currently have a bounty on their head of a thousand gold pieces... Would you like to tell me where they are?"

"Hopefully, far from the reaches of you and your Assembly."

"My reach has no limit, Battier. All of the ocean answers to me. Remember that." He walked over to the heavy iron door. "I met your boy, Eddie. He's a bright young man. Initially, I thought he got all that from his father. Now, I can see you've contributed. With the proper guidance, he could make a fine captain for our Navy. Should I come across him again, I think I might be the one to shepherd him along."

She brought her knees up and rested her bound hands on them, "I have full confidence my son will be great without your leadership. In fact, I'm willing to believe he'll be far better off not having it."

"It would be a shame for a mind such as his to go to waste and not be used for the betterment of our homeland. He could be a Grand Captain, probably quicker than anyone. He could excel past your eldest, even my own son, perhaps." Alistair rested his hand on the latch. "Because I can also see the trajectory of things. You could say it's a gift I have. It's what makes me a great commander. I see potential."

The low creaking sound the door made as he opened it was haunting. His silhouette left the room, and he slammed the heavy door, leaving her in darkness.

Adelaide began to cry. Not tears caused by Alistair Cross, but for the fate and well-being of her children. She sent a plea to whoever or whatever would listen. She thought of the gods of the warring clans but never believed they would offer their help. She hadn't prayed to them for years.

She thought of the Creator, the god worshiped in the Unified Provinces and the Assembly. She was married to Mathias under his blessing by Priest Erich. However, that was all the interaction she'd had with the deity. *Perhaps he'll listen.*

Be with them. Give Xavier compassion, for I know he has the capacity for love. Give Caldwell trust in his family and the ones who want the best for him. Keep Avery level-minded so she doesn't make any rash decisions. Allow Isla to speak without words and with her actions. Give Eddie courage, for that is all that holds him back. Help me... please... please...

TWELVE
THE CHAMPION II

Soon after arriving in the capital of Helmburough, Xavier was informed by Assembly officials that his mother, brother, and sister had been taken into custody under suspicion of conspiracy and treason upon the heels of a pirate attack on Molten Bay. He had a difficult time coming to grips with the prospect of their crimes being genuine. However, he also knew that to question the Assembly would be the way of a fool.

Since the moment his boots hit the docks of Whitefin Harbor, he knew something was off. He made the voyage across the underbelly of the United Provinces and through the Beaker Gulf, yet something about this time was different.

The troubling news hadn't helped him in his preparation for the duel. Being confined to a small ship would surely impact his movement. He would never vocalize any trepidation, but he didn't feel ready.

Lieutenant Chiesa's assistance in easing Xavier's occupied mind failed. Xavier could tell that the news of the attack had affected his trainer since Fili, his foster son, was back in Molten City.

"All you should visualize in your mind is the sword your opponent is wielding," Chiesa instructed. "All you should hear is the clanging of the dull blades clashing against one another. All you should feel is the ground beneath your feet. All you should smell is the odor of thousands of men that have fought in that arena before. And if you can taste the iron of blood in your mouth, make sure it's Declan Cross'."

Any other time, Xavier would let those words fuel him, but today, they were lost on him.

Xavier spent the eve of his duel walking the busy streets of the capital alone. The stark contrast between the province of the capital and Molten City was astounding. Frankly, the entire province of Helmburough was luxurious compared to Roguewave. The wealthy thrived and lived amongst each other. Everyone wore the finest of bright fabrics and coats that never seemed dirty. The roads were paved smooth and actively cleaned by workers at all hours of the day. All the beauty in the world lived and prospered here.

One thing that wasn't mentioned in the letter was the Capital Fair, which was to begin the night of the duel. Every province had its fairs for a variety of different reasons. They all paled in comparison to Helmburough's. And while commerce was always strong here, there was a bustle in the streets of excitement for the upcoming festivities.

People gave Xavier a respectful nod as he passed. The world was aware of his feats as a fighter. *That's right. Know who I am, know what I can do.*

Ahead of him were the tall gates to enter Helmburough City. A sacred place only reserved for the world's elites and the Assembly's members. Sentient Tower stood even higher above the gates. It was another wonder built to house all the knowledge the world had to offer. The overwhelmingly white and gold buildings reflected the sunlight to a profound degree, making all the other colors pop and make him feel as if he was walking in the Creator's heaven.

Also in the heart of the city was another wonder of the world: Martyr Arena. A massive colosseum that could house an audience of eighty thousand. The roar of the crowd that shook Xavier's bones in combat was unlike anything else.

A small shove from behind made Xavier turn quickly. He looked down to see a boy staring at him with wide eyes.

"Watch where you're going, boy," Xavier said.

The wonder on the boy's face never left. "A-A-Are you, Champion Battier?"

"Aye."

"You're my favorite fighter. I've seen your past six duels in the arena. My father even likes you, and he doesn't cheer for anyone!"

"Good."

"I want to be just like you. I want everyone chanting my name. I want to raise my sword in victory in Martyr Arena."

Xavier nodded and lifted his chin in the air to gaze upon the colosseum arena in the distance. "Not the worst goal."

There was a ball at Xavier's foot that the boy had presumably been playing with before bumping into his back. Xavier picked it up and handed it to him.

"My father says all I need to do is work hard, and I can be as great as you!"

Xavier towered over him. "My father told me similar things."

"So, they're right?" The boy's smile grew as if the prospect of being champion duelist could be grasped in front of his eyes.

"No," he said, and the boy's smile died. "If that were true, any moron could achieve greatness. Plenty of men work hard and get nowhere. It takes much more than hard work to be where I am. Something about you has to be different or special. To assume anyone could be great by one quality is the thinking of an idiot. That's something your father won't tell you."

With that, Xavier turned his head and continued forward.

It was a short walk from there to the gate. A guard greeted him, and Xavier never looked back.

"Is that how you talk to your fans?" a familiar feminine voice spoke.

Creeping toward the gate at his back was Francheska Krusade, daughter of Assembly Leader Charles Krusade, the most powerful man in the world. Her attire appeared more masculine, which was to be expected as she single-handedly thrust herself into a position of power that had not existed prior. She was the first female captain recognized by the Assembly and the Unified Provinces. And being a female captaining her own ship with a crew of testosterone-filled Navy men was not easy, but she exceeded expectations. Perhaps many, especially men, questioned her elevated position, not to mention the fact that nepotism was present in the promotion.

Xavier never doubted her position or prowess. She came from a lineage of power, but she was self-made. There was no disputing that. She had also earned the respect of her crew at a meteoric pace, gaining the moniker of Cheska "The Banshee" Krusade. His father spoke often on the importance and difficulty of respect from a naval crew. Respect was a relationship that had to be tended constantly.

"Cheska," Xavier replied.

"You win a duel, leave, and never write to me?" she wore a fake frown that quickly shifted into a devious smile. "I'm disappointed in you, Battier."

All five of the Krusade children had black hair, and Cheska's bangs always hid her left eye. She was the least subtle person Xavier had ever met, but her eye cover gave off a mystery he couldn't help finding attractive.

"Relax, Xavier. I'm not going to lose it on you. Although, I personally would like to see how I measure up to the Champion. Father and Chamberlain claim you're merely boys playing in the sand."

Chamberlain was the eldest of the Krusade children and already a respected Army general at the age of twenty-three.

Xavier cracked his neck. "Well, I'd be happy to oblige you and your brother and see if the Krusade children are as combat-ready as others claim you to be."

"Well, Chamberlain gave me this yesterday morning." Cheska peeled back her bangs and revealed a swollen black and purple eye.

"I see. And how does he look?"

"Unfortunately, still handsome and pristine. That's what the other girls tell me."

Xavier scoffed. "You have friends?"

"I didn't say that."

A pause followed. All Xavier could think to ask while clearing his throat was, "So, how have you been?"

"I've been well ever since I accepted that I was never going to receive anything from you. I've kept myself busy. Got a new hobby," she said, giving him a coy smile.

Xavier didn't apologize. He attempted to move off that topic of their relationship entirely. "What hobby is that?"

She crept forward and rubbed the palm of her hand across his chest and around his body. Xavier couldn't fight the rousing chill she sent through his body with her touch. She talked at his neck as she was too short to reach his ear. "Killing pirates," she said with an eerie, unshakable confidence. "I'll see you tonight."

Cheska looked up to the battlements of the capital gates and yelled, "Open the doors for Champion Battier!" Then, she softened her tone once more. "My apologies for your current situation."

Her eyes glimmered for a moment as she took her leave and ran her palm across his belt.

The large wooden gates slowly creaked open, and Xavier looked upon the haven-like quality of the city that appeared as if he was entering into another realm. He placed his chin high in the air as well and entered the living quarters of the rich and powerful.

Night fell, and a feast was served in Sentient Tower. Xavier and Lieutenant Chiesa sat alone at a table near the front of the Grand Room with wandering eyes and whispers aimed at them. Xavier didn't have to wonder what they were talking about. *My treasonous family.*

"Don't pay them any mind, Xavier," Chiesa said. "You have a job to do tomorrow."

Xavier didn't reply. He continued to watch the elites with powdered faces and wigs, sporting long violet jackets with gold trimming, doing their best to pretend like he wasn't the main topic of their gossip.

"Let them talk. It's on you to control the outcome of the duel," his lieutenant said.

"Do they hate me?" Xavier asked softly.

"What?" Chiesa replied.

Xavier scanned across the room. The roof was high and broad, extending over five hundred feet. It had a massive painting of the sea and all the Grand Ships engaging in a battle against lesser vessels on open water, and it had taken over a hundred painters and almost a full year to complete the masterpiece. No other display of art in the world rivaled its magnificence. However, art and creativity were something that didn't mean much to Xavier. *My little brother can enjoy art and remain a coward.*

Gold ivy traveled up the alabaster columns from the marble floor. Xavier looked down to see his reflection on the floor. He fixed his hair and adjusted his jacket.

"Xavier Battier, it's a pleasure to meet you."

He turned around in his chair to see a pair of three-tallied officers at his side. The man extended his hand. "Where are my manners? I am Tevon Cassell, and I am to be the new governor of Roguewave in the absence of Governor Tytus."

Absence?

Xavier stood and shook his hand and was shocked to discover the future governor's left arm was missing elbow-down. Cassel acknowledged Xavier's curiosity. "War can truly be horrific, Battier, but don't worry, I can still hold my own with my strong hand."

"Pleasure to meet you, sir," Xavier replied.

"Not to disparage your family's name further, son, but it's nice we still have a Battier loyal to the Assembly. We're all the better for it." From his tone, it was hard to navigate whether the governor was being sarcastic or not. "I'd like you to meet my officers: Officer Kindrake and Officer Sauloman."

They both stepped forward and greeted Xavier. Sauloman, who looked to be an eastern coast man, perhaps Axelford, shook his hand with a stone face. Officer Kindrake looked like something out of a nightmare. His face was burned and scarred to the point of no return.

Cassel continued with a flat line for a mouth, "I watched your father command and fight up close. How he combated pirates was a thing of beauty. If you ever need anything or are looking to be of service somewhere, don't hesitate to ask."

"Thank you, sir," Xavier replied.

A tapping of silverware on glass quieted the hall. For the first time, the hundreds of eyes were no longer focused on Xavier. Instead, everyone's head turned to the vacant and elevated table at the northern end of the hall. Governor Cassel and his officers took their leave back to their table.

"Ladies, gentlemen, if you would all rise to pay respect to our devoted and beloved Assembly Leaders."

The sound of hundreds of wooden chairs sliding across

the floor occurred all at once. It was a race for all the people in the room to pay their respects first.

Xavier took his time. *So many influential people that turn into beggars and brown-nosers when someone more powerful walks into the room. It's pathetic. The cycle must never end for these people.*

"Please welcome Grand Overseer Benjah Kearse, Grand Forerunner Linus Lewden, Director of the Academy Dawkin Bashford, and the Head of the Assembly, Charles Krusade!"

The ovation lasted far too long for Xavier's liking.

The Assembly members found their seats as the clapping began to die. It took Charles Krusade raising his hand and motioning everyone to be seated for the obnoxious gratification to end. Xavier looked to one of the tables at the front of the room and saw the Krusade family occupying the whole table. The matriarch, Ella, sat like a proper wife of the leader of the world with an unwavering smile. Chamberlain sat next to her, adorned with many colorful badges, gold and silver alike, on his royal coat. His curly black hair made women of all ages swoon.

He made eye contact with Cheska, who winked and blew Xavier a kiss from across the room as that sinister, closed-lipped smile shot him like a musket. He averted his eyes and shifted his focus away from the entire Krusade family, even though it appeared they were all present, including the younger ones, Genevieve, Maximillian, and Theodore.

Grand Overseer Kearse stood to his feet not long after. "Tonight is a special occasion," he said. "Tomorrow, we have a fantastic round of duels lined up to kick off the festivities for our annual Capital Fair!" A round of applause blared throughout the hall. "But, before we get to the revelry, perhaps some combative arts must be on display. Perhaps the thundering of the Martyr Arena needs to be heard from coast to coast. Perhaps some blood needs to be shed!" Xavier clapped slow, using his weak hand to slap his opposite palm. He never committed to the excitement of the surrounding elites. "Now, these fine young men have dedicated themselves to the entertainment of our Unified Provinces, and more importantly, they are to defend it with their lives one day, maintaining our proud country. Let's give these young men a hand."

Applause broke out again, but Xavier knew that none of those gestures of appreciation were for him. Benjah Kearse was the youngest of the Assembly members by at least ten years. He was in the early stages of balding and had silverish eyes that always seemed in the middle of charming and sinister.

Kearse continued with clear control over the room. "And I would be remiss if I didn't mention the duel that will be kicking off our festivities."

The Overseer stepped out from behind his pedestal and down the steps. He weaved between the tables and seemed to take pleasure with all the eyes in the hall solely focused on him. The other members at the table didn't appear to be enjoying themselves as much as Kearse.

Xavier was surprised Kearse turned and stared directly at him while meandering between tables. "Ladies and gentlemen, I ask you, what do you get when an unbeaten young man with everything to prove steps into an arena against an opponent that wants nothing more than to beat the best?" Kearse looked around the room and got nothing but silence. "Anybody?" he asked with raised brows. "You get a lot of excitement."

Reluctant laughs sprouted from across the hall.

Kearse returned to the front of the room. "When called upon, would the two men involved in tomorrow's highly anticipated duel please join me up here at the front." Eyes darted around the room. "First, our challenger, Mr. Declan Cross."

Xavier looked upon his opponent and saw a young man with a similar build. Only Declan had long blond hair that was tied up in the back while strands of hair still dangled in front of his eyes. He wore a deep blue coat with obnoxiously large gold buttons that held three wide straps across his chest. His hands were firmly tucked behind his back, and he didn't look up from the floor.

"Now, if you please, welcome our champion, Xavier Battier!"

Xavier stood, and only Lieutenant Chiesa, along with a few awkward, isolated claps, followed. No matter. He made the walk in crippling silence. *If they want to applaud him, that's fine. I'll silence them when Declan Cross yields to me in the sand.*

His boots clicked on the foggy marble floor. Xavier stood in front of his opponent with his chin high in the air.

"A historical eve to a historical tomorrow. Oh, how I can't wait to see how all this transpires!" Kearse said with a clenched fist. "Great people of this grand province, please, put your hands together once more for these two exceptional fighters!"

The duel was something they could cheer for, at least. Declan's head still hadn't raised to meet Xavier's eye. *Is he afraid? For his sake, he better get over that by tomorrow.*

He stepped forward. The applause tapered off. Nose to nose, they stood. Xavier was slightly taller and used the little height advantage he had to assert dominance.

"Easy, now," Overseer Kearse said with that sly grin stuck on his face.

"Are you afraid to look at me, Cross?" Xavier said.

Still, Declan didn't raise his head. First, Xavier saw the corners of his mouth creep up on both sides. Only then did his head follow, and the two young men were eye to eye.

Xavier didn't even lie to himself. He had faced many opponents and had had countless matches for training and competition. Looking into the eyes of the one standing in front of his face, Xavier saw Declan wasn't afraid. In fact, he was hard-pressed to read any emotion from him.

"My condolences to you and the rest of your family. Times are difficult," Declan said. "Good luck tomorrow, Battier."

Xavier stood alone on the observatory of Sentient Tower, miles above the world. The wind whipped past him, and his coat was never at rest on his back. The short exchange he had with his opponent kept eating at him. He mulled over Declan's friendly gesture, wondering how he should feel. *My condolences? Good luck? Who says those things to someone you're about to fight?*

The only thing that could ease his thoughts was the setting sun on the horizon of the Aster Sea. Xavier wasn't one to appreciate nature's beauty; that was more Isla or Avery's strong suit. However, the array of reds, yellows, oranges, and violets was nothing short of mesmerizing. It looked as if the Creator spilled his watercolors while painting the world into existence.

Seagulls flew in the foreground of the descending sun. Even from this high up, Xavier could still smell the fresh moisture of the ocean in the air.

"I have to say, I've lived here all my life, and I still never get used to that setting sun. There's nothing quite like it."

Xavier turned his head to see Grand Overseer Kearse with his trademark grin.

"My apologies, Overseer, I didn't know you were there," Xavier said.

"No need." Kearse stepped forward and stood shoulder-to-shoulder with Xavier. "Are you prepared for tomorrow?"

"Absolutely, Sir."

"Yes, I know you are." Kearse proceeded to pick the polish off the railing. "I am sorry about what has happened to your family, especially the news you received recently. It's just terrible. I'm sure it's an awful feeling."

"What feeling is that exactly, Sir?"

"Betrayal, son." The word didn't feel right as it hit his ears. "Your mother has committed treason, not only against you and your family but all of the Unified Provinces."

Xavier hesitated. "May I ask what she did, Sir? I'm not trying to question you, but for my mother to be labeled for such a heinous crime is… difficult for me to come to terms with."

Overseer Kearse took his time before answering his simple question. "You are aware of the pirate raid on Roguewave?"

"Yes, Sir."

"Well… it's believed your mother had a rather large hand in orchestrating the savage attack."

Still, Xavier had a problematic time believing it to be true. However, the Assembly had all the answers to everything. They'd established and built the foundation on which their society operated.

The Grand Overseer's duties were to manage interpersonal responsibilities between the governors of all the provinces. His father once explained that the Overseer's job was to "babysit the governors," a task he was led to believe was probably the most difficult out of all the main Assembly members.

"Why was my sister arrested?" Xavier asked, more out of curiosity than concern.

"Just as a precaution. Your brother Caldwell was taken in as well. Still no word on your youngest siblings, though. I'm supposed to receive an update on their whereabouts at any time."

"Precaution? Does that mean she could be a conspirator…" Xavier stopped himself. "Apologies, Grand Overseer. I don't mean to overstep any boundaries."

"It's quite all right, son. Not a crime to be curious about your family." Kearse stepped forward and rested his hands on the stone railing. "Are you close with your siblings?"

He didn't wait long to reply. "No."

"Why is that?"

Even if his last answer was quick and at the ready, somehow, this one caught him off guard, like he was being asked to solve a complex equation on a test back in the Academy.

"They don't much care for me."

"Why?" Kearse persisted.

"I don't know."

"Of course you do."

Xavier stood in a haze, never taking his eyes off the setting sun.

Kearse stepped closer and put his hand on Xavier's shoulder. "Your life in Roguewave has been difficult, and I'm sorry about that. But now it's time for you to move on from that place and your family."

"Sir?"

Overseer Kearse turned. "From this day forward, Roguewave will no longer be your home. It would be in your best interest to remain here and do something worthwhile that could appease Helmburough and your country. People that are not very high on you right now. You're the son of a rebellious, foreign traitor."

The words hurt him further, although he'd never admit it.

"What am I to do?" Xavier asked.

Kearse's grin returned. "Whatever a young man with your skillset should do."

THIRTEEN
THE AIDMAN II

Ricky Meeks and his merry band of entitled greencoat morons pushed Caldwell in the back as they walked through the ruined corridor of Molten Fort. They jabbed him with the ends of their rifles. Caldwell was thankful they weren't equipped with bayonets.

The sun was shining through the large blast wounds the fort sustained in the onslaught. Even in confinement, Caldwell learned that pirates were the culprit of the attack. It surprised him to hear such a thing. Everything he was led to believe was that the pirate's numbers were dwindling.

A raid of this magnitude should be beyond their capabilities.

Caldwell stumbled on felled beams and crumbled stone as the breeze from the bay hit his face for the first time in days. He had to catch himself, for his energy was fleeting. Since his arrest three days ago, he had been fed once, and the small bowl of seaweed soup left him desiring something with more sustenance.

"Having trouble staying upright, Battier?" Ricky said, like the pompous soldier he enjoyed being.

Caldwell didn't reply.

Being left to sit and simmer in the darkness while a battle

raged outside nearly drove him mad. All he could do was focus on his family and friends, hoping more than anything, they were okay. Isla and Eddison's innocence was etched into his mind. He was thankful in a way that Isla couldn't hear destruction and the cries of people running scared. That was all he heard for hours that day. He could imagine Eddie clear as day, curled up in a fetal position, shaking in fear.

But there was a guilt he felt for what occupied his mind the most. It wasn't his mother. It wasn't his best friends. No, it was Carlie Domines. Even after their brief interaction, he couldn't help but replay her visage over and over in his mind. Her big hazel eyes, her thick brown hair that naturally curled toward the bottom, and the way her cheeks swelled when she smiled. He hoped the picture of Carlie he conjured in his head did her justice.

The wooden door ahead of him had a pair of golden tallied greencoats on either side. The two golden stripes on their collar told their rank. Tallies, more commonly called marks, were awarded through service and acts of bravery. The most a soldier could receive before being promoted or given permission for retirement was five. It was a prestigious honor to be awarded a mark, and there had never been anyone in Roguewave given more than one. *These two must've sailed with Alistair Cross aboard the* Hydra.

The bottom half of the door was blown off, and only the splintered top was left behind. "We'll take the prisoner from here," Cross' naval officer said.

"We can take him to the judge. It's no problem," Ricky said.

"And *I* said we'll take him from here. Any part of that you misunderstand, soldier?"

Ricky stepped back, and he and his little band of boys walked away with their tails firmly tucked between their legs.

The two soldiers allowed Caldwell to walk past them into the hall. The space was large, easily the biggest room in the fort. It was on the interior, so the room had not been damaged during the raid. Postured up in his seat behind a massive oak desk at the end of the room, in his powdered wig, was Judge Barnes. He was a lanky man who seemed to disagree with the sun.

"Mr. Battier, step forward, please," Barnes said.

The room was packed with around thirty greencoats, all with at least two golden marks on their collars. Every single one of them had their hands resting on their hilts and their eyes trained on Caldwell. *Ricky Meeks is a far cry from these men.*

At the end of the table stood Alistair Cross with his hands positioned behind his back. His shoulders were broad, and he commanded respect. Blackened blood and dirt stained his once beautiful and pristine coat.

Judge Barnes had a single piece of parchment in front of him that he inspected through his bifocals. "Caldwell Rosen Battier," Barnes said in a monotone voice. "What a name that is." What followed was a long silence that left Caldwell jittery. "Do you know why you are here?"

"No, Your Honor," Caldwell replied. He glanced at Grand Commander Cross, who gave away nothing in his blank expression.

"This is a sentencing hearing for you to answer for the crimes of your mother, Adelaide Battier. And to prove to me, under the laws of the Unified Provinces, that you have no prior or current plans to conspire against this great nation."

"I beg your pardon, Your Honor?" was all Caldwell could say.

"It's believed your mother may have played a role in the terrorist attack against Molten Bay and Molten City proper that was carried out by the pirates. To the extent of her involvement, we don't know at this time. However, without a shadow of a doubt, your mother knew of the attack before it happened. A heinous act that saw the death of hundreds of Roguewave citizens and soldiers who are the most hard-working and resilient people of the Unified Provinces. This plot also saw the capture of Governor Tytus."

Judge Barnes was a respected man, but Caldwell questioned every shred of his legitimacy.

"I assure you, I don't know of my mother's involvement in any such thing. Nor do I believe these accusations are true."

He leaned forward and perched his neck out. "Do you believe I would just do this on a whim?"

Even with the distance, Caldwell took a half step back. "No, Judge Barnes, but my mother is a good person with a kind heart. She wouldn't–"

"Are you aware of your mother's roots, Caldwell?" Barnes interrupted.

"Roots?"

"Where she comes from, boy," he said aggressively. The curls in his powdered wig bounced in place as he removed his bifocals. "Surely, being her son and being at the top of your class in the academy should acquire you some knowledge."

The soldiers stared back at him. Some had bandages all over their bodies, but their stoic nature remained.

"She is from Caste Valley, Redrainn, home of the Trezbe Clan."

"Correct. Tell me, Battier, what are the Trezbe people known for?"the judge asked, smirking.

"She tells me the cuisine is excellent."

Barnes bypassed the gavel and slammed his fist down on the table. "Enough! What are they known for?"

His quickness to anger made Caldwell's nerves spike. The reality of the situation hadn't been realized until now. "Of the warring clans, the Trezbes are believed to be the most ruthless. It's said they enjoy battle so much they sing during it."

"Did you, by chance, ask your mother about the validity of such things?"

"No, Your Honor, I didn't."

"Seems like you're in denial about several things involving

your mother... I would say the warring clans and the pirates have a lot more similarities than differences. Two sides of the same coin, you might say."

Caldwell wondered if he could say anything that could sway Judge Barnes' notions about his mother, or even himself. "My mother is no savage, Your Honor."

He watched as the judge's eyes moved to Alistair Cross. "Grand Commander Cross, you knew the boy's father. You've conversed with his mother. I'll ask for your input in the sentencing of Caldwell Battier."

Caldwell leaped forward. "Sir, if you please–"

"Grand Commander Cross has the floor!" Barnes barked as quick as an arrow, slamming the gavel down on the desk. "Without him at the helm of the *Hydra*, Roguewave would be a ruin right now."

Alistair took a step forward. The soldiers all around the room straightened their spines and stood more at attention. "Mathias Battier was a great captain, and I would be remiss to not mention the fact that he may have been a better man."

Caldwell locked eyes with him from the center of the room.

"He was loved by all," Cross continued. "Even the ones he captured had kind words for him. However, perhaps he showed too much kindness and too much trust in people. People that aren't from this country."

Cross made his way around the room, walking in front of every soldier along the way. He was a head taller than everyone, so he looked down upon all the soldiers like he was their crowned king.

He enjoys this.

"Take his widowed wife, for example. He put his trust and loyalty in her, and how did she repay him? She betrayed him. Betrayed his great name and everything he stood for." Alistair held court by stepping in front of Barnes, erasing him from Caldwell's vantage point. His stature loomed large in the center of the room. "Mathias Battier was a captain during the Third Pirate Rebellion and brought pride to his ship and all the men who sailed under it... All the while, his wife was conspiring with his enemies."

"Lies!" Caldwell raged.

The gavel struck hard on the table again. "Silence!" Barnes yelled.

"Battier, I can understand your pain. Being lied to for your entire life is tough to swallow," Alistair said evenly.

The muscles in Caldwell's jaw were in the early stages of locking.

"What should be done with him, Grand Commander?" Barnes asked.

Alistair stopped once he finally circled the soldiers. He moved to Caldwell and stared into his eyes, only inches from his face. A long exhale left Alistair's nostrils, and Caldwell could feel the warm air hit his forehead, and a hint of tobacco followed.

"I say we should leave his fate up to him, Judge Barnes."

Caldwell could see Barnes fight off a pompous grin.

Alistair presented a solution: "If he disavows his mother and her actions and accepts whatever fate shall befall her, Caldwell shall be allowed to continue representing and serving the Unified Provinces without repercussions. That's what his father would want. And besides, should a son with such potential suffer for the sins of his mother?"

"You're an aidman, aren't you?" Barnes asked.

Caldwell nodded.

"I hear you're a good one. Think of all the people you could help should you make the right decision here today."

Alistair stepped away and returned to his powerful stance behind the table next to Barnes.

"And if I refuse?"

"Caldwell, you don't want to know the answer to that question."

I do.

"The Assembly doesn't take betrayers and attacks against the Unified Provinces lightly. Grand Commander Cross can speak on that," Barnes said. "The fate of someone who sympathizes and supports those vile people shall meet a similar outcome... You're smart. You know what happens to them."

Caldwell raised his head and tilted his chin high in the air, just like the soldiers around him and how his father instructed him and his brothers and sisters to do. "I don't believe my mother did the things you claim she did."

"Boy, the evidence against her is overwhelming," Barnes said.

"Show me, then," Caldwell said without breaking much of a sweat.

"Are you refusing to do as we ask… siding with your treasonous mother?"

A chill went down the back of his spine. His stomach turned, and his palms started to clam up. "I am."

"Battier, think about what you're doing," Alistair chimed in.

Out of the corner of his eyes, he could see the soldiers looking at one another.

"Condemn your mother, Adelaide Battier's, actions here and now in front of men that can witness your loyalty," Barnes commanded.

His ears became warm, and with a shortness of breath, he said, "I will not."

Barnes looked to Alistair before grabbing his gavel.

The silence built.

"Very well. Then, under the eyes of the Assembly, the Creator, and these fine soldiers of the Unified Provinces, I, Judge Barnes of Roguewave, sentence you to hang by the neck until dead."

FOURTEEN
THE SILENT ONE II

The closet had become somewhat of a second home for Isla
and Leo as the random search parties came to the Emerson
estate a couple of times daily, but there was nothing they
could do. The alternative was capture.

Oliver had begun the process of lodging formal
complaints to Judge Barnes and Grand Commander Cross,
claiming that the searches of their estate were unlawful and
unjust. However, it seemed his formal complaints fell on deaf
ears. For in times of war, Cross said that "everything was
justified."

Oliver was a respected man, arguably the most respected
man in Roguewave. Isla's mother and father often talked
about how he did more for the province than Governor Tytus
or Judge Barnes.

Livian informed Isla that her mother was a prisoner in the
black cells of Colwerth Prison. *A wretched place for wretched people.*
A place my mother does not belong.

Her eldest brother was the only one who was for sure safe
in Helmburough. Despite how he treated others, including the
rest of their siblings, Isla always recognized he was kind to her.
Perhaps he took pity on her, but she didn't hold that against

him. Avery was apparently aboard a ship en route to Autera, forced to live out the rest of her days with the Trezbe Clan in the south across the Beaker Gulf. Eddison was nowhere to be found, and Livian said the greencoats were still searching for him. And Caldwell was to hang on the morrow for "collusion against the Unified Provinces." But that made no sense to her. Caldwell wanted nothing more than to help others and be friends with everyone he came across. Not for a moment did she believe her brother was capable of such things.

The reality of the horrible situation came to her at night when she attempted to sleep in a bed that wasn't her own. She couldn't enjoy the cushioned bed while the rest of her family was enduring the brunt of such awfulness. *If Father were here, he'd make it right. That's what he did — made things right.*

The kindness of Livian and Oliver was not lost on her. Isla knew the trouble they were putting themselves in by helping her. The respected doctor and his renowned professor wife were sheltering a potential enemy of the Unified Provinces. A crime that would not have light consequences.

Isla sat in the dining room, looking over the book Livian made for her. A subtle vibration alerted her to the front door opening. Every time she felt that sensation, her neck grew warm, and her shoulders ached. Her mind always went to the worst-case scenario of someone coming to take her.

She could breathe freely when Oliver walked into the dining room. There were dark circles under his eyes, and Isla could tell he had lost a little weight on his face over the past few days. He didn't notice Isla until he was done rubbing his forehead halfway across the Ghonian rug of pristine color and quality.

His eyes widened, and he forced a pleasant smile. "Hello, Isla," he signed while straightening his spine. Oliver pulled down on his waistcoat and removed his damp and sweaty cravat. He sat down on the felt couch, and when he did, it was like all the stress of the past week accompanied him.

"Where's the boss of this household?" Oliver asked.

He was always in good spirits, and he also had a charming sarcasm that never failed to make her smile, even if it wasn't the most appropriate thing to do at the time.

"She's in the garden," Isla signed.

"What's for dinner?" he asked.

"Lamb stew."

"I can live with that."

Housekeeper Martha was hard at work, cutting onions, carrots, and garlic and dropping them into a pot. She was meticulous to an almost unnecessary degree. Martha didn't even allow Yula, the woman she had been best friends with since she was a girl, to stir the pot.

When the warrants for Isla and her family became public, Oliver had to have a discussion with Yula and Martha about their discretion, making sure the two of them didn't speak a word about Isla being sheltered in their home.

The conversation was rather quick because, after all these years, Isla had become like a daughter to them. They could communicate with Isla as well as any of her immediate family, even though their worldly tongue wasn't as smooth. They were from one of the Free Islands, known as Onuh Island, where they spoke in the Sandshore tongue. Many of their words on the islands had different meanings on the mainland, so it had been difficult for them to adapt. Luckily, most Roguewave natives near Molten City weren't known for their polished vocabulary.

Martha had short dark hair with around twenty earrings that went all the way around the borders of her ears. It was not uncommon to see people from the islands adorned head to toe in jewelry, most of which consisted of family heirlooms.

Yula, whose head was shaved close, wore a ruby ring in her eyebrow that contrasted against her alabaster tone, which was from a rare skin disease she had been born with. Where Martha could talk for days, Yula was much more reserved and never the first to speak. Isla and Yula shared more in non-verbal cues than words.

Oliver gripped her shoulder. His head was down, and he rubbed his eyes with his other hand. When he looked up, his eyes were red, and he looked as if he was on the verge of tears. "I'm so sorry about Caldwell. He doesn't deserve what is coming to him."

Oliver spent almost as much time with Caldwell as he did with Isla. Caldwell did a lot of his aid training under Oliver and always praised him. She remembered her father once saying, "Oliver is equal parts a good man and a good practitioner. Anyone with those two qualities should be mirrored. Because sadly, it's hard to find anyone proficient at both."

Then, it hit her.

The reality of her brother dying tomorrow and being gone from this world, along with her father. She broke down, struggling to grasp air as she fought shortness of breath.

Oliver lifted Isla's head. "Please believe me when I tell you I've done all I could. I spoke to Judge Barnes and pleaded my case for his innocence."

There was no doubt in her mind that Doctor Emerson did that very thing. But at this point, there was no consoling her anymore. "What am I supposed to do? I don't have a family anymore," Isla signed with shaky hands and teary eyes.

Oliver struggled to meet her eye. He removed his tricorne hat and slicked back his greasy black hair underneath. He talked with his hands alone. It seemed he couldn't bear mouthing his words. "I wish I could bring them all here right now for you. I wish I could defy all the laws of this world and put them all in this room. But I can't." His eyes darted to the doorway leading into the kitchen, where Livian now stood with a basket of assorted vegetables. "However, we can help you. We will do everything in our power to protect you and give you a life worth living."

Livian put down the basket on the kitchen counter. Yula and Martha took notice of the conversation but continued working. "We don't desire to replace your family, Isla." A lone tear fell down Livian's cheek. "But we want you safe. We can keep you safe."

Emerson Estate butler, Chives, strolled into the parlor. He carried a letter on a silver platter that seemed unnecessary. He offered it to Oliver. Chives gave Isla a respectful bow and took his leave.

Oliver widened his eyes while reading the letter. He ignored Isla's tug on his arm and kept reading. She waited for a response. "If this letter is to be believed, a new governor and administration are on their way to Roguewave." His nostrils flared and shook his head side to side over and over. "Local government officials are to be voted by the people… not forced on them. The Assembly makes up rules and laws as they go."

FIFTEEN
SHARKEYES III

It took a week to travel from Roguewave to the northern shores of Autera. The southern continent, now under Assembly and Unified Provincial jurisdiction, operated vicariously through the needs of the landmass looking down upon it from beyond the waters of the Beaker Gulf. From there, it was another week or two on foot to the lands of Redrainn, home of the Trezbe Clan.

Avery hadn't spoken in days. No other prisoners accompanied her on this mandatory journey, and she wasn't about to speak to the greencoats that forced her here.

Avery had always wanted to travel the world, but not like this. She always imagined herself at the wheel of a Grand Ship, perhaps her father's vessel, the *Abyss,* giving orders to her crew and voyaging beyond limitations. A free woman, with nothing holding her back from seeing all the wonders of the world made by man or the Creator. However, she found herself in shackles, landlocked, and confined in unknown territory where the sea only existed in her memory.

The dry air seemed heavy and almost toxic to breathe. The sun was harsh and abused Avery's naturally tan skin. She thought of her father and his paleness and wondered how he managed when he first visited here so many years ago.

The irons on her wrists had become quite heavy after wearing them for three weeks. Blisters and sores crept up to her forearms. She received one meal a day and only two small cups of water. With Redrainn's heat, she was losing more water than she was taking in.

A rifle jabbed her in the back. Greencoats didn't care about the pain they caused.

The shackles were attached to a long chain attached to a horse that rode ahead of her. The small group of transport soldiers laughed and conversed atop their steeds as Avery wobbled on foot. Occasionally she would be flogged for straggling. It bothered her how easy it was for the men to do such a thing without remorse.

Men like these would never sail under my father.

There was nowhere to run. In every direction was nothing but flat ground covered in hard dirt and minimal trees that stretched as far as the eye could see. However, she knew the Botan Rainforest was to the east and the Skiatation Mountain Range to the west. Neither appeared close as they were not in view.

If I could make it to either of those, perhaps I could evade them in the terrain.

The man in charge of the prisoner expedition, Captain Ike, informed the group they were to arrive in the capital of Redrainn by nightfall.

"You'll be seeing Grandmother and Grandfather here soon, Battier," Captain Ike said with a crooked smile. "I'll warn you. They don't look much like a tarquin and tarquiness anymore, so don't get your hopes up."

Her mother always said her mother and father were the leaders of the Trezbe Clan, but she never mentioned their official titles. *Tarquin? Tarquiness?*

She kept her gaze forward.

"You haven't spoken in weeks, Battier," a common greencoat with rotted teeth said. "Perhaps you should lose the scowl and cheer up. You're home now where you and people like you belong."

The thoughts racing through her mind were malicious. She had a lot of time for contemplation, and at times she wanted to cry because of her situation. However, her desire not to appear weak was more powerful than her sadness. She prayed for her siblings' safety, all except Xavier's. She'd tried communicating with Eddie every day, but there was no response. The phenomenon of the foggy echo no longer took place, and it broke her heart.

And when she felt at her lowest, she thought of the bravery and strength of her mother, as well as words of wisdom from her father.

She recalled once asking her father what his favorite animal was. His reply was a coated rat. The rodent had a hard exterior and was found in all corners of the world. He fancied the rat because of its ability to survive extreme environments.

I shall be a coated rat, Father. A coated rat with shark eyes.

The ground began to crack. Massive fissures riddled the ground. Ahead was the fire-lit capital of Redrainn called Caste Valley. The trees and greenery became more frequent. Most of the homes consisted of huts that shared no differences aside from their gradual increase in size towards Caste Valley center.

Captain Ike trotted through the darkness. "Take the Battier girl to the Sodaro home."

Four greencoats with their rifles up toward the black sky escorted her to the middle of Caste Valley. Many Trezbe people shared features she recognized in her mother. A darker complexion with matching eyes, a square face with a distinct jawline, and the ability to wear an emotionless face.

She saw tired men and women soaking their feet in buckets positioned over fires, children in leather and fur pants still in between huts playing despite the grim atmosphere. An elderly man's back was being tended by two girls younger than Eddie as it bled from gruesome and thin lashes.

A hut at the valley's center was larger than the rest. Avery approached with her hands still bound. Braziers were lit at the curtained entryway. Where the other clan homes could maybe house a family of four, this hut looked big enough for double. A man facing away from her was bathing in a barrel with only his head exposed. It steamed as the cool air made its presence known.

"Sodaro," a greencoat said to the man in the Aelic tongue. He was ignored. "Alexious Sodaro! At attention, Tarquin. It's your favorite Lieutenant Colbe come to offer you a gift!"

As he rose from the barrel, the man's scarred back, littered with healed lash marks, was on display. He was a broad-shouldered and tall man. Avery wondered how he managed to squeeze himself into that compact barrel to bathe in the first place. The greencoats tightened their grip on their rifles.

One greencoat removed her shackles while Colbe carried on, "Welcome your little half-breed granddaughter home, Alexious."

Her grandfather had a weathered face with a thick white beard contrasting his skin. Then, an older woman emerged from behind the leather entryway.

"Ah, and the reunion is now complete. Hello, Eralia," Colbe said while giving Avery a shove in the back, forcing her to her knees.

Avery was surprised as two hands lifted her upright once more. Her grandmother, whom she had never met before, embraced her like family.

"Your daughter put herself and your grandchildren in a

very challenging place because of her treason. But then again, we aren't surprised," Colbe said. "Enjoy your new life, Battier. It won't fulfill your hopes or desires, but perhaps the offspring of savage traitors shouldn't have the luxury."

Avery wanted nothing more than to wipe the arrogant look from his face with a hammer.

From the darkness, around six Trezbe men appeared with scowls and surrounded the greencoat guards. The soldiers' confidence quickly shifted in the opposite direction as they now had their rifles at the ready.

"Not to worry, occupiers, our claws have been removed. We aren't as savage as we used to be," her grandfather Alexious said.

The greencoats didn't turn their backs to walk away until the darkness shrouded them completely.

On their exit, Trezbe people arrived from every direction. Her grandmother and grandfather both held her and made sure she wasn't hurt.

"Are you whole? Water!" Eralia called.

Avery hadn't spoken Aelic in a long time. Her education was never a priority, even something so close to home as her mother's native tongue.

"I'm fine. Just tired," Avery said.

"You must be," Alexious replied with a frown.

As he stood looking down at her, the longer his gaze lasted, the more his eyes filled with tears. "I always knew my daughter would return to me in some way. By the gods, I knew it. Here she is." He gently grabbed her wrists and rubbed his thumb along the blistered skin. "We'll get you something for this." He looked to Eralia and back to Avery with a soft smile. "What's your name?"

"Avery."

He turned and addressed the small crowd that had gathered. "My people, we are struggling. However, we must not lose hope. It's times like these when we must enjoy the things the gods give us. Homecomings. This is Avery, my dear Adelaide's daughter—my granddaughter. I want you to all clutch one another a little tighter this evening. If you're lucky to still have any loved ones left, make sure your love is not uncertain. All we have is each other now!"

Eralia ushered her inside the hut. "Come, Avery. We have much to discuss."

SIXTEEN
THE COWARD BOY III

Eddison's eyes fluttered open in a swaying hammock of the cramped crew quarters aboard the cog. The back of his head was tender to the touch as he ran his palm over the lump in his curly hair.

He panicked. His hands gripped both sides of the netted hammock, and he went to rise out of it, but it jerked the opposite way underneath him. Eddison couldn't get his feet under him in time to stop the fall. Luckily, his forearms cushioned most of the blow.

Avery? He tried to call out to his sister but got nothing in response—only the creaking of a ship from below deck. *Avery?*

Nothing.

Eddison stumbled towards the sunlight shining on the staircase leading to the deck. The ladder appeared hopeful, as if he were to climb it, he would ascend into the heavens, be reunited with his family, and sail to the Golden Shores.

He bumped his head on one of the low beams but continued up the stairs.

"Aye, there he is, boys!" Eddie heard a man yell from the deck.

The sunlight blurred his vision as he emerged from

underneath. All he saw was an unrelenting flash of white and yellow.

"Ah, rise and shine, Battier!" the same voice yelled. "Those words seem rather literal in this context."

The world started to come into focus.

The five strangers around him paid him no mind as they were all focused on manning the ship. Eddie's stomach turned. He ran to the railing and retched into the water, spewing his stomach acid into the beautiful blue waters.

"I don't know if the seas made you sick or that shot to the head I gave you... Either way, my apologies, Eddison."

His eyes focused on Leven Parke. He was operating the wheel and keeping the ship on course to their destination, wherever that might be.

"Where are we?" Eddie asked.

"East," was the only response he got.

What first tipped him off was the silence. Every sound, whether it was the waves hitting the side of the cog or the ship itself, was loud. It was all amplified by the soundless echo chamber manifesting itself around them. *East?*

"There isn't anything to the east," Eddison said, still in his groggy state.

"Is that what they teach you now in fancy boy school?" Leven said with a smile. "You haven't been properly introduced. You've been below deck for nearly two days now. At one point, you got up and relieved yourself in one of the apple barrels with your eyes closed, then you got right back into the hammock and went to sleep. We all had a good laugh about that."

Eddison didn't remember that in the slightest.

"Welcome aboard the *Dogtooth*, Eddison. A humble yet sturdy ship captained by me," Leven went on. "Behind you, working their hands to the bone, as usual, are my sailors, Cemitri, Ali, Robbie, and Pat." Even with a small crew the ship was still cramped with all the equipment, storage, and endless ropes.

"Slowed to five knots, Captain!" Pat yelled. He had a burn scar that covered his entire back.

"We're going to be limping to shore, boys. Just have to work with it."

"Aye!" they replied in unison.

Eddie looked ahead, farther east to the small island that seemed to be their destination. "Find a smile, Eddison. You're about to meet one of the last great captains this world has to offer."

The *Dogtooth* slowly sailed right into its heart of the island. The eerie and soundless void of this place left Eddie on edge. Granted, that was his default position. However, nerve bumps formed on the back of his neck.

Thick forest surrounded them. Branches hung over the ship, and from time to time, a small critter would drop its dinner onto the deck and jolt Eddie.

"Relax, Eddison. There's no one here that wishes you any more ill will. Quite the opposite," Leven said.

Eddie had a difficult time putting his faith in a man he hardly knew and knocked him unconscious.

Travel was slow through the watershed. However, up ahead was a familiar sight that caught Eddie's eye. Sails peeked through the tree line. The waters widened and formed a large catchment of open water big enough to anchor four tall ships and one square rigger. The tall ships were badly damaged. Their sails were torn, and the hulls looked crippled beyond repair. Eddie wondered how they were still afloat.

"A-Are those the same ships—"

"That engaged Molten Fort and the *Hydra*? Yes, what's left," Leven said.

The *Dogtooth* was compact enough to sail between the larger vessels and creep right on up to the rotted jetty. Heavy thumps beat against the hull. He looked to Leven.

"Eddie, there's going to be things you see today that may be beyond your imagination. Accept it now."

The thumping continued and was followed by the scraping and clanking of metal. Creatures were surfacing from the water and climbing the ship. The crew maintained their calm demeanor.

Eddie backed up against the main mast in the center of the *Dogtooth*, awaiting the upcoming arrival. *Breathe,* was something his father and his sister always told him to do when he was nervous. Eddie's eyes were glued to the side of the ship, and the sounds stopped altogether. He gripped a cord behind him.

Then, hands reached over the sides of the cog. They were fleshy, wet, and webbed, greenish-brown with faint scales. These creatures pulled themselves onto the deck. They stood upright, like men. Their heads were bald, rounded, and they had what looked like gills on their necks.

This cannot be real. Surely this is the afterlife.

Around twenty boarded the ship. Eddie's lower jaw dropped and shook as it dangled. They returned a curious gaze. Their yellow eyes had small black pupils, and yet their shoulders were large and rounded. They wore soaking wet, tattered clothes of men.

Leven spoke first, and it was in a language Eddie had never heard before. It was hard for him to even consider it a language. It didn't sound like words, merely noises made with the back of the throat.

A runt amongst them peeked out from behind the others. It never took its eyes off Eddie. When it blinked, its eyelids opened and closed vertically.

Leven spoke to them in a manner that matched a normal interaction any seafaring man would have with another. His crew followed suit, and they even exchanged handshakes as men would.

Their hands are so gross and slimy.

The one that hadn't broken its gaze on Eddie went for a handshake. Eddie was frozen.

"Go on, lad. We don't leave hands unshaken around here," Leven said.

In the Academy, it was taught that alternative races were killed or driven away at the conclusion of the Grand War. Hundreds of years ago, Renera was host to giants, daemons, gravers, and mackereli alongside humans. However, tensions began to rise over land distribution. The textbooks claim that the alternative races occupied most of the western lands and wanted to pursue eastward expansion, especially due to the rapidly growing population of humans. The alternative races grew contemptuous of the humans, and prejudice began to form, and conflicts rose.

Then, the Original Five Provinces united against the incursion. The war led to many inventions and weaponry that tilted the tide in human favor to nearly eradicate them all to extinction. Eddie's great-great-grandfather, Malachai Battier, commanded a great battle against the last remaining band of giants at Lake Ghonia. His father said he slew the final giant, Golidrum, in single combat while knee-deep in lake water. The story goes that he sliced through the back of its legs, immobilizing the behemoth, and proceeded to drown in the shallow.

Eddie extended his hand. It was exactly the way he imagined. It reminded him of the times he and his family would go catch and release fishing. Taking the fish from the hook was always the worst part. Most of the time he had his sister do it for him. So, he kept his head low and wasn't looking forward to doing that again. He wiped his hand on the back of his pants.

"Eddie, these are the mackereli," Leven said. "They are friends of ours. Treat 'em like such."

"O-Okay," he stammered. The bulk of the mackereli helped the crew dock the ship, and Leven put his arm around Eddie.

"Let's head ashore."

The walk through the dense forest on this small island was longer than Eddie could've ever imagined. The absence of the wind gave him eerie chills. The only sound to be heard was the chuckling exchanges between the crew and mackereli. They talked as if they'd known each other their whole lives.

The forest opened into a clearing. It was the home of a massive campsite that housed hundreds of log cabins with an abundance of small fires lighting the primitive thoroughfare. Eddie's eyes moved up the trees to see tons of houses elevated up high. Every man and woman wore cutlasses and pistols on their hips. They were going about their business until their eyes found Eddie.

Some that were wearing hats or bandanas removed them and placed them over their hearts, and lowered their heads as Eddie walked by. "Why are they doing that?" he asked Leven.

"Out of respect."

"For me?"

"No. Your father."

A watchtower stood proudly on the far end of the makeshift town. It had three stories with winding stairs curling around the entire structure. By this time, hundreds of people – men, women, children, and mackerel – had emerged from their cabins, tents, and treehouses to look upon Eddie.

"Let's head on up," Leven said, leading the way up the many steps.

Once the pair of them reached the top, a large map table filled most of the observation deck. A man wearing a long, dark blue officer's coat stared longingly at the open sea.

"Are you the only Battier that made the trip here?" the man asked, still facing away.

Eddie looked to Leven, who urged him to reply. "Yes, I am," he replied in a shaky voice.

"I hear they call you Coward Boy, Eddison Rogers Battier."

The man turned. He had a thick beard, and Eddie could smell the sea on him. He approached with a heavy step, looking at everyone around the table. A thin roof of branches and leaves covered their heads from the elements. The walls were open to observe the island and ocean for miles in all directions.

"Leave us," he commanded softly. Everyone obeyed his command as they collected themselves and moved past Eddie.

"Tell me, how does one acquire that unfortunate nickname?" the man asked.

"I'm n—not much of a fighter, sir," Eddie replied.

"So, you don't fight back, is what you're saying?"

"No."

"Word is you don't have to because your sister is usually there to rescue you whenever you need."

Eddie dropped his head.

He stepped closer. His movements were slow and methodical. "It's a shame she couldn't be here with you. Seems like we could use someone like her. Not you. We can't use cowards. Cowards have no place in our way of life and our mission." He planted his palms on the map table and stared over the typography with a cocked brow. "No matter. You're the son of Mathias Battier, and that counts for

something. Perhaps you've heard of me. Perhaps you haven't;
it matters not. I've fought in two wars enduring countless
battles. I've been tortured, marooned, and hunted. Songs,
both fantastical and horrific, have been written about my
exploits. I have been the Unified Provinces' most wanted
fugitive for years, yet I remain."

He stood right in front of Eddie and glared down at him.

"They will tell you that many dead bodies are in my wake,
but they'll never utter how many people I've saved. Destiny
has placed you here under my command, believe it or not. By
the grace of your father, I will do my best to usher you along
as well as I can. I am Captain Marstellar Lockett, leader of
the Rebellion and the bane of the Assembly's existence."

Marstellar walked to the tower railing and utilized his
observatory.

"I know this is probably the last place you want to be, and
I know that these people intimidate and possibly frighten you.
Don't despair. You're going to spend a lot of time on a ship
surrounded by strangers and people you won't desire to get to
know. You might as well get over that wave of fear now
because you're going to be miserable if you don't."

Eddie didn't want to be with these people at all. The pirate
captain was right about that. He wanted to be home,
surrounded by his family. At this point, he wouldn't even mind
training under Xavier anymore as long it meant he was home.

"For how long?" he asked.

"How long for what?"

"How long until I can see my family again?"

Marstellar stroked his beard. "Someday, perhaps, but that
day won't come soon. Whether you like it or not, this is your
family now. I know that's not what you want to hear, but I will
never lie to you."

As Eddie stood in the middle of this Windless Isle, his chin
quivered, and his eyes watered.

"No," the captain said sternly. "Now's not the time for tears."

The top of the tower seemed to be the headquarters for Marstellar's dealings in the heart of the island. It also served as a watchtower, with a clear view in all directions. Rifles and swords lined the walls, and the map table in the center was king.

Marstellar went to a sea chest in the north corner. Eddie thought it might be buried treasure found in the belly of caves worlds away — something fitting for a pirate.

The lid cracked open, and there was no shine of gold. Marstellar returned with only a letter. The prospect of seeing true pirate booty vanished before his very eyes.

"Perhaps you should read this," Marstellar said, extending the letter to Eddison. "I was with your father when he read this for the first time as we sailed south."

"What is it?" Eddie asked.

"Just read, son."

Dear Mathias,

Be joyful. Yesterday, our son was born in good health. He has a full head of dark curly hair already. The doctor says he will turn plenty of Roguewave girls' heads when he gets older.

Avery has already taken to having a younger brother because she will not let anyone else hold him for the time being. She and Xavier have already fought over the situation, so things on that end have not altered.

Eddison Rogers Battier, born on the fourth day

of winter in 81AA, awaits his father to meet him for the first time.

With undying love,
Adelaide

"Every letter your mother ever sent to your father is in that chest," Marstellar said, closing the lid and sitting atop the chest.

Eddie's chin uncontrollably wrinkled. "I thought it would be gold."

"No, there's plenty in this world that is far more valuable than gold."

"I thought that's all pirates cared about?"

Marstellar took the letter from Eddie's hand and folded it neatly. "Freedom is our most important currency, son. It's what your father died for."

Eddie shook his head. "I don't understand."

"Your father fought for the betterment of this world. That's all you need to know for now."

The floor creaked behind Eddie. He turned to see the woman with six swords standing there. She bore a striking resemblance to his mother.

"Ah, Cella," Marstellar said.

"Apologies, Captain, I did not mean to—"

"Not to worry. I have a task for you."

After he put the letter back in the chest, he grabbed Eddison's shoulders, squeezed them hard, and ushered him forward. "Eddie, this is Cella Djar. She's our weapons master on the *Madfrog* and a good one at that." She looked Eddie up and down coldly. "We sail soon, and you need to be ready. Cella is going to start training you around a sword."

"But—"

"No. There is no arguing to be had. This is an opportunity

to train under a person that may be the best swordsman on the sea. You will not cast it aside." As Marstellar made his demands to Eddie, he looked at Cella with an intense glare. "And you will train him as well as anyone else, understand?"

Keeping her cold demeanor, she replied, "Yes, Captain."

The seven-foot man made his presence known. "This is her husband, Leak Djar, our quartermaster," Lockett said. "He is in charge of keeping ship operations running smoothly. Both he and Cella are of the Idush Clan in Autera."

The Idush? Mother hardly spoke on the other clans from Autera, but when she did, there was never anything kind relayed about the Idush.

"Despite any feelings you may have towards the boy's mother, you will treat him as a member of this crew and son of Mathias Battier. Do I make myself clear?" Marstellar asked them.

What did my mother do to them?

Both Cella and Leak had furrowed eyebrows that made their presence more intimidating. Through gritted teeth, they replied, "Yes, Captain."

"Good."

As they exited, a young and old version of the same person entered in their place.

Lockett continued to introduce him to more pirates. "This is Jameson Roke and his son Mathias—yes, after your father. But on the *Madfrog*, we just call him Matt."

Matt extended his hand first. "Pleasure to meet you, Eddison. I've heard a lot about you." His eyes fell. "I'm sorry about your loss."

"Matt is our boatswain," Lockett said. "He keeps a log of all our equipment and crew. You'll learn from him as well. You'll be shadowing him from now on. Even after setting sail."

Jameson stepped forward. "Ah, young Battier." He squeezed Eddie's hand tight. "The resemblance between you and your father is true."

"My brother talks about you all the time," Eddie said.

"Does he?" The upper left side of Jameson's face didn't seem to move. The three scars that ran diagonally from forehead to cheek had evidently caused irreversible damage.

"He wants to beat your dual record."

The scarless side of Jameson's face smiled. "There was once a time when all of that was very important to me. Maybe it was around the time I met your father when all of that seemed to fade."

Heavy, wet footsteps slapped the floor behind his new shipmates.

Mackereli.

"Last but not least," Lockett said.

Nervous, Eddie did his best and said, "Hello," in the mackereli tongue. His voice was shaky.

Everyone stopped. The world seemed to stop. They tilted their heads with their mouths agape.

Did I do something wrong? It took a lot of effort to speak from the back of his throat and gurgle through whatever greeting he believed he gave. *I must've not said it right.*

"What was that, Eddie?" Marstellar asked.

The mackereli cocked its head, and its eyelids blinked.

"Just… trying to say hello."

"I can see that. You did it successfully. How'd you do that?"

"I just listened." With all eyes on him, he grew nervous, even more than he already was. "I-I-I can l-learn quick, especially when it comes to languages."

Marstellar smiled, a smile bordering on either pride or intrigue. The pirate captain spoke in mackereli himself. "Can you speak Aquatic?"

"Bits and pieces."

"Well, Eddie, this is Caspus, king of the last mackereli school. You will shake his hand just as you would a man's, understand?"

"Yes," Eddie replied and, at the same time, extended his

hand. He couldn't tell for certain, but he believed just the hint of a smile formed at the edges of Caspus' wide mouth.

Lockett and Caspus met each other's gaze.

"Eddison Rogers Battier," the Captain grinned. "We may have use for you yet."

SEVENTEEN
THE PIRATE KING I

The introductions involving Eddison Battier had to be done. Marstellar wasn't keen on having a timid boy be a part of his crew. With the inevitable dangers on the horizon, it was another responsibility tacked onto a monolith of duties. Soon he would send Eddie with Cella to begin his sword training which would be far more rigorous than the coward could imagine. *We learn difficult lessons in difficult ways.*

"From what you've told me, Marstellar, he seems like a good kid. Too good to be here," said Roke, trailing behind him, the only one amongst his brethren to use his first name. Most everyone just called him "Captain" or "Captain Lockett." There wasn't a rule against using his first name, but the respect he garnered was the driving force behind the formality.

"You're right about that," Marstellar agreed. "But he's Mathias' son, and I'm not turning a blind eye."

"Neither will I."

Marstellar looked to his friend of many years, "Good. However, I do find it bland that my first mate doesn't challenge my authority more often."

"Well, you always sound reasonable to me. I'll leave the challenging of your authority to Leak and Cella," Roke said.

Marstellar noticed Roke's contemplation.

"Is it wise to have Cella train the boy, Marstellar?" Jameson asked. He was raised in Roguewave, but make no mistake, he's half Trezbe, and Cella is Idush. She hates the Trezbe Clan more than anything. Not to mention the fact that Cella and Adelaide have crossed sword and axe before, and it didn't turn out so well for our weapons master."

"That is why she must help the Battier boy. Regardless of what we were once, we are pirates now. We all have former rivalries, prejudices, and anger that we must overcome. It is what Mathias set out to do." Marstellar looked down at his arm to gaze upon the hydra tattoo with seventeen heads, angrily ascending to his wrist. "Those people with their powdered wigs in their massive halls want to make us out to be the real danger to civilized society. To tell everyone we're animals setting out only to destroy and steal our way through life. I will do my best to make our intentions nothing of the sort. I want those elites, with nothing but the need for their own to prosper—that see us as demons—to look back one day and realize we were ahead of the wave crashing down on them. I want them to know that it was the rebels that saw everyone as equals. And no matter the background, location, race, or appearance, they could come together and make such a beautiful reality possible. I want them to look back and realize it was the bloody pirates that showed them the way."

"Aye, very well," Roke said.

"Remember, we are not doing this for us. We are doing this for Matt, Eddie, and the next generation. A generation that doesn't look promising at the moment, but perhaps we can change that."

The newly founded civilization on the Windless Isle was something that gave Marstellar a sense of pride. In collaboration with the mackereli, he believed they built a place that could satisfy everyone's needs. Though small, the isle was blanketed by trees, giving them more than enough to develop their condensed city.

The buildings were constructed around the various creeks that flowed from the cove in the island's center. They were large enough that the mackereli could travel up and down them with haste. Only the pirates used the homes and buildings. The mackereli spent most of their time in the cove, for they lived in pods dug beneath the surface of the water.

The captain and first mate walked along the southernmost creek, away from the island's center. Doctor Samms liked his privacy. Having studied in Helmburough Academy, Samms had grown used to the finer things in life and didn't much partake in the revelry of high seas piracy. Marstellar left him to his own devices and studies when on land. He even allowed Samms' cabin to be built away from everybody so he could do what he enjoyed without distraction. At one point, people knew his first name, but even the captain had to admit that after all these years, it had been lost to time.

It was a humble cabin. Like the rest of the island, and though Marstellar was proud of what he and his people had accomplished, this place to him was nothing more than a checkpoint toward the end goal. A destination that would require great sacrifice.

Roke put his knuckles up to the wooden door and knocked. "Doc?"

It didn't take long for the locks on the other side of the door to begin clicking.

Doc opened the door, Samms' finely curled mustache making its presence known.

"I like the curls, Doc," Marstellar said.

Doc smiled, and the mustache curled even more. "Thank you, Captain."

"How's our prisoner doing?" Roke asked.

Doc removed his bifocals and rubbed his eyes. "Well, I had

to gag him because he wouldn't let me focus on my work. He likes to talk."

"That doesn't surprise me. He's a politician," Marstellar said. "I'd like to speak with him."

"Very well."

Doc's cabin matched his mind. Though he was calm and collected in most circumstances, his mind was cluttered with creative ideas, mostly revolving around his work. He thought of crafting new forms of medicine, or explosives, and they kept him awake at all hours of day and night. He liked to refer to himself as the "doctor that could destroy things and put them back together." That was partially the reason Marstellar left him to his own devices, to use that creative mind, because he believed Doc could stumble upon something groundbreaking and give them the upper hand, whether that be of the medicinal or destructive type.

The interior did not match any normal living area. There were workbenches along every wall. The tools varied from blacksmithing hammers to glowing glass vials that only Doc knew the contents of, as they weren't labeled. Captain Lockett wondered how he managed to sleep since there was no room for a bed anywhere. *Perhaps he doesn't sleep.*

"Any discoveries, Doc?" Roke asked.

"I may have found something that keeps our fish friends more comfortable on deck." Doc reached for a small blue vial that had a light glow and handed it to Marstellar. "Take a swig."

"What is it?" he asked.

"It's water with a little added concoction I made."

"I can see that. Is that what's causing the glow?"

Doc smiled. "Aye. The mackereli won't be comfortable on deck and will most likely get sick on the extended voyage. This mixture of water and stagnant lily will reduce the effects if not eliminate sea sickness entirely."

Marstellar shook the vial and watched the glow intensify. "Are you certain?"

"Do you doubt me already, Captain?"

"Of course not." He handed the vial back. "Open the hatch, if you don't mind."

The skinny frame of Doctor Samms moved to the opposite corner of the room. "Very well. Very well. Don't mind me. I'm merely the man who does all the important work around here," he added.

"That may be true, my friend," Marstellar replied.

A lever angled upward from the wall. "I'm just glad you recognize that, Captain." Doc pulled the lever down, and a square door opened in the middle of the cabin floor. "Happy interrogating."

The underground staircase built into the foundation of the island was a feat of pirate architecture. While their reputation was one of stealing and murder, that was merely propaganda to keep people afraid. Marstellar had people from all backgrounds in his company. There were miners from the Ink Mountains in Bluemoore and Swiftwater Province that worked in the bowels of the ship, loggers from Northwood that used their craft to build and repair his fleet, fishermen from Whitefin Bay, as well as the lakes of Ghonia to assure that the crew, no matter the waters, never starved. And there were educated men from the capital like Doctor Samms, Pick de Gerrard, who used their wisdom to propel their proficiency. There were men and women from Rustling and Drybrun who just wanted to fight, and the clan folk from Autera who wanted to be left alone.

The space beneath the cabin was cramped. However, it served its purpose of housing Marstellar's prisoner. Jameson tore the burlap sack off Governor Tytus' head. His fat and pale face revealed itself.

"Hello there," Marstellar said as the governor blinked his eyes to have them focus in the dark. He was doused in sweat, his lips were cracking from lack of water, and wispy hairs formed under his double chin. "Jameson, would you mind giving Tytus some water?" Roke put the waterskin up to Tytus' lips, and the Roguewavian drank his dehydrated fill. "I do apologize for the climate. Even down here it seems like there is no escape from our haven's humidity. You must believe me. I don't want to treat my prisoners poorly. I'd hate for those awful things the Assembly say about us pirates to be true."

Water dripped from both sides of Tytus' mouth. "And what haven might this be that you and your wretched people call home?"

"A place far enough away that you and others like you can't be heard."

Tytus laughed a wheeze-filled cackle that was near torture to Captain Lockett. "That place does not exist, bloody pirate. There is no place in this world that is not in the shadow of our empire."

As the cackle continued, his arrogant nature seemed to rub the first mate the wrong way.

"Perhaps we can beat him first, then ask questions, Captain?" Roke asked.

Lockett knelt in a very froglike pose with his elbows resting on his knees as his back dropped. It was a position he often found himself in, which led to his famous nickname: Madfrog. As he spent as much time at sea as he did on land, he felt the name was justified. After wearing that nickname for so many years as a youth, he thought of no better title for his latest flagship.

"As I said, Roke, let's not give him any reason to believe the lies told about us."

"Lies?" Tytus scoffed. "You vile creatures raided Molten Bay! Everyone knows the destruction you caused."

"And I'm sure the Assembly makes it sound even worse in their letters and papers that spread across Renera."

"So, was your little raid simply executed to capture me?" the governor asked.

"Yes, it was."

"I'm flattered," Tytus said sarcastically.

"I figured you would be, judging by what I've heard."

"Is that so? And was else did you hear? I doubt your information is entirely accurate."

Still, in his Madfrog kneel, Marstellar said, "You were born Melvin Tytus in the year 46AA—Son of Lord Ike and Lady Merriad Tytus of Pennway on the western coast. You were the middle child of seven children and the least important in your parents' eyes due to your lack of ambition and entitled demeanor. Your other siblings remain near Port Spryte, where your family's estate still resides. After the death of former Roguewave Governor Cooper, your father cashed in many favors requesting you to fill the void. Many believed it was to elevate your family name, but that wasn't true because your father openly admitted to his fellow lords in Pennway that he didn't care about your new title. No, he was simply happy his disappointment of a son was on the opposite end of the world, rotting in Roguewave."

It didn't seem possible that Tytus could pale further, but as he turned silent for the first time, it was *very* possible.

Marstellar finally stood upon seeing the defeat in Tytus' eyes.

"I know who you are," the governor said grimly.

"Is that right?"

"You're supposed to be dead." Tytus shifted his weight to the opposite side and adjusted his bound hands behind his back. "I, like everyone else, heard the rumors of your demise at the hands of Alistair Cross. When whispers arose that you had somehow managed to survive, I asked the grand commander myself about them. He said that the rumors were false. That there was no possibility that the Pirate King Marstellar Lockett could be alive."

Marstellar returned with a grim voice of his own. "He was right about that, Governor."

"Then what happened that day when you found yourself captive of Alistair Cross? And how did you manage to survive? Very few who exchange cannon fire with Alistair live to tell the tale."

Marstellar looked to Roke, who dropped his eyes. "A story for a different day, perhaps. You should be asking different questions."

Tytus thrashed around, seemingly wanting more than anything to be out of his restraints. "And what question should I be asking?"

As cool as his reputation believed him to be, Marstellar said, "Do you desire redemption?"

"Redemption for what?" Tytus asked with attitude.

"For yourself. Wouldn't you like the opportunity to truly accomplish something great?" A silence befell the underground space before Marstellar continued, "Or perhaps your family was right about your lack of ambition."

"I am a governor!" Tytus yelled.

"A governor who means very little to the Assembly."

Tytus cocked his head sideways. "What did you say?"

Marstellar extended his hand for Roke, and his quartermaster placed a newspaper in his palm. He flipped open the newspaper and read: *"Governor Tytus was found slain in his mansion at the hands of the monsters who call themselves pirates. His tragic death will now lead straight into an election of qualified candidates looking to restore Roguewave and Molten Bay to its former glory."*

Marstellar then turned the page, putting the words right in front of Tytus' eyes. "I apologize that the Assembly cared so little about you that they decided to write you off as dead. Almost makes you wonder if they cared about losing you in the first place."

Tytus hung his head. He was a broken man, defeated, and nowhere to call home.

"I know these people. Believe me, if you are to return to the Unified Provinces, they will kill you because you are making liars out of them." Marstellar drove his pointer finger into Melvin's chest. "That cannot stand. You know this. You must. I believe you can help us and can be a valuable ally in giving us the information we need to change the landscape of our world. There are going to be things I ask you to do. I promise it won't be anything beyond your capabilities. And you never know, you may like the potential of everything Mathias and myself set out for you."

Tytus slowly brought his head back up. "Set out for me?"

Marstellar smiled. "That's right. You work nicely into our plot. There's far more to this world than meets the eye. There are lands uninhabited, lush, with life ready to be claimed. It's just up to us to take it. I'm just going to need you to tell us the navy's patrol schedule for all their routes, especially the Grand Ships."

Melvin scoffed. "I don't know them off the top of my head. I know they are pushing more vessels farther east because of you all. Perhaps the newly elected governor will have a navy mobilization ledger or the captain of the fort if he's still alive."

"Is there not one in your mountain of papers and ledgers we took from your office?"

"Most likely, yes. However, they must be updated bi-weekly. Mine would be out of date at this point if you want to pin down exact locations of ships in eastern waters."

"Then, time is of the essence now more than ever. I have a mission for you. You and Jameson will return to Roguewave and declare for all to hear the Assembly's crimes by any means necessary. You will take these papers and get them published in the newspaper and get them released by any means necessary. One of the finest killers this world has to offer will be escorting you on the sloop as soon as we are done here. He has permission to end your life if you don't comply by any means necessary." Marstellar stared into his eyes and his soul. "You never know, in your solitude and contemplation on your way back, perhaps a sense of clarity will come over you, and extreme measures won't be necessary because, contrary to popular belief, we aren't so ready to kill as much as the Assembly is. You can be a massive step in the right direction for course correction. I know who you are, Melvin. You're a man desperately looking for significance. There's nothing wrong with that. We all are. How will you go about claiming it?"

Marstellar looked at Jameson again and nodded at him to give him the key to Tytus' shackles.

"Don't believe everything you hear. I told you I need your help. I'd like to give you that choice to become something far greater than the society you came from could offer. I have a mission for you, one of Mathias Battier's making, to set into motion a grand plot. So, the only question remains: do you want redemption?"

EIGHTEEN
THE CHAMPION III

The silence beneath Martyr Arena did everything but ease his nerves. *This is what you do, Xavier. You win,* he told himself a thousand times over.

Lieutenant Chiesa's words of encouragement fell on deaf ears.

There was a knock at the door that felt like an earthquake. "It's time, Champion Battier," the arena guard said.

It's time. Be perfect, Xavier demanded of himself.

A loud chattering of spectators conversed above his head as he walked down the dark tunnel toward the combat zone. Their words were too muffled by the stone foundation, but he wondered what they thought.

Son of a traitor.

The time to think about such things was pushed from Xavier's mind. The arena master's introduction sounded. Xavier's shoulders stiffened, but he rolled them out. His palms became clammy, but he wiped them on his brown combat pants. The belt to his sparring saber was loose, so he yanked the strap as hard as he could. He tested the thin layer of padding he sported around his ribs and shoulders. With each hand, he slammed his fist into his protective equipment until he felt pain somewhere.

"My fair ladies and gentlemen of Helmburough, welcome!" the master began as his words were filtered through echo pipes that carried the sound throughout the stadium. "Today is a glorious day—a monumental day where we get to kick off our Capital Fair with a match for the ages! This is the day our undisputed champion squares off against an undefeated, fresh, and hungry challenger!"

The crowd went into a frenzy after each word.

"Today, records are being pursued! Names are looking to be made! A fight we shall have!"

Xavier squatted and stood back up quickly over and over again, breathing in through his nose and out of his mouth.

The arena master carried on, "Well then, let's go ahead and get to it, shall we!"

Xavier had never heard them this loud. Dust fell into his hair as the stomping above his head shook the entire arena. Nearly one hundred thousand people cheering for the outcome of a fight between two combatants never ceased to bring him pause.

"Our challenger, fighting out of our very own Helmburough City, ladies and gentlemen, Declan Cross!"

This was to be Declan's first time fighting in Martyr Arena. Of all his previous opponents, Xavier knew the least about him. However, with the ovation his opponent received, one would've thought he was a veteran with countless victories.

"Now, a fighter who needs no introduction, coming into the arena with forty-eight straight victories and no defeats, ladies and gentlemen, our champion, Xavier Battier!"

Xavier ascended the dark tunnel, and sunlight hit his face. However, it didn't strike him quite as hard as the unrelenting boos coming from the audience. Their synchronized hatred towards him vibrated his ears. Chants of "traitor" rang out.

As customary, the champion was to walk up to the challenger and face off in the center of the combat zone. The sand crunched beneath Xavier's boots on approach. He looked upon Declan Cross and felt not an ounce of fear. His blond hair was tied back, and he sported similar combat attire. He could hear girls of all ages swooning and cheering on his opponent. They seemed to enjoy his parted bangs, currently attempting to conceal his blue eyes.

Nose to nose, they stood. All at once, the crowd's chanting stopped. It was so quiet he could hear a baby crying from sixty rows up.

A booming crash above their heads sounded, and the crowd erupted once more. It was the arena panels opening wider so the sun could cover the entire combat zone. This feat of engineering added to its significance of being the ninth wonder of the world.

Snare drums snapped through the echo pipes. It was soft at first, allowing the audience and the fighters to prepare for what was about to happen next.

"Take your paces back, gentlemen. Start as the final drums cease," the arena master said.

"Good luck, Battier," Declan snuck in before stepping back. His words seemed sportsman-like and genuine.

Xavier gave him no reply. *Be perfect. You are Xavier Royal Battier. Be perfect.*

Now the bass drums sounded. The rhythmic pounding was enough to make anyone, combatant or not, ready for a fight. Gradually, the beat quickened. The melody was to a song written after the great victory in the Battle of Driftwood during the First Pirate Rebellion titled "The Smoldering Howler." The *Howler* was the flagship of Captain Fant, leader of the rebellion.

Xavier found his heartbeat syncing with the war drums. He could feel his blood pumping through his veins.

Then, the drums stopped. All noise died.

Xavier dug his back foot in the sand and sprinted forward towards the prodigal son.

When their dull swords clashed and rang out for the crowd to hear, wild shouts for violence erupted.

The first exchanges of their swords were the feeling-out process.

Declan handled the first exchange better than anyone he'd faced before. Every fighter had a different style, different stance, and different intensity. No single fighter was the same, like flakes of snow. Declan was balanced, and good from everywhere. His posture was proper, like a good ole lad taught by suitable instructors in fancy robes with a curriculum of combat.

However, as they exchanged, Xavier was caught off guard by how Declan showed flashes of burning intensity before reeling it back into an even-keeled and relaxed sensibility.

He's trying to catch me off guard and be unpredictable. Admirable.

If Declan was a proper fighter with flashes of aggression, Xavier was a concentrated one that showed glimpses of vulgarity. Declan swung downward, and Xavier parried it to the ground. He spun and struck the royal son to the side of the head with an elbow. As Declan stumbled backward, Xavier was met with a torrent of boos. The populace thought it a dirty strike.

It's a fight, you bloody fools.

The quickness of the push kick that sent him skidding back on his heels as a reply had Xavier confused.

He's fast.

The fight between them raged. Neither could get an edge over the other. When Xavier thought he was in a good position, setting up his combinations for a final strike, Declan was there to counter. When Declan's silky and effortless movements looked as if they were leading to a beautiful ending, Xavier's controlled chaos prevailed.

Their swords clashed, sending sparks into the air. The pair of them got locked in close quarters, trying to out-muscle the other. Declan seemed to catch on that Xavier's strength would prevail. Swiftly, he kicked the inside of Xavier's leg and put him off-balance. Xavier grabbed onto his arm and pulled him to the ground. Both of them dropped their swords in the process.

More boos came from all corners of the arena. Many spectators that were partial to bloodshed enjoyed the display of swords rather than matches reverting to grappling. Xavier rolled over into the top position and rained down punches like a man possessed by a curse. Declan's ability to block and narrowly dodge his strikes made him furious. His arms became heavy, and for the first time in a while, in the heat of battle, Xavier's lungs burned.

Declan trapped Xavier's arms, swung his legs around his throat, and began choking him with his thighs.

Xavier was stuck. He tried to pry out of the hold with his strength, but his arms were shot. The last resort was to posture up, plant his heels in the sand, hoist Declan off the ground, and slam him into the dirt.

It worked.

The challenger's air left his lungs as he hit the ground, and released his chokehold. Both of the prime combatants attempted to work back to their feet, but catching their breath was a bigger priority for the pair of them.

Xavier looked around the arena in his moment of exhaustion. Ahead of him were the seats reserved for Assembly members. The powerful men sat in the shade with twice as many maids at their service. Leader Krusade sat there eating from a bowl of grapes in his powdered wig, drooping to one side with his family, including Cheska. Ferham Ullys was too preoccupied with the maids to care about the match, and Benjah Kearse wore a grin with his eyes glued on Xavier.

The crowd and their anticipatory gasps snapped Xavier back to reality. Stumbling to his feet, he turned to see Declan, sword in hand, coming at him full swing. He felt the wind pass his cheek as he dipped to the side just in time.

Xavier countered Declan's sword with a fist. His punch landed flush, and the fresh-faced, pretty boy now had a crooked nose with blood leaking from his nostrils.

The sand had nearly concealed Xavier's sword, and it took him a moment to find it. He swung as soon as he grasped the handle, attacking Declan with a near-endless barrage of swings. After each one, Xavier thought he was getting closer to landing a clean strike that would end the match. But his long-haired opponent managed to hold him at bay.

His shoulders, his arms, and his legs were heavy. He planted his sword in the ground to catch his breath.

They were both locked in a blank and exhausted stare. Declan recovered faster, lunged forward, and disarmed Xavier, throwing his sword back into the ground.

Then, the challenger's sparring sword slammed into Xavier's padded rib protector. Even with the protection, he felt something give way. He clutched his side and followed his sword to the sand.

He tried to stand, but his body wouldn't allow it.

No. No. I don't lose… I can't.

The arena master stepped forward and declared the bout over. The crowd roared for its new champion. Chants of "Cross! Cross! Cross!" rang to a deafening crescendo.

Declan stood over him, covering his nose with one hand and offering Xavier help to his feet with the other. "It was an honor, Battier. You're the best fighter I've ever fought."

Xavier was in excruciating pain. He managed to eventually roll over and lift himself to his feet, bypassing his opponent's handshake. "Piss off."

He walked back to the corridor while the cheers for the new champion were unrelenting, beating his ears like an unwelcome insect. He held his side the entire way as almost every movement cut his breaths short.

Xavier Battier, bruised, bloodied, and beaten, made the walk alone. Not a soul in Martyr Arena cheered for him, for not a soul cared.

NINETEEN
THE AIDMAN III

The carriage swayed back and forth on the unpaved Hansen Road. The destination was Salty Pointe, the farthest point north in Roguewave. It was the place where criminals and traitors went to hang over the oceanside cliffs. *A glorious final view.* Caldwell sat with his hands shackled in his lap as the fatal side of a blunderbuss jabbed into his torso.

Ricky Meeks and his flock of unknowing dolts were far away from this transport. No, this task was left to more capable men. The three men crammed into the carriage with him were all two-marked soldiers. Normally, that wouldn't be anything to praise. However, Grand Commander Cross awarded these maroon tallies—a rank given sparingly. The word was that a single mark awarded by Cross was equal to five under any other officer.

"I sailed under your father to Tyver Island after Marstellar Lockett set Grand Harbor ablaze. I would never say there was a commander better than Alistair Cross, but Mathias Battier may have been his equal," the soldier with the cocked blunderbuss said. He was in desperate need of a new coat, as the one he sported had suffered far too many tears.

Caldwell didn't know how to reply. "Thank you," he said.

"It's not a compliment. Apparently, he could get a crew of hundreds to abide by his every command but couldn't control his own family. Now, the name of Battier will have nothing but negative and treasonous connotations. Just like that… a great man never even existed."

A rage inside him billowed, enough to forget about his pending death.

"But I admire the loyalty you've shown to your traitorous and foreign mother. You've obviously made the right decision." The soldier's expression never changed, but Caldwell knew sarcasm when he heard it. After all, his sister was Avery Battier.

He missed his family as he rocked hard from side to side. His mother was most likely to meet the same fate as him, so he prayed to whatever god listened that they would travel hand in hand into whatever afterlife would accept both of them.

"Salty Pointe," the soldier with the torn coat said, taking a swig from a flask. "I've seen many a man hang from those cliffs. Traitors, pirates, cultists, witches. They say the mackereli feast on the remains of the rotting flesh that falls into the ocean."

The mackereli, the fish people. A myth just like the thousands of others that superstitious Roguewave natives seem fond of. Caldwell thought being an academic made him above all of that. His mother was quite the opposite; there was no shortage of folklore amongst the warring clans to the south. He never questioned her or what she claimed to have seen as a girl in Autera. He had too much respect for his mother.

"Mackereli are long gone, Winston," the quiet soldier glaring out the window said.

"Don't be so sure of yourself. I've seen a lot on the open ocean. Can't claim that any of it was real, but I've seen a lot of things."

The carriage became quiet once more. Caldwell couldn't get comfortable, and he had a nervous twitch in his neck. The thought of the inevitable rope constricting him was already irritating him.

"Not to worry, Battier. The pain won't last long," Blunderbuss said.

The carriage came to a halt. Caldwell heard the driver call out to the greencoat sailors next to him. "Tree down on the path. Come help move it!"

The road had narrowed, and the tree line had packed them in tight. The woods steeped upward on both sides.

"Winston, stay with Battier," Blunderbuss said before stepping out of the carriage with his long legs and lumbering body. Caldwell didn't realize how big the sailor was until his head was above the window as he stood outside.

He could hear the struggle of the men attempting to navigate the tree from the middle of the road. From the sound of their grunts, the tree was a jinks cypress, the largest on the east coast, which didn't hold a candle to the echo oak of Northwood.

"I hear you're a good fighter, Battier. Especially for an aidman."

"Not as good as my brother, I'm told."

"Well, he is better than most. I'm sure he'd give some of our crew trouble with a blade," Winston said. "Word around is that you could too."

"It doesn't matter now," Caldwell said grimly. Smoke hit his nostrils as the remaining soldier lit his long tobacco pipe with little regard for the situation.

"Aye, perhaps you're right," Winston said. "Such a waste."

I can hear you.

The air seemed chillier than usual. The forest was lush green and always damp from the never-ending drizzle of rain falling from the sky. There was a rare type of badger that hunted smaller vermin in these forests. It had a distinct yellow stripe that went across its eye-line, like the warpaint of his mother's native Trezbe Clan. Caldwell always told his younger sister Isla that he would take her adventuring out into these woods to find the war badger. Isla was obsessed with finding one. Not for its yellow stripe across its face but because it had another distinct feature: no ears.

"We may need to have the horses pull it," the carriage driver said.

Caldwell heard the deep voice of the blunderbuss soldier say, "This tree... This tree was cut down."

"What do you mean?" the driver replied.

"I'm saying—"

Gunfire burst from the forest. Four shots got off before his guarded escort returned fire.

Caldwell went to look out the window, but a flintlock was shoved into his cheek.

"You don't move, Battier!" Winston said with a brooding scowl.

"Ambush!" the driver yelled. Another gunshot roared and presumably found its mark on the driver as a tumbling sound followed.

What is this? Caldwell didn't know if his fear should be heightened.

"What is this, Battier?" Winston demanded.

"I don't know!"

Winston's pistol was still trained on Caldwell, but as the soldier was focused on the skirmish going on outside, the young aidman took his opportunity. Caldwell grabbed the barrel of the flintlock and ripped it from Winston's grasp. The soldier unsheathed his knife and thrust, but Caldwell was quick on the trigger.

Smoke filled the interior of the carriage. For a moment, Caldwell couldn't see a thing. Winston struggled to find breath as the musket ball found his throat. Heat radiated on the back of Caldwell's neck.

Did I just...

Caldwell went to open the door, but it wouldn't budge. He

was trapped with something unknown occurring outside and a dying soldier in front of him. He attempted to waft the smoke away to get a better view out the carriage window, but it didn't seem to help.

When the smoke cleared, it was plain that Winston was dead, the gunfire was becoming less frequent, and the moans of greencoat soldiers were snuffed by kill shots and kill thrusts. His escort was being executed, meeting their end before him.

The natural creaks and moans of the forest were the only thing he could hear. He gripped the flintlock, reaching into Winston's jacket to retrieve his powder horn and wads for another shot. He reloaded the enemy's gun, which was much harder with bound hands.

"Caldwell?" he heard.

His best friend poked his head through the carriage window. His face was caked in charcoal that acted as camouflage, but it was smeared from the sweat. He had a red bandana around his neck and wore an all-black shirt.

"Are you all right, brother?" he asked.

Caldwell couldn't believe his eyes. He questioned his condemned mind, believing he was crafting some fantastical illusion as a way of coping with his pending death. "Emil?"

His friend looked at the lifeless body of Winston in the seat ahead of him. "We're in this together now," Emil said with a rare seriousness. "Come." Emil extended his hand and helped Caldwell out of the carriage. "We weren't going to let them hang you, brother."

Caldwell stretched his legs. Maynard and Fili were rounding the other side of the carriage, matching Emil with their red and black attire. "Are you okay?" they said, putting their hands on his shoulders. He moved forward, away from their consoling gesture. Soldiers littered Hansen Road with gunshot and sword wounds.

We're all killers now.

Fili offered Caldwell a bag stuffed with clothes, including a set that matched their current attire. "We figured if someone were to get word of this, putting the blame on the pirates would only buy us time," Fili said. "Plus, since the Assembly believes your mother as a conspirator in the attack, it's not inconceivable that they would make an attempt to free you."

Caldwell looked upon his friends with pale faces and sword and gun in hand. "You have all potentially ruined your lives for me... You know that, right?"

"No. We don't know that. We're still in control of our lives." Emil retrieved another battle harness behind a tree up the hill. Standard battle harnesses were equipped with a pistol with additional shot and powder, a naval cutlass, a dagger, and travel-friendly medical supplies. "We have to leave. They'll send a search party once this carriage doesn't show up by nightfall."

"What did you have planned?"

"Ride this carriage all the way to Vester, where we can get passage from Port Randolph to the Free Islands."

Port Randolph was not a short trip. Normal travel time on these roads would take roughly a month. Motivated pursers would follow once word reached Judge Barnes or Alistair Cross that Caldwell was not swaying lifelessly over Molten Bay.

"You're all fugitives with me now," Caldwell said.

"Aye, we are," Maynard said.

"I don't know how to thank you."

"You don't need to," Fili said.

"We have some of the stuff we took from your house. Clothes, boots, anything we could find," Emil said, retrieving a bag from behind a tree. "Seems like the greencoats searched it pretty good. Your house was unrecognizable from the inside. Seemed like they were looking for something."

"What word of my family?" Caldwell asked with trepidation.

His friends looked at each other, which failed to ease him.

Fili spoke first. "Your mother is in Colwerth… Avery was deported to Autera… Xavier… well…"

"What?" Caldwell stepped forward.

"He denounced your family and your mother's actions, effectively pardoning himself…"

Caldwell exhaled deeply from his nostrils, with air so warm it almost burned. He grabbed the large wheel of the carriage and squeezed it until the jagged corners hurt his palm. "Damn you," he softly whispered to his brother, hoping he could hear it clear across the continent. "What about Isla and Eddison?"

"No one has seen them since the raid," Fili responded. "Search parties are looking for them daily. But Caldwell…"

"Say it."

"There were casualties in the raid. It is believed that—"

"That Isla and Eddie didn't make it," the blunt blacksmith apprentice, Maynard, finished.

Caldwell wasn't convinced. "No, they did. They made it." He believed it in his heart.

Emil nodded with a smile riddled with false confidence.

"I have to go find them. I have to try," Caldwell said.

"You can't," Emil stated.

"Like hell I can't."

"Caldwell, I understand you want to save them, but if you get caught, you'll die right then and there. We could *all* die." Emil spoke for Maynard and Fili. "We have just changed the course of our lives because of you, and I'd do it again, no question. So, Port Randolph is our destination if we have any hope of a life well-lived."

"You are my family, Caldwell," Fili said, resolute eyes meeting his. "You're the reason I did this, and now you may be our only hope of getting passage to the islands."

Caldwell dropped, taking a knee in the dirt. They all stood in quiet as the wind picked up. Caldwell felt a drop of rain on his cheek.

A low rumble of a thunderstorm was coming from the water. Caldwell never said a word. He didn't want to speak about the choice he was making because he felt it to be a selfish one. He looked each of his friends in the eye, and all he gave them was a nod.

TWENTY
THE WIDOW IV

The constant drip in the opposite corner was beginning to drive her mad. Adelaide thought about moving her mouth under it to receive a steady dose of water at the very least. However, her legs were too weak to lift her from her seated position, planted against the stone wall.

There was no difference or change in darkness from her eyes being open to being closed. *You're not blind. You're not blind.*

Her mind was occupied by the welfare of her children. She wondered if Eddie had made it safely into the hands of Marstellar Lockett. She knew "safe" might not be the best of words to use when handing her son over to pirates for protection. But it had been her best course of action, and if the stories and songs were true about the pirate captain, she either made a great or grave decision.

Everyone, from Roguewave to Helmburough, from Leafland to Cape Talon, knew of the song "The Reaper's Sails." A work of which the pirate captain was the direct inspiration. She remembered Mathias singing it to her at night, and he would always chuckle at the conclusion. She never asked why he did, but now, in this dark place, with her son in Lockett's hands, she wanted the answer more than anything.

She sang it to herself softly.

Through spyglass, I saw a man, made up in all black. He had no dread, for it followed at his back.

He had no sword, nor pistol on his hip, just crew in red, with scythes and torches well lit

Lockett be his name, and fear became, all in his wake.

They slashed and burned, on Tyver shore, that silk that was now no more.

They slashed and burned, on Tyver shore, that silk that was now no more.

They slashed and burned, on Tyver shore, that silk that was now no more.

When asked by the five, who declared the act of war in the autumn fall, the Pirate King replied, "My name is Marstellar Lockett, and I'm coming for it all."

Under Reaper Sails, and Reaper rule, oh, that scythe flag snapped as it flew. His crew it cursed the Assembly, and its obedient children too.

The king's ship sailed away, to enter the fray, and burning Tyver, pleaded for him to stay. Yes, it sailed away into a horizon blue, and they pleaded for him to stay.

The heavy iron door unlatched as Lockett's song concluded.

Her eyes adjusted to the shadowed, torch-lit face. It was the face of someone she hadn't previously met. His foggy facial details began to focus.

"Ello, Adelaide. How is your stay in Colwerth so far?" His mouth was crooked, and his lips were subtly perked outward. Somehow, he managed to smile and frown simultaneously.

"The food is rubbish," she said.

"That so?"

"Perhaps adding salt to the *salted* pork would help."

"Ah," the man replied as he took a step into the center of the cell. "I'm Warden Edward Tell, so I'll see something done about our... renowned salted pork. But, you see, Adelaide, salt is not to be wasted on the likes of you, is it?"

"On the contrary, Warden, it's the likes of you that have been using excess salt to pour into the wound you've made in my chest."

Tell held the torch on the left side of his face that sported the frown. "Relax, Adelaide. I come with good news."

She scoffed. "You've brought my husband back to life, have you? Are my children all safe inside my home? There is no good news for me anymore, Warden Tell."

He pulled a rolled paper from his coat pocket. It was wrapped in an emerald ribbon and had a noble wax seal. "We here at Colwerth hate to see you go. However, everything has a price." Tell handed the paper over to her to unravel. He leaned down close to her and switched his torch-bearing hands. Now, the sinister-looking grin side of his face was way too close for comfort. "You're to be transported to Leyfield, Helmburough. You are to serve on the Hannah Estate for Lady Hannah herself."

Adelaide read the contents of the letter, and Warden Tell seemed to be genuine about its message as it reassured his words.

Charlotte Hannah. I know that name...

TWENTY-ONE
THE SILENT ONE III

She ran her fingers through Leo's curly hair. Isla hadn't seen her family in weeks, and the rumors of their whereabouts were all over the place, none of them positive. She would privately ask Yula to inform her of the news and gossip on the streets. Yula lived for the rumors of the province. Whispers told her that many people believed Xavier was the only Battier remaining. That meant Caldwell's execution was carried out, and the rest of her family died under other circumstances. However, Yula also told her that there had been no confirmation of Caldwell's death and that there were some follow-up rumors that he somehow escaped the noose.

Isla wished for it to be true more than anything. At nights she would lay awake, thinking of how she and Caldwell could break their mother out of Colwerth Prison together. The delusions always faded as she realized that if Caldwell were to have escaped, the last place he should be was Roguewave.

The Emerson Estate had a lot to offer. Far more than Isla needed as she spent most of her time meandering about the mansion with only Leo at her side. Both Livian and Oliver made a lot of money. To Roguewave standards, they were extremely wealthy, possibly only second to Governor Tytus in terms of income.

Tytus had yet to be seen since the pirate raid. When Isla asked Oliver about his potential whereabouts, he replied, "There's no limit to the possibilities of what those pirates could have done with him. However, it doesn't seem like the Assembly cares since they had his replacement so readily available."

Oliver also spoke of the destruction the seaside markets suffered and how they were in ruins, claiming all of it to be splintered wood, shrapnel, and bone chips.

The last time she had been there was when Avery and Eddie stopped at the small tent owned and operated by the witch. Isla couldn't stop thinking about the woman, with her frizzy blonde hair and yellowed teeth. *I wonder how she held up in the raid. Are those animal bones that dangled from the roof now scattered about? Are those strange vials of liquids broken and dried on the stone street?*

She had been locked in the house for weeks now. The greencoats' interest in the Emerson Estate had mostly subsided. Oliver and Livian didn't seem to be persons of interest in Isla's disappearance. While she was thankful for them and their home, the estate fever was kicking in. She wanted some element of freedom. Having to spend the rest of her life indoors would be a death sentence. She wasn't the extreme outdoorsman like Avery, but she could see herself becoming her equal.

Sneaking out of the estate would not be a problem, but Isla would have to go alone. If she were to take Leo with her, she would most certainly be recognized. She would have to really mind her surroundings without the help of her canine assistant. However, the urge to find answers overwhelmed her soul.

Isla's first step was to invade Livian's massive closet that was nearly the size of her family's home in the Seventh Quarter and borrow some clothes.

Isla walked the streets and found most of it in repair. She feared the anger Livian and Oliver would have should they find out about this little adventure. *They can't expect me to stay there forever.*

She knew, in a way, this act would seem selfish, but she was on a mission to find her family or any information leading to them.

Isla's eyes widened upon seeing the countless display of wanted posters with her and Eddie's face. Below them read the words: *WANTED UNDER SUSPICIONS OF TREASON AND COLLUSION.* Luckily, the artist who sketched her and her little brother did not do them justice. Greencoats walked past without any awareness of Isla and her many warrants. She kept her head low, and the brim of the hat covered her whole face. She wished she could hear the whispers and gossip spoken about her family. However, Isla would have to work harder than that to discover more, but she was used to that.

She wandered the remains of the market for nearly an hour. The only semblance of flourishing business was the Flying Molten Crab Pavilion. *Nothing can keep molten crab vendors down for long.* People flocked to the local-sourced crabs like they were sacks of gold coins. The positive was that all the eyes that occupied the market didn't look Isla's way.

Isla remembered exactly where the witch's tent was set up, and after about half an hour of meandering through the market, she had found the spot. However, the witch was nowhere to be found. Only an elderly man selling colorless rugs remained.

A chill went down the back of her spine. Isla looked

around at the people. Still, none of them paid her any attention, but the chill remained.

Are you looking for me, silent one? she heard a familiar voice say in her mind. The tone of it was so distinct that Isla recognized it right away.

It was her.

Don't be alarmed, child, and don't look around. You're doing an excellent job of not being noticed. Wouldn't want to change that.

This experience was new for Isla. *She's undoubtedly a witch.*

Is that what you think I am? Oh, child, that's hurtful.

Can you hear my thoughts? Isla asked.

You sought me out, did you not? I can commune with all who desire my counsel.

Where are you?

Not far. Come find me, Battier. Come find me, the woman said.

Before she could even ask how to find her, Isla knew.

At the base of Pointer's Hill was the poorest sector of Roguewave. A cesspool of filth and immorality. The Bellows. A place that made her home in the Seventh Quarter look like the platinum streets of Helmburough City. The high hill blocked the sun for over half of the day, so shadow covered the Bellows. It was hard knowing if it had been affected in the recent pirate raid or if this was its default appearance. Buildings and homes were sundered, and most of them had a constant smoke rising from them.

The people—*people* being a generous term—hardly even spoke. Of course, Isla wouldn't hear them either way. However, there was little communication between them. Everyone kept their eyes on the ground, only glancing out their peripherals to see where they were walking. Unlike most bay people, they had a pale complexion and seemed to have disdain for everyone. As eerie as they were, Isla didn't have time to worry about them.

There was an urge to stop at the tattered main gate of the house to her left, just off Elmore Street—the urge manifested by way of shortness of breath and pressure on her chest.

The house itself was nothing special. The grass in the yard was dead, the shutters were either chipped or nonexistent, and the door was cracked open. Isla went ahead into the unknown and never looked back.

It was void of color and filled with gray and dust. The only thing giving off light was the orange and red glow from the dining room.

Isla rounded the corner, and in the center of the room was a woman facing the fire, rocking away in a wooden chair. *Welcome, Isla Battier,* she said, speaking inside the mind. *Come seeking me out, have you? Is it because of the poor circumstances that have befallen your family?*

How did you know I was looking for you? Isla replied.

As I said, I can always be made aware of the few who seek me.

Isla didn't really think that to be true, but she couldn't deny the fact that the woman had some magical abilities, even if Isla wasn't much of a believer.

It's easier for someone like you.

What do you mean? Isla thought.

I have a sense about people and their capabilities. Most people are quite uninteresting with a lackluster trajectory. I did not get that sense from you and your siblings the day you visited my tent. No, quite the opposite.

You gave my sister a necklace—said it would protect her from evil.

And it shall.

No, it won't. Avery gave it to my little brother, Eddison.

The woman laughed. The high-pitched cackle broke through Isla's deaf ears. She collected herself. *I suppose it will do the same for him. Perhaps one day, he will let you know how it shielded him from darkness.*

Isla shifted into a serious manner. The allure of the woman standing in front of her faded. Her thoughts were on her family once again. *That's why I'm here…* Isla didn't know what to call the woman, even in her mind, and she stumbled over her words.

Please, call me Sadollah.

My family is in trouble. I came to you to see if there is anything you could do to bring them back.

Sadollah stopped rocking in her chair and stood to her feet. As she turned, she revealed her baggy eyes. *What is it you want from me?*

A simple question that Isla couldn't find the answer to. *I don't know. Something.*

Were you under the impression that I could just snap my fingers and your family would appear right here, including your father? Her lips curled, and the skin under her nose nearly wrinkled into a spiral. *I'm afraid that it isn't possible, Isla.*

Then, what is possible?

There is no magic in this world strong enough to give you what you want. Believe me, if I could bring your father back, I would. Sadollah's face dropped, and the witchy woman wore a look of melancholy.

You knew him?

Sadollah's bushy brow raised. From thin air or another dimension, she manifested a musket ball between her thumb and forefinger. *I was your age when I moved to Roguewave. I was born in Ghonia, where I was landlocked in the center of the Unified Provinces. I had never seen the ocean until I arrived here.*

Sadollah walked to the desk underneath the fogged glass window. She let go of the metal ball, and it remained in the air next to her. Her weathered hands took hold of a mortar and pestle.

There was a line of glass jars that all had caps of different animal heads. Sadollah dumped the contents of the jar with the eel's head into the mortar. It was a chunky yellow powder with the consistency of sea salt.

What are you doing? Isla asked.

Sadollah didn't answer, and she turned the pestle around in the mortar until the chunks were broken down more. *I apologize. This will seem a bit surreal at first.*

What? Isla replied.

Sadollah threw the contents in the mortar over her shoulder, and the yellow dust filled the room. It started to whirl at an unimaginable rate, overpowering the dark space and conjuring light.

Step forward, Isla, Sadollah said.

Isla refused. She didn't trust this woman enough to follow blindly – until everything in front of her morphed into the fresh and clean markets of Molten City proper.

She was no longer in some broken home in the shadowy Bellows. The sun had never shined brighter. The people walking in the markets never looked happier, and music was playing.

What is this? Isla asked.

Step forth, and I will show you, Sadollah said.

Still, Isla remained.

Her refusal to move ended when she saw a young man in a royal emerald coat walking amongst the citizens. She only saw the back of his long auburn hair. The voices were muffled, but everyone greeted him as if he were a king, and he took the time to shake their hands.

Isla finally stepped forward into this altered place. For the first time, she could hear the sounds of the busy market. Her deafness was no longer present. Not far off, she could hear the ocean waves, the seagulls dancing above them, and she cried.

Her eyes returned to the man. He was busy courting a swarm of people, and as she approached, the voices became clear.

"Grand Captain! Grand Captain!" they yelled for his attention.

He carried a level of celebrity that rivaled rich lords in the West.

Others just called, "Mathias, when does your voyage to the south depart?"

"Are you scared to deal with those savages?"

"How do you know if they'll even be reasonable enough for an audience?" they asked.

He put his hands up and softened the tone of the group surrounding him, and like loyal dogs, they obliged.

Father? More tears flowed. She cried out for him, attempting to get his attention. But no one took notice. Everyone just carried on about their day, their beautiful day.

He can't hear you, Isla. No one can. This moment has long since passed, Sadollah said.

Isla circled the group in order to get a better look at him.

"First off, their savage nature is only a rumor, so let's refrain from labeling them that," Mathias answered. "However, if all goes well, we'll have more lands to explore and more life to experience."

They all smiled and shook their heads. Some out of a genuine belief in what he was saying and others merely being appreciative of his optimism. Isla finally got around to get a good look at her much younger father. He was clean-shaven, the sun had yet to tan his skin from countless voyages, and his eyes had never been bluer.

A young boy approached him from behind his mother's leg.

"Aren't you afraid of the pirates?" the boy asked.

Her father leaned down, put his hand on the boy's shoulder, looked right into his eyes, and said, "I assure you, when the pirates see the sails of the *Abyss* on the horizon, it's they who quake."

"What about Marstellar Lockett?"

"Believe me, a cold chill goes down his spine as well."

While the people stared at her father with the wonder and amusement she once did, Isla couldn't help noticing the massive tower over the bay. A tower that she had never seen in Roguewave before. It stood amongst the clouds and was a nearly perfect rectangle with all the provincial flags flying along its eastern side. A raging fire spiraled into the sky at the very top, and its intensity never wavered.

Sadollah, what's that tower? she asked.

That, Isla, is the East Flame Tower—another wonder of the world that acted as the epicenter for communication and trade.

But wasn't the East Flame Tower–

Isla didn't even finish her sentence before a massive explosion shook the world beneath her feet. She watched as everyone darted around, petrified. Mothers instinctively grabbed their children. Men looked at one another with questioning glances. Stray dogs barked at the unknown in the distance. Yet, her father took one step forward as the initial reverberation faded.

Then, the tower wavered. Smoke rose from its base, and the breaking of its foundation sounded like cannon fire.

"Everyone to safety!" her father yelled.

People screamed and cried out as they ran in the opposite direction. Her father, however, ran towards the falling tower, towards danger, towards the unknown.

The tall beacon favored the eastern side, and Isla gasped at its descent. It was as if time had slowed. She ran behind her father as he fought through the dense market crowd, shouting for them to get to safety.

The tower crumbled before it hit the ground, but when its mass collided with the land, people tumbled over from the shockwave.

Citizens struggled to get to their feet, including her father. Gunfire whistled past, and Mathias sprung up, drawing his sword and flintlock.

"Invaders!" a Roguewavian yelled. "Pirate invaders!"

Sure enough, rounding the corner, ahead of the billowing dust from the felled tower, was a band of around thirty men with their faces covered in black cloth getting the better of Roguewave greencoats.

Mathias gave another warning to the citizens around him to retreat to the fort. His gaze shifted to nearby greencoats, whom he began to rally. "These men mean to cripple your way of life and leave us fearful of them! Are you afraid?" Mathias asked them.

"No, Grand Captain!" they replied.

Her father said no more. It wasn't needed. The dust and smoke shrouded the imminent battlefield and overpowered the bay. Not only had the tower fallen, but the remnants of it burned an unrelenting flame that made it rain ash.

Mathias removed a red sash from his belt and wrapped it around his face to filter out the smoke. It gave him the appearance of a rebel himself as he fired his pistol and entered the clouded fray.

That is who your father was, Isla... That is who he was.

Her young father transfixed Isla. How brave he was, how strong he was, how righteous he was. *Everyone was right about him.* Mathias clashed swords with pirates with almost zero visibility. Isla found her shoulders tense as this historical battle replayed itself over in front of her very eyes, and her father was in command.

Soldiers ran around blindly, nearly cutting down their own comrades in the process. Ordinary citizens were caught in the crossfire, and the greencoats had to fight as well as save lives simultaneously.

A young girl was in the middle of the dust-ridden battle, crying for help, consumed by the raging fight. Across the narrow street, a group of pirates set up a line of shots intended for Isla's father and the soldiers around him. She watched as Mathias disregarded the incoming barrage.

"Get down!" he yelled to the girl as he ran to her. His men urged him to take cover, but he ignored their warning.

Five shots rang out, and Mathias couldn't get to the girl in time to spare her from taking a musket ball to the back. The young girl dropped and squirmed on the ground. The pirates advanced over her, and Mathias Battier was there to meet them. The enemy outnumbered him five to one, and yet Isla saw that her father didn't care.

Had they attacked him all at once when they had the chance, perhaps they would've gotten the better of him, but they proved no match. Isla had never seen the look of rage on her father's face before as he cut men down left and right. As her father, he had offered nothing but soft smiles and inspired grins.

He deflected every strike swung his way and thrust his sword back at the enemy with ferocity. He dispatched the band of pirates in a matter of ten moves and went straight to the girl. Mathias hoisted her in his arms and carried her behind a building. She cried and begged for the pain to stop, and he reassured her that everything was going to be okay. He began to work on her wound and nurse her to the best of his ability.

"You're going to be all right, love. It's just a little stinger," he told her as she was still crying uncontrollably. "Aidman! I need an aidman over here!"

Shortly after, a greencoat appeared with his massive aid pack over his shoulder. "Where was she hit?" the aidman asked.

"Her back," Mathias replied.

The aidman was young, maybe around Xavier's age. Nevertheless, he went to work, removing the ball from the girl's back. The first thing he did was ask her to eat a pepper pear seed, which had pain-numbing qualities.

The aidman focused on the wound, and the girl was still petrified. Mathias grabbed her face and pulled her in close.

He removed his sash to reveal his face. "You're going to be all right, love, I promise. You're doing great. I've seen many a man get shot, and they cried far more than you are now," he said with a laugh, attempting to put her at ease. It seemed to work because she smiled for the first time. "What's your name?"

"Sadollah," she replied through a veil of expiring tears.

A greencoat approached. "Captain, there are people trapped in the rubble!"

The aidman looked to Mathias and assured him, "I can help her, Captain."

Her father looked the girl in the eyes and said, "I'm going to come back and check on you, Sadollah. I promise."

"Don't leave me," she begged.

"We need to help as many people as we can. There could be kids younger than you trapped and in need of help. We should help them, right?" he asked, nodding.

Sadollah agreed.

"I promise I'll be back."

Her father let go of her, stood to his feet, pulled the sash back over his nose, and continued into the unknown.

Then, the vision stopped. Isla was back in the dark and worn dining room of the woman she hardly knew.

Again, I say, that is who your father was, Isla Battier. Sadollah walked over to her, dropped the musket ball in Isla's palm, and put her finger under her chin. *You want to find your family? You want to save them?*

More than anything.

Then, defeat the enemy first.

TWENTY-TWO
SHARKEYES IV

Avery was put to labor the next day after arriving in Caste Valley. Her forced labor consisted of knitting caravan bonnets. It was a tedious task as the canvas had to cover the entire caravan arch. The Trezbe women focused on the canvas while the men constructed the caravans themselves. A certain number had to be completed each day, or else there were consequences, most of which were of the lashing sort, and hardly anyone remained unmarked by the punishment. There was a substantial learning curve because the Trezbe Clan had not known what a wagon or caravan was prior to the Occupation nearly twenty years ago.

Over the past several weeks, Avery had been growing closer to her mother's side of the family. She had no expectations as to what she was being forced into, but she found a quick kinship with the family that she had been isolated from.

Her grandmother, Eralia, who remained sturdy in her old age, knitted next to her on a stump. The cool air in the oasis was a stark contrast to the dry heat, where the greenery was a welcome sight. Her hands were wrinkled but still strong.

"Why are the Trezbes being forced to move away?" Avery asked.

Eralia looked around. She eyed the spring that cultivated fruits, including wild berries and vegetables aplenty. Trees of varying sizes and formations provided many uses for the Trezbe, as they never wasted their prized resources.

"Because of *that*, my dear." She pointed at the spring in the center of the vast oasis. "*Pili eh Fora*—the Spring of Many Gifts. All that we have needed, the spring has provided, my dear. It has been the source of most of our wars against the other clans. It's why we are the most hated, and it's why we are the most feared."

Sunlight glittered off the water, unknown birds of every color seemed to dance in flight all around, and it tasted as pure as fresh rain. It was hard to even imagine the heat of the Okamara Desert not far from here.

"Food and water are hard to come by in the desert, the Skiatation Mountains are hard to traverse, and the Botan Rainforest is near unlivable due to the wildlife. Our ancestors found this place to settle, establishing it as the most strategic position, and as time went on, families raged against one another, forming opposing clans. Sooner or later, we became enemies. The last conflict we had against the Idush was nearly the end of us. This occupation won't end unless we unify," Eralia said, her eyes scanning the monitoring greencoats, who flogged slow workers.

Avery became solemn and angry upon watching the treatment of the Trezbe people. "Was my father like the rest of them?" she asked.

"Avery, I hope you know the answer to that question," Eralia said. "Of all the people that landed and followed after Mathias Battier, he was one of the few good ones."

Avery issued her first smile since arriving in Caste Valley. "Mother never talked about life here."

"Is that so?"

"When I was younger, I would ask her all the time, but she never went into detail. Eventually, I just stopped asking..."

Her newly initiated grandmother continued to knit, not saying a word. Then, a grin crept up from the corner of her mouth. "You have her spirit, my dear. I can sense it in you. I'm sure Adelaide didn't discuss it much because, for many years, we were in intense conflict with the Idush since she was small, much smaller than you. And your mother led many battles against them."

Led battles?

"They've wanted this territory for hundreds of years. They've come close, but thanks to warriors and leaders like your mother, they've never taken it. They're a sour group of people, and I doubt the best company. The compliment they'll get from me is that they are excellent sword crafters and wielders. Though they are fewer in numbers, we had a hard time combating them with our tre-axes."

There was a soft crunch of foliage behind them, and as Avery's head turned, a greencoat slammed the butt of his rifle onto the ground. "Get to work! Less talking for the both of you!" he commanded as he continued walking through the green.

A tingle made its way up her leg. She looked down to see a bug with many legs on its elongated body. It had four massive eyes that made up much of its head. Avery believed herself to be brave, but she wasn't immune to a healthy skepticism of unknown insects. She backhanded it and hoped she'd never meet its acquaintance again.

"It's all right, my dear. A quopoda can't harm you." Eralia smiled, found the creature in the grass, and placed it as high as she could in a tree. "Their mouths are too small."

Avery's doubt remained. "If you say so."

She didn't really know how to knit, so Avery shadowed her grandmother the entire time, learning and practicing simultaneously.

"I remembered when I first saw him. He always had a red tone to his pale skin from being sun-blasted. He was one of the few that could speak our language shortly after arriving because he assimilated himself into our culture. He was quick to subdue conflict on either side, and we trusted him," Eralia said.

There was a delight that came over Avery in the reassurance that her father was exactly the man she presented to them. It was nice to have such knowledge when the world was attempting to convince them her family was something they weren't.

"He earned Alexious' trust when he nursed Adelaide back to health. Not only that, but he made it a priority."

"Back to health?" Avery asked.

"Yes, my dear. She had been wounded in battle after she and Ianthia led an attack against an Idush village in Runkor Valley."

"I have a difficult time believing Mother was a fighter," She slowed her work.

"That's because, in the provinces, any display of culture could be used against your family. She also didn't want to be seen as a threat, so she left her tre-axes here."

Avery's understanding was limited. "Was she a good fighter?"

"She was an excellent fighter. She once defeated the Idush sword master in single combat."

The images of her mother fighting in her prime raced through Avery's mind and brought a smile to her face. All her forced labor ceased as she planted her knee on the ground.

"Now, your grandfather is going to try and convince you that it was all him that taught her how to fight, but don't sleep on my abilities either. I taught her several of the most effective moves that she used to defeat many enemies. Oh, if I was thirty years younger, I'd knock some of these greencoats on their asses."

Avery couldn't hold back her laughter. Greencoats scowled at her from a distance.

Eralia continued with tales of a young warrior Adelaide. "She and your Aunt Ianthia were very competitive, and that made them strong. Not to mention they were smart, which always helps." Her grandmother pointed her finger to one of the girthy purple vines that wrapped around nearly every tree in the oasis like a snake. "You see, the Idush village in Runkor was backed against a plateau, and those paranoid warmongers reinforced entry on all remaining sides, making it an almost impregnable structure. So, Adelaide came up with the idea to ascend the Runkor Plateau on the opposite side. On a cloudy night, they used the vines to rappel down into the village and execute their attack with a small force of Trezbe warriors."

Avery wondered if her grandmother was lying or, at the very least, exaggerating.

"They were trying to end it all by killing Romin Fjarr, the Idush tarquin," Earlia said.

Beyond amused, Avery asked, "What's a tarquin?"

"The leader of the clan. Alexious is the Trezbe tarquin, and I tarquiness."

"You're a queen?"

Eralia scoffed, "Well, my dear, don't I look like one?" she replied, flipping her greyed hair.

They had another quiet chuckle together, still trying to remain at work so as not to grab the ire of the greencoat guards.

"So, my mother didn't succeed—in killing the tarquin?"

"She succeeded in killing his son Roz, whom she believed to be Romin. It was dark that night, and they looked almost identical, as father and son often do. Adelaide sustained severe wounds after fighting Romin's daughter, Cella, who was attempting to avenge her brother and took over as sword master."

For the first time, Eralia became solemn. She leaned in

close. Her tanned skin was unblemished by wrinkles or age spots. "These are harsh times, Avery. And it looks like things are going to get much worse before they get better. I know this is all new to you, but we need to stay strong."

"Yes, ma'am."

"I'm not going to tell you again! Get to work! I'll gag you if I have to!" the skinny-necked greencoat, Colbe, said.

Eralia rolled her eyes. "I'll tell you, Avery. I haven't fought for a very long time. Should that day come where I must, Colbe is mine."

"I'd like to see that. I may join you in that if you don't mind," Avery replied.

"I think we are going to get along just fine, granddaughter."

Avery returned to her knitting. This was the tedious work she used to avoid, like the plague back in Roguewave. She hardly tended to her studies, and to her, she was better for it. "How did Father help Mother when she was injured?"

"There were many aidmen from the provinces. They were under orders not to assist or heal any clan people under any circumstances. Your father broke that rule and issued any aidmen sailing under his command to help anyone, no matter what, should they need it."

Avery dropped her head. Through a clenched jaw, she said, "I miss them."

"It's okay to admit that. I miss Adelaide just as much as you. And though Alexious and I had our reservations concerning your father, he was a great man."

Avery shifted away. "They called Mother a conspirator. They called *me* a conspirator against the Assembly and the Unified Provinces. I am no such thing. I know Mother wasn't either."

Avery made eye contact with many of the fellow Trezbe women working their fingers to the bone. They did the task as if it was second nature, nearly sleepwalking through it all. She pitied them. Being under the thumb of such oppression was something that shouldn't be.

Eralia put her arm around Avery, the comfort she expressed nearly identical to her mother. "Those people in their fancy buildings and fancy clothes can create whatever it is they desire in the world. Whoever gets in the way of their vision, they will dispose of."

"Is that what you think happened? You think Mother got in their way?"

"Maybe, maybe not. Perhaps she didn't even know. But I'm willing to bet your father had a hand in what's happened to your family—to our family. Mathias Battier pushed back against the powers that be. The powers that be cannot allow that."

Avery leaned forward, "are you saying you think my father was killed?"

Her grip tightened around Avery's shoulders. "I'm an old woman now, Avery. Soon my wits will leave me, but I know for certain your father was killed. I knew from the moment the greencoats mocked us and told us our family was returning home because of Adelaide's treason on the heels of his heart attack."

Again, there was a rustling behind them, and they were interrupted by Colbe. "All right, get them up! Put both of their palms on the trees!"

Avery was jerked to her feet under both her arms and thrown face-first into the closest tree. She barely got her hands up in time to save her nose from making contact with the thick bark. They weren't easy on her grandmother either, as she followed just behind.

"Face the tree!" Colbe yelled. "Allen, Jicks, make sure the Battier girl knows how this works."

"Just let it happen, my dear," Eralia said, already out of breath.

But as the first greencoat laid hands on her, Avery

involuntarily elbowed him in the middle of his face, knocking him back a few paces.

"Avery, don't!" Eralia pleaded.

Avery stopped and placed her palms on the tree with the aggressive assistance of the other greencoat.

"Five lashes for the tarquiness, twenty for the Battier girl!" Colbe demanded.

Eralia pleaded for Avery's punishment to be less severe, but those cries fell on deaf ears, for the greencoats made their decision.

The man Avery elbowed – Allen, she believed – wiped his bloody nose and gripped the flogging staff. He seemed eager to take his anger out on Avery as she looked back at him. "Face forward!" he yelled at her.

Avery stared at the greyish bark in front of her eyes, taking in its bumpy characteristics and flashes of subtle moss.

A sharp pain flamed in her back that hurt worse than anything she'd felt in her life. She tried to focus on the tree and not the intense horizontal stinging.

Nineteen more, she told herself.

TWENTY-THREE
THE FORMER IV

His loss crippled him physically and, more so, emotionally for days. Xavier remained secluded in his small city home that overlooked the beach. The liveliness of Grand Harbor made the action in Molten Bay appear insignificant. Whitefin Bay was where ships of all shapes, sizes, and significance sailed.

He stayed in a place gifted to competitors from other provinces as lodging while in the capital. It was a hard place to feel gloom as families outside his window frolicked along the white sand under the sun and bathed in translucent waters.

Still, Xavier brooded at everyone's recreation.

Today was the first time he considered leaving his temporary home to look at something other than his beaten and shame-filled face. The stairway on the humble deck touched the sand, and in a few short steps, he stood on the beach, listening to the peaceful waves crash against the shore. A few seagulls glided overhead and squawked as they flew. To the west, he saw the Sea Bridge as it stretched beyond the horizon, just like the water. It was around fifty miles long and a half mile wide. Though it was functional, the bridge was under endless construction and in a constant state of repair. Two trade galleons were used to haul in planks of ungodly amounts of echo oak. Its sheer size made it a feat of modern engineering.

The Sea Bridge was built to establish a strong trade route in and out of Autera without constant voyages that required excessive resources and limited storage capacity. Plus, the Third Pirate Rebellion, though weak, was still alive. Trips anywhere via ship still required multiple support ships to avoid conflict. The rule was that for each trading vessel, there would be two combat-ready ships called aidships sailing alongside it. Those precautions proved justified after the attack in Molten Bay.

Sailors hated being assigned to aidships. Regardless of what happened in his home province of Roguewave, pirate attacks had drastically declined since their institution. The boredom and the tedious nature of sailing back and forth to the same ports and not seeing anything new grew old. It was, of course, not what he wanted. He wanted to captain his own Grand Ship and be at the forefront of hunting pirates and all who wronged his country. The very values that had been instilled in him since his education through the Academy took root, values that he feared his family had forgotten.

Xavier pondered all manner of things on his walk on the beach. Being alone never really bothered him. He liked being independent, and that had been the case for most of his life, but never more than now. In the land of Renera, with all the provincial citizens, he, unlike the rest, had Autera blood, Trezbe blood. He wasn't scowled at or treated poorly. He had never been. However, as informed sunbathers looked his way, their eyes quickly shifted in the opposite direction, back towards the water.

On the horizon were a trio of ships. He couldn't see their sails, but he knew they were trade ships headed to gather resources from Autera.

Ahead was a boy playing with a stick that presumably washed ashore. He was no more than eight years old as he swung it around like a sword. The boy would switch stances and pretend as if there were enemies all around him and he was successfully slaying them all.

As Xavier got closer to him, he saw that it was the same boy who stopped to talk to him shortly after he arrived in Helmburough on the eve of his duel. His harsh words for the kid weren't very encouraging, but he believed them to be true. The boy seemed oblivious, even though Xavier was only standing a few feet away.

"Good swing," Xavier said.

The boy spun around, and he held his makeshift sword straight out in front of him. The boy quickly lowered it upon seeing him. *I wish Eddie had the same craving to fight like this one.*

"Champion Battier? Sorry I didn't see you," the boy said.

There was a moment before Xavier answered. The ocean breeze cooled his head as he remembered he was a champion no longer. "Xavier is fine," he said.

"Uh, yes, sorry, Xavier."

"You don't have to apologize. What's your name?"

"Eli."

Of course, it is, Xavier thought to himself. "How old are you, Eli?"

"Twelve," he replied sheepishly.

"You ready for official combat training when you turn thirteen?"

"Yes," Eli said with a shaky voice while the tide ebbed and flowed.

Xavier nodded. "I'm sensing some hesitation." He had no issue motivating himself, but others, not so much. "You can't have that."

"I just want to be good," he said.

Eli's potential remained ambiguous.

Xavier didn't offer any reassurances or false promises. "Can I see your weapon?" he asked as jokingly as he was capable.

Eli smiled and handed over his damp stick. It was crooked but also straight enough for a kid's mind to imagine a sword.

Xavier gripped it tightly as he swung it towards Eli's neck. "How would you defend this?"

Eli parried with an imaginary sword.

Xavier chuckled. "The upper half of your body did well. It's your lower half I'm worried about. Look at your feet. What's wrong with them?"

"Um, I don't know, sir."

Sir? At least the boy has manners.

Gently, Xavier pushed Eli in the chest, and the boy fell into the sand. "Make sure your feet are farther apart, or else you'll get put down just like that."

"Yes, sir," Eli said, remaining on the ground.

"Are you going to sit all day? I'm not going to help you up. No one will. Don't expect help from anybody."

Eli scurried to his feet in such a hurry that he kicked up sand all around him. Xavier admired the tenacity.

And for the next hour or so, Xavier helped Eli, teaching him the basics of fighting as best he could. The boy's smile never left his face upon the conclusion of their training session.

Xavier returned to his temporary home as the ocean breeze, and sun seemed in conflict with one another, as one brought the scorching heat while the other continued the coolness of the day.

His boots were caked in sand, and he couldn't wait to remove them as grainy sweat sloshed between his toes.

It wasn't until he hit the steps that he noticed Grand Overseer Benjah Kearse sitting in his rocking chair, smoking a berry wood pipe. His silver eyes reflected blue as he admired the ocean. "This is quite the view as well, Battier, wouldn't you say?"

Xavier straightened his arms to his side and bowed his head in a hurry. "Grand Overseer, sorry I didn't see you."

"How could anyone notice me with that right there?" he said, pointing to the ocean.

"Everyone should notice the Grand Overseer, sir," Xavier said.

"Perhaps you're right. But what's a man to a natural wonder such as the ocean? What's a stray cat to the plain's lions? What's a musket to a ten-pound cannonball? What's a cog to a Grand Ship?"

Xavier nodded, unaware of what Overseer Kearse was going on about.

"That was a close match. There is no shame in losing such a contest. All of Helmburough City is abuzz recapping the historical duel." Kearse spoke with his eyes still on the ocean. Xavier said nothing. "Though that doesn't matter to you, does it?"

Xavier took a moment. "No, it doesn't."

"What hurt worse—the loss or the fact that not a soul chanted your name after it was done?" Kearse asked. "It takes a lot to step into Martyr Arena and fight in front of that many people, some of which are so high up in the stands they can't tell who is who, and they only hope for is a splash of red to satisfy their thirst for violence. Hardly anyone knows the self-sacrifice it takes to get to where you are at such an age."

For the first time, Kearse looked at Xavier. There was a power to the Overseer that he couldn't register. He was slim and not a man of stature, but he established dominance over the entire coastline as he stood.

"Jameson Roke never lost a duel, and the people couldn't get enough of him. Willam Staker had the most consecutive wins under a minute. John Fawl was seven feet tall. All of them were loved. And who cheers for them now? Where are they now?" He held his arms out wide. "Hell, I'm the Overseer, and I don't know. The theory is that Red Sand Roke died in a tempest. Do you think anyone mourned the potential loss of his life?"

"I don't know, sir."

Kearse placed his hands on the railing. "Your accomplishments in Martyr Arena do not define your legacy. You know that, don't you?"

Reluctantly, Xavier replied, "Yes, sir."

"Then what does define your legacy?"

Xavier took a moment to answer as the sun was beginning to make its descent over the horizon. "Service?"

"Right. Service to your country. Protecting citizens from those that will harm them and actively conspire against them. Understand?"

"Yes, sir."

"Good," Kearse said. He took a moment and looked Xavier in the eyes. "Why don't you sit down, son."

Son? Xavier thought. "Everything all right, Overseer?" he asked while rocking backward.

The man drove right into the topic at hand. "Your mother is being transported to Leyfield to serve the Hannah Estate. The urge to visit her might one day find you. Do not give in to the urge. You are to have no contact with her."

Xavier clenched down.

"Avery has been successfully transported to your mother's clan in Autera. Your youngest siblings, Isla and Eddison, are still unaccounted for, but between you and I, Xavier, man to man, the pirate raid on Molten Bay wasn't kind to many Roguewave citizens. It's believed that both of them died. It may be best to come to terms with that as soon as possible."

His stomach dropped. He did his best to keep his posture erect and not look fazed in his seat. He might not have been close to them, but he by no means wanted his family dead.

"And Caldwell?" he asked.

Kearse cleared his throat. "Caldwell made it clear that he would not speak against your mother's treason and was sentenced to death."

Xavier's heart stopped beating for a moment. The creak in the chair as it rocked back and forth ceased.

"I know that's hard to hear, Xavier, but anyone who sides with a conspirator is one themselves."

Xavier agreed, but this was his brother. Somehow,' he didn't think the rules should apply entirely. "But my mother wasn't sentenced to death," he pointed out.

"Only because the Hannahs went through endless barriers to claim her as their own and spent a tremendous amount of money. Wealth can get you a lot of things in this world." Kearse said while adjusting his gold cuff lengths. "Regardless, my main reasoning for being here is because of Caldwell. Through some miracle, your brother escaped the noose."

"Beg your pardon?" Xavier said, unaware of what that meant.

"Caldwell was scheduled to hang at Salty Pointe. But his escort was attacked, and the loyal soldiers that were carrying out his justice were murdered. It's believed your brother's friends freed him, as they have not been accounted for. They have all been labeled enemies of the Assembly and Unified Provinces and must be brought to justice immediately." Kearse stepped close to the chair and asserted his dominance. "How do you believe we should proceed?"

Xavier was caught off guard by the question. He didn't know how to respond, so he fumbled around with his words.

He stepped closer, stood tall over Xavier, and leaned in. "Do you agree that your brother and the rest of the traitors should be brought to justice?"

Xavier gauged his response. "Yes," he said.

"Many people are not on your side, Xavier, including members of the Assembly who believe you should be stripped of all academic and athletic rankings and undergo strict loyalty evaluations. You know as well as I do that any progress you have made so far would come to a halt, and the prospect for advancement in your military service will be much more challenging. It will be as if you never went through the academy at all."

His fingernails scraped along the armrest, effectively chipping his nails and driving splinters into his fingers.

"However, I raised a compromise to my fellow members. A test, if you will. A test to have Xavier Battier prove his loyalty and finalize his pardon." Kearse's words were sharp and affecting. Xavier was all ears. "Should you accept this test and pass, you will be granted a high-ranking position as boatswain under the command of a respected captain."

"What is the mission, Overseer?"

"Trackers believe your brother and his treasonous friends are heading northwest. You will ride for Brickford and try and cut your brother off before he reaches Port Randolph in Vester. You must bring him back here to face justice or carry it out yourself."

Xavier said nothing, and he stared back at the crashing waves. *Kill my brother?*

"It's a difficult thing, I'm asking. But it would be best if you did it for your well-being. Declan Cross will lead your expedition and speak on your behalf should you manage this task proficiently. So, I ask you, Xavier, what's a traitor to a loyal countryman?"

TWENTY-FOUR
THE AIDMAN IV

Caldwell and his friends followed along the outskirts of Terkwill Road. Travel was slow. The four of them trekked through the forest to avoid being seen by any greencoats and local or provincial law. The quiet was somehow deafening as Caldwell's voice in his head kept telling him over and over again that his life had changed forever.

Never going to be the same.

It had been five days since Emil, Fili, and Maynard saved him from his early demise. Five days since they'd all taken lives. They wore the coats of dead men. In doing so, Caldwell felt some validity to being labeled the renegade the Assembly claimed him to be. They were all coping with the bloodshed differently. Emil showed hardly any sign of change as he was the one taking point on this expedition to Vester. It seemed like he was putting all of his thoughts and energy into getting them to Port Randolph in one piece as opposed to self-reflection.

Maynard dealt with it the hardest. He kept softly repeating, "What are we doing?" or "What have we done?"

Emil snapped at him on several occasions in an attempt to

shut him up. Perhaps because he was asking himself the same questions and he didn't want to hear them.

Like always, it was hard to put a finger on Fili's headspace. As the orphan raised by Lieutenant Chiesa, he never showed excessive emotion.

Caldwell was proud to have loyal friends who risked their lives and future for him. He loved his siblings as much as an older brother could. But there was something unparalleled about the fellowship, a core group of friends on the heels of suffering. They had suffered grueling academic trials as aidmen, bone-breaking combat training, and rigorous schedules, and now, they had all fought, bled, and killed together. The blood that united his friends was not familial. It was the blood that they'd taken together that was somehow thicker and more potent.

Night fell. Emil suggested they make camp farther into the woods so that they couldn't be seen from the road. The party agreed, and they pushed deeper into the dense forest. The travel northeast wasn't kind to their coastal likings. In the province of Brickford, there was already a chill in the air. They rubbed their arms over their sleeves in an attempt to stay warm as the breeze cut through the thin green coats of the men they had slain.

Emil was the map bearer on the route. Geography wasn't Caldwell's strong point. While he was top of his class when it came to medicine and practice, his map skills, though proficient, were not on equal footing with his youngest siblings.

As they followed the road at a discreet distance, they saw something that wasn't on the map. Through trees that had shifted dark was a cabin. No light emerged from the windows. If it was vacant, it had the potential as shelter for the evening. But it reminded him of those cabins in the woods from scary children's stories.

"You think anyone is in there?" Maynard whispered.

"Hard to tell. They may have turned in early," Emil replied, eyeing the house with the intensity of a hawk. "What does everyone think?"

"You want to knock? See if anyone is home?" Fili asked.

"We're disguised as soldiers. We could demand they open the door," Emil said.

Caldwell didn't like that idea. "Are we sure we want to go about things that way?"

"I understand. But we haven't got a full night's rest in days. This may be our best and only opportunity. If it rains with this cold air, we could die."

Emil's argument was convincing.

"Let's get a closer look before we do anything," Caldwell said.

All of them agreed and tied their horses to nearby trees.

Caldwell and his friends remained low, stalking the house as if it were their prey. They had their rifles at the ready with bayonets leading the way as swords dangled from their sides.

Still, no movement or sound came from the cabin. The grass was overgrown and knee-high. Bugs of various sizes and shapes leaped out from their place of hiding in front of their faces. One managed to fly into Maynard's mouth. The composure he showed upon having the unknown insect nearly nest in his mouth was impressive, as he was prone to lose control.

They approached the door. Emil slammed the bottom of his fist into the wood. None of them said a thing or gave any clue as to who they were. Caldwell saw the latch on the door and decided to check if it was locked. With ease, the latch lifted, and the door quietly creaked open.

It was a humble home. The inside was no larger than Caldwell's back in Roguewave. It didn't appear to be lived in, but it didn't seem abandoned either. The furniture was still intact, and there were fresh logs in the fireplace. There was a kitchen area with a wooden table and cooking utensils and cabinets lining the walls.

"Check for food," Emil said while Fili was already in the process.

There were two doors on either side of the fireplace. Maynard approached one while Caldwell searched the other. They cocked their rifles in synchronized fashion. Maynard's door opened while Caldwell's luck with unlocked doors had run its course.

"Locked?" Emil asked.

"Yeah, the latch won't budge."

Then, a swaying commotion came from outside along the dirt road.

"Get down," Emil said in a harsh whisper.

Through the open window was a lantern bobbing back and forth as it dangled above a wagon. It seemed to be a lone man as the light illuminated his black mass.

"It's a man," Fili said. "Just one. Doesn't look armed."

"Be ready, just in case."

The man, whom Caldwell guessed was the owner of this cabin, dismounted from the wagon and approached the house with no suspicion.

"Maynard, can you get a good look at him?" Caldwell asked.

"Eh, it's too dark. He looks older," Maynard whispered back.

Then, from behind Caldwell, the locked door burst open. "Don't hurt my father!" a young girl said, or what Caldwell believed to be a girl. It was hard to tell because the child was covered in linen bandages from head to toe.

"Simone!" the man from outside yelled as he entered the house.

Fili wrestled the man to the floor while Caldwell kept the child at bay with the butt of his rifle.

"Please, I don't have any money, I swear," the man pleaded.

Fili had his back with his forearms pressing down on the man's shoulders.

"We aren't here to take anything from you, sir. Fili, let him go," Caldwell said. Emil lowered his gun but reluctantly and with a clinched jaw. "Rifles down, guys."

Emil was the last to put his down on the ground, yet he, with Fili's help, hoisted the man to his feet. His child ran past Caldwell and embraced him.

"Are you all right?" he asked.

"Yes, Father," she replied.

He put his hand on her chest and covered her from the boys. "Put your hood on, Simone," he said.

"Sorry we broke in, sir," Caldwell said. "We thought the house was vacant."

The man wore confusion on his face. He examined all of their attire one by one. "You're not greencoats or coppers?"

"Greencoats?" Emil said, sharing the communal puzzlement of the group. "No, sir. Despite our attire, we aren't associated with them in the slightest. Have greencoats been bothering you? Or have you committed a federal crime?"

The father was hesitant to engage in conversation. His arms wrapped tightly around his little girl. "Not necessarily, but my daughter, Simone, has an… affliction. We once lived on the border of Helmburough and Ghonia when word got out about her. They told me their concerns about her possibly infecting other people, so they said they would come for her, but we fled before that happened."

Emil was intrigued. "Take her for what?"

"I'm not sure. Do you lot promise you're not from the capital? Or are you here under any government mandate?" The man asked, squeezing his daughter against his body, who remained shaking and peeking out from behind his waist.

"We promise," Caldwell said, encouraging his friends to nod in agreement. "What's wrong with her? Simone, you said, right?"

"Yes. Simone. I'm Alred," the man said. "It's a rare disease. I don't know the name. I've tried everything to get her help. Seems like I asked too much because her sickness garnered negative attention."

"Is it contagious?" Fili asked.

"I don't think so. Otherwise, I would have it."

"May I see her?" Caldwell asked.

Alred squeezed Simone's shoulder. "I don't think that's a good idea, young man."

"Caldwell..." Emil said with a glare.

"I'm a student of medicine, sir," Caldwell explained. "Maybe I can help."

There was a soft smile on Alred's face. "You're an aidman?"

"We all are."

Fili spoke up. "You might as well, sir. We're all aidmen, but Caldwell is a scholar of medical knowledge."

Caldwell held out his open hands and got down on one knee. "I know we just met, and the circumstances are very strange, but maybe I can help."

Alred looked down at Simone, who was already halfway out from behind her father. It seemed like the potential for being helped urged her along.

She extended her bandage-wrapped hands that were grey and blackened around the edges. They had a musk to them that told Caldwell she had been wearing them for a while now.

"Could I get some light in here?" he asked.

Wasting no time, Alred ignited the fireplace using a rod of flint he had hanging from a nail in the wall. He then proceeded to light every candle in the cabin. It wasn't much light, but it was better than nothing.

Caldwell unwrapped Simone's bandages. He looked at her, and he could see hope in her eyes. He could only wish the hope he was giving her wasn't false.

Simone's skin was not a welcome sight, nor anything Caldwell had seen before. It had a reptilian texture and color. It was dark green and had brown bumps that scattered about, oozing pus. "When did this first occur?"

"Four years ago, maybe. She's had this for nearly half her life now. We fled the capital three years ago."

Caldwell struggled with discerning what this affliction might be. He had a few theories rolling around in his head, but he quickly cast them aside as not all the symptoms aligned.

"Any idea, Caldwell?" Emil asked.

No, it can't be what I think.

He stared at the floor, getting lost in his own mind of possibilities. There was no rhyme or reason, but he thought of his mother, whom he missed more than he was willing to admit. Perhaps it was from the suffering this father and daughter were going through. Caldwell hoped more than anything that his mother was safe and that she wasn't rotting away in a cold dark cell with no one to comfort her.

He thought of his youngest siblings, Isla and Eddie, who weren't good at taking care of themselves on their own, especially Eddie, without Avery to nurture him. It was the unknown that kept him awake at all hours of the night, not the cold.

"Caldwell?" Emil asked to snap him out of his near-catatonic state.

Back in reality, he looked into Simone's eyes. "Can you undo the bandages around your face?"

As she peeled the damp wrappings away like a waking mummy, a sticky, sap-like liquid remained. Not much grossed him out, for he'd seen a lot as an aidman, but this made his stomach churn. When her face was revealed, it was more of the same – green like the back of a lizard, but luckily for her, less pus.

"Have her symptoms gradually worsened over time? Or have they been like this since the beginning?" he asked her father.

"She's been like this since the start," Alred said.

"I've read about something like this, but not from a medical book, and I don't think it's a disease," Caldwell said.

Alred looked to Caldwell's friends as if they'd offer an alternate theory. "Not a disease? What is it, then?"

Caldwell rubbed his tear ducts. "First, I want you to know that whatever I say might be incorrect. I'm well-informed – that doesn't make me an expert. That being said, my little brother used to read books about exotic animals and plants in the Botan Rainforest in Autera from a zoologist named Dr. Poplinn. Simone's symptoms don't seem to be that of a disease but of a fungus."

Alred stared a hole through Caldwell, exposing his entire pupil. "That's your assessment? Are you serious?"

"I know it sounds outlandish, but that's why her body is changing. The fungus is using her body as a host. If I recall correctly, it's called Lacerfungi—the Gila fungus. She must've been exposed to it somehow."

"How would she be exposed when Simone's never been to Botan Rainforest?"

"That, I don't know, sir."

Alred's frustration for his daughter grew. "Well, is she just going to be like this forever? How would one even go about curing such a thing?"

"She won't be like this forever," Caldwell whispered at the ground before returning to Simone. "Would you mind lifting your arm, please?"

She hesitated, like she knew what he was curious about, and slowly removed her baggy cloak.

Under her arms was a collection of formed fungal caps

with gills sprouting from the pit of her arm like it would at the base of a tree. They were beige with dark orange lines in a trio of circle patterns on the top. Maynard and Fili had to look away.

"What do you mean, *won't be like this forever?*" Alred asked.

"I mean, if something isn't done soon—this has gone on for far too long."

"And?"

His pinky ran along just over the top of the infected area as a sort of medical display. "I would say Simone's time as a host for this fungus to reproduce is coming to an end... Judging by what I'm looking at, she doesn't have long."

Alred was in denial at first. After that, he pleaded for a solution or a cure that Caldwell did not have. "What do we do? How do we fix her?"

"Again, I don't know. I'm sorry."

"Could you at least try? Anything? This is my daughter. She's not even ten years of age."

Emil spoke for Caldwell. "There's nothing we can do, sir. We can't stay. We have to be on our way as soon as possible."

"Why?" Alred asked.

"That, we can't tell you," Emil replied.

Caldwell felt horrible. He'd yet to come across anything so substantial in his young career as an aidman. It was far beyond his depth of knowledge, and perhaps it was beyond anyone's. Still, it didn't erase the shame of being worthless to someone who needed his help. He wished there were something he could do. "There may be doctors, shamans, druids... I don't know, someone that could help you on the Free Islands where we're heading."

"Caldwell!" Emil burst out. "You can't tell them where we're going. He could tell the greencoats where we've gone!"

But it was too late for that. Caldwell had made his decision.

He stood and stepped closer to Alred. "They won't tell

anyone. They're coming with us." Then, he leaned in and whispered to the man, adding, "Or Simone is going to die."

TWENTY-FIVE
THE SILENT ONE IV

Isla remained in the tall grass atop Pointer's Hill, looking through a spyglass at the harbor where Oliver was to meet the newly appointed governor – Governor Cassel.

They arrived by a man-of-war called the *Sea Viper*, not quite the prowess of a Grand Ship, but a solid second in terms of size and firepower. Isla counted around two hundred soldiers marching across the battered harbor. Even at such a distance, she could make out his formal, violet doctor's sash. The soldiers marched in a direct line, stomping their feet along the way before pivoting and parting, allowing a small collection of men to walk between them. Isla counted five. The one in the lead kept pace ahead of them, wearing a royal emerald coat. Isla was too far away to notice any distinct facial features. However, something that couldn't be missed was that he didn't have a left arm. The coat that signaled royalty was tied in a knot at the forearm.

Oliver and Governor Cassel shook hands.

Behind the governor were two men looking in every direction as if they were paranoid. *Must be his personal guards.* They couldn't differ more in appearance. One was a darker-complexioned man with what looked to be trimmed facial hair, and the other's skin was mangled with waves and divots as if his entire head had been burnt.

As the greetings seemed to be going normal and peaceful, Isla couldn't help but think, *Defeat your enemies first.*

Things were beginning to find themselves back to normal after what the people in the markets were calling the Molten Raid. There were signs nailed to posts and still-standing shops with the words *Retaliate, Death to All Pirates,* and *Remember the Molten Raid!*

The debris was almost cleared, and commerce, though sparse, returned to the bay. The reflecting orange light off the backs of the molten crabs seemed to be a welcome sight for the citizens as no one paid attention to her in a hooded cloak.

The choppy and dark waters remained, and it seemed the *Hydra* had left. *I always heard nothing could stand against the* Hydra, *and yet, the bay burned anyway.* But it was an amphibious assault, or at least that was what her brother Xavier once informed her was the name of an attack on water and land.

Isla didn't know if her mother was still in Colwerth Prison or if she'd sailed away in the custody of Alistair Cross. Livian told her both scenarios were likely but didn't know more beyond that. Her secret guardians had to keep their appearances up and continue working so as not to arouse suspicion. Isla remained left to her own devices with dense-haired Leo, who was suffering estate fever just as much.

Her cooking skills had improved as she spent a lot of her time in the kitchen with Yula and Martha. Everything from baking sweet bread, chicken pie, venison with molten sauce, and the countless variations of molten crab dishes.

Isla preferred chicken to crab, but her mother always informed her that she wouldn't be complaining if she grew up somewhere where seafood was sparse. Her mother and father always reassured Isla and her siblings that "they were better off than most."

There was a saying in Roguewave, but really it applied in

every province. That saying went, "It could be worse. You could live in Dryburn." Even though Roguewave was considered the poorest, Oliver informed her economically, their province was on the rise due to trade, while Dryburn lived up to its name of being a harsh landscape with barren soil and bitter people.

Isla was at the end of the marketplace when she arrived at the Governor's Quarter. It was a collection of villas around four stories high that overlooked the bay. They had been untouched during the raid but were currently the main focus of renovation as the new governor was to be resuming his office work there. It was under armed guard all day and night. Isla eyed the greencoats as she circled the tall hedges bordering the property from about a hundred feet away.

This is going to be harder than I thought.

Her father's study was on the fourth floor in the eastern villa. Formally, she and her family were allowed access at any time, but now, as labeled conspirators, she doubted that clearance still applied. She saw the white building with yellowed vines growing up the side. She remembered how her father's back would face the street from his window while the nostalgia tugged at her heart.

Isla's mission was to find any reasoning as to why these horrible events had been happening to her family. She knew, and her mother and father assured her that being deaf didn't make her stupid or unaware. No, quite the opposite. Her mother once told her, "Should you use your eyes properly, you'll find you can see more than anyone."

A greencoat scanned the streets at his post beneath the ivory archway between the front hedges. To avoid his gaze, Isla rounded the corner, following another guard making his way around the squared-off villas. At every corner, he would turn and look in all directions. Isla caught on quick and ducked into the hedges that doubled her height.

Ahead, below her father's window, was a trellis that

climbed upward along with violet Zfora blooms. The timing had to be perfect. Almost too perfect for her to take the chance. It would be too easy for anyone, guard or bystander, to notice her climbing the trellis. She had to consider an alternate route.

To her luck, the first floor offered her plenty of entry points. But, as the guard was making his way back around the bushes, she bet all her eggs in the hope that the nearest window was open. Perhaps the spirit of her father was smiling down upon her because the glass slid open with ease. Her body involuntarily jumped through the tight space, and she rolled into the room without knowing the prospect of things going on inside.

As she came to, the world around her leveled. She recognized it as an empty dining room with beautiful unused dishes and pristine mahogany furniture. A breeze cut through the room, and she quickly returned to shut the window.

She appeared to be alone in this place. It took her a moment to find her bearings in the dining room and its relation to her father's office. Dust fell through the cracks of the ceiling. Distinct and repetitive thumps followed. People were walking above her.

Of course, the first door she cracked, Isla clocked the rusty and unkempt hinges that would surely screech, opening it further. However, there was no one currently walking the hall. The pathway along the multi-colored Ghonian rug to her father's study came back to her. Isla kept low. She knew more than anybody how to stay quiet. Her feet tip-toed like a dancer as she moved through the halls and up the stairwell.

The third-floor door swung open on approach, and her only option was to duck behind the door itself. It was a greencoat who proved not to be proficient as a security guard. All he did was peek his head out and investigate the stairway before shutting the door again. Isla carried on with her mission.

At the top of the stairs, the fourth and final floor appeared empty. The halls were ghostly and void of life, not at all like it was when her father spent time here. Granted, it had only been a few months out of the year he spent in Roguewave through all of Isla's childhood.

She shouldn't have been surprised by her father's office being locked. But what the security might not have known was that her father had six more keys made for his office door. Isla reached into her pocket, removed one of those spare keys, and entered.

Looking at the state the office was in, Isla wondered why she was surprised or expected anything different. It was stripped bare. The paintings of the *Abyss* and the family portrait were gone. Some of the floorboards were ripped up and tossed to the side. The cabinet and armoire drawers were emptied and strung out in the middle of the room. A few papers and letters addressed to him of seemingly little importance were left behind.

The only thing that remained was the desk that matched the rest of the study, empty and bleak. The wood was dark, near black. She took a seat in his chair that looked to be made of the same cedar. For a moment, she could almost feel his presence, and even in the gloom of his empty office, she smiled.

I miss you, Father, she thought to herself, hoping he could hear her from somewhere.

Isla wondered why they would desecrate his study. Perhaps it was to get back at her mother for her treason.

She ran her hand across the smooth finish of the desktop until the inkpot halted her progress. Isla recounted how it seemed all her father did was write letters as if it was the main task assigned to a Grand Captain. She lifted the cap, and no ink remained. *I suppose that's fitting.*

Something about the inkpot caught her eye – it was tilted off-center. Isla attempted to move the inkpot around, but it wouldn't budge. Perhaps her desire for answers left her hopeful that something would secretly appear. As she was about to give up, and her youthful way of thinking failed, she felt a click in the desk as she rotated the pot clockwise. It continued as she turned it more, and then, something dropped on her foot underneath the desk.

Next to her boot, she saw a large ledger with a string seal wrapped all the way around, thick and filled with stacks of papers. It was brown leather with a blank cover. Isla tucked it under her arm, and as her head popped up from under the desk, a guard stood in the doorway. They were both surprised upon seeing one another. He shouted to his fellow guards.

Isla didn't know what to do. She had been caught red-handed. He ran for her, and she used the desk to stop his advance. She rotated around it, and he followed suit. Knowing she couldn't do this forever and thinking how his backup would arrive shortly, Isla attempted a high-risk maneuver.

When the greencoat was where she wanted him to be, she flipped the desk over, pinning him in the corner. Isla went for the window, but his arms gripped her tight around the chest from behind, and the guard hoisted her in the air. Her diversion had little effect as she was helpless in his arms.

She thought of a move Avery taught her once that was for when someone bigger had her in this position. Isla put her legs together, brought her knees over her head, and swung them down as hard as she could, using her core and momentum. The greencoat loosened his grip to stop his face from slamming into the hardwood floor. Isla sprung to her feet quicker than he did, which left her an opening to throw her shin into his manhood.

He folded into himself like a molten shrimp. Isla wasted no time leaving the villa as she entered it, jumping through a window. She grabbed the trellis and slid down until her feet touched the ground. She didn't even bother looking around for anyone who might have seen her.

TWENTY-SIX
THE WIDOW V

Her stomach churned as the choppy seas weakened her constitution. This was only the second voyage in Adelaide's life, both of which caused similar outcomes of vomiting stomach acid. The difference this time was that her hands and feet were shackled the entire journey to Helmburough. She couldn't peek her head over the ship and spew the contents of her stomach into the ocean. No, she had puked on the cabin floor in the prisoner's holding. Luckily, a waste barrel was in the corner of the room.

Adelaide didn't seem to get nervous anymore. She had fought in many battles and seen enough horrible things to push her through various anxieties, but she had to admit that it wasn't the rocky ship alone that gave her that nauseous feeling; it was the destination and who was awaiting her arrival.

She'd never met Charlotte Hannah, now Lady Hannah. She only knew her by name and as her late husband's former betrothed. They were set to be married long ago before his voyages south. Mathias informed her that the marriage was for political reasons under his father's orders, and he had no affection for Charlotte.

Those who were convicted of treason faced the gallows in the Unified Provinces. So, Charlotte Hannah, originally from a royal family and married into another, must have pulled rank to achieve such an arrangement.

Her sweaty forehead leaned against the interior of the hull. Her weakened body had barely seen light in weeks. Adelaide believed it to be a strategy to further break a prisoner's spirit.

I shall not be broken.

The voyage to Helmburough could've lasted days, weeks, a month – Adelaide had no idea.

A pair of greencoats held her arms and dragged her up the wide *Hydra* stairs from below deck. The sunlight hit her face and was unforgiving in its greeting. The ocean breeze was welcome to combat the heat, which seemed to have a vendetta against her. She almost wanted to pray to the sun god, Toltili, as she once did as a girl in Caste Valley. The smell of the fresh ocean air was similar and foreign at the same time. She had been living in Molten Bay for years, but the smell of crab remained on the tips of her nose hairs and overpowered the aroma of the ocean.

"That'll be all, men. Back to your stations," Alistair Cross said.

Adelaide had forgotten the scale of the Grand Ships. The deck was the size of a cathedral's interior. The crew of around a thousand men was never cramped. It was a fully rigged ship with one cannon for each of its crew members. Mathias used to tell her about the different types of ships and how they sailed, but that was years ago, and the *Hydra* was a cut above the rest. The five Grand Ships ascended beyond first-tier ships like the man-o-war or treasure galleon. No, these were ships built for gods, perhaps *the* God.

"When's the last time you stood on the deck of a ship this size?" Alistair asked.

Still twitching her eyelids to adjust, she answered, "Years."

"Was it before or after you and Mathias married?"

"Before," she said.

He scoffed. "Yes, of course. Because Mathias stepped down from his title of Grand Captain to spend time with your family… What a price to pay." He turned to face her, his stone-like face glaring strong. "Walk with me."

He began up the steps to the quarter-deck. The helm was being operated by Alistair's sailing master Gerick, who shared his captain's scowl and standoffish nature.

"I'm not going to apologize for how my crew looks at you, Trezbe," Cross said.

He still doesn't want to consider me a citizen.

"We sailors and soldiers spend the majority of our lives at sea, lives contested by endless obstacles living, natural, and even unnatural. A common sailor will see more in a lifetime than most regular citizens that have not been troubled by the sea."

Adelaide looked around at the crew of the *Hydra*. Between their duties, they would shoot her a hate-filled glare. She feared that the thousands of rifles lined against the guard rails would soon be aimed at her. "That is the reason they look at me so?" she asked. "Because you all live hard lives? I could *never* understand that."

Gerick's nostrils flared as he listened in the background of their conversation.

Cross waved his hand in the direction of the massive and tireless crew manning the ship. "Each of these men learned to hate anyone that doesn't sail under a provincial flag. It makes it all the much easier when trouble arises, and that hate unites them."

"Yes, I'm sure hate is a brilliant motivator for brutes."

"Ah, you hate them and me all the same. You just don't admit it."

"I don't know them," Adelaide said sharply.

"But you know me. And any man who sails under Alistair Cross, you can't bring yourself to like, surely."

She said nothing and ignored the fact he spoke in the third person.

Yet, Alistair continued. "My duties are to protect my country by whatever means and methods I must. I'm sure you've heard rumors of the things I've done. Perhaps they're fabricated, perhaps not. But in the end, thousands of people in the provinces sleep better because of it."

"Is that what you tell yourself? Is that your justification for the horrible things you do?"

"Of course I do." He never lacked conviction. Adelaide could sometimes see that glint in the eye of a person who didn't fully believe in what they were saying. Alistair Cross was not one of them. "Gerick, make sure we port as far southwest as we can in the Grand Harbor."

"Yes, Grand Commander," was all the sailing master said.

"Well, Trezbe, you aren't far away from the rest of your life serving the Hannahs. I suppose it's better than a traitor's death."

There was a long, drawn-out exhale as the Grand Captain stared out over his kingdom.

"You killed him. A father of five," she said through gritted teeth.

"Believe what you want," he said while scolding a few of his soldiers who were taking a breather below the mainmast. "The bottom line is that you're guilty because you cannot be trusted. As I said, maybe you had something to do with the pirate raid. Maybe you didn't. The fact of the matter is that you share no love for our country, and we share no love for you."

He was a powerful man. He ruled with fear that seemed to

manifest itself as wind for the *Hydra's* sails. "Tell that to my husband, who was a more righteous man than you or any of your contemporaries claim to be. A man whose love got him killed."

"Allegedly," he said coldly as he stomped towards her. "You speak as if we are equals. As if what you say means as much as the words leaving my mouth. I've done my due diligence being cordial with you. I will no longer be so kind. You haven't been the daughter of a tarquin for a very long time. In every sense, I am above you. You are not my guest aboard the *Hydra*. You are my prisoner. Should you forget that, I'll reinstitute the plank walk with a cannonball strapped to your feet."

There was a witty comment to be made rattling around in her head, but she held it in, seeing no upside. Adelaide swallowed it with only the continuous Beaker Gulf breeze to ease her.

The *Hydra* ported at the jetty in the Grand Harbor. Adelaide glanced across the harbor that stretched beyond the horizon. Thousands of ships of various sizes and status launched and landed in an orderly fashion where the chaos was controlled. As she looked out at the vastness of the empire, she saw it as symbolic. For though her prism, she viewed the Assembly as controlling the world with systematic chaos.

Flags of all seventeen provinces flew in their diverse and distinguished color scheme. On the opposite side was the royal emerald flag with seventeen condensed landmasses, representing the Unified Provinces, bordered by five horizontal gold lines.

The Free Islands' flags had different shades of blue depending on the island it represented and the water's color. She saw the Tyver Island flag flying high and proud. Its cargo of Tyver rum was of high value in Renera. She wondered if the amount of gold in their hull weighed their galleon down on their way home.

She was escorted down the steep ramp onto the dock, surrounded by greencoats on all sides. The four of them were three-tallied lieutenants and were as cold as their captain. Their marching legs stepped onto the wood ramp at the same time on their descent.

"The Land of Commerce and Grandeur" was Helmburough's slogan. Vendors with small carts yet large signs pitched their products. Whether it was the catch of the day, sun sashes, fish and hunting gear being hawked, or renters looking to provide expensive lodging along the coastline for weary travelers, there was money to be made—lots of it. The commerce here made everything in Molten Bay seem insignificant.

At the bottom of the ramp was a large carriage and a collection of private security.

Is this all for me?

"You with the Hannah Estate?" Lieutenant Rollinn asked.

"That we are, Lieutenant," said the guard with the untucked shirt as he stammered in his respect to the high-ranking officer.

"Very well."

"Yes, very well," said a woman's voice.

Adelaide came to attention and looked up to see a beautiful blonde woman emerging from the carriage. She wore a long grey dress with a floral design of blue daisies going from her waist to her feet. "Unshackle her. She's not aboard your obnoxiously large ship anymore, so she's not your property."

The four lieutenant's faces soured. It was plain that they had never been spoken to by a woman in that manner.

"Lady Hannah, these are Alistair Cross' lieutenants:

Rollinn, Fairday, Bester, and Stills. Perhaps you should speak to them with more–"

She stopped her head of security right there as she marched, using her umbrella as a makeshift cane. "I'll speak to them how I desire. Relay to your commander that the exchange went through. Good day, Lieutenants," Lady Hannah said as she unfurled her umbrella directly in front of their faces on her turn before returning to the carriage.

The carriage rode smoothly on the paved road. Adelaide was informed it would take the better part of a day to get to the Hannah Estate in rural Helmburough. The route they traveled wasn't spectacular as they avoided the popular landmarks in the city, like Martyr Arena, the Seabird Library, or the inland shores, and Sentient Tower, which could be seen in passing, but not closely admired.

Xavier is here.

"I'm disappointed," Charlotte said, swaying in front of her.

"Beg your pardon?" Adelaide said as the back of her head rested on the padded interior, the most comfort she'd had in weeks.

"I was told the clannish woman from the southern continent that stole my husband away was beautiful." Charlotte didn't make eye contact. "I prayed that she wasn't equal to me… and here you are, dirty, bruised, tortured, yet your beauty remains."

She noticed around Charlotte's eye was a hint of blue that was concealed by her overly applied makeup. Adelaide was sure it was a bruise, but its origin she did not know.

Charlotte cleared her throat. "I assume there are a lot of questions swirling around in your head as to why you're here."

"There's a few."

"Well, don't feel so thankful," Charlotte said. "I'm in need of a handmaiden. I require a lot, and others weren't doing their duties to my standard."

"That's why I'm here? To do whatever you'd like?"

It was the first time Lady Hannah smiled. "Tell me, Adelaide, is it such a harsh alternative to death or your lifeless body swinging over Molten Bay?"

The smile faded. Charlotte looked out the window and stared at the trees. "I love my husband. I'm not denying that. But my life with Mathias Battier was taken away from me. And the woman responsible is sitting right in front of me." She had an icy stare that shifted to Adelaide. "Did he tell you he was supposed to marry me when he met you?"

"Not right away."

She scoffed. "He must have been smitten with you."

"I can't speak for him now," Adelaide said, frustrated.

"Of course, you can. All women know that look in a man's eye when he desires you."

Adelaide pushed that conversation aside best she could. "Why did you do this? Why did you go through so much to bring me here?"

"Is it not obvious, Adelaide? You seem smart. Mathias wouldn't have married you if you weren't. I simply wanted to see how I compared to you. If you were all of what people said you were. It would have eaten away at me the rest of my life if you had died, and I never got the chance to look upon you."

Adelaide cocked her head. "You went through all those obstacles to do this—to look at me."

"Money grants you a lot, my dear. I know you've never known that power. But the more money you have, the more your desires can become a reality, no matter how petty or insignificant."

She was right. Adelaide didn't know the power of excess.

"I'm from a place where the most desirable commodities are far less extravagant."

A brief exhale shot from Charlotte's nostrils. "Is that right? Well, you're in Helmburough now."

Their escort was grand. *Excessive* might be the proper term. Around fifty private security were armed with rifles and swords as they rode. *All those guns to protect one person.*

Adelaide observed Charlotte as she continued to stare out the window. Nearly an hour passed before the noblewoman's eyes started to water unprompted.

"How many children do you have?" Charlotte asked, wiping the soon-to-be tears away. As her sleeve fell down her arm, Adelaide could see the hint of a healing bruise going around her wrist.

"Five," she replied confidently, believing all her children were still alive.

"Five of them?" Charlotte repeated back. "I hear people have issues with one. How do you manage five?"

"I do what I can."

TWENTY-SEVEN
THE COWARD BOY V

The four tall ships still standing, the *Whale, Bloodsucker,
Drifter,* and *Hope*, were all in repair. Eddie was surprised at the
progress made on them in just a couple of weeks. The pirates
and the mackereli worked tirelessly together, which seemed to
be all day and night. The *Whale, Bloodsucker,* and *Drifter* were
almost ready to sail again. The only thing left to be done was
to patch the sails that were riddled with cannonball holes. The
Hope had very little of it left. All that could be spared was
being stripped from it, including all the contents of its hull.
The pirates made sure all the rum was accounted for and
dispersed evenly amongst the remaining ships.

The square-rigger called the *Madfrog* was moved out of the
inland cove and to the eastern side of the island under
Captain Lockett's command.

Eddie still spent his days with anxiety flowing through
him. However, to his surprise, it had been eased by the way
the pirates treated him. Most of them were kind and seemed
to care about his well-being – aside from the Djars of the
Idush Clan. And as he stood on the deck of
the *Bloodsucker* with a sparring sword in hand and a fiery-eyed
Cella staring back at him, he believed that even more.

"Get your sword up. I'm not going to tell you again." She scolded him for the majority of their training session. She didn't yell. She didn't have to; the deep bass of her voice was enough.

"It's heavy," Eddie said.

"Then, you are weak. Get stronger or die." And the Idush warrior charged him with two swords. It took everything to get his sword up in time to block the first pair of swings before falling to his back, dropping his weapon along the way. "You fall, you die."

Eddie wanted to be anywhere else. It wasn't that he didn't want to be a good fighter, but the inevitable violence proved challenging to overcome. He didn't want to find himself in situations where wielding a sword was the solution to the problem.

The dull blade wobbled on the deck next to him.

"Get up!" she screamed, coming down with a strike on his head. He rolled out of the way, and Cella's blade bounced off the railing, sending woodchips airborne. "You can avoid trouble for only so long, Battier. Sooner or later, you're going to have to fight back."

She slammed the flat part of her blade into Eddie's shoulder, and it stung worse than any insect. He curled up and started to rub it as if that could somehow alleviate the pain.

He was angry, not just about his sword training, but everything that had happened to him. In a fit of rage, he grabbed his sword and rushed Cella, swinging wild, trying to connect with any of them.

She parried them effortlessly. "There's that Trezbe war blood. I hate to see it, but I'm glad it's in there for your sake."

She spun at him, faking as if a sword strike was coming at any moment. Eddie was back against the ship's edge with nowhere to go. Her swords stopped at his throat. "Can you swim, Battier?"

"No," he replied.

"Who is raised with water all around and can't swim?" Cella lowered her blades and relaxed her shoulders. Then, in one swift motion, she kicked him in the center of his chest.

The air in his lungs escaped from him, and he fell back over the railing. The back of his neck slapped hard against the water as he submerged. The darkness frightened him as much as the lack of swimming ability. As he sank lower, thrashing, the water became black.

Eddie struggled to find which way was up. Luckily in his flailing, he felt air on his hand, and he followed. He sucked in a huge breath as he surfaced.

His panic didn't cease there. His chin bobbed below the water, and it leaked into his mouth. Cella stared down at him, along with the rest of the pirates and mackereli working on the ships on all sides.

"Help!" he cried.

"Help yourself, Battier!" she replied.

His first course of action was to try and grab anywhere on the ship to see if he could hold his head above the surface, but his hands kept slipping on the mossy outer hull.

"Help!"

"Don't help the boy!" Cella demanded.

Eddie couldn't tell if they were obeying her order or not due to the water smacking him in the face. A splash behind him was on the opposite side of the cove near the *Drifter.* But he didn't see anyone.

His heavy arms were shot, and his lungs were burning. He could no longer keep himself up, and he sank below the water. The dark enveloped him on all sides. It almost seemed like something was pulling him down by the shoulders.

A wave of bubbles left his mouth as he continued crying out for help. But his tears and his cries were lost, becoming one with the water.

He started to feel lightheaded.

Then, a pair of arms wrapped around his chest. Eddie

didn't know if they were real or if perhaps it was an angel transporting him to the afterlife.

He surfaced and gasped for air. He found himself on the cove bank and a mackereli standing over him with its yellow eyes.

In his best Aquatic, he said, "Thank you."

A gurgly reply of "You're welcome" eased his mind. He couldn't speak the language well and had only picked up a few words and phrases. After each exchange, his knowledge grew.

"Are you hurt?" the young mackereli asked.

Eddie could tell he was young by the shade of green and blue of his scales. The mackereli's colors faded to grey as they aged. Males could be identified by the shark-like fin that curved backward on the top of their head, while the female mackereli were bald.

"No, I'm fine." Eddie checked his body, making sure everything was still there. "Yep, I'm all here."

The mackereli laughed. Not like a person, though. Their laughter seemed to exit the gills on their necks and sounded like repeated exhales through someone's nostrils.

"Good." The mackereli extended his webbed hand. Eddie obliged and was lifted to his feet. "My name is Sephor."

"Eddison Battier," he replied.

"I know."

You know?

There was a shuffle to his left, and the boatswain Matt Roke emerged through the thick brush. "Eddison, are you okay?" he asked, concerned. He lightened his tone upon seeing the mackereli. "Ah, Prince Sephor," he said, crossing one arm across his body and bowing.

Prince? He's the son of Caspus, then.

Cella Djar wasn't far behind Matt, but she took her time. "You can thank the prince all you'd like. Perhaps one day, you'll learn there won't be anyone around to save you." With two swords dangling from her belt and two strapped to her back, she left him. "We're done for today."

Matt took a closer look at him to inspect if anything was the matter. "She's a real peach, isn't she?"

"I suppose that's a good word for it," Eddie replied.

"Is this your first time meeting Sephor?"

"Yes, it is," he said, looking back at the mackereli prince.

"He seems nice," Matt said outside of Sephor's comprehension. "We have a hard time communicating with them. The captain and my father can speak the language, but I'm afraid to admit I'm not the brightest star when it comes t'learnin'."

Matt had shaggy hair and a morning shadow for a beard. His forearms were beyond their years as he had been performing ship duties for the better part of a decade.

Sephor spoke once more. "It was a pleasure to finally meet you, Eddison Battier." The prince turned and dove back into the cove.

"Where did he go?" Eddie asked Matt.

"That, I don't know. Wherever they want, I suppose." They watched as the water settled and the ripples dissipated. "Anyway, I have to check inventory on the *Hope* and see if there is more we can use on the other ships. Would you mind helping me? I promise you don't have to fight."

"What makes you think I'm worried about that?"

"No offense, Eddison, but it's quite obvious."

"That's fair." Eddie dropped his head. "I don't see myself getting any better, is all. I'm not like my brothers and sisters."

Matt put his arm around Eddison and began to walk with him. "No one starts good, Eddie. My father was the best duelist in the world for a long time. Maybe he's still the best fighter, but even he said he wasn't good at first." The reassuring words of the boatswain were more comforting than any words Eddison's brothers ever offered him. "And if you're so worried Cella is going to kill you in training, I can help you get better in my spare time. I don't have much else t'do anyway."

Eddie's face softened. "You'd do that?"

"Of course, m'brother."

~

Matt had lit a torch in the hold to provide them with a source of light. "Captain Lockett wants me to make a final sweep of the cargo to see if anything of value got left behind."

It was a dark and cavernous place. Their boots were submerged as water leaked through the crack in the hull. "There's no possibility of this thing sailing ever again, is there?" Eddie asked.

"Eh, you'd be surprised. I've seen ships in worse condition than this be repaired and sail away like nothing ever happened to them. We won't be spending the time and effort into fixin' this one, though."

"Why's that?"

"Time's of the essence. Have to make sure we set sail soon before the mainlanders get us."

Eddie followed each precise step Matt took. "Mainlanders? Is that what you call people from Renera?"

"Not the best name, I suppose, but yes. Half of our crew is from the mainland, so it's not entirely right casting them as the enemy."

"You knew my father?" Eddie asked.

"Yes, of course. He was a great man. He and my father were the best of friends growing up, he told me. My father is the reason Mathias and Marstellar had an audience."

Eddison was still foggy on the details. But of everything alluding to his father being a conspirator who was working with pirates for some type of gain, he was still unaware.

There were countless wooden crates. Some were still intact

and sealed shut, some were open, and others were blown to smithereens while their debris floated in the water.

"I'm positive this didn't get checked as I wanted," Matt said. "We pirates aren't too thorough, Eddison."

Eddie ignored his sentiment entirely. "What was my father doing? What were his intentions with the pirates?"

Matt cocked his head. "You don't know?"

"I don't know anything."

The boatswain nodded in a manner of sympathy. "Well, he had big plans, Eddison," was all he said.

"What kind of plans?"

"He had many tasks to achieve in his master plot," Matt continued walking about the hull, cracking open crates, and searching through standing water with his feet. "One was to establish more lands outside the Unified Provinces' jurisdiction because he informed us it's only a matter of time before they take the entire world. He assured us of lands to the west that were ready for occupation, and while we don't have any evidence, Captain Lockett believes it to be true. Another thing your father wanted to ensure was the liberation of the clan folk like your mother. But ultimately, everything your father wanted to accomplish, and now what we are still trying to achieve, stems from one common goal."

"Which is?"

"To bring the Assembly crumbling to the ground."

"Why?"

For the first time, Matt, who was always very chipper and positive, became serious. "Because they do horrible things."

Eddie inched forward. "What kind of things?"

"I don't think I should be the one to tell you, but hell, they're the reason you're here."

"Matt, please. You're the only one here who has offered me answers."

Matt nodded once more. "Very well," he said while leaning his shoulder on the post. "I'll tell you the things that are rumored first, and then I'll tell you the things I know for certain."

Eddie attempted to get comfortable on an empty crate. "Okay."

"Besides the slavery, they're forcing on the clan folk or the fact that they slaughter innocents that aren't Reneran, it's believed that the members of the Assembly are having secret experiments carried out on people to test the potential benefits of foreign plants and things."

To Eddie, that sounded outlandish. "What kind of things?"

"I don't know. Captain Lockett thinks they're trying to attain power. Power like cheat'n life."

"Cheat life?"

"Y'know, by prolonging it, making themselves immortal."

Eddie's head snapped back. "How exactly would they do that?"

"Don't ask me. These are things your father told us."

Eddie knew his father to be a truthful man. He always taught them the value of honesty, even when someone knew they didn't want to hear it. "Honesty is a first step to bravery," he used to say.

"What of the other rumors?" Eddie asked.

"Well, apparently, there are..." Matt struggled with the words. "Monstrosities in the western ocean and around Ecrosis."

"And?"

"And the Assembly's looking for ways to use them to their advantage. Don't ask me how because I have no idea."

Eddie didn't want to believe it, but his imagination ran wild. "I've met one of the main Assembly members, and he seemed normal, I suppose."

"Which one?" Matt asked.

It was a simple question. But as Eddie thought of the

answer, knowing that Alistair Cross was a known pirate hunter and killer, he feared he might offend his new friend.

Eddie cleared his throat. "Alistair Cross."

Matt stood as still as the chipped pillar he was leaning against, and his torch dropped, putting his face in darkness. "I assure you, Eddie, you're wrong."

"I'm sorry. I had a long conversation with him, and he didn't seem too—"

Matt cut him off. "Alistair Cross is responsible for the death of many of my friends."

"I didn't mean to—"

"You should see the things he does to innocents," Matt said with a scowl. "Innocents like Captain Lockett's wife and son."

Eddie was caught off guard. He didn't know Lockett had a wife and child. "What happened to them?"

The torchlight returned to illuminate Matt's face. "That's not my story to tell." The boatswain took a few deep breaths to gather himself, and the slight smile returned. "Let's look through these crates, Battier?"

"Yeah."

The crates were sealed shut with nails and difficult to open. The boxes were very prone to giving splinters to anyone who gingerly ran their flesh across the wood. Matt used his sturdy gully knife to pry the boxes open. The contents changed with each crate. The first one held ten rum bottles.

Matt's agape mouth merged into a smile. "The lads may kill us if they found out you and I left these behind."

"Why?"

"You keep pirates from their rum, and they're prone to go mad."

"I thought rum was the source of madness. That's what my father said."

Matt picked up one of the hefty bottles and examined it.

"Well, he's not wrong." A look came over him as if he just had an idea. "Suppose you're the one that found these..."

"What are you on about?" Eddie asked.

"Lotta the crew are hesitant about you. I mean, they'll give you the benefit of the doubt because of your father, but they don't trust you, especially with your reputation. But if we claim you found this crate of rum and you brought it to my attention... they'll treat you like their own flesh n' blood."

Anything I can do to get them to like me.

The following two crates consisted of rotten food. There was bread nearly consumed in all by ants and maggots that had claimed the salted pork as their own. The smell of the sour meat made Eddie gag and come close to vomiting, but he held it in.

Matt put the lid back on the two crates. "Best keep those two closed."

While Eddie was still recovering from the smell and trying to keep his breakfast down, Matt opened the final crate in the hold. "That's what I like to see," he said, whistling lowly. "Eddison, get over here."

He straightened up and looked in the crate to see an assortment of weaponry and straps. Matt removed a harness of thin leather that had a shoulder guard as well. He placed it over Eddie's body to get the measure of it and tightened the straps around the waist. "Hopefully, we can loosen this once you get meat on y'bones," Matt said

He was familiar with the sword and gun belt his father and brothers wore. However, he'd never seen one that went over the shoulders and down to the waist.

"This is a prize, Eddison. I'm tellin' ya."

"Why's that?"

"Oh, these harnesses have better control. Your effects won't be bouncing all over," he said, tightening the final strap that was sealed with a belt loop. "Now, let's complete the en... ensymbol... onnsemble?"

"Ensemble?"

"There it is," Matt said, rather cheery, as he removed a sheathed cutlass. Then, he reached back in and returned with a holstered flintlock pistol.

Eddie was hesitant. "I'm not so sure about that. I don't know how to use it."

Matt attached it anyway. "Well, the concept's simple. You pull back on the hammer, aim, and shoot. You're smart. You shouldn't have any issues. If so, I'll teach ya not to worry."

Eddie stood there with a sword and pistol at his side for the first time. He raised his chin in the air like Avery and his brothers instructed him to do. He enjoyed the soldier-like quality and power it gave him as the thought of bloodshed weighed down his bones.

Matt seemed to take notice. "Eddison, it's going to be okay."

He forced a smile, genuinely trying to trust his new friend.

"Let's go surprise some pirates with more rum while we can."

TWENTY-EIGHT
SHARKEYES V

Her back was still stinging from the flogging she received at the hands of Lieutenant Colbe. Thoughts of revenge flowed through her. It took hours for her hands to unclench fully, and when they did, soreness found her, and her fingers involuntarily closed.

Night fell. Eralia forwent her own pain to rub ointment on Avery's back. It was tender to the touch, and she had to fight the urge to arch her back. "The first time is always the worst," her grandmother said.

Alexious paced in circles inside the tent, furiously rubbing his thumbs together. "We must fight. If this continues at this pace, our people will be enslaved beyond the point of no return or die off entirely."

"What can we do?" Eralia said. "The numbers aren't in our favor. We can't combat their guns either."

"It's gone on far enough. They are removing us from our homes—homes that have been ours for a thousand years."

The ointment stung, but the pain quickly subsided as the cooling and medicinal effects took hold.

"Are you all right, my dear?" Eralia asked.

"They shouldn't be able to get away with what they're doing," Avery replied.

"I know, Avery," Alexious agreed in a fumed state. "Not even a week! Not even a full week and our granddaughter is flogged for minor defiance. When will it stop? When will they move us? When will they eradicate us all? When they claim the entire continent!"

"Surely there is something we can do," Avery insisted, eyeing her grandparents. "They don't know these lands. That has to mean something to the Trezbe."

Eralia gave Avery a fresh shirt with no bloodstains.

The ointment was made from the fat her grandmother said was an Oka deer. The smell was similar to that of rotting meat. The scent of oasis lavender failed in its attempt to mask the stench.

Alexious picked up Avery's bloodied shirt off the ground and looked at it with longing before scoffing. He looked into Avery's dark eyes and went to an unlocked chest that acted as a nightstand beside the fur-covered bed. She couldn't see the contents of the chest from where she was sitting. He lifted the inside compartment out of the wooden box and placed it on the floor. He stopped, and the longing in his gaze manifested once more.

He returned to Avery with both hands full and misty eyes. "It may seem like an odd keepsake, but this was your mother's shirt after her first battle when she was fourteen years of age." Alexious offered both shirts for Avery to admire, and she did.

The sizes were the exact same. Her mother's top also had bloodstains and sported an aged yellow tint. There was a feeling of pride in where she came from. She always respected Mother, but as she learned more, her admiration for her grew.

"I also have these." Alexious handed her something wrapped in a series of leather straps. She unraveled it, and the pair of tre-axes were easy enough to hold with one hand each.

"Those were also your mother's. I've managed to keep those hidden well after this disarmament."

Having a scholarly knowledge of nearly every weapon, she knew the majority of the metal at the head of the axe was iron aside from the tip, which was steel. The poll, opposite the blade, had a hard surface for hammering, and by rotating the knob at the bottom of the handle, a knife could be removed. They were some of the most versatile weapons, and they made the Trezbe a nightmare on the battlefield.

Alexious squeezed Avery's shoulders. "Those, of course, are a pair of the finest axes we have ever made. You may think them twins, but they are quadruplets. Ianthia wields the other two. Adelaide left them behind with us when she left with your father."

Their beauty was unparalleled. Carved into the smooth wood handle was a tree where the branches traveled up the neck. The axe head had etchings of symbols Avery didn't know aside from the Trezbe crest. That symbol was littered across Caste Valley, even under provincial and Assembly flags. The crest was a tree growing out of a pool of water to represent the oasis and its Spring of Many Gifts.

"Hopefully, you won't have to use them anytime soon," Alexious said. "But if you need to, I'm sure your mother would be honored if you had them."

While the pain softened, the soreness remained. Every time she arched her back, her muscles constricted.

Alexious knelt in front of her upon seeing her grimace. "I am so sorry, Avery."

She accepted his apology, even though she didn't believe it necessary. The weapons fueled her like kindling to a dying flame. She opened her arms and hugged him, axes still in hand.

"Easy now," he said with a laugh as the axe heads were close to the back of his neck.

Avery's focus shifted to the problem and issues at hand.

The fire in her belly grew. "What are we going to do about this?" she asked.

His gaze softened, and a grin followed. "You're my granddaughter. There's no questioning that." He patted her shoulder once more. "I don't know what to do. I can't see a scenario where we fight back and don't lose the majority of our people." He paced around the tent once more. "It's a terrible thing being a leader when something like this happens. No matter the circumstances. No matter the conflict. I am at fault for what has taken place. And perhaps that's how it should be."

"You're not at fault," Eralia said as she prepped the harness for the axes, adjusting the sizing around Avery's waist and shoulders. "And we still have hope. Ianthia is still out there. We would know if they'd caught her. They wouldn't miss that chance to grab us by the hair and gloat."

"Perhaps," Alexious said.

"Aunt Ianthia?" Avery asked. "What do you mean she's still out there?"

"It didn't happen all at once. The foreigners we thought were potential allies turned out to be lions disguised as sheep. They were looking to colonize at our expense all along." Alexious turned grim. "First, they took a patch of land for themselves along the northern shore. We didn't mind, and I allowed it as a peace offering. But that's the problem with lions, Avery. They don't want to share their prey. They want it all for themselves."

He stopped telling the story, turned, and stared into the lit fire in the middle of the tent. The smoke rose past his head and disappeared through the opening in the ceiling with the moonlight shining through.

"They started mobilizing their troops and claiming more and more territory for themselves, and our boundaries drastically shrank," Eralia said, taking over for her husband. "They claimed dominion over the smaller clans' territory first, the Ryma, Qay, Cindah, and the K'izin. The three largest and more centralized clans – us, the Idush, and the Ruamont – offered more resistance but were taken all the same. After making the climb, Ianthia started a resistance of Trezbe and tried to unite the clans, but her efforts hadn't proved fruitful. I guess even a foreign occupation doesn't erase thousands of years of bloodshed."

"The climb?"

"The Keewaul. The vision quests we Trezbe take to the top of Mount Calibre. That is where she found her destiny."

Avery scrunched her nose. "And she's had no success at all since the climb?"

"Some of the smaller clans put forth their numbers. Still, that isn't much of a resistance." Alexious said. "We need the Idush and the Ruamont to swallow their pride, or else. All the clans are being relocated to the same place. If we can't put aside our differences by then, we will all die together."

"That's what they want. That's to their benefit," Eralia said.

Thundering hooves shook the ground beneath them and settled outside the tent. From the looks on her grandparents' faces, it seemed irregular. Quickened boots circled them. As everything seemed to halt outside, a single voice yelled, "Trezbe Clan, please come outside. Though my tone is friendly, it shall change if you do not comply!"

"That's Captain Weese," Eralia said with wide eyes.

"Who's Captain Weese?" Avery asked.

Alexious went to the tent entryway. "He's overseeing our removal," he said, marching towards the entry and throwing the tent flap over his shoulder.

"Alexious," Eralia called him back. It didn't work.

Avery gently placed her weapons down at her feet, and her grandmother helped her stand. In all the discussion, she had forgotten about the pain in her back. She wondered how her grandmother was still holding up without any sign of discomfort.

The night air brought ease that was snuffed by the sight of hundreds of greencoats cramped between the web of clan tents with rifles at the ready. The watchtowers that were strategically placed throughout Caste Valley were stocked with musketeers in the wraparound nests.

Avery was met with a smiling Lieutenant Colbe just outside the main tent. "Hello there, half-breed," he said softly and followed that by blowing a kiss.

Emerging through the sea of green was who she believed was Captain Weese. He was tall, and his ponytail went down to the middle of his back. He made himself comfortable in the humid Redrainn climate as his sleeves were rolled up to the elbow. His mustache curled.

Weese removed a three-tallied pin from his captain's coat and placed it on his shirt collar. "Congratulations are in order," he said in Aelic, scanning the Trezbe people, who were exiting their homes in a fatigued state. All of them wore matching dirty shirts and short cotton bottoms as their animal skin and leather armor were no longer allowed. "You all have done a fine job of crafting your traveling necessities. Now it is time to put them to good and final use. Your new home awaits you in Okamara."

Trezbe eyes looked around at one another.

"Beginning tomorrow, you will start the relocation process, meaning at first light, the first wave of you will leave Caste Valley, followed by the next wave, and so on and so forth. Okamara is a fine plot of land gleaming with life, inspiration, and possibility." A smile curled his mustache, and his fellow greencoats shared their commanding officer's delight.

As he walked, Weese locked eyes with many of the clan folk. He had no fear in his eyes as hate stared back at him. "It will be a long night for all of you. Make sure you have everything you need, which won't be much due to limited space. But I'm sure you more primitive folk will thrive nevertheless," Captain Weese said, rolling his sleeves even tighter. "You know, my Trezbe friends, we live in a hierarchal world. Look at you all. Look at us. Our systems and the way we go about existing aren't so different..."

To Avery, he seemed to be rambling and didn't look like he had a point.

"Aren't they?" he asked rhetorically. "The mighty Trezbe Clan ruled over Autera, and the noble Assembly stakes its dominion over Renera."

He enjoys addressing everyone.

He seemed to have aspirations of being an actor or a politician based on his performance. "But let's not forget how the hierarchy of things works. Things cannot be equal. One thing will always be greater than what's beneath it. I suppose from your vantage point, it's easy to see your place on the steep mountain of significance. Especially now, as you look up at the empire casting a shadow over you." Captain Weese paused for a moment and basked in the hostility. "Which brings me to the more difficult yet necessary aspects about maintaining hierarchy."

Weese glanced back at a collection of his men and gave them a look that they already knew while the Trezbe were left in confusion.

The first person they rushed and grabbed was Alexious. He contested and fought back. The butt of a rifle slammed across the side of his face and knocked him unconscious.

"No!" Eralia and Avery yelled as they both went to help, but they were stopped by the sharp edges of bayonets inches away from their foreheads.

"You two aren't going anywhere," Lieutenant Colbe said. "This may hurt worse than the flogging."

Five more men around Alexious' age were brought before Weese. Avery assumed they were elders of the Trezbe Clan.

The home crowd of clan people were upset and pleading for answers, but the greencoats held them at bay.

"It's time to usher in the new," Weese said. The greencoats lined the six Trezbe men shoulder to shoulder, including her grandfather, who were all on their knees in a haze. "You have no use for the past any longer. Your future awaits you in Okamara."

The captain signaled a group of his men to ready their rifles and take aim at the elders. Avery glared down the bayonet, inches away from her nose. Shouts for mercy filled the night sky.

Captain Weese wasn't hearing any of them, and he said, "Fire."

Muzzles flashed, and smoke filled the air. The quiet disbelief was haunting as Avery looked back at Eralia, who had gone pale.

The smoke cleared, and all the elders, including her grandfather Alexious, no longer moved in the dirt. The laughing amongst the greencoats made Avery's stomach churn.

"Bury their bodies and memories here." With that, Captain Weese casually put his coat back on, cracked his neck, and climbed atop his horse. "Good night" was the captain's last words as he and his troops dispersed.

TWENTY-NINE
THE FORMER V

He awoke to a knock at his front door. Xavier had fallen asleep on his deck that faced the ocean. The morning dew made him damp. Part of him wondered if it was sweat from his horrid nightmares. He never remembered his dreams, and perhaps it was for the best. When he was little, he would find himself shaken awake by his mother and father from screaming fits while sleeping. Those were now fleeting memories, lost to time.

"Xavier?" Lieutenant Chiesa said.

He stood from his reclining chair and wiped the moisture from his face with the palm of his hand. "Around back," he said, ushering his longtime trainer through the white sand alleyway.

As Chiesa walked up the steps, wearing a faded brown jacket and tricorne hat, he asked, "Everything all right, son?"

He looked like a common man today. Chiesa wasn't wearing his lieutenant's coat, and he looked a bit under the weather. His face was pale, and he had bags under his eyes.

"Yes, Lieutenant. Are you all right?"

"Don't go through with this, Xavier," Chiesa's masculine voice cracked.

"Beg your pardon?"

"You shouldn't have to prove your loyalty like this."

Xavier looked off, observing the ships sailing leaving and entering the Grand Harbor, wishing he was aboard the one drifting into the horizon.

"You know who helped your brother escape the noose?" Chiesa went on.

"I have an idea," Xavier admitted.

"Fili hasn't responded to my letters since I left Roguewave. I know he's with Caldwell."

"Looks that way." Xavier put his shirt on and tightened the laces around his neck.

The beach had come alive. Families frolicked in the calm waters and sunned on blankets while seagulls in abundance flew overhead. *All this peace has to come at some price.*

As Xavier looked out over the vast, light blue ocean, the heavy steps of the lieutenant crept behind him.

"Fili is my son. Caldwell is your brother."

Xavier raised his eyebrows and crossed his arms. "And?"

Chiesa leaned forward, fingers curled into fists, "That means something."

"What's it mean, exactly? They all committed treason."

"Treason?" Lieutenant Chiesa leaned his back against the railing and put his chin high in the air, letting the ocean breeze run across his face. "And how are you supposed to exercise this justice? Kill them?"

"Or arrest them," Xavier said.

"Arrest them and bring them back here to be hanged!" Chiesa snapped, eyes alight. "They die, either way, Xavier!"

Xavier tried not to show an ounce of emotion. He didn't want to offer his lieutenant anything to interpret. A wave crashed, filling the silence between them.

"I sailed alongside your father, fought with him, bled with him. I knew him quite well."

Xavier rubbed his face and shook his head like a wet dog attempting to get dry. "What of it?"

"Over twenty years ago, we engaged a pirate vessel in the Tearing Sea. Certainly, you know how the Tearing Sea got its name?"

Xavier knew, but he wouldn't say. He didn't want to give Chiesa the satisfaction of compliance in the conversation. But in his mind, he said the famous words associated with that body of water: *filled to the brim with the tears of those who've sailed these waters.*

"You wouldn't believe how cold it was," Chiesa continued. "Every drop of water that landed on you from an unforgiving wave burned. It was so cold. But we overcame the sea and the pirates all the same. The pirate captain, Captain Trance, died in the fighting. Your father and I assisted in clearing the hold. It was in the dark when we heard the sounds of a crying baby. As a barren man, unable to have children, I thought some cruel god was mocking me in the silence or some ghost with a sick sense of humor haunted me. But the cries continued, and we found the lone child. Your father looked to me and said, 'A gift from above comes in peculiar ways, aye?'"

Xavier said nothing.

"Show your brother mercy. Show Fili mercy. Please."

"What would you have me do? Defy the Assembly?" Xavier loudly whispered, making sure to keep his voice low as his eyes scanned their surroundings.

"Find a way to let them go. Let them escape to the Free Islands. Give them a chance."

Xavier cocked his head in disbelief. "*You're* telling me this? You? The man who taught me always to execute the mission at all costs—to *win* at all costs. How dare you?"

"You're right. I have taught you that," Chiesa said as he looked off and shook his head. "But if you can't see that there are exceptions to the rule, that there are things more important like family, then I'm sorry, I have failed you." Chiesa wiped the sweat off his forehead with his forearm. "Xavier, I'll ask you again. I'll do whatever it takes to help, just don't go through with this."

Xavier contemplated his lieutenant's wishes while looking out over the water. It was to the east he saw a ship heading west to pass under the Sea Bridge. It wasn't a Grand Ship but a treasure galleon sailing to claim resources from somewhere beyond. His longing for the sea grew.

"I've been given orders. I'm sorry. I can't," Xavier said as he kept his gaze away.

"Xavier, you're capable of so much, and yet you don't realize you do so little that means anything."

His heart blackened as the words poured from Chiesa's mouth. All his hard work, all that time and sweat, and blood he'd wasted on a man who wouldn't even recognize it. "Good day, Lieutenant," Xavier said before retreating into his beach house.

~

To our loyal countryman, Xavier Battier,

We, the powers that be, understand the task given to you and know its challenge. It's not easy bringing justice to anyone, let alone flesh and blood. We ask that you bring honor back to your father's name by further casting aside those that would tarnish a legacy so strong. Please accept these gifts on our behalf and use them to shine Assembly light.

Moonrise was bred and trained by the most exceptional horse breeder Leighton has to offer, Ran

Harrison. The rifles were smithed by Lloyd Cunninghall, the man who revolutionized firearms. The blade, as you may know, is a helm sabre, a straighter and more effective combat blade forged by Ilya Stipe. We hope all these things can provide you with all that you require. We hope these offerings show you the respect we have for your potential.

Lastly, the pistol, though aged in its appearance, fires proficiently. It should have value to you, as it was your father's during the Pirate Rebellion. It was used to defeat his enemies. To defeat those who put their desires above their country and to cast aside traitors.

With Respect,

The Assembly

Xavier took a deep breath and tucked the letter into his breast pocket. A galloping rider sounded on the Grand Road as he waited outside the city gates near the stables where Moonrise was kept. The beautiful stallion's black coat glistened in the midday as he frolicked in the pen before being prepared and brought to him.

All of Xavier's new weaponry was secured to perfection on the custom-made saddle. His rifles were strapped to the left side, while his sword was on the right.

Sitting atop the slowing horse, peeling off the road was Declan Cross. Xavier's former opponent pulled the reins on his steed and hopped down with a swiftness that wasn't at all surprising after seeing it first-hand.

"Greetings, Battier," Declan said with a genuine smile while offering a handshake.

Xavier nodded. "Morning."

Declan's long blond hair was still tied back on the top, while the rest of it was straight down to his shoulders. "You look well met. That's an incredible stallion and sword you have there."

Xavier was actually inclined to agree with him.

Declan petted Moonrise and eyed the sword in its sheath. "May I?"

"Sure."

Declan drew the sword that sang upon its removal. It shined as his steed did in the Helmburough sun. The hilt was dark silver, and the guard curled and formed crashing waves going into the blade to represent his home. The slight curve that Declan observed led him to look upon the signature.

"There's no mistaking Ilya Stipe's work, is there?" Declan said, giving the sword back.

"I'm surprised you don't have one," Xavier replied.

Declan tapped the sword dangling from his side. It wasn't a drab sword by any stretch of the imagination, but there was nothing special about it either. "My father doesn't believe I deserve the honor quite yet."

Xavier nodded, but he didn't agree with the reasoning.

"Do you have everything you need?" Declan asked. "Looks like it's going to be a long mission for us. We'll have to take the Grand Road all the way through Ghonia, and then it's either Brickford or Vester."

"I travel light," Xavier said shortly. "There are plenty of stops along the way, so we shouldn't have to worry about food until we get to Fort Pierce."

"I was thinking the same thing. Glad to know we're on the same page." Declan frowned, dipping his head. "I apologize for how they've run your family's name into the dirt in the papers."

Xavier stopped him with a hand. "I don't read those."

"Still, I'm sorry."

Xavier ended that conversation before it went any further. "Will the others arrive soon? I figured they'd be with you."

Declan went along with the change in subject, shaking his head. "I don't know. I was instructed to meet here and wasn't given any more information."

"You mean, you don't know the others coming with us?"

Declan scratched his scalp and shook his head side to side. "No, I don't."

I figured the man leading this mission would at least know the soldiers accompanying him.

"I'm going to get into some shade before they arrive," Declan said. He leaned against a hitching rail underneath the stable awning. "Did your father teach you how to fight?"

Xavier was annoyed by the attempt to make small talk. But he obliged. "Some. How about you?"

"Some. When he was home, that is. Most of my formal training came from Lieutenant Beamer."

Xavier knew the name. Silas Beamer. He sailed as weapons master for Talon Kuake aboard the Grand Ship *Chimera.*

"He taught me more than my father ever did," Declan went on. "Is that the same for your lieutenant?"

Xavier cracked his sore neck. "No," he said.

"Well, either way, perhaps our rematch is on the horizon."

"Perhaps," Xavier said, watching the horses graze the large grass fields outside the capital walls. "I don't know if I care much anymore."

The frown and nod of understanding manifested itself once again on Declan's face. "Good," he said.

Xavier wondered what his fellow duelist meant, but he didn't think about it too hard.

Two men rode upon them quickly out of nowhere. They were riddled with battle scars on their faces and wore three-tallied pins. They were a hardened-looking duo.

"Declan Cross?" one of them asked with little to no enthusiasm.

"Aye," Declan replied.

"You're commanding this mission?"

"I am."

There was a long stare from both of them before they glanced back at each other. They were Xavier and Declan's elders by at least ten years and didn't seem pleased about serving under someone so young. They were well met, with four rifles strapped to their horses and two swords apiece.

"Very well. I'm Wiggins," the first man said. "And this is Aaron."

It seemed Aaron didn't do much talking.

Avery would call this one a sourmope.

Declan left his shade and went to his horse. "Well, I suppose there's no reason to stand around. Xavier, anything you'd like to say?"

"No."

"Very well," Declan said, taking command of this mission. "Let's head out."

Xavier climbed atop Moonrise. Declan rode out ahead with Wiggins and Aaron behind. Xavier took one last look at the horses in the nearby pen, free in every sense of the word. His gaze turned forward, and he set out north with his new companions on the Grand Road.

THIRTY

THE AIDMAN V

Caldwell bathed in the river with the moonlight casting bright and blue. The water was cold. He couldn't submerge himself fully, so he scooped handfuls from the river to wash. The hastened travel had taken a toll on him and his friends, along with their new companions, Alred and Simone. As de facto leader to Port Randolph, it was still over a hundred miles northeast, so tonight, he sought solace alone.

If his mapping was correct, the Greenmore River was tapering off and thinning as it stretched westward. All Caldwell desired now was to be on the next ship to the Free Islands, for the provinces only brought him exhaustion, spite, and saddle sores.

"What did you lot do?"

Before Caldwell had come to the water's edge, he thought everyone in his company was asleep, so the sudden question in the dark sent a jolt through his body.

"What do you mean?" Caldwell said to the middle-aged Alred.

"I mean, I'd like to know what you and your friends are running from," Alred asked, planting the butt of his rifle in the dirt. "You're fair traveling companions, but over the last day, one subject has been off-limits, and that is why you're trying to get to the Free Islands. Seems to me you're trying to avoid the Assembly as well. I'd like to know why."

Caldwell didn't have any reason to lie to the man. Given Alred's circumstances, it figured him an honest man. "I was given a choice to denounce my family and serve the Assembly for the rest of my days or die."

"Doesn't sound like much of a choice," Alred said, squatting on a large rock and resting his gun across his lap.

"Aye, no, it doesn't."

"The powers that be are good at that, only giving one real choice that fits with their desires."

Caldwell drenched a piece of cloth in the river and placed it across the back of his neck.

"I don't get how your friends fit into all this, though," Alred continued.

"They freed me on my way to hang at Salty Pointe."

"Huh, some good friends you got," Alred muttered as he relieved himself behind a tree. He spoke rather loud at a distance. It wasn't as quiet as Caldwell would've preferred. "I'm sure word has reached every port and harbor, looking for you, including Port Randolph."

"They don't know what we look like," Caldwell said.

"Eh, maybe they have wanted posters printed on posts or in the papers. Perhaps you all should board different ships. If they don't know what you look like, then they'll be looking for the four of you traveling together."

He felt like an idiot for not thinking of that beforehand. Caldwell liked to believe he contemplated everything thoroughly enough, but perhaps not. Lucky for him, Alred was already making himself useful.

"That's good counsel," Caldwell said.

As he continued his private business in the bush, Alred said, "I've gotten good at hiding and staying anonymous. Believe that."

Caldwell returned to the water, and, from his kneeling position, he watched the river flow. The sounds of nature enveloped the night as the crickets clicked all around. Frogs croaked and hopped in and out of the water. The atmosphere brought a sense of peace in the echo chamber of despair in his mind.

Sitting atop a log, popping out of the river, was a spiked owl with brown and black feathers and serrated horns poking out its head. It stared at him with its head turned upside down. *A strange sight that is.* The owl's head was unwavering as if it were leering into Caldwell's being.

It was then he realized it wasn't an ordinary spiked owl.

No, a recon owl.

"Get into the trees!" Caldwell yelled to Alred. He grabbed the musket that was leaning against a nearby tree and took aim at the owl.

As if the bird knew what was happening, it soared straight upward. In the dead of night, the booming blast echoed for miles. He removed the ramrod from under the barrel and loaded another cartridge of black powder and musket ball.

The owl was getting away. Caldwell tracked it with his rifle as it continued west. He fired again. Another miss caused him to curse himself.

Caldwell loaded another. Only this time, he ran along the bank of the river to follow the bird.

His friends had awakened by this time and were following behind him.

Emil was the first to question, "Caldwell! What is it?"

"Recon owl!" he replied.

There were a series of rocks and jagged boulders he had to climb to get a clear shot. Only the moonlight illuminated the owl, as it was becoming a black pebble shrinking in the distance. Caldwell was able to line up his shot with the low-hanging branch of a tree in front of his face. He lined his sights and placed them directly on that wretched beast.

The small spark from the hammer striking the breech and the muzzle flash was nearly blinding. As his eyes came to focus and the blur faded. The owl, still in flight, disappeared under cover of night.

A feeling of uneasiness originated from his stomach and crept outward into a warm heat radiating on his neck.

He turned to his friends, who were staring at him wide-eyed and at attention. "We need to move."

The owl was flying in the direction of Fort Pierce. It would now be able to escort the greencoats or whoever to their location, even while they were on the move. *If time wasn't on our side before, it's certainly not now.*

A downpour slowed them to a halt. Caldwell wanted to keep pushing onward, but the wagon's wheels were sinking into the mud.

"Caldwell, we have to stop!" Maynard yelled through the rain.

"No! We need to keep going!"

They carried on.

Through the muck and the rain, the terrain of the forest became denser and slicker. Caldwell found it hard to find his footing as they ascended a steep hill.

"Is there a way around it?" Emil yelled.

"Perhaps we should go farther south and see if the land levels out!" Alred proposed.

"South's the opposite way! Can't go south!" Caldwell yelled.

The horses were aggravated and showing their discomfort as they resisted every yank on their reins.

The trees were claustrophobic. Brickford wasn't known for its expansive woods.

The rain peppered Caldwell's head to a near-torturous

degree. His clothes were soaked, and his companions looked discouraged.

Fili's arms were shaking uncontrollably from the cold. Maynard was the only one still atop his horse. That didn't last long as his steed became so agitated that it bucked. He tried his best to stay on, but his grip didn't prove strong enough, and he was thrown off hard.

He slid down the wet and muddy hill. Maynard looked like a corpse as he never attempted to catch himself. Emil went to help but fell along with him. They struck trees on their way down the hill. Though Emil was able to soften the blow due to his consciousness, Maynard wasn't so lucky. He was caked in blackened mud from head to toe, and only the illuminating lightning strikes revealed his location.

"Maynard!" Caldwell yelled to no response.

"Caldwell, we need to stop! We've got to get warm and dry out!" Fili called out.

"Let's get into the wagon. We can use the oil lamps to warm up!" Alred said.

Caldwell didn't hear their proposals. He sprinted into a slide down the hill, passing Emil, who was picking himself off the ground with aid from a low-hanging tree branch.

He couldn't find traction himself. Caldwell rammed into his friend with his knee on accident. Maynard had disappeared into the muck. "Maynard!" Caldwell yelled.

He wiped the mud off Maynard's face. Much of it was in his mouth and far up his nose.

As Maynard came to, panic seized his eyes. He whipped his head from side to side, scraping away the muck on his face and wheezing for breath.

"What happened?" he asked.

"You fell!" Caldwell replied, leading him back up the hill.

Not one, but two strikes of lightning in rapid succession struck a tree around thirty feet away. *Lightning never strikes the same place twice. Huh.* Caldwell wondered if that was just another lie told to him.

Emil took Maynard's hand and pulled him up from the sinking mud, then Caldwell. "*We* have to get in the wagon!" Emil said.

The rain hadn't let up. Caldwell stood there while his friends awaited his order. He didn't ask to be in command, but he was. The only thing he ever wanted in life was to help others. That had been taken from him. His three friends gave up their lives to save him, and now he was responsible for them. While he was grateful, he hadn't asked for that either. And now, a father and daughter had put their trust in him. Caldwell had given them hope. Hope that, in the end, could prove false.

He didn't reply to Emil. He marched past him up the hill to the two horses that were stagnant in the storm. They were so still that Caldwell wondered if the thunder had petrified them.

He grabbed their reins and pulled.

"Caldwell!" he heard them repeatedly yell, commanding him to come inside.

With all his strength, he yanked and pulled on those reins. His feet sunk into the mud so deep it was up to his knees. The horses didn't budge.

"Damn it, come on!"

More yells. "Caldwell!"

He blocked them out. To him, the most important thing was getting to safety, getting the ones who put their trust in him to safety.

The rope was tensed straight. Caldwell couldn't pull any harder.

"Come on!" he yelled once more.

After that, he mistakenly held his breath while gripping the rope. The last thing he remembered before falling on his back was how he could feel the veins in his arms and neck bulging.

From his back, he stared into the sky, watching the flashing pockets of light burst behind the clouds. The trees swayed back and forth from the relentless wind. The mud covered his entire body, but he didn't resist sinking into the world. It was almost cathartic as the mud clogged his ears, and all he could hear was the echoes of the natural world.

He closed his eyes, and he screamed at the sky as loud and fierce as he could. He did it over and over again until the cords in the back of his throat began to rattle.

"Why! What did we do?" he shouted at the storm. Caldwell didn't even know who he was asking or whether he even wanted a response. Perhaps he was asking the many gods of the warring clans, or maybe the Creator.

The only reply was thunder. And with that hollow answer, he cried. On any other day, he would have felt ashamed for doing so, but on this night, he couldn't help it or fight it off. The rain spattered across his face, and he felt lucky his tears were indiscernible from it.

As he lay there and cried, thinking of his family, he opened his eyes to see his friends standing there with extended arms. "It's okay, brother," Emil said.

Caldwell took their hands, and his brothers hoisted him from the mud.

The heat in the carriage was more than welcome. The six of them were covered in blankets they had fortunately taken from Alred's home. Caldwell was still trying to find his way up after his emotional low.

"Suppose you all well know by now that the weather is pretty unpredictable here," Alred said.

"We gathered that," Emil replied with a straight face.

The rain pelted the roof of the wooden carriage. Caldwell

was still shaking from the cold and wet. However, out of the downpour, he felt more at peace. The rain that, moments ago, was an obstacle was now a song. In his haze, he hummed an improvised melody. He noticed the heads around him perk upward, and he didn't care.

He looked at the afflicted Simone, who seemed to be smiling for the first time since they'd met. She looked to her father, and Alred returned with a smile of his own. The gentle and high-pitched voice of the girl filled the undersized canvas auditorium. She postured up against the side.

"You don't know what you've started, Caldwell," Alred said with a chuckle.

> Cast a shadow, cast away,
> The lamps have all died; light's gone today
> But I see a pleasant place
> A place of lush, where no one's cried or wears
>   a solemn face
> Masses have passage
> Embers and ashes
> No clashes of classes
> We are primal, forever, and final
> for all our days

She sang those words over three times, putting them all near-catatonic. When she finished, it was silent other than the sound of rain. Fili broke the silence with a cheerful clap, and the rest joined.

"Brava!" they all told her. "Brava!"

THIRTY-ONE
THE SILENT ONE V

Isla was able to claim one of the many spare rooms of the Emerson Estate as her own for now. She stayed locked in her room, furnished with the finest wooden furniture. Her bed was fitted for a queen. It had posts at all four corners with a canopy at the top. Leo curled up on a wool blanket at the foot of the bed. He could enjoy the comfort of wealth, but her mind was too preoccupied to enjoy much of anything. Isla feared he wasn't getting enough exercise being cooped up, but Leo seemed to handle the change of pace well.

Isla sat at a desk that took up as much space as the bed. It wrapped around her as three long shelves on the desktop had been emptied for Isla's hobbies. The only problem with having that amount of shelf space staring directly at her was that she had no hobbies. Prior, she often pondered what she could fill the shelves with, along with her bored and static mind.

After meeting Sadollah, her mind had one goal. One goal only.

Defeat your enemies.

She ran the palm of her hand across the leatherbound cover of the ledger she found in her father's office. She untied the strap that wrapped around it several times and opened its contents.

She rifled through for a long time, consuming page after page, hoping to find anything of value. The papers seemed to be letters discussing trade, routes and manifests of ships throughout the waters surrounding Renera. Page after page revealed similar results. Nothing written on them appeared to be anything worth keeping secret.

A few letters were between two people known as Eustice Pike and George Verbal. One of their exchanges read:

Dear Mr. Pike,

Travel has been well. The seas have been kind, and the winds gentle yet firm. We are en route to Tyver Island to trade for a lump sum of silk for the Assembly. We had to stop at Port Spryte in Pennyway to purchase some hearty steaks and rum so we can hopefully see this trade through. And though the best rum in the world comes from Tyver, we were running low, and you, as well as I, know that keeping spirits up on an expedition is critical to success. Unfortunately, on the journey, some of our wheat barrels spoiled from inadequate containment. Apologies. My boatswains did not do a proper inspection—more letters to follow.

Best Regards,

Captain Verbal

She spent hours looking through all of them, trying to

decipher something of importance. Then, she became discouraged. *Maybe I'm not smart enough to see what's going on in these letters or even mature enough.*

Isla left the ledger open on the desk and leaned backward on the rear legs. She looked at the high ceiling and felt a nudge on her lap. Leo put his big paws on her thigh to place the chair on all fours. *Always keeping me safe, aren't you, buddy?*

His spongey fur was softer than ever. Livian made sure he was bathed often to keep the house clean. Isla petted him along the spine as he circled the chair, pining for attention. He rested his head in her lap and seemed to intend on staying forever by the way his hindquarters dropped.

Defeat your enemies. Defeat your enemies. Defeat your enemies.

Having looked over the papers for several hours, Isla decided to cut her losses and take a break. The days since separating from her family brought more rain. Today was no different. A cloudy overcast made that dower atmosphere remain.

In the parlor, she saw Oliver and his eyes affixed upon the weekly paper. Isla's quiet nature left her in secret. However, Leo's nails tapping on the hardwood floor gave away their position.

Oliver crinkled the paper and glanced up with his spectacles on the edge of his nose, and quickly removed them.

"Is everything all right?" she signed to him.

He folded the sheets and rested them on his crossed legs. The spectacles that he removed from his face were folded in the same delicate manner and pocketed in his jacket.

"Uh–yes," he stammered.

"Did you meet the new governor?" Isla asked.

"I did."

"And?"

He laughed. "He's a politician. So, my first impressions

were a bit skewed, but he appeared not to be the man he presented to everyone."

Isla wasn't exactly sure what to think of that. "What's that mean?"

"I supposed we will have to wait and see, love." His smile faded as the newspaper gripped his attention. "I don't want ever to lie or keep anything from you, Isla," he signed. "You've been through too much for that disservice." Oliver motioned her over and revealed the paper's title of *The Weekly Rogue: THE FALL OF THE HOUSE OF BATTIER.*

Isla took the thin pieces of paper and read through the vast article regarding "Adelaide Battier's treason" and how she was a "disgraced foreigner who spat on Mathias Battier's honorable name." It went on to say she had orchestrated the pirate raid on Molten Bay and that she would "rot in Colwerth Prison for eternity," and that the "clan folk are not to be trusted."

The article's author, Desmond Riley, emphasized, "That brave day. The day when the pirates brought down the East Flame Tower, it was Mathias Battier who rallied troops to push them back into the sea. The Savior of the Bay, we called him. And his foreign wife sought to ruin his legacy along with those same pirates who managed to capture our beloved Governor Tytus."

She looked at Oliver.

"It's a smear campaign, Isla, at your family's expense," he signed.

"Smear campaign?" Isla signed in return.

"Propaganda used to damage your family name."

"Why?"

"That, I don't know, my dear."

The writing went on further, speaking on how her brother and sister, Caldwell and Avery, were "partnering conspirators. Avery, the eldest girl, was sent back to Autera to live out the rest of her days with her own people of the Trezbe Clan, which is more mercy than the savage deserved. The two youngest children of Mathias and Adelaide Battier are still unaccounted for and are either kept in hiding or are most likely dead. If they died and were naive to their mother's actions, let us hope they find peace in life after. If they sympathized with their mother's cause, then good riddance to both of them."

The entirety of the following page was devoted to Caldwell. It accompanied crude and inaccurate portraits of him and his friends who had gone missing since Caldwell escaped imprisonment. A bounty of twenty thousand gold was placed on his head, and five thousand for his friends.

Isla ran her finger across the picture of her brother. Though the drawing didn't look exactly like him, it was still enough to bring forth sadness. However, with that, there was pleasantness seeing his face again. Caldwell had always been more occupied with education, but he was a good brother. Isla wished she were with him right now, along with the rest of them.

Get free, brother. Get free, Caldwell. Run.

The third and final page regarding the "Disgraced Battier Family" was a shift in tone for one member of their family who had "proven himself worthy to the Assembly and Unified Provinces."

It continued to talk about Xavier's commitment to the provinces and his denouncement of his family's action. And though he might be guilty by association, no one should cast a stone against him quite yet. "His loyalty has been tested, and he has paid his dues to deserve the potential for a pardon."

Isla didn't know what that meant. All she knew was how disappointed she was. While she knew Xavier to be selfish and had issues with her other siblings, he was always very kind to her.

Isla folded the paper and handed it back to Oliver.

"Desmond Riley is employed by the Assembly, Isla,"

Oliver signed. "I'm sure he was told to write this. It was his quill that graced the page, but the Assembly's words, believe that."

"How can they lie like that?" Isla's emotions swelled. "How can he write such things that aren't true?"

"I wish I had an answer that could satisfy you. But the harsh truth, Isla, is that they do it simply because they can. If it's any comfort, I know your family is not what this paper says they are. Whatever you need, Livian and I will continue to provide. The Battier name will not fall into nothingness if I have any say in the matter." He went on to pace around the room and stared disheartened out the window. "The capital bringing someone from Helmburough to govern here raises a lot of alarms. Above all else, it's an insult to democracy to allow such a thing to happen. We, the people of Roguewave, are supposed to decide our governor, not a group of people that don't even live here."

"What's that mean?" Isla asked.

"That means things are going to get even more difficult for us."

As dread crept back into her head, she remembered the letters upstairs.

Isla disengaged conversation with Oliver altogether and raced to her room. Leo kept pace right beside her.

She rummaged through the letters that had been exchanged between two men, and at the bottom, their names were signed. It didn't occur to her until now that neither of the names were her father's. Eustice Pike and George Verbal.

"What's this?" Oliver asked after following her up the stairs and placing a hand on her shoulder.

She made a decision at that moment. "I don't want to lie to you," she signed.

"What is it, Isla?"

"I..." Her hands stopped moving for a moment. "I broke

into my father's office and took these letters that were in a secret compartment."

Oliver's eyes widened. "You *what*? Isla, you could have gotten yourself captured or worse!" he scolded her, but he had too much love for her to commit his full anger. All he could do was stand sternly and place his hands on his hips. And as he leveled his emotions, he asked, "How did you even get into his office? It's under guard all day and night."

Isla didn't reply. Her slumped head was her response.

Oliver's hand lifted her chin in the air to make eye contact once more. "You are the silent one, aren't you? No one sees you coming," he signed with a smile. "Now, are you going to show me what you got?"

I couldn't have found myself in the hands of better people.

She turned to the desk and handed him around half of the letters exchanged between the two mystery men. "It's not my father's name at the bottom. Why keep these if they aren't his?"

Oliver examined them for a long while, going through every paper and reading the contents. Then, without saying anything, he left the room with the papers still in hand.

Isla went to grab him, but he was out of reach. She followed him to his study in the next room that overlooked the lush fields and gardens at the front of their estate. He went through drawer after drawer but didn't seem to find what he was looking for.

He stopped. At the edge of his desk was a tin box, which was the most ordinary thing in the room. He removed the lid and shuffled around what looked like small knickknacks and papers before removing one of them. He held a yellowed paper up to the letters and examined them.

Oliver made his way over to Isla in a hurry and motioned her to compare the letters from her father's desk and his own. She looked at him.

"That letter in the box was from your father. It was when

he wrote me years ago to ask for mine and Livian's assistance with helping you and your hearing," he signed.

She thought the sentiment was nice but didn't know how it was relevant. "I don't understand," Isla signed back.

"Look at the handwriting. It's clearly your father's. It appears he was using an assumed name. In this case, Eustice Pike. I could be wrong, but it seems like the recipient of these letters, George Verbal, is reporting back to your father on what's going on at sea and updated locations. While your father, Eustice, is giving this George what routes to take and where to go next."

Things were beginning to come together.

"Was there a manifest along with these letters, Isla?" Oliver asked.

"Manifest?" she signed.

"A list of things aboard the ship, what's it's carrying in its hold, passengers and crew aboard, something like that?"

She knew precisely what he meant and raced back to her room. The papers in the very back of the ledger were what she now knew were manifests. It was a detailed document offering up all the information Oliver was asking about, but as Isla looked at it with fresh eyes, still nothing came to her mind, and nothing seemed out of place. She didn't recognize any of the crew's names. The cargo consisted mostly of food, extra sails, freshwater, exotic plants, and animals. Her frustration grew as she struggled to put more pieces of this puzzle together.

Isla handed them over to Oliver to see if he could discover anything. In her defeated state, she looked over the ledger. It was a simple brown leather case, and it gave little to nothing away. That was until she noticed a tiny slit that ran across the interior of the ledger. Inside was a thin sheet of metal around the size of a pamphlet.

Rum - New Recruits

Silk - Ship in Need of Repair
Sugar - Guns
Wheat - Assembly Interference
Tobacco - Ember Dust
Salt - Ammunition
Meat - Losses
Unknown Animal - Mackereli Adult
Unknown Plant - Mackereli Child

She scratched her scalp. After all the struggle of not being able to figure out this mystery, she felt something—a rush. She became warm on the back of her neck, which continued throughout her body. It was the intensity of solving something more complex. A sense of pride came over her, and she thought of her little brother for a moment. *Eddie might've figured this out a long time ago. He was far better at this kind of stuff than me. I miss him.*

Isla held up one of the letters sent from George Verbal to Eustice Pike again.

Dear Mr. Pike,

Travel has been well. The seas have been kind, and the winds gentle yet firm. We are en route to Tyver Island to trade for a lump sum of silk for the Assembly. We had to stop at Port Spryte in Pennyway to purchase some hearty steaks and rum so we can hopefully see this trade through. And though the best rum in the world comes from Tyver, we were running low, and you, as well as I, know that keeping spirits up on an expedition *is critical to success. Unfortunately, on the journey, some of our wheat barrels spoiled from inadequate containment. Apologies, my boatswains did not do a proper inspection—more letters to follow.*

Best Regards,

Captain Verbal

Tapping Oliver on the shoulder, Isla demanded he scan it. His eyes widened farther, and he went for ink and a quill, underling the keywords: *silk, steaks, rum, wheat.*

"Seems like this Captain Verbal was telling your father his ship was damaged in a battle against Assembly forces and sustained casualties. If that is indeed what *losses* mean."

"But they also gathered some new recruits for their journey."

"Right, you are, Isla." He looked at her with a serious demeanor. "I suppose the question now is who is this Captain George Verbal, and why were he and your father speaking in code? Unless I missed my guess, they had something big planned."

THIRTY-TWO
THE WIDOW VI

Hunter-gatherer culture was familiar to Adelaide. It was how she used to survive as a Trezbe. She spent more of her time as the hunter, stalking mountain bulls, deer, and rabbits. Working for the Hannahs in endless fields of corn and wheat was a different kind of survival but amplified by way of being a foreigner in a foreign way of life. There was nothing to shield the long day sun from beating down on her and her fellow slave laborers.

It seemed clouds were rare in Leyfield, Helmburough. The skies were blue, and the agriculture rivaled the vast fields of Ghonia, where most grains were grown, and all of the cattle grazed for hundreds of miles.

Here, on the Hannah Estate, the poorest of the poor worked the fields and were compensated very little. Slavery in the Unified Provinces had been abolished for ordinary citizens. However, criminals could still be subject to slave labor. Even though she had it difficult, she only worked a half-day in the fields, and the rest of her time was spent serving Lady Charlotte.

It had been just over a week now for Adelaide at the Hannah Estate. While Charlotte didn't require much of her, she ensured the work was demeaning. Whether it was cleaning chambers (outhouse included), brushing the lady's hair as she bathed, preparing three meals a day, or standing right behind her with a decanter of wine at dinner, Charlotte took full advantage of the situation.

Adelaide wiped the sweat off the back of her neck. Near the well on the western side of the mansion, other slaves of all colors and nationalities were getting a much-needed break.

A pale man, who wore a sash over his head to block the sun, handed her a cup of water. "Here ye go, Adelaide," he said.

"Thank you."

Christoph was his name. He was originally from the swamplands of Beaker Province. "The Land of River Runners," it was called. The rivers in Beaker were so vast that an entire trading system depended upon it, with the traders of the delta thus being dubbed "river runners." Christoph was a former river runner himself and traded on those inland waters for many years.

"Another day in sun-abusing paradise, wouldn't you say?" he asked with a smile.

"Sure," she replied while taking a drink. The water, even though there was nothing special about it, never tasted better. As it ran down the sides of her chin, she said, "Can I ask you something, Christoph?"

He edged closer. "Of course."

"Why are you here? You said you were a successful river runner for many years. How did you manage to find yourself doing slave labor in the Helmburough heat?"

He peeled his sash away. "I'll make a deal with you," he said, revealing his hairless face. Even his eyebrows were bare. "I'll tell ye how I ended up here if you tell me how you did?"

Adelaide had kept quiet since leaving home. She had gotten good at it. Christoph was the only other slave she'd engaged with since arriving, and that was because he went out of his way to approach her. He was a garrulous talker but also equally as kind. It didn't make the situation any more comfortable as far as telling him the specifics as to why she was at the Hannah Estate. She considered lying, but she didn't feel that would serve much of a purpose.

"They believe I committed treason against the Unified Provinces. They believe I orchestrated a terrorist attack."

He showed a smile of teeth like yellowed corn kernels. "And did you?" he asked, leaning down and dipping his sash in a bucket of water.

"No."

"Good." Christoph's bald and shiny head reflected the sun back at Adelaide. "What did you say your last name was?"

Again, she hesitated. "I don't believe I said."

Christoph didn't skip a beat as he wrapped the damp sash around his head once more. "Very well."

"You lot have an hour! Then back to it!" Groundskeeper Ulrick said while marching along the wraparound porch of the large plantation-style home. He was a stern but tolerable man. He made sure everyone was doing their work to preserve the Hannah Estate, as he had been employed by the family for nearly four decades. Then, he addressed Adelaide. "Lady Hannah will be needing help with her dress before dinner. It's a big occasion, so do your part well."

Big occasion?

Christoph refocused her mind off the duties for the evening. "I ran the waters of the Emper Delta for my whole life. I could get you anywhere you needed to go and faster than anyone. I mostly killed alligators and traded their skin for silver. A usual day consisted of me hunting all day and trading at night. Trouble arrived for me when I fell in love with another pale runner like myself. I wanted to give her more than just alligator meat and silver. No, I wanted to treat her like she was the queen of the delta, and I king."

With that, Christoph became lost as he stared at the wheat field, watching it grow.

"What happened, Christoph?" she asked.

"Well, in my pursuit of excess, I met a runner named Talison. He ran everything: alligators, spices, rum, cloth, and even flowers. Ever seen a delta rose, Adelaide?"

"No, I haven't."

"They grow in moss at the base of trees in the delta marsh. In the shade, the petals are dark blue, but the moment they are exposed to sunlight, their color changes to bright purple with white edges. It's really something." He stopped once more and ran his hands along the flowers, weaving his fingers between the pedals. "Anyway, Talison was the wealthiest among us, but it wasn't from trading fancy flowers. It was because he smuggled in pirates all throughout the delta. It didn't take long for me to work my way into his trust and join him in his criminal activity. And for about a year, I gave my queen anything she ever desired but never asked for."

"What was her name?" Adelaide asked as she glowed from the memory.

"Kholia," he said, looking at her with the bluest of eyes.

"Lovely name," she replied. "Did you get caught?"

"You guessed it. I went to retrieve a pirate and smuggle him farther inland, but waiting for me was Captain Cheska Krusade and her men. The leader's daughter herself. She's not as charming as you might think. That woman has black eyes and a matching heart."

Sharkeyes.

"I didn't even get to say goodbye to my Kholia," Christoph continued. "To her, I left and never returned."

"How did you end up here? I'm surprised they didn't hang you."

"I was initially supposed to die at Riverswell, but it just so happened Mr. Hannah was traveling through the countryside and needed more slaves, so I ended up here…" Christoph cracked his neck. "Where I'll work the rest of my days."

Adelaide paused, "Does it have to be the rest of your days?"

Christoph smiled. "Unless you have plans to the contrary, Battier?"

Adelaide tightened her corset. It constricted her torso like a python of Botan Rainforest, a place she never wished to venture again. She was forced to wear it along with an aged yellow dress with a puffy waist at dinner. Lady Charlotte told her she wanted Adelaide to look presentable when she stood behind her, eating a five-course meal.

Charlotte sat in front of her mirror, powdering her nose and putting on her oversized earrings that stretched her lobes. "What clan was it you are from?"

Adelaide had told her once before, but she found that Charlotte wasn't the best listener. She mainly focused on her thoughts and what she was going to say. The world operated through the prism in which she saw it, no other way.

"The Trezbe Clan," Adelaide replied.

"Trezbe Clan, what?"

Adelaide clenched her jaw before looking down and flaring her nostrils. "Trezbe Clan, Lady Charlotte."

"I'm sure the custom of proper manners is foreign to you. For your sake, I hope you improve," Charlotte said condescendingly. "So, how does it work in the Trezbe Clan? Is there a leader?"

"Yes. A tarquin."

"Is that so? Did you know your tarquin?"

Adelaide knew Charlotte was attempting to pass the time while she finished getting ready. "He was my father."

Charlotte slowed her powdering process for just a moment

before continuing. "Is that so? Nice to know royalty is cleaning my dishes. It makes me think I'm in good hands."

There was a glare above a tight smile, looking back at Adelaide in the reflection of the mirror. She didn't let the words get to her. It was going to take a lot more than a few verbal jabs to break her spirit.

"They say there's no joy like motherhood. Is that true?" Charlotte asked.

Adelaide was taken aback at the randomness of the question. "I suppose that's true. It's very difficult but worth it. Joy, however, is no longer present."

Charlotte's gaze in the mirror softened. "Would you have considered yourself a good mother?"

Why all this talk of motherhood?

"I would do anything for my children," Adelaide said.

"That doesn't answer my question now, though, does it?"

Adelaide adjusted her corset around her waist as it was riding upward and left Charlotte on deaf ears.

"I read an interesting article in the *Weekly Rogue* this morning titled, 'THE FALL OF THE HOUSE OF BATTIER.' Now, I debated even telling you about it. However, I wanted to learn about what happened to those children you love so much, and it tells quite a bit."

There was a little motion from Charlotte's hands, and from her seated position, she held up a copy of the paper she was talking about for Adelaide to see. "I'll make a deal with you, Adelaide."

She wanted nothing more than to leap forward, rip the paper from Charlotte's hands, and feverishly read everything that was said about her family, even though she fully expected most of it to consist of lies. She decided caution and a cool head would prolong her life. Staying alive and out of harm's way was the only way she was going to help her kids.

"What deal is that?"

Charlotte finally stood from her chair and turned to face

Adelaide. Her makeup was caked on her face, and her new persona of a proper royal was made complete. "You do what I ask and serve me well, and I will keep you in the know. I will inform you of whatever I find out about your children. I will not help you beyond that, but that I can offer."

Adelaide needed to learn her plans for the future and what they entailed. She didn't know if she planned to escape or wait to earn Charlotte's trust. That could prove to be a bigger gamble that might not be fruitful. Seeing as this was the best, and near only option for now, she figured she might as well take advantage.

"I can live with those terms," Adelaide agreed.

"There's one more thing," Charlotte said.

"Yes?"

"A man is coming here to dine with us tonight on his journey back home to Northwood, an associate of my husband named Count Lucien Stahl. You are not to speak unless spoken to, and if he addresses you, make sure the response is short with no room for a reply. Barton is very anxious about hosting him, so the less intrigue, the better."

"Count Stahl? The name is familiar."

"That is because he's the richest man in the world, and he has no rival in the wealth department. Not even Charles Krusade. I'm sure Mathias was acquainted with him at one point or another."

"His name rings a bell, but I wasn't aware of his high status. How did he obtain such wealth?" Out the window, the endless rows of laborers worked tirelessly to maintain the expansive property in the fields that went as far as the eye could see.

"He founded the North Echo Trading Company and is the exclusive supplier of echo oak. Nothing of importance gets made without echo oak. For instance, the Grand Ships, the Sea Bridge, and the Flame Towers. His name is attached to anything that is significant in this country. However, I hear he's not a man to overly flaunt his wealth. I hear he's an eccentric man with unique tastes. He has such gravity in Northwood that the province as a whole has adopted his gothic aesthetic. They say if you enter Alterborn, the capital of Northwood, you either want to leave immediately or have the urge to stay forever."

"I've never heard it described in such a way. I'm sure my husband had been there, but I never heard him discuss it or Count Stahl."

"From what I gather, he's a very private man. Those people of Northwood never see the sun and like being left in the dark. It seems they will go to great lengths to keep it that way." Charlotte handed Adelaide the newspaper. "That's not important, though. This, however… may be a difficult read. But make sure you're right for dinner, understand?"

Adelaide nodded.

As Charlotte went to leave, she stumbled forward into the wall and clutched her back. She used her hand to brace herself against the door and hold herself upright.

Adelaide didn't know whether to help her or stay put. "Are you all right?" she asked.

With labored breath, Charlotte straightened her spine to retain her perfect posture. She then patted her hair with her gloved hands. "I'm fine," she replied before exiting the room.

The dining room was not much of a room at all. Perhaps it would be better to call it a hall, as the room was far too large for the table of ten it seated. On the northern wall was a fireplace that stretched halfway up the high ceiling. Even though the night didn't soften the day's heat, a fire was customary for the atmosphere.

Adelaide had been informed by groundskeeper Ulrick and the rest of the servants there would be no need for a harpist as the fireplace put out enough crackling sounds alone. And as she stood along the edge of the wall behind Charlotte's chair, she found that the groundskeeper was correct. The logs were massive, and the cracks and snaps echoed as embers trickled out.

There was a servant at the ready for each person of importance sitting at the table. Adelaide knew everyone's face by now, but she had little to no interaction with them because she was on her schedule put forth by Charlotte. They were kind and would smile when she looked at them, but there was no relationship yet built.

All the servants stood with their shoulders back and head forward while waiting for the dinner party and honored guests to arrive. No one said a word as the fire continued to rage.

Then, the double doors opened, and the gaggle of wealth filtered into the room. The dinner party followed, consisting of Lord Barton Hannah, who rounded the table and sat at the head with his back to the fireplace. Charlotte shot a glance at Adelaide before sitting down in front of her.

Adelaide thought about the newspaper article. Her husband's name, which she proudly shared, was synonymous with disgrace and treason. *Lies. Lies and deceit from up high. I will find my children. I will give them a place to call home once again, even if I have to burn down every Assembly building and monument in all seventeen provinces.*

Three men followed. Two wore lieutenant badges with three-tallied pins to match. *Men of importance indeed.* The last of them was a lanky and slow-moving man with broad shoulders. His black hair was soft and remained untouched by the humidity. His age was ambiguous. She guessed between mid-forties to mid-fifties.

"Please, have a seat, Count Stahl," Barton said.

Stahl softly scooted the chair backward and sat prim and proper at the opposite end of the table facing Barton. "Please, call me Lucien. I appreciate you allowing Lieutenant Gamble and Magnolia to dine with us this evening. If the Assembly be just, I'll have them under my permanent employ."

There was something about the man that didn't sit right with Adelaide. The moment he walked into the room, there was an aura that absorbed any positive energy, and the orange glow coming from the fireplace wilted. However, Count Stahl didn't present himself as darkly as Adelaide's senses. He wore fitting clothes that most high-end gentlemen would wear. His jacket was dark blue, the closest shade to purple. It had red stripes with gold trimming that were an aggressive fashion choice.

"So, Lucien, is the North Echo Trading Company treating you well?" Barton asked.

A servant, whose name escaped Adelaide, went to pour wine into his glass, but Stahl waved it away. "Darling, if the bottle hasn't been aged for at least ten years, I'd rather not."

The servant girl hesitated, looking to Barton for reassurance, none of which he offered. "I don't know the age of the wine, sir," she said with a shaky voice.

"Today's water will suffice," the count said. "Things are moving as desired. The oak of Northwood shall continue to progress this great country of ours into the future."

The room quieted. Charlotte eyed the company around the table. She seemed to gauge her entrance into the conversation carefully. "I hear you made a big sale here recently, Lucien. Perhaps one that made your pockets even larger. Is your lumber going to the construction of the sixth Grand Ship like it's rumored to be?"

"That it is. The sixth *and* the seventh Grand Ship. Soon, the sea will be ours, and any other countries across the water or rascal pirates shall think twice before challenging our prowess."

Barton raised his glass, and the dinner party followed. "As if they don't already. Assembly be praised."

A term for the rich and powerful.

Count Stahl kept his glass low and didn't show the Assembly the praise a loyal royal usually would. "Again, thank you for having me on my journey to Helmburough City to finalize the deal. I must say, this has been one of the more well-kept estates I've stayed. So, perhaps some praise should go to you, Barton. I'm sure the lieutenants would agree with me on that matter."

"Aye," they said in unison.

"You are more than welcome to stop by and dine with us again on your journey back home," Charlotte said.

"I'll hold you to that," the count replied.

Barton grabbed Charlotte's hand, clutching it tight. Too tight, judging by the tremble in the lord's grip. "Make no mistake, Lucien. This estate has been in my family for generations, and I keep operations running. However, my wife here keeps its aesthetic strong."

"A woman's touch is always needed."

With that, the first course was served. It was a link of sausage with a dollop of red sauce Adelaide was unfamiliar with. As she looked upon their meal, her eyes met the count's. She darted her gaze away, hoping it would amount to nothing.

He dined with the respect and proper manners expected of a royal. The pace he used to cut his protein was slow yet calculated. "This sausage is fantastic," Stahl said, wiping his mouth and downing his course with a glass of water.

"Thank you. It's from our neighbors at the Bridger Estate around thirty miles west," Charlotte said.

The smell was inviting. Not to mention, it looked to be perfectly seared on all sides. Adelaide couldn't help but salivate.

"Well, write to the Bridgers tomorrow and tell them I'll pay them handsomely to have this sent to Northwood as fast as they can," he said with a chuckle. The count seemed to be enjoying himself, but his eyes never stopped moving across the dining room. There was nothing his gaze didn't see.

"As you wish," Barton replied with shared laughter.

The room settled. All that was heard was the smattering of silverware on fine plates. The next three courses were chicken broth with cornbread, turkey with peas, and thin slices of pork shoulder with black beans. The conversation was cordial and mostly consisted of topics regarding the wealthy and powerful, subjects that Adelaide couldn't identify with or keep her attention.

It seemed like an average high-class meal until the count inquired about personal information. "Lady Charlotte, I'm curious as to where you acquired the servant woman at your back," he asked, speaking as if Adelaide was a decorative statue along the wall.

Adelaide didn't look up at him. She heard the shudder in Charlotte's voice after he posed the question. "She's from the east coast. Before that, she was much further south."

"I see," he said in a very calculated manner. "And what eastern province does she hail from?"

Adelaide's head finally perked up, and she saw Charlotte glance at her husband before meeting the count's eyeline again. "Roguewave."

"Ah, Roguewave." Count Stahl examined her. Even from a safe distance, Adelaide was perturbed by the man and fought the urge to tremor. "The blackness of her eyebrows and the prominent cheekbones don't match any typical Roguewavian." His tone was a serious one. "How is the molten crab the locals take so much pride in?"

He awaited Adelaide's response, and she remembered what Charlotte told her about keeping her answers brief. "It's very good, Count Stahl," she replied, most respectably, adding a courtly bow.

Even though he wasn't finished with the meal, Stahl placed his fork and knife on the table. Resting his hands in his lap, he took a very relaxed posture as he continued to stare at Adelaide.

Charlotte attempted to alter the course of the conversation. "The blueberry cream pie is possibly the best you'll ever have. I have to make sure it's taken away from me after one slice."

The count ignored her, eyes only on Adelaide. "Not originally from Roguewave, I see. So, where might that be?"

Barton and the lieutenants were silent. It seemed they were confused at the count's reasoning for pressing Adelaide for information.

"Ah... So, I'll ask again," Stahl said. "Where are you from?"

"Before Roguewave, I lived in Autera."

Stahl smiled. "And what savage clan are you from, woman?"

"Trezbe."

"I see." He nodded for a while. "What did you say your name was again?"

She wondered if she was supposed to lie or not. Charlotte didn't prepare her for this, and she couldn't make eye contact with her to get a good read. "Adelaide."

His smile grew even larger. "Would that make you Adelaide Battier, widow to Grand Captain Mathias Battier?"

Adelaide said nothing.

"Forgive me if I'm wrong. I like to think of myself as a well-learned and educated man who stays up-to-date on current affairs. But I could've sworn that you were supposed to be rotting in Colwerth Prison for conspiring with the pirates against the Unified Provinces."

Lieutenant Gamble and Magnolia placed their hands on their sword hilts.

"There's no need for that, men." The count waved them back down into their seats. He addressed Barton and

Charlotte once again. "My question is, how did this Adelaide Battier land in your possession?"

There was a long pause.

"I purchased her," Charlotte admitted.

Barton looked at her with disdain.

"Must have been quite a large purchase to rip someone from Colwerth and for the Assembly to be at peace with it."

"It was. It helped that Alistair Cross owed me a favor," Barton said, wiping his face clean and folding his napkin.

"May I ask why her? Why this Trezbé woman?" the count pressed.

"Personal servants are hard to come by?" Charlotte said, placing her fork down after eating her last piece of pork.

He nodded with little satisfaction at that answer. "Oh, I doubt that… How much, then?"

"How much for what?" Barton asked.

"How much would you like for the Battier? I think someone like her could be beneficial in Alterborn."

Barton went to speak, but Charlotte interrupted, "She's not for sale."

"Everything's for sale," the count said.

She leaned away from Barton ever so slightly. "She's not."

Barton grabbed her wrist and squeezed it tight enough to show his knuckles turn white. "I apologize for my wife's poor manners. What are you willing to spend for our... prized servant?"

"I'm not sure, really. I haven't dealt—"

Charlotte cut him off mid-sentence. "She's not for sale. That's final. My apologies, Count."

Adelaide could see Barton squeeze harder.

Count Stahl seemed amused, regardless. "Very well," he said, dapping his face with his napkin. He scanned every individual in the room, even his personal guards. "If you all don't mind, I am a weary traveler and would like to turn in early."

As his anger towards his wife shifted to a general defeat, Barton said, "Of course. Groundskeeper Ulrick can show you to your quarters."

Stahl left at Ulrick's escort. The pair of lieutenants decided to retire along with him as Barton and Charlotte remained in their seats.

"Leave us," Barton said. The servants all left one after the other, and Adelaide followed their lead. "For all the trouble you've caused, I would assume it's not too much to ask that you shut the door on your way out," Barton commanded Adelaide as he leered at her underneath his protruding brow. He finished his glass of wine and ripped the bottle away from a servant to fill his glass himself.

She closed the double doors behind her. The door latched closed, and on the other side, a chair scooted violently across the floor, followed by a clash of more furniture being pushed aside.

The thuds and echoing slaps grew quieter as Adelaide returned to her room.

THIRTY-THREE
SHARKEYES VI

The road, if one could call it that, led south to the desert land of Okamara. The walkway was one of cracked dirt foundation, littered with coarse sand and dead grass. Avery's newly fashioned sandals clapped against her sweaty heels with each step. They were a far cry from the terrain boots she rarely removed. She ushered her grandmother's mule by the reins as it pulled the wagon behind them.

Even in her grief, Eralia was strong. Her spine was erect, and she was aware of all her surroundings, observing the endless queue of wagons being removed from their home.

"Are you all right, my dear?" her grandmother asked.

Avery felt as if she should be the one proposing that question. She wasn't the one who just lost her husband of nearly fifty years, not even a full day ago, but somehow, Eralia managed far better than she did. It was almost as if the entire series of unfortunate events gave her a clarity Avery was still attempting to discover.

"I'm fine."

Avery hadn't known her long, but her grandmother presented herself as a confident woman with a kind heart.

Her father always told her never to mistake anyone's kindness for weakness. Those words stuck with her.

But one day, a few months prior to her father's death, the two of them strolled through the woods north of Molten City. It was a day when he was quite solemn and not as talkative or present. That wasn't her father. There was a moment when he had to stop and lean against a tree for a break. In the quiet of the woods, with no context and tired eyes, he said, "Never underestimate anyone's potential for violence."

She brushed off that exchange and never thought about it again until now.

I miss him.

The greencoats that rode alongside the traveling party received the bulk of her grandmother's ire as she glared at them. Yet, they continued to bark orders and commands at a dwindling Trezbe Clan. The enemy soldiers made it sound like the Trezbe chose to leave Redrainn under their own free will.

Nothing was said about the journey to Okamara. Avery heard rumors that the journey could last weeks, maybe months depending on the pace. Either way, Trezbe folk were going to start falling left and right from dehydration or general exhaustion, and she didn't believe the greencoats were going to do anything about that.

The days were excruciatingly long. From morning to nightfall, Avery no longer had the constitution to remember what day it was anymore. She guessed it was either the sixth or seventh day of the journey. The desert heat beat down on them and effortlessly sucked all the moisture and energy from their bodies. Avery's youth kept her upright, but even she was faltering.

The oasis of Caste Valley was well in the distance behind

them as massive dunes encircled them. They stood more like mountains than piles of sand. The horizon fluttered in and out of focus as waves of air rippled the scenery. Avery wasn't familiar with the phenomenon, and she thought her eyes were failing her, along with the rest of her body.

Their water intake was far less than what was needed. The waterskins they all wore around their waist only lasted until midday. Those with heatstroke were only tended to by fellow clan folk and left to die in the sand by provincial soldiers.

Avery observed the now pale faces of weakened Trezbe. Even the wagons that were once fresh with cream-colored canvas were now faded and scraped from the desert's wrath. The proud and honorable people she'd only known for a short while dropped face first. However, at the end of bayonetted rifles, families of the ones claimed by the desert were forced to move onward. And none had any energy to deny the demands of the soldiers.

There was no resistance to be had, no fight or skirmish to be won against the persecutors—more than anything. Eralia, who days ago sat up straight in the wagon, now slouched and struggled to keep her hips aligned and spine erect. Avery's legs moved beyond soreness and into numbness. She feared stopping or taking a break, for the momentum required to reclaim their pace seemed to be an impossible dune to ascend.

Avery's eyes fluttered open and shut. *Can I really fall asleep walking?*

The mule's reins slipped from her grip, and the wagon continued past her. Her legs were heavy. Hiking through the sand was getting to her. As she licked her lips, there was no moisture left.

Then, a thump ahead of her kicked up sand. She raised her head to see her grandmother fighting for life on the ground.

Avery dropped to her knees. "Grandmother!"

Through shakes and pokes, Eralia didn't even open her eyes.

Avery called for help, but hardly any noise exited her mouth. Her weakened cry fell on deaf ears. Soldiers continued, not paying the two of them any attention or compassion.

Behind her, she heard none other than Lieutenant Colbe say, "Keep it moving, Battier. Old people die. No sense delaying it."

"She's not dead! She needs water!"

With that, Colbe removed his waterskin dangling from his painted horse and drank it. They were large gulps where water ran down his cheeks. He then poured a substantial amount on his head to cool himself. Finally, he tossed it to her. "There, have at it."

The grin made her quake with anger. It wasn't even worth putting the waterskin to her lips because there wasn't a drop left.

Avery eyed the sword hanging from the horse's side that was just out of arm's reach. *I can go for it and deal with him now.*

Colbe took notice of her gaze. "Please, do us both a favor and go for the sword, and we can see what happens next."

Avery stood there in a locked gaze. She ignored the pain in her back from the lashes as she postured up.

Avery made her decision.

She stepped forward.

A subtle tremor shook the earth, accompanied by an unfamiliar sound.

Colbe's arrogant demeanor shifted to concern. His eyes widened, and he looked at his soldiers.

Chanting, accompanied by an array of whistles, grew in volume. If it hadn't been for Colbe and his greencoats' reaction, she would have thought the sounds to be in her own mind that was brought on by the desert heat.

"Line up on the eastern side of the wagons! Formation! Get in formation!" he ordered.

Avery looked to the east and saw a line of horses descending one of those mountainous sand dunes. She wasn't the best with numbers, and her eyes were suspect at this point, but it looked to be over a hundred strong heading right for them.

The chanting grew louder. Some of the Aelic words being screamed in rhythmic stride were recognizable.

"Blood! Sand! War! Blood! Sand! War! Blood! Sand! War!"

Then, to the west, another line of horses mirrored those on the east. The greencoats prepared for engagement on both sides. Their heads went back and forth as they feared the attackers on both sides.

The western riders repeated, "War! War! War! War! War! War! War!"

In the commotion, Avery forgot about her grandmother, who was still lying motionless on the ground. However, for the first time in a while, she saw Eralia's lips moving along with subtle movements from her chest. Avery kneeled to listen to what she was saying, and in Aelic, her grandmother repeated, "Blood… sand… war… war… war."

The first gust of wind since the beginning of the journey drifted across the desert sand. The riders descended upon them so quickly that they seemed to hover above the ground.

All Avery could think to do was cover her grandmother for protection. The remaining Trezbe along the wagon train cheered passionately for the riders. They returned chants of war and battle.

The greencoats ordered the Trezbe under their command to quiet down, but to no avail. Those who didn't were kicked or struck with the butt of a rifle, but their discipline was unsuccessful. The new attackers seemed to light a fire of adrenaline into the weakened Trezbe.

The clicks of around a hundred greencoat rifles sounded. Lieutenant Colbe shouted, "Steady!"

The ground shook more violently as the riders grew closer, and their chants grew louder.

Malcolm, Colbe's elder second-in-command on this journey, appeared to deal with the stress of the pending attack much worse than his superior. His rifle bobbed all around. Her father would often talk about how many unseasoned soldiers would get something called "buck fever" during battles where they were unable to steady their aim.

With that, both Colbe and Malcolm gave the order to fire, and plumes of smoke erupted from the barrels. A few of the western riders flew backward off their horses as the bullets struck them.

But as the rest sped onward, the guns had no effect on their resolve or momentum. The riders were a mix of men and women, both hollering. All of them sported blue paint from the bottom of their noses to their hairlines. Their armor consisted of thick animal hides along with leather bracers. Tre-axes bounced up and down on their hips as they fired their longbows.

The riders yelled a command to the Trezbe on the trail. She couldn't make out the words, but everyone who could, dove for cover under the wagons as the riders nocked their arrows. With all the strength she had, Avery dragged Eralia behind the closest wagon wheel. It wasn't the most effective cover, but it was the best she could do at the moment.

Arrows peppered the greencoats and the wagons above. Soldiers fell from their horses, prompting clan folk on the trail to take advantage of their opportunity by finishing them off with whatever means available.

The remaining soldiers fumbled through their reloads, but it was too late.

The riders were upon them.

Their braided hair stayed tight to their scalps as they

leaped from their horses with tre-axes now in hand. The greencoats drew their swords or used their bayonets, and the melee erupted in full force.

Avery retrieved one of the water skins off the soldiers' lifeless bodies and delicately put it to her grandmother's lips. Even with her eyes closed and seemingly unconscious, she drank all its contents.

Clashing of steel and bone deafened her. No Trezbe warrior's braids were the same. The patterns were as unique as the flowing waves in the desert dunes. Some had close rows that went in jagged lines down the back of the skull. Others crisscrossed into one large ponytail. Their hair was black as the night sky. Along with the various stylings of rows and braids, their locks wore adorned with painted bones that stuck out from their hair like a porcupine.

Where did they come from?

The Trezbe warriors, men, and women alike, fought with a ferocity and speed Avery had never seen before. Their tre-axes were the perfect counter to the single-weapon-wielding soldiers. Their ability to trap the opponent's sword or rifle left the greencoats unprepared and confused as a swift and fatal counter always followed from one of the three lethal points. This standard batch of foot soldiers was no match for the hardened natives.

Greencoats ran around in a frenzy, attempting to find shelter from the barrage of clan combat, but there was none to be found.

Of the men and women who fought against the greencoats, one stood out amongst the rest – a woman around her mother's age and who shared nearly all her features, aside from the hair, which was braided down the center of her shoulder blades and cut to the skin on both sides. The blue paint on her face formed sharp lines around her cheeks. Avery, who wasn't fearful of much, couldn't deny her intimidating nature.

Every strike, every kick, every swing of the woman's tre-axe had lethal intentions. She was a master.

Ianthia. My mother's twin sister. My aunt.

Ianthia went rogue and engaged multiple greencoats alone. Her fellow warriors attempted to keep pace behind her, but there was no mirroring the desert lioness.

Her axes were extensions of her arms. Swords that swung her way were trapped and repelled. Ianthia would claim her opponent's weapons by way of gripping them with the axe heads. Those unlucky greencoats never even witnessed the brutal counters, for they were already dead.

The last thing in the world Avery wanted to do was leave her grandmother, especially in her state of defenselessness, next to the wagon wheel. However, there was no more focus on them. The soldiers were more than occupied with the Trezbe warriors, and Avery had something stowed away three wagons back.

Avery crawled in the sand underneath the wagons. Bodies, lifeless and living, dropped on both sides beyond the wheels. Some were greencoats taking their final breaths, while others were locked in combat, trying to achieve the dominant position.

As the corpses began to mount and blood wetted the sand, no sense of pride or gratification came over her—just a need, a need for it all to end.

The sand stuck to her body. As she trudged along the desert floor, her forearms and chin got the worst of it. The seemingly indestructible grains scraped against her teeth and were quite possibly more uncomfortable than the chaos of battle.

Finally, under the desired wagon, Avery found what she had secretly stowed away before leaving. She reached up and retrieved her mother's axes, which were tied to the underside of the wooden wagon bed. The handles of the ancestral weapons in her hands somehow calmed her. She ran her fingers along with the engravings, and an empowered hum swelled in her gut. Her mother's spirit was with her; she couldn't be convinced otherwise.

Between the wheels, Avery rolled out from underneath the wagon and rose to her feet. The sea of axes dominated the declining number of swords. A few male warriors even managed to snap some of the cheaply made blades.

Around twenty yards away, Lieutenant Colbe combated Trezbe warriors. They underestimated his prowess. Avery was quite shocked that the man who had women, both young and old, beaten frequently could prove his mettle. Unlike his subordinates, he managed to cut down many of the Trezbe that came his way. He would make use of quick stabs as opposed to big swings. That way, he wasn't open for counterattacks and traps from the rival axes.

An urge came over her that she couldn't resist. With that, both malnourished and exhausted, she still managed to explode forward after digging her heels in the sand.

He managed to shove his blade through two more Trezbe on her way toward him, and he turned just in time.

Avery brought one of the axes above her head to swing down upon him, but he was faster. He spun off to the side and managed to duck out of the way. She pivoted towards him as he laughed.

A throbbing pain emerged in her side. Warm liquid fell from her ribs, dampening her clothes as his swift slash opened a decent gash.

"Battier. You are so far out of your depth," he said matter-of-factly.

The pain across her side was manageable for now. She tried to forget about it and push it to the back of her mind like a repressed memory.

She rushed him once again, swinging wildly with no pattern or even semblance of strategy. Her father always instructed never to let the enemy get a read on her attacks.

However, as she used up a lot of her energy and didn't find purchase, Avery feared she misinterpreted her father's counsel.

She became lightheaded, and the axes that moments ago gave her a spike in energy now matched the weight of cannonballs.

Colbe took the opportunity to go on the offensive. He walked her backward, sending stab after stab, which she barely managed to block and evade. Avery's confidence waned.

He kept her at the end of his blade. A few of his jabs got through Avery's novice defense, slicing her on the forearm and shoulder. She bit the inside of her lip in a failed attempt to conceal her pain. The last thing she wanted to do was give Colbe that satisfaction.

As blood dripped down her body, Avery mustered up the strength for another charge, hoping the lethal end of her axes would find their mark.

Only this time, Coble grappled her under both arms and flung her past his hips. The sand did not provide a soft landing as the air left her body. Her axes were no longer in hand. She had failed her family as well as herself.

Colbe's shadow blotted out the sun as he stood over her. "Perhaps you'll fare better in the next life," he said as he reared back with his sword, looking to end her life.

Avery couldn't fight back anymore. She stretched for one of her axes.

Just as Colbe's sword began its descent for her heart, he froze.

It took a moment for Avery's eyes to focus. A blade jutted out of his chest, fresh blood staining the uniform whose authority he had so proudly lorded over her. His eyes wide, breath coming in gasps, he collapsed.

As his body hit the sand next to Avery, she saw the life leave his eyes. She looked up to see her grandmother, though weakened, had managed to find the hardiness to claim her revenge before collapsing to her knees.

"I knew I'd get you," Eralia said.

Avery went to her. Even in her state, the will to nurture her grandmother persevered. She held her tightly in her arms.

A group walked towards her, led by her aunt Ianthia. Her leather breastplate pulsed in and out. Blood caked her entire body, but she carried herself like the blood didn't bother her. Perhaps it didn't.

Ianthia knelt next to them and looked at Avery with intrigue. She averted her gaze as her mother's life held on by a thread. "Mother, are you all right?" she asked, coddling her.

"I'm far better now," Eralia replied. "Ianthia, this…" Her breaths became labored. "This… is Avery. Your niece."

The smile remained. "I assumed as much. Looking at her is like looking at my reflection in the water ten years past."

The small amount of anxiety faded after the introduction to Avery's lioness of an aunt.

"Let's get everyone out of here," Ianthia said as she looked at the party of weakened Trezbe folk. "Where's Father?"

THIRTY-FOUR
THE COWARD BOY VI

Eddie looked out over the misty ocean waters from his post atop the watchtower. Boredom set in hours ago, but his fear of letting someone arrive unannounced kept him vigilant. He passed the time by carving all of his family members' names into the wood railing with his sister's dagger. It was imperative that he kept the dagger close by; he never removed it and even slept with it at his side. For now, it was more of a keepsake than a weapon.

Everyone took shifts in the nest, aside from the higher-ranking pirates. Usually, the task was done in pairs, but the captain wanted a trench dug all the way around the island village. That was where the crew found themselves this evening while Eddie was stuck amongst the trees. The height scared him, but he was growing tolerant. He dangled his feet off the side of the tower and clutched onto the lowest bar of the railing. His chin rested on his forearms as he never once looked straight down, only ahead.

A pair of heavy boots thumped as they hit the wooded steps. Eddie turned, expecting it to be Matt, but no, it was Captain Lockett. He sprung to his feet and straightened his spine. Eddie still wasn't sure how to address the captain, but he did so as formally as he could.

"At ease, Eddie."

Captain Lockett's dark coat with silver trim gave him the appearance of something far more sinister than this personality reflected. His sword, a straight cutlass with an extended handle for a two-handed grip, never left his side. The matching dagger laid horizontally on the backside for concealment. When bladesmiths constructed matching swords and daggers, they were given the moniker of *big brother* and *little brother*. While Eddie admittedly didn't enjoy putting the weapons to practice, he loved the craft and artistry behind bladesmithing.

"How's everything lookin' out there?" the captain asked.

"It seems like there's nothing, but it's hard to see with the fog on the water," Eddie replied.

The captain grabbed the railing beside him and looked across the water. "You seem to have a pretty keen eye. Would you agree?"

"I don't know what you mean," Eddie said, genuinely confused.

"You see things that maybe others don't."

"I'm not sure."

The captain finally met his gaze. "Your father used to see things for what they were. He could see through fog, buildings, people—as if he had a gift. Do you understand what I'm saying?"

"Father was good at knowing what was real and what wasn't."

A hint of a smile came over the pirate's face. "Yes, you are correct, Eddie. I'm also telling you that your father saw through lies. He saw through deceit."

How could a Grand Captain of the Assembly come to dine and befriend the people he was at war with?

"How did you and my father become close?" Eddie voiced

aloud. "He did not speak well of pirates when you all were brought up in conversation."

Lockett's smile remained as if the memories pleased him. "You may not believe this, but he reached out to me and asked for an audience through a covert letter over twenty years ago."

He stroked his chin, attempting to remember the details of decades past.

"He wanted to meet in secret on Tyver Island," Marstellar continued, "so I had my crew ready. I also convinced the men in charge of the Tyver Fort to keep their guns trained on Mathias' ship as soon as he arrived. But when I saw that he was arriving without his Grand Ship, under a blank flag, I knew he was to be taken seriously. We met in a tavern on the island filled with my men while he came alone. Right then and there, without even exchanging words, I respected him. The cannon balls between his legs. My word."

Eddie smiled wide in admiration upon hearing more of his father's bravery.

"I was hostile to him at first, I'll admit," Lockett said with a chuckle. "He was a man destined to be my enemy—he a navy captain and me a pirate captain. However, not far into our conversation, I noticed how serious and passionate he was about his aspirations. He informed me of the expansion south into Autera and how he didn't agree with the methods to achieve the Occupation at the clans' expense. He told me that the Assembly was planning on using the clan people as slaves to build structures and extend the empire. Those who weren't cooperative would be relocated to some desert with obviously minimal resources."

"The Assembly would do that?" Eddie replied.

"Ah, yes, Eddie, oh yes," Marstellar responded with a frown. "Your father seemed to be one of the few that stood opposed to the idea of using the clan people in such a horrible way. After all, he was the only man from the provinces who'd fallen in love with a clan woman."

Marstellar put his hand on Eddie's shoulder. "But that's the thing, Eddie. Your father cared about people and saw who they truly were. He knew the clan folk to be aggressive but not the monsters and savages the Assembly made them out to be. You see, it was their mission alone that made your father rebel. It was the fact that they were lying about it to every citizen in every province. Their papers depicted your mother's people as the subject of nightmares people tell their children. That they've killed so many good Assembly soldiers for sport and cannibalized rival clans and none of it was true."

He stammered over his words. "My father was conspiring against the Assembly and the Unified Provinces? Isn't that treason, Captain?"

"Yes, it is, son, and your father paid for it."

"My father d-died of a heart attack."

"Did he?" Marstellar replied in his swift manner.

What followed was a stare that lasted a rather long time. Eddie didn't find himself in many staring matches often because he quit before they began. That result didn't change when facing down the pirate king.

The captain walked to the other end of the watchtower. He looked down at someone and gave them a nod from up high.

"What is it, Captain Lockett?" Eddie asked with his nerves taking form.

"Eddie, when my crew raided Molten Bay, we did so with the purpose of accomplishing several goals. Goals that your father and I thought essential to see our vision through." Lockett rested his hands on his sword pommel as he faced Eddie. "Now, I realize that a raid places our image in a light I'm actively trying to avoid. However, it had to be done. Our plot will come to its inevitable conclusion, and we'll not only be the victors but also the heroes."

Eddie heard collective footsteps making their way up the

winding watchtower. With no wind on the island, it was easy to hear everything, even at a great distance.

"My main goal was to capture Governor Tytus along with his schedules and letters of the things happening throughout the sea, from Molten Bay to the Aster Sea. I wanted information out of him involving the Grand Ships and their locations, their trade routes, escorting assignments, and when they were docked, all so we could avoid them when we began sailing west. Because if we meet one of the Grands on open water, they'll put us at the bottom of the ocean in a hurry. At first, it was supposed to be a covert operation. We pirates were to sneak in under the cover of night and capture Tytus. Grand Commander Alistair Cross thwarted that plan. Not to mention the fact that his presence brought on far more armed guards at the governor's office. So, our best course was to make a little noise and create a distraction."

The captain paused for a moment and breathed in through his mouth, then exhaled through his nostrils.

"Of course, there was an added element of collateral damage that I'm not proud of, but in order to achieve greatness, some things have to fall. But Tytus was still the main goal. I had countless questions for him that needed to be answered. There was one, in particular, I knew he wouldn't know the answer to, given his merit. He's not viewed as a high-ranking governor due to the lack of respect given to Roguewave, along with his reputation as a fat and lazy indulger. When I asked him what happened to your father, and he answered with a blank and unknowing stare, I knew he was telling the truth."

"I don't understand, Captain," Eddie said.

"I know, son," Lockett replied. "This should help."

Two of the captain's crew, Brent and Stoops, carried a man under his arms with a bag over his head and dropped him down to his knees. His hands were tied behind his back, and the black sack on his head wagged in every direction.

"Who is that?" Eddie asked, feeling nervous heat go down his spine.

"I knew there would at least be one man that truly knew about your father's demise. Even if he was the only one, I was going to find out regardless—the man who inspected your father's corpse. You see, Eddie, the Assembly failed to account for the lengths I would go to find the truth. To find that man."

Lockett pointed at the bag-headed man and motioned for his men to remove the sack. As it was peeled away, the confused, sweaty, and wrinkled face of Coroner Ullman was revealed.

He panted like a dog in the heat.

Captain Lockett walked forward into the gap between Eddie and Coroner Ullman. "Mr. Ullman, do you know who this young man is?"

Ullman blinked as he focused on Eddie, and his head fell.

"Answer the question, please," Lockett pressed.

"Yes. I know him," the coroner replied, defeated.

The captain towered over him. "Who is it?"

"One of the Battier boys."

Eddie locked eyes with Captain Lockett, who said, "You don't even know which one he is? I guess it should come as no surprise. You obviously didn't care too much to learn… His name is Eddison. The youngest of Mathias and Adelaide Battier. Would you like to tell Eddison here how his father really died?"

Really died?

Some words left Ullman's lips, but they were so quiet that they were inaudible.

"Say it!" Lockett demanded.

And like a whipped animal, Ullman responded immediately: "He was poisoned. I diagnosed it as poison."

Eddie's eyes watered and swelled.

"They threatened to hurt me and my family, I swear! I promise!" Ullman cried.

"Who did?" Lockett asked.

Ullman wiped the sweat from his forehead with his bound hands. "I don't know. They wore masks and said that their power was limitless should I not cooperate."

"Were they working for the Assembly?"

Ullman didn't answer right away. "Please let me go home," he pleaded.

"Answer the question," the captain said in a much quieter voice. Somehow, his softened tone was equally as intimidating.

"I think they were?"

"How can you be certain?"

"I'm not," Ullman said. "But they gave me a lot of money for doing what they asked. I don't believe anyone could gift that amount other than the Assembly."

Lockett seemed satisfied with that answer. "I'm glad we caught you when we did. I noticed that you sold your home in the Second Quarter and put a down payment on land just outside Helmburough City. Seems like you were quick to utilize your newfound wealth, as well as flee the scene of your lies."

The pirate king meandered back to Eddie. He left Ullman to wallow in self-pity, which manifested itself as snot and tears streaming down his face.

"Do you believe you deserve to live, Coroner?" Lockett asked. Before Ullman was able to respond, Marstellar's gaze landed on Eddie. "I guess at this moment, it would be more appropriate to ask you that question, Eddie. Do you think Mr. Ullman deserves to live?"

Thrown off by the gravity of the situation, Eddie just stood there wide-eyed.

He twitched back further when Captain Lockett removed his ivory-handled pistol from the front of his belt and placed it in Eddie's hand. "It's your choice, Eddie. What do you think should happen to the man who lied to your family?

Who is employed by the very people who had your father killed?"

Before Eddie was given a chance to reply, Captain Lockett cocked the gun in Eddie's grip and forcefully aimed it at Ullman.

"Please, don't!" Ullman pleaded.

The black barrel shook at the end of Eddie's extended arms, even with it partially held up by Captain Lockett. In any other circumstance, Eddie would be admiring the custom gold trim wrapping around the gun, but not now. No, now he was afraid.

"I-I-I-"

Lockett cut Eddie's stammering short. "Make the choice, Eddie. Decide for yourself this man's fate, as well as what you are." Eddie shook more. Ullman continued begging for his life. "Breathe, son. Who are you? What are you capable of?"

The shaking continued, and he closed his eyes.

Who am I?

What am I capable of?

He asked those questions over and over for what seemed to be a thousand times.

Sound died.

When he opened his eyes once more, he no longer shook. At that moment, Eddie no longer had that overwhelming fear that kept him from accomplishing the things he wanted. *I want to be free. I want to be free of crippling fear.*

The gun in his hands was steady, aimed right on target. Captain Lockett's hands no longer assisted him. His index finger could feel the pressure on the trigger that was more than willing to give way. There was power in having such a decision in the palm of his hands.

But this was not the way his mother or father would carry out such a situation.

Eddie handed the gun back to Captain Lockett. "He doesn't deserve to die."

"How can you be certain?" Lockett asked.

"Because I'm not certain, Captain," Eddie replied. His sentiment might not have been one of confidence, but his faith in his decision was absolute.

Lockett smiled and nodded in agreement. "Very well, son," he said as he motioned his men to take Ullman away.

With that, Eddie went back to his post, looking in all directions. He stood with his chest puffed out, embracing his watch guard status. Eddie didn't stop hearing Ullman say thank you until his voice died out in the distance below him. Lockett remained behind him as the silence returned.

"Everything all right, Eddie?" Captain Lockett asked.

"I have two more hours left on my watch, Captain," Eddie replied.

A cool breeze brushed his face and gently moved his curled hair.

Not so windless, I suppose.

"Mind if I stay and lend an extra pair of eyes?"

Eddie nodded. Captain Lockett, the pirate king, whom many feared the mere mentioning of, stood right alongside him with a soft smile and content eyes.

It was then that Lockett asked, "Eddie, do you desire redemption?"

THIRTY-FIVE
THE PIRATE KING II

Marstellar Lockett's vision would require a great deal of sacrifice from himself and all those who sailed under his flag. His confidence was unshakeable. There wasn't a man alive that could convince him his motives were false or misplaced. But being aware of the massive wave he was to crest in the near future gave him unwelcome anxiety.

He maintained a tried-and-true self-belief that, with time to contemplate and navigate his voyages, he and his crew could achieve nearly anything. However, he wondered how long his brothers and sisters would trust him once they found themselves in those dark and unknowing waters with monsters in pursuit, both metaphorical and very literal. Monsters whose sails cast a shadow over the ocean and those who stood against them with a broadened chest were branded enemies of civilization. Even as his bulging scar still burned on his breast, not a soul on the land or sea could convince Marstellar Lockett he was the enemy. Not a soul.

As Lockett stood on the quarterdeck, watching his crew work tirelessly towards the end, he thought, *there be monsters ahead.*

"Captain, all the gun barrels have been swabbed and

cleaned. The new sails on the foremast are nearly complete," said Gerrard.

The full name of Marstellar's sailing master was Pickrill de Fulbright Ambrose Gerrard IV. For short, he just went by Pick de Gerrard. However, even that proved too long for pirates. The crew decided to address him as merely Pick or Gerrard. Or, as Marstellar liked to call him, Mr. Gerrard. He believed it gave his sailing master a little more respect that came with his station.

"Very well, Mr. Gerrard. Sail on," Marstellar replied.

On the water, there was probably no better sailing master in the world than Pick. He was the only one whose navigation ability equaled Marstellar's. And for that, he got the respect he was owed.

The upcoming voyage would see the mackereli filtering on and off the ship. As an amphibious race, the fish people got tired of both land and water after a while. Marstellar had a few concerns heading forward regarding his mackereli allies. For starters, he was worried that their lack of experience on a ship could cause them to get sick. He didn't know for certain if it was a possibility with them, but it was a concern regardless. Marstellar had seen it enough, most first-time sailors struggled with the motion and rocking the ship underwent at sea, and it usually led to vomiting and fatigue.

The ship was over capacity with crewmen. If the mackereli were to filter in and out of the water, it must be done in an orderly manner and in shifts, or else it could significantly slow their progress. That wasn't even factoring into account the six added guns stolen in the raid, which was another key addition in the execution of the Cannon Fire Plot.

There was no sign of Eddie Battier and Matt Roke in the cove, where Marstellar expected they would be training. While he was there, he acknowledged the other crews and offered greetings. The mackereli, who were usually feeding on land at this time of midday, seemed to all still be under the surface. Marstellar scanned the bank, contemplating where the boys would be other than the cove.

"Everything all right, Captain?" Quartermaster Jordo Patan of the *Drifter* asked from up high on the poop deck.

"Have you seen Matt and the Battier boy?"

"Maybe an hour ago, Captain," Jordo replied.

"Where'd they run off?"

"I think they followed the inlet to the coast."

"Thank you, Jordo."

"I can offer you some men to help you go look for them if you'd like," the quartermaster suggested.

"That's all right. It's nothing urgent," he replied.

From his vantage point, it was hard to see who was on watch in the tower. It didn't look like anyone was there at all, but then again, it was designed to be near impossible to see from a lower point of view. He decided to take a closer look on the way back and make sure his watchers weren't sleeping or anything of the kind.

He kept onward along the bank, enjoying the quiet briskness of his walk. About half a mile ahead of him, the inlet opened into the ocean. This day alone would see him walk from one side of the island to the other.

There was still no sign of the boys anywhere. *They made sure to get far enough so Cella couldn't find them.* He chuckled to himself. His laughter faded because he felt ridiculous laughing while no one was around.

He pondered a moment, wondering whether the boys would be training to the north or south of the inlet.

Something caught his eye on the mushy water's edge. Heat came over him as countless bootprints littered the ground going north. They emerged from the forest, crossed the inlet, and went into the northern foliage.

Marstellar was no tracker, but he knew this could be anywhere from forty to fifty men, based on the tracks alone.

The tightness of the formation seemed to illustrate covert movements.

These aren't the prints of my crew.

A bad feeling came over him.

His prized watchtower seemed to have failed him. He made haste to the beach, with the hairs on the back of his neck standing up.

As he emerged from the foliage, he saw a ship anchored to the southwest about a mile offshore, flying an Assembly and Helmburough flag. Three longboats rested under the cover of palm trees.

We're under attack!

THIRTY-SIX
THE COWARD BOY VII

Matt continued to simulate stabs to Eddie's torso with his sparring saber. His youthful instructor assured him it was the same kind of sword he might come across on the seas, for the navy and pirates used them. The Navy men were issued a more curved blade to complement the compact space of a ship, while the army had a straighter sword.

Eddie struggled getting the hang of the basics. Even coming from a family of fighters, it didn't come naturally to him. His stance seemed off-balance, and his strength nonexistent. The footwork was the most challenging aspect for Eddie to grasp. The repetitive failing got to him as he struggled, struggled, and struggled. He could never string together any combinations or parry more than a single strike.

"Don't be too hard on yourself, Eddison," Matt reassured. "It's like learning a new language."

New language? No. I'm actually good at that.

They took a break to sit and snack on some bread and jerky. Ever since arriving on the Windless, Eddie had yet to stop sweating. Though, the quiet was unlike anything he had experienced in his life. He was almost scared to think that someone would hear them.

Matt stood. His recovery time was nothing short of extraordinary. "All right, let's try that again. Remember, after you parry or dodge, grab and isolate my sword hand. Then, use it as you wish. You remember the counters we went over?"

"I remember. Whether or not I can do them is a different story," Eddie replied as his grip clenched the sword hilt so hard his fingers seemed stuck.

"No, it's the same story, not to worry. It doesn't have to be fancy or look good, either. It just has to work. Got it?"

"Got it."

With that, Matt took his position in front of Eddie once again. He feinted with his shoulders a few times to make it difficult for Eddie to time the thrust. Then, the real one came, and Eddie shifted left and used Matt's forward momentum to bring him close, grabbing his wrist in the process. He put tension on Matt's elbow, hyperextending it while putting his dull blade to the back of Matt's neck, along the spine.

There was a wide-eyed glance from Matt's profile as Eddie held the sword in its lethal place. It was a counter Eddie had not been illustrated, but one he came up with at the moment. As Matt stood there not responding, Eddie worried if he did something wrong... again.

However, Matt grinned. "That was incredible, Eddie. Where did that come from?" he asked with a laugh.

Eddie released him and loosened his grip on the sword. "I got a good teacher, I guess," Eddie replied with a sense of pride. He was beginning to realize, the more confident he got at something, the more he behaved like his sister and understood her.

"See, you can do this, Eddison," Matt said. "You don't have to doubt yourself."

He still wasn't convinced, but he smiled and nodded to appease his trainer.

Limbs snapped in the foliage.

"What was that?" Eddie asked as the sounds continued.

Matt yanked the back of his collar and dragged him behind the cover of a large oak. He put his palm over Eddie's mouth to silence him from whatever he might have seen.

From the dense trees emerged a line of provincial soldiers. This group seemed to be more covert and didn't sport the traditional greencoats. Instead, they wore tight-fitting, camouflaged jackets tucked into a large belt with weapons and additional shot lined all the way around their bodies. Their bayonets also had a serrated hook that curled downward.

They kept low to the ground and moved at a methodical pace. A woman with black hair led the men. She had the tightest of ponytails and appeared around ten years younger than the men she commanded.

Eddie was only aware of one high-ranking woman in the military. Avery wouldn't shut up about her and had a love-hate relationship with her. She was jealous of the woman's station but also wanted to prove she could beat her in a fight. Xavier angered Avery every time he mentioned the name Cheska Krusade and how her ruthlessness would make Avery run screaming in the other direction were they to lock horns. If the rumors about her were true, Eddie hoped to the Creator she didn't discover him under cover of the trees. She wore a four-tallied pin on her lapel, and since his father shared the same rank in his service, that spoke volumes. None of the men following her through the forest had under three marks.

These aren't common foot soldiers.

Captain Krusade and her men snuck further north, back into the thick forest, keeping a low profile. They appeared and disappeared like the flash of an ember drifting away from a flame.

After a couple of minutes of standing behind cover, Matt grabbed Eddie's shoulder and said, "We have to go tell Captain Lockett."

"Tell him what?" Eddie replied in a shaky voice.

"We're about to be under attack."

The prospect of battle made Eddie's mind go to that place he hated most. Fear overcame him with just a few choice words. His stomach turned, his ears grew hot, and he had the urge to vomit.

A series of clicks amplified more fear than he could ever imagine.

Then, a hard metal barrel was pressed into the back of his head.

"Don't move," a gravelly voice said. "Chop 'em down."

That signaled the greencoats to push on the back of Eddie's and Matt's knees and place them on the ground. Two soldiers held Eddie by the shoulders and two on Matt. *Surely, they know we can't cause much trouble.*

The soldier with the hoarse voice walked around to face them.

"Don't say anything!" Matt demanded.

The soldier knelt at their eye level and said, "Oh, you're going to want to say something, boys." He adjusted his black cravat and coughed. It seemed that there was a previous injury the soldier was dealing with, and the article of clothing covered the wound. He had cuts, fresh and old, all over his face. "Who are you two?"

Eddie shook. He looked over to Matt, and his eyes were staring at the cravat-wearing soldier.

"Perhaps you both misunderstood," the man said while removing a pistol from his belt and placing it on Matt's thigh. "I don't like the way you're looking at me, boy, but I'm going to ask again. Better yet, I'm going to ask a different question. Where on this wretched island is Marstellar Lockett?"

Eddie panted while Matt's steely demeanor remained. He could feel the soldier look back at him while his eyes were glued to the floor, but Eddie said nothing.

The gun cocked, and Eddie flinched. The soldiers laughed at him for jumping at such a quiet sound.

"We got a timid one right here, men. Perhaps he's more willing to talk."

A soldier grabbed a handful of Eddie's hair and pulled him up to look the cut man in the eyes.

"Where is Lockett?" he repeated.

Eddie held firm, and though he was shaking, he didn't speak.

But then, the soldier yelled, a drastic shift in tone, "Where's Lockett?"

And with that, Eddie couldn't fight it anymore. "He's on the eastern coast of the island where the *Madfrog* is at anchor. He's usually on the ship around this time."

A smile came over the scarred soldier's face.

Matt's head dropped in disappointment. Eddie already wished he could take it all back more than anything.

"Thank you," the man said as he stood to his feet and winked. "Do it quietly, men. We don't want to let the rest of the pirates know we're coming."

The soldiers leaned their rifles against the tree and removed their knives.

"No, please!" Eddie cried out.

The cold and sharp steel touched the side of his neck, and a booming shot rang out behind them. Gurgling through a flood of blood pouring through the hole in his neck, the soldier dropped the knife.

Everyone stopped. The enemy turned their heads to their dead companion.

Before anyone could discern the blast's origin, another roaring gunshot found its target on Matt's potential executioner. Except this one landed center mass.

Erupting through the smoke at full speed with his sword and dagger drawn was Captain Lockett.

The soldier holding Matt attempted to get off a shot with his rifle, but the captain closed in too quickly, and the shot fired into the ground upon Lockett's initial strike on the barrel. His follow-up slash ran up the soldier's chest.

The men holding Eddie released their grip and went for the captain along with the scar-faced man.

Scarface swung on the captain's head, but Lockett parried it off to the side, countered with his off-handed dagger, and sliced him through the neck, adding a final wound to his body as he spewed blood.

Lockett proved fast enough to strike the other soldier's belly before he could even get off a swing.

Captain Lockett gave no time for reflection as he commanded, "Boys, with me. To the *Madfrog!*"

With that, the captain led them back to the inlet, away from the rest of the provincial soldiers. There was no doubt in Eddie's mind that the rest of the enemy would be in pursuit of them, especially when they found five of their men dead behind them. Matt led the way while Lockett took the rear. The captain's eyes scanned in all directions as he pushed Eddie in the back to drive him forward.

They reached the inlet that led back to the cove.

That was when gunshots whistled past them, piercing nearby trees and water. Eddie looked back to see if he could find where the shots were coming from, but the makeshift camouflage jackets seemed to work nicely for the provincial soldiers. All that was visible was the flashes of smoke and orange.

Eddie's vision was then blotted by the captain's body, who shielded him from any potential shot that would find him. At that, his guilt grew a bit more.

"Matt, get in the water!" Lockett yelled.

It wasn't a short leap to the other side of the bank. Matt tried to clear it anyway. He ended up coming up short and getting only about halfway there, and then he had to wade to the other side with a fever.

Lockett pushed Eddie in the back, and he went face-first

into the water. In an instant, his nose was filled with water, and a burning sensation followed. He fought his way back to the surface and could only manage to get just his head above water.

Lockett shielded him again as he splashed into the water behind them. The captain began slapping the water with both palms over and over. It was as if he was attempting to take flight or a beaver patting its tail.

The shots grew closer. Captain Lockett pulled Matt in close by the shirt collar.

Eddie could see on Matt's disheveled face that he was just as confused with the captain's plan. Water splashed him and Matt in the face as the gunshots formed tighter groupings. The soldiers weaved through the trees and readied more muskets.

"Captain!" Matt yelled frantically.

The soldiers were nearly done loading their next round of fire, removing their ramrods that packed the powder and musket ball. As Eddie turned his head, he and Matt were dunked.

He was disoriented. Strong and new arms wrapped around his waist. The acceleration forward under the water was shocking. They cut through with unnatural speed at minimal resistance. It didn't take long, at the rate they were swimming, to make it back to the cove. On a normal swim, it would've taken close to half an hour to get back, but they didn't have to come up for air once.

They surfaced, and Prince Sephor, along with his father, King Caspus, released them all. With his large frame accompanying broad shoulders twice the size of an average man, he was more than capable of swimming with two men under his arms. Both Sephor's and Caspus' greenish skin glistened in reflections of crimson, orange, and yellow.

All four of the ships in the cove were ablaze, along with the watchtowers that raged the brightest and hottest. Those covert soldiers were no longer in hiding as they were in intense combat with the pirate crews. At a casual glance, the elite group was proving their superior combat abilities over the pirates.

Heartbreak and anger burned on Captain Lockett's face. It was as if he was reluctant when he turned to Caspus and, in Aquatic, said, "Get your school to the eastern side of the island to the *Madfrog*."

There was no reply, only a nod from the mackereli king. Eddie looked to Sephor and offered his thanks once again, and the prince smiled back before submerging.

"To the shore, boys! Stay close to me!" Lockett commanded.

Eddie planned on following any of the captain's orders.

He was soaked. His boots were filled with water, and Eddie could feel his softened skin peeling against the leather interior. But the captain drew his sword once again, and Matt followed. Eddie had no choice but to do the same.

The clattering and steel blades were all around them. Eddie and Matt shadowed Lockett's back as he engaged whoever came his way. Whatever soldier was stupid enough to try and make themselves famous by killing the captain found themselves dead in a hurry. Eddie had to remind himself that these were no normal soldiers Lockett was slaying either. They were some of the best, but there appeared to be a steep hierarchy of combat, and the captain remained high above them.

Lockett's counters were faster than anyone he'd ever seen. He'd never seen anyone utilize all aspects of their body in a fight. He was great with a sword. That was a fact. But the captain punched, kicked, slammed, and ripped chunks of flesh off the enemy with his teeth.

Where did he get his training? He's an animal.

"Get to the *Madfrog*!" the captain yelled to any pirate still breathing.

There's not enough room for all of them.

There must've been another fifteen men who tried to claim the life of Marstellar Lockett as they weaved through the battlefield. No one succeeded.

The three of them made it to the tree line that covered the eastern side of the island to the shore.

Two soldiers emerged from the burning tannery, noticed the captain, and went straight for him. It was as if he had a flashing beacon on his head.

Eddie stood there, watching his captain and his friend fight for their lives. His blade shook in his hand as he did. The two men Lockett was engaged with were superior fighters than any of the men he previously clashed against and were giving him a hard time. Matt was struggling from the start as the soldier he fought doubled his age.

Eddie offered no help. He couldn't.

The soldier parried Matt's strike, grabbed him behind the head, and elbowed him with his opposite arm, knocking him to the ground. Then, he stepped on Matt's chest, aimed the lethal tip down, and raised his arm.

Eddie swung his sword as hard as he could under the soldier's arms. The blade didn't cut deep, for he was short, but it was enough to save Matt's life.

Anger filled the soldier's eyes as he focused his fiery gaze on Eddie. He swung at him, pushing him back on his heels. Eddie parried once, twice, but the third swing was so hard it knocked his blade out of his hands.

Before he found himself too helpless, a shot from the forest robbed the soldier of his kill for the second time in a row. The man dropped face-forward into the ground and rolled around in agonizing pain due to the fresh bullet wound in his spine.

Leak Djar tucked the pistol behind his back and moved on. He didn't acknowledge Eddie any further and kept fighting, swinging his boarding axe with controlled rage. Eddie wanted to run into the forest and get to the ship as fast as he could.

Captain Lockett observed the village he had constructed and the ships that sailed under his command burn and cripple into blackened wood. It was obvious that he was conflicted. He didn't want to give in and let the people he despised take something from him, but in the end, he had to move on.

"To the *Madfrog*!"

Those three words made Eddie as happy as he could be, given the situation, but there was a mobilization of troops at the village center.

Cheska Krusade's alabaster visage contrasted with the blood spatters on her face. "Marstellar Lockett! The dead pirate bastards at the bottom of the ocean wait for you!" she yelled in a youthful yet banshee-type tone.

All eyes moved to the captain, awaiting his response to the demand.

She seemed to salivate seeing Captain Lockett in the flesh. "What a great day for a Krusade to kill a king!"

"Everyone, to the ship!" the captain said in his retreat. "Eddie, let's go, son! To the ship!"

Captain Lockett had chosen to fight another day, and Eddie was perfectly content with that.

Eddie, Matt, the captain, and a few remaining pirates cut through the forest as fast as they could as Cheska's men pursued.

The tree line cleared. At the crude jetty were a pair of longboats to ferry them back to the *Madfrog*. The captain untied the longboat to the dock and started rowing as if their lives depended on it.

Cheska's forces made it to the shore to set up a firing line.

"Boys, get down!" the captain said.

Bullets splintered the longboat. Eddie and Matt huddled together. Countless isolated whacks riddled against the hull. Fortunately, none of them managed to pierce the wood.

Lockett made himself a small target, but there was only so much they could do having to continually row.

These pirates are as good as any men that I've ever come across.

"Captain! Grab the rope!" a crewman yelled from the *Madfrog*.

The eastern waters were choppy and difficult to row against. With weakened arms, the captain grabbed the rope.

The longboat slammed against the ship.

"Boys, go up first. Hurry!" Lockett commanded.

Even in his weakened state, he's putting us first.

Eddie climbed the ladder to the main deck as fast as he could, for they were still in the range of gunfire. Matt followed close behind, using his shoulders to boost Eddie up quicker.

He got to the top, and Mr. Gerrard was there to assist him over the side of the ship. "Stand clear of the side, Eddie," he said.

Leak and Cella Djar helped the others up the ladder on the main deck. It appeared that all the members of the *Madfrog* were aboard, including the mackereli, who filtered onto the ship on the opposite side.

Captain Lockett was still in the process of climbing as he yelled, "Jimmy! Open the gun ports! Full complement!"

The gun master, Remy Blondie, with ironic, jet-black hair, responded with, "Gun crews at the ready!"

Pirates mobilized to the gun deck. forty-four guns lined the starboard side. Five men were assigned to every gun: one loader, one sponger, one gunner, and two ropers. The loader placed the gunpowder and the ball into the barrel. The loader used the hammer to push the ball and powder farther into the barrel. The ropers held onto a rope that ran under the cannon to control the recoil and pull the cannon closer to the gun port. The gunner lined up the shot properly before firing and lit the gunpowder to fire the cannon.

Eddie would have thought that there would be little discipline on a pirate ship. However, ever since he arrived on the Windless Isle, that notion was disproven each day. The pirates manned their stations with proficiency. There was no denying Captain Lockett's command over his crew.

Everything was loaded, and the guns were at the ready. The only thing that left the crew waiting was the captain's command. The island shore had around fifty soldiers still shooting their rifles at the *Madfrog.* At their range, with the size of their musket balls, there was little threat from their shots.

Beneath him, Eddie heard the squeaking hinges of the gunports finally opening, along with the rolling of the cannons being pushed forward.

The soldiers took notice, and an obvious retreat was taking place as the greencoats made for the cover of trees, but the captain wasn't going to allow them to make it far.

Lockett's boots finally graced the main deck, and he yelled, "Fire!"

All nine guns exploded in a rolling sequence. The cannonballs soared over the water. Their impact on shore was devastating, sending sand fifty feet in the air. Trees shattered into woodchips, and soldiers flew in all directions like pieces of rotten fruit.

Smoke concealed the view of the shore. Eddie looked at the captain, whose steely-eyed gaze remained as if he could see through the smoke.

"Mr. Gerrard, get us underway!" Marstellar commanded. He moved his attention below to the gun deck. "Jimmy! Continue firing! Make the island crumble into the ocean if you must!"

Both replied the exact same way: "Yes, Captain!"

Eddie continued to watch the destruction. The anchor was raised, and the sails caught wind. The *Madfrog* made its way along the southern shore.

Eventually, Jimmy's gun crew ceased fire. Eddie took one last view of the beach and watched the smoke begin to clear. The cannonballs did a number on the shore and brutalized the island. Trees were cut to pieces, massive craters were in the sand, and the greencoats were scattered all along the coast, red and motionless.

Eddie stared longer. His eyes didn't move away from the Windless Isle. He thought about the fact that now two homes had been taken from him.

"Are you all right, Eddie?" he heard the captain say at his back.

Eddie dropped his head. "No."

There was a pause from Lockett. Eddie felt the captain's hand grab his shoulder, but he pulled it back.

"I know, son."

"I'm sorry, Captain."

"Sorry for what?"

Eddie was holding his tears in well for once. "Earlier, the greencoats pushed me to tell them your whereabouts on the island... and I told them. I'm sorry. I was afraid."

Captain Lockett perched next to Eddie along the wood railing. "It's okay, son," the captain replied. "D'you want to know why you're afraid?" Eddie didn't have to answer before Lockett continued, "It's because you're smart. Knowledge and intellect are your curses. You can see everything in your mind before it even happens. The countless scenarios of any given event that you're involved in replays until the moment's passed you by."

Before, Eddie had trouble expressing why he always felt constant fear, but in just a few words, Captain Lockett perfectly comprehended Eddie's struggles.

"Eddie, your potential for success in this world is higher than probably anyone I've ever known. You just have to have that realization of what you want and make it yours."

Eddie gave him a nod.

"You want to know what I saw today, son?" Lockett continued. "I saw a boy, known to all as a coward, save Matt's life by striking that greencoat soldier with a dull blade.

Perhaps you knew the ramifications of the act, that the soldier would come right for you. Either way, you were brave, son." Gritty and hardened, Captain Lockett swallowed and said, "I'm very proud of you. And knowing your father, I'm more than certain he would be proud as well."

The tears that Eddie was doing so well at holding in finally fell down his cheeks, and he sniffled out, "Thank you."

Captain Lockett turned to face Eddie. "I could use that intellect to help me with something. Something beneficial to the entire crew."

"What is it?"

"Leak just informed me that he saw our watchmen in the tower were killed before the attack occurred. It was how Cheska's forces were able to slip through unannounced."

Eddie's brows furrowed.

"I'm going to need you to apply your critical and creative thinking skills to solve a very new mystery amongst this crew. For there's a traitor in our midst."

THIRTY-SEVEN
THE FORMER VI

Xavier and his companions ate a late dinner in the commissary of Fort Pierce after a long day's travel on the Grand Road. The older officers, Wiggins and Aaron, kept to themselves and hardly spoke to Xavier or Declan. They were always on the opposite side of the fire, shooting down any attempts of a conversation by Declan, and when they traveled, they also kept their horses back at a distance.

"They're real rays of sunshine, aren't they?" Declan murmured while chewing on some elk jerky.

A commissary waitress around Xavier's age gave him a soft smile as she filled his cup with more water.

He averted his gaze. "I suppose they do their job well," Xavier replied.

"What makes you think that?"

"They haven't done anything on this journey. They haven't made a fire, cooked, checked the routes, or made conversation. However, they've cleaned their guns and sharpened their swords twice daily since we left Helmburough."

"So, they're good fighters, at least?" Declan asked.

Xavier crunched his broccoli. "That's exactly what I'm saying."

Declan leaned back, glanced at Wiggins and Aaron, but returned to Xavier. "Does it bother you?"

"Does what bother me?"

"Their focus on the mission at hand. That mission of potentially killing your brother."

"We all have our mission. No matter what it is, I would prefer the ones carrying out the task to be capable and ready to do so, as opposed to the opposite."

Declan nodded.

The iron commissary doors creaked open. It was a dark space, only lit by a pair of windows and a limited number of torches along the wet stone walls. It took four guards of Fort Pierce to deliver a single message. They stood behind Xavier, and they were too close for his liking.

"Declan Cross?" one asked.

"That'd be me."

"There's a recon owl perched for a hunt."

Declan scoffed in a manner that he might have believed the soldiers to be joking. "A recon owl?" he said with disdain. "What of it?"

The guards behind the speaker stayed quiet and seemed they desired to be anywhere else, but the greatcoat officer pushed through. "Well, sir, the owl is facing northeast. I know that is where you're heading, so perhaps it would not be a bad idea to follow its trail. See if it leads you to your fugitive?"

Declan wiggled his jaw. "Forgive me. I am rather young to be commanding a mission of this caliber... but my father once told me that recon owls are about as reliable as a straw boat in a hurricane."

That statement left the men hesitant.

"Let me ask you, sir," Declan continued, "what's your success rate in capturing fugitives by way of recon owl?"

Whatever pride the greencoat had left was swallowed at Xavier's back. "Not high, sir."

"Humor me. Throw me a percentage."

The guard cleared his throat again and looked through his peripherals to his quiet companions. "One in ten."

"One in ten?" Declan took his time gulping down his cup of water in its entirety. "First off, that's not a percentage. Secondly, if you were me, would you take a chance on the beast possibly leading you farther away from the fugitive?"

"I'm not sure, sir. It's our job to inform you about every possibility. We are more than capable of scouting for the track if that's what you desire."

"I understand all of that. And I want to apologize if I seem dismissive or you feel underappreciated." Declan rested his fork on the table, leaving his flank steak to grow cold. He then clasped his hands together and leaned forward on the table, taking a posture as if he was praying yet giving the soldiers his undivided attention. "This mission is of high value from the greatest power the world has ever known, so hopefully, you can understand the pressure we are under. So, thank you for informing me, and I will let you know what we decide."

The soldiers made their exit out of the commissary.

The moment the iron doors shut, Xavier said, "We should follow the owl."

Declan was surprised. "Beg your pardon?"

"The guard said the owl was facing northeast. That's the direction we're heading anyway. Perhaps it will take us off course, but if it does, it won't be by much."

Declan contemplated, and as he did, so did Xavier. He thought about his brother and his crimes. He hated that Caldwell essentially forced him to prove his worth to the Assembly.

The bench Declan sat on scooted back, squeaking across

the stone floor. He turned to Aaron and Wiggins, who were finishing their supper. "Get ready to ride on."

The pair did what Declan asked but took their time doing so. Xavier could see how much it bothered Declan, but he also appeared to understand. "Are you ready?" he asked Xavier.

"I'm ready. Just give me a moment."

"Very well... you all right, brother?"

"Yeah... I think I just... I think I just miss my fath... never mind." Xavier stopped himself. He no longer wanted to express any vulnerability, especially with the task at hand. "I'll meet you all at the stables."

Before Xavier was left alone in the commissary, Declan stopped on his leave, "Don't be ashamed, Xavier. I wish I had the luxury of missing my father."

As his companions left, Xavier was alone in the commissary. The quiet was welcome. However, as his mind raced, suppressed thoughts began to manifest.

What would Father think? Would he hate me, or would he praise me for my loyalty to my country?

I am not selfish.

I am not.

Caldwell is a traitor, and the Battier name will endure. I will make it so.

He remembered all the blood and sweat he and his brother Caldwell had shared over the years. And though they were never close, Xavier felt that counted for something.

Can I bring justice to my country? Can I kill my brother if I must?

Xavier slammed his cup onto the table. The impact sent an echo throughout the room. He stood, never answering his own questions, just presenting them. With that, he made haste to the stables.

THIRTY-EIGHT
THE AIDMAN VI

The sun vanished through the western trees, whose density was beginning to give way. Red and yellow markers lined the tree trunks going north to south. It was confirmation that Caldwell and his companions had crossed over into Vester Province. Brown and peach markers went along a similar pattern ten feet away that archaically illustrated the boundary lines between Vester and Brickford.

"Everyone, wave Brickford goodbye."

A chorus of sarcastic goodbyes followed, and Caldwell looked back to see Fili waving.

"How much longer until we reach Port Randolph?" Maynard asked. The extensive travel through endless forest had gotten to Maynard's psyche as he never stopped looking over his shoulder, and heavy bags had formed under his eyes as his paranoia ruined his sleep.

"Another day or two," Alred said. "Depends on how the weather maintains."

Maynard scoffed. "Our luck, a typhoon will strike us in the middle of the continent."

Caldwell didn't want to appear optimistic. Everything that had happened to his family left him immune to such pleasures.

However, the prospect of setting sail soon left him with a minimal amount of optimism.

Simone lagged with her father. Despite her affliction, she never complained about the grueling pace of travel. Caldwell admired her tenacity, but as her sweat dripped down her prominent reptilian brow, he knew she needed a breather, perhaps for the night.

"Let's find a good place up here to camp. Hopefully, we can make it to the port in the next few days," Caldwell said.

The sound of rushing water ebbed to the north after his suggestion. Caldwell brushed through neck-high foliage, and thorny bushes slashed through his coat and the top layer of skin. The water grew louder as he pressed onward. But in his excitement, he lost his footing, and his boot slipped on the failing rocks beneath him. Those thorns that sliced and cut him ended up being his saving grace as he clamped down on them. His palms were bleeding, but it was far preferable to being amongst the rocks skipping down the cliffside.

From what he could judge, it was a hundred or so feet to the river below. Based on their location, Caldwell took an educated guess, believing it to be the Crying River. Admittedly, geography wasn't his strongest, but he remembered something his brother Eddison once spewed to him. The waters of the Crying River flowed rapidly and coldly as its mouth was connected to the unforgiving Tearing Sea.

The sound of the rushing current below made him snap from his recollection. The rocks on either side of the cliffs were taking a beating from the stream. His companions struggled through the thorns behind him.

"Are you all right?" Emil asked, picking a thorn from his pant leg.

"I'm fine."

On one side, they were surrounded by a cliff, the other a thorn-filled forest.

Alred surveyed the location and asked, "Is this our spot for tonight?"

"Looks that way," Caldwell replied.

Still fighting through the forest, Maynard said, "Bloody hell, yes."

Simone shot him a judgmental eye. She didn't like or admire that type of language at a young age.

Maynard regretfully and awkwardly apologized to the girl who was seven years younger. But in terms of maturity, Simone might very well be the elder.

THIRTY-NINE
THE FORMER VII

The owl flew overhead with its destination well in mind. Even on horseback, the bird kept its distance and lead. They were closing in on a crossroad that was accompanied by a sign that said, "Welcome to the Province of Vester." Below it was the Vester slogan: "The Land of Giants."

Vesterans, on average, tended to be seven inches taller than people in other provinces. The people of Vester descended from a race of giants called Vynkards. They were a nomadic group of people and were rumored to be some of the continent's first people, well before the establishment of the Assembly and the unification of the provinces. An archeological dig hundreds of years ago, just south of Port Randolph, revealed hundreds of giant humanoid bones buried with thousands and thousands of battleaxes that were six feet long. While Vester didn't attract many tourists, it had a fascinating history that sparked the imagination of thousands.

The Vester flag proudly flew above their sign. It was Xavier's personal favorite of all the provincial flags, and he knew he wasn't the only one. It was a yellow giant stepping between mountain ranges on a red field. Below the slogan were two arrows facing opposite directions—one toward a road leading to Port Randolph and the other to Vester Capital. The owl carried along the east, in the direction of Port Randolph, and the group followed.

Xavier's inner thighs were beaten from the saddle. He'd grown up riding, but traversing through the heart of a continent was something else.

Declan's eyes never stopped moving from owl to road. It was as if he thought the bird would vanish, and their pursuit would all be for nothing.

Perhaps that isn't so unlikely.

Officers Wiggins and Aaron kept right on their tail. So close that if Xavier or Declan were to stop suddenly, a catastrophic collision would take place. It appeared that the prospect of accomplishing the mission and locating his brother had drawn their bloodhound noses.

Daylight was fading.

As the owl led them off the main path, the party had to make do with a narrow side road that led towards Brickford.

For three hours, they followed that cursed bird until it circled overhead in the same location.

Declan pulled the reins on his horse.

Xavier followed while patting Moonrise on the neck and stroking his mane. "Good boy," he said.

"He's circling near Crying River. If your brother so happens to be under that owl's gaze, the projected route would be correct," Declan stated.

"It would."

Declan pressed further, "You going to be all right?"

Xavier didn't reply. *I've come this far, haven't I?* He clapped his heels on Moonrise's side and went ahead.

FORTY

THE AIDMAN VII

Caldwell struggled to strike the flintlock properly with the newfound gashes on his palms, courtesy of the thorns. Clashing rocks into one another to create an ember had never proved so difficult. In school, he had been ahead of his peers in every way since the beginning, no matter the subject. It was a gift he had but also a curse.

"Let me give it a go," Emil said with an outstretched arm and open hand.

Caldwell didn't want to hand it over so easily. For he believed a few more strikes, and he could conjure the fire they needed.

"Your hands are covered in gashes, and you haven't slept in weeks, and you've led us the entire way. Plus, you've made every bloody fire on this journey. You could at least let me make one." Emil's tone sounded both equal parts scornful and affectionate. "Because contrary to popular belief, I was ranked second in school behind you. One of those subject areas just so happened to be bushcraft, but second doesn't mean I don't know how to make a decent fire on my own."

Caldwell conceded all the same. "Very well."

"You were really ranked second? I thought you failed fire-making?" Fili asked.

"No, I failed first aid."

Maynard laughed. "How can you be an aidman and fail first aid?"

Emil smashed the stones together, sending an ember that ignited the kindling in a surge. "I didn't fail first aid. I failed one – yes, *one* – of Doctor Emerson's practical exams."

As the fire grew, Emil placed a couple of smaller logs on top for it to build. Everyone, including Alred, Simone, and Fili, circled around the campfire. The farther north they traveled, the colder it got, and Caldwell hated the cold. It wasn't icy weather like Northwood experiences in the winter, or the Frigid Twins suffered year-round in the far north of the Stonic Ocean.

"Which practical exam was that?" Alred asked.

"Well, if you must know, it was extracting a musket ball from a fresh pig carcass. I didn't remove the shot from the body in the time allotted. So, if you get shot, you better hope it's not me standing over you to save your life."

"What you're saying is I should cry out for Caldwell if I get winged in the shoulder?" Alred asked, smiling.

"No, go ahead and call out for me. I'd love a chance to redeem myself."

"Better hope you don't get shot, Alred," Maynard replied. Emil himself laughed. "I saw the pig carcass he failed on, and you would've thought that pig was shot by a battalion instead of one musket."

"He's not wrong," Emil admitted.

Fili finally inserted himself into the conversation. "Wouldn't it be horrible to be that pig? To die just so some practicing aidman could receive a failing score on your corpse?"

The laughs grew louder as the fire itself intensified, illuminating their faces and casting a glow on the surrounding foliage. At Caldwell's back was a black void off the cliffside into the flowing river down below.

Emil defended himself. "Well, the pig still tasted great, so it wasn't a total failure. Although I did crack my back molar on the musket ball. I never extracted it while chewing some pork shoulder."

The smiles and chuckles faded. A dead quiet followed.

They were so close to their destination, and Caldwell didn't know that their answers and desires would be solved upon reaching Port Randolph or arriving in the Free Islands. Nevertheless, they were close.

Caldwell took a sip from his waterskin. He looked at his friends, Emil, Maynard, and Fili, all staring at the fire with a tired intensity as if the flickering flame warmed them internally as well as externally. He had to look away as emotions overwhelmed him. A thankfulness for his friends came crashing into his soul like a rogue wave. It just seemed to intensify as they approached their end goal.

Alred provided Simone with paternal warmth as he held her tight, despite her afflictions.

Even at his age, where he believed himself too old for that type of parental comfort, Caldwell would give anything to have his parents with him. His father sitting on the ground next to him, spouting his wisdom once more while his mother gave them all the confidence and comfort they'd ever need. The exhausting journey made him more emotional than usual, and it took everything he had not to cry. He dropped his head to hide his eyes. After a few minutes of letting the emotions pass, he finally raised his head and took a deep breath.

Caldwell's gaze returned to his party. He scanned past them to the tree line at the edge of the fire's shadows.

A flash of fire coinciding with a boom jolted him alert.

Emil clutched his chest as blood began to seep through his shirt.

FORTY-ONE
THE FORMER VIII

Xavier followed Declan through the forest, both with rifles in hand, as Wiggins and Aaron continued to follow suit. They crept through slow, and the owl found its landing spot, perched on the top of a high tree facing northeast. Each step was methodical. Xavier avoided any loose sticks and dead leaves on the forest floor. He tapped his trigger finger on the side of his rifle, wanting to resist the nerves and inevitability of the situation.

He's a criminal who's brought shame to my family. Shame to my father's name.

A sound made them all pause and look at one another in the dark forest. Xavier's eyes had adjusted to the night, and he could see the details of his companions' faces. Declan had a look of questionable command, seemingly unaware of what was to happen next but nevertheless accepting the outcome. The older officers, Wiggins and Aaron, wore faces of stone and appeared ready to kill, which didn't put Xavier at ease.

Laughter was ahead. So, their approach grew more delicate, like they were stalking a jackal.

Beams of firelight filtered and swayed through the trees. At first, Xavier was in denial as to what he was seeing. There, seated on the rocks with his head dangling, was his younger brother. Around him were his brother's three best friends. Two others had their backs facing the forest. Xavier couldn't make out who they were and had no guess as to who they might be. It looked to be an adult male and a young child as his arm was wrapped around him or her.

All right then, brother.

Declan crept close. "Is that your brother?"

Wiggins merged between them to await the answer.

"Yes," Xavier confirmed.

Officer Wiggins gave a nod to Aaron, and before they took their firing position, Wiggins turned to Xavier and said, "We have our mission: kill all who are traveling with the target and confirm that you indeed killed Caldwell Battier."

The words hit like a knife to the belly. "We should take him back to the capital to await justice. Killing him shouldn't be the first course of action in the plan."

"Plans change," Wiggins replied in a matter-of-fact way. "He's going to hang in the square anyway upon returning him. We are here to make sure you two don't ruin this mission. My advice: don't let that happen. Let me and Aaron do the work. Declan, you hang back, and we will give you, Xavier, the chance to prove your worth."

Wiggins cut between Declan and Xavier as they looked at one another.

Xavier whispered, "Wait, wait —"

But it was too late.

Aaron positioned his rifle on a low-hanging branch, took aim, and fired.

For a moment, the world stopped. The sound of the blast echoed through the trees and out towards the cliffs.

Emil, Caldwell's best friend, had his hand over his heart and fell to his side.

Wiggins quickly lined up a shot aimed at Fili. Xavier

thought of Lieutenant Chiesa and how he pleaded for Xavier not to hurt him.

His arm was moving before his mind could register it. He struck Wiggins in the back of his head with his rifle, and the officer dropped.

The confusion caused Aaron's second shot, intended for Maynard, to miss high. Xavier and Aaron locked eyes, and the second officer flared his nostrils and gave him a look of hatred. "Bloody traitor!" he yelled.

Then, he heard the familiar voice of his brother yell, "Alred, get Simone out of here!"

Xavier didn't recognize the names, but the two ran north, away from the conflict, while Caldwell, Maynard, and Fili drew their swords.

Declan ran to pursue the two called Alred and Simone. Xavier and Aaron unsheathed their swords and stepped out of the forest to reveal themselves.

He saw the shock and utter dismay on his brother's face that his friends shared. From Caldwell, the look turned to rage, and his brother ran at him full force with his sword at the ready.

Aaron cut behind him and engaged both Maynard and Fili, who were both competent fighters, but Xavier didn't believe it would end well for them.

Caldwell swung hard. The initial clash of swords sent embers flying, and the force knocked him backward.

"What have you done?" Caldwell yelled.

"What have *I* done?" Xavier roared back, swinging his newly forged blade with purpose.

You are the traitor!

He had tunnel vision. His awareness of anything other than his brother in front of him didn't process in his mind.

He kept Caldwell on his back foot, making him parry along the cliffside. But his brother smartly edged off one of his blocks to pivot away. The cliff descended the farther south their fight went. Xavier made sure to keep the higher ground.

He was always able to beat his brother in training. Though Caldwell put up a good fight, the result always remained the same. However, with the loss of Emil and the anger that was so visible, this version of Caldwell was new.

Xavier swung high, but Caldwell ducked under it relatively easily due to the low ground. Xavier anticipated it and fired a push kick right into his brother's sternum.

Caldwell fell over backward down the hill. Xavier followed him, minding his step along the way. Even with the careful movement on his descent, he managed to roll on his ankle twice.

Caldwell recovered fast and was back on his feet by the time Xavier closed in on him once again. His brother slashed at his midsection. Xavier managed to shift back just in time, but Caldwell's fist hit him square in the jaw.

The crack was followed by a solid and stout object sloshing around in his mouth. If he was to return to Helmburough City, he would be doing so with fewer teeth. Nothing was left but to spit it onto the ground and watch it clatter against the rocks.

Blood trickled from his mouth, but Xavier didn't pay it any mind and pushed forward. "Give up, Caldwell. Let me take you in."

"They're going to hang me!" his brother shouted.

"There's no guarantee of that. You could prove you're still loyal, and you had nothing to do with our mother's treason."

Caldwell scoffed. "If you believe that, you're either very naive or very stupid. Having known you better than anybody, I'm going to assume the latter."

"You betrayed our country by siding with her!" Xavier said, waving his sword.

"Never given a trial. Never found guilty of treason. If you truly believe our mother orchestrated everything that happened, you are lost. But even if she did, what's more treacherous, betraying a system of corruption or your own flesh and blood?"

Xavier marched forward.

"And if you don't know the answer to that question, you are merely a mindless sword."

Xavier was done negotiating. Now, his slashes and thrusts had malice behind them.

Caldwell was still holding his own. Any other time, this bout would have been over, but he was not only parrying all of Xavier's best strikes, but he was on the offensive.

Both of them had pistols dangling from their side. Xavier couldn't speak for his brother, but he didn't have any intention of using it. Pistols eliminated the ultimate goal and question.

Who is better?

Xavier slashed towards Caldwell's midsection again, and the younger blocked with his offhand, supporting the impact at the end of his blade. Xavier saw an opening and took it.

In his sideways stance, he quickly shifted behind his brother, nearly touching his heels together and making himself small. For a split second, Caldwell's back was exposed, and Xavier slashed him.

Caldwell arched his back in pain and jumped forward to duck out of the follow-up strike.

A warm sensation came over him as if he was happy to have missed.

That was nearly it. He would have been dead.

Caldwell turned fast and swung vertically from underneath. The tip of his brother's sword caught Xavier's chin, and blood poured down his neck into his shirt.

Caldwell attempted to thrust his blade into Xavier's belly, but he parried, shifted to the side, wrapped his arm around Caldwell's neck, and began to choke him. He went to drive his sword into his brother's back and end it all, but Caldwell spun in his grasp and parried the blade to the side and then headbutted Xavier.

His nose exploded into a bloody mess.

In the moonlight, his brother's blade shined and glistened a white aura like it was enchanted with some sort of angelic power.

Is his sword magical?

The thought crossed Xavier's mind for a split second, and he felt like a moron. As he got a better look at the blade, he thought, *No, that's nothing more than a regulation-issued saber.*

Caldwell went for another attack. Xavier closed the distance, locked his brother's arm, and flung him over his body. Caldwell slammed flat on his back, and the wind left him. Xavier disarmed him in the process and then kicked his sword away.

But he made a mistake.

After tossing his brother, he let go of him and broke the distance. It gave Caldwell enough time to recover and tackle him.

They went tumbling further down the hillside. They continued to exchange blows while somersaulting.

They both achieved so much downhill momentum that they didn't stop falling until the ground leveled off at the bottom.

Xavier was the first to recover, even if he appeared worse for wear. On all fours, he gazed back up the steep hillside that led to the rocky cliff. The moon was shining just above the horizon. Its white glow lit the battlefield of sibling rivalry. His prized sword was no longer in his hands. It sat about halfway up the hill, maybe fifty feet away. The grunting and movement he heard from Caldwell shifted his focus away from his weapon.

Xavier disregarded his sword, knowing that his brother was swordless as well. Xavier stood over him and kicked him in the midsection. He then took the dominant position and put his knee on his brother's belly, and started raining punches down upon him.

As his brother was preoccupied with the safety of his face, Xavier took the opportunity to drive a hard shot into Caldwell's stomach. If there was any air remaining in Caldwell after the beating his torso had received, it was surely gone now.

Never let the opponent get a read on you.

Xavier never let up.

He shot into the air as Caldwell attempted to buck him off, but Xavier held firm. He never let up. His shoulder hurt, so he used his power hand to grab Caldwell's shirt collar and started hitting with his left. It would be impossible to keep up the pace of his barrage.

As the punches became less tenacious, the throbbing in his thigh intensified. A dagger gleamed in the moonlight.

He must've reached back and removed that when he attempted to throw me off.

He didn't know if he should address the issue of the dagger or bring his brother to heel. He contemplated for too long.

Caldwell grasped the handle of the dagger once again and twisted. Xavier couldn't stop from screaming in agony.

He wrestled his brother's hand off the dagger. He was unsuccessful and decided to kick Caldwell in the face with his boot heel. Caldwell went flying back. However, his grip was still strong on the hilt, and his momentum pulled the dagger out of Xavier's thigh. His screams echoed over the Crying River.

He removed his pistol from behind his back and took aim at Caldwell. His brother stood to his feet with nowhere to go. A sixty-foot drop off the cliff was at his back, and Xavier held a gun at his front. They both stood there for a moment, catching their breath and observing their wounds.

Caldwell, with labored breath, said, "If he saw you right now, he would feel nothing but shame that you were his son."

Xavier was beginning to surpass anger.

"Mother would slap you across the face," Caldwell went on. "I haven't disgraced our family. *You* have. You want to shoot me? Do it. You'll only confirm what you are: a broken bastard who doesn't deserve the name you so desperately believe you're protecting."

Xavier's anger turned to hatred.

He hated Caldwell Battier—his brother.

The pistol remained steady in his hand. His index finger felt the resistance of the trigger.

Caldwell was in his sights.

He remembered his mission.

Xavier pulled the trigger.

His shot found purchase in his brother's chest. Caldwell curled over. The shot's momentum drove him backward, and his foot slipped off the cliff's edge. He tried to catch himself but was too slow. The side of Caldwell's face smashed against the rocks, and he tumbled over the side.

Xavier stood there a moment in his firing pose.

Eventually, he lowered his pistol, walked to the cliff's edge, looked down into the Crying River at the bottom of the gorge, and saw his brother flowing facedown and downstream.

The tension in his shoulders gave way. The pain in his face and his leg seemed to dissipate altogether.

But a feeling far worse than any physical pain washed over him: guilt. No matter how hard he fought or tried to convince himself he was in the right, the feeling wouldn't subside.

What have I done?

Xavier limped his way to the camp that once occupied his brother's group. Officer Wiggins was dead in a pool of his own blood. Next to him lay Maynard, who had met the same fate as his pale face stared lifelessly into the night sky.

There was no sign of the two unknowns or Declan, who went after them. Xavier questioned if all this was right or if their mission was successful at all. He didn't know anymore.

Sounds of shuffling came from the forest to his left. Officer Aaron emerged from the woods with his rifle, armed and ready, aimed directly at Xavier. "Did you do it?"

All Xavier could do was hold his hands up, signaling his intent not to fight back.

"Did you do it?" Wiggins asked.

"Do what?" Xavier replied.

Aaron pulled the hammer back on the rifle and took a step closer to within point-blank range. "You know what I'm talking about. Did you kill Caldwell Battier?"

Xavier didn't want to answer the question. If he were to answer the question, it would be a reality.

"Answer!" Aaron yelled.

"Yes," Xavier said, his voice cracking for the first time in years.

"Show me."

"I can't. He's… floating downriver."

"That's a lie, isn't it? You let him go."

"He's dead."

The words left his mouth, and everything was real. *I killed my brother.*

Aaron pressed the rifle to Xavier's head. "All right, Battier. I'll do a casual search myself then to know if you're telling the truth. Then, I intend to return to the capital and move on to the next mission because that's what a good soldier does. *Great* soldiers can accomplish more than what the mission requires."

He saw the change in Aaron's eyes but didn't comprehend what the soldier was saying.

"Perhaps the world no longer needs any Battiers. Perhaps

eliminating all of them would be best for the Unified Provinces."

Xavier closed his eyes, and the shot fired.

He stood there a moment, feeling no pain. As the second wave of adrenaline washed away, he wondered why he wasn't dead.

A sudden drop occurred in front of him.

Xavier opened his eyes to see Aaron with a fatal gunshot wound and his body smoking in the dying campfire.

Declan stepped out from the trees with his smoldering pistol. "You all right?" he asked.

Xavier didn't respond, not even a nod.

"It's done?"

Xavier didn't want to repeat it. "Yes…"

Declan nodded. "I'm sure that was difficult. I am sorry. The father and daughter got away from me. Looks like one of his friends got away as well. Do you know which one it was?"

"Fili."

"Is he going to cause us any problems?"

Xavier needed clarification. The blows he'd taken to the head from his brother didn't help matters. "What do you mean?"

"Way I see it, we can tell our superiors whatever we want," Declan said. "Wiggins and Aaron are dead. We may be scolded for their deaths, but we will be equally praised for carrying out this mission."

"And what about how they died? I assume that will be fabricated?" Xavier asked.

"Brother, this mission was about getting your name restored. Most of the praise, fabricated or not, should go to you. We will have plenty of time to come up with our version of the way things transpired here, but it will always be told that your brother's men killed both the officers, and you alone avenged them. Believe me, I'm fine with not living up to expectations. I'm used to it."

As Declan went to retrieve his horse, Xavier asked, "Why are you doing this? Why do you want to help me so much?"

His boots stopped on the rocks, and before he turned around, Declan looked off to the moon. "I saw how you were during our fight, as well as after. You put so much pressure on yourself. I don't know why you do, for I don't know your story. But based on how you reacted, I could tell we were one and the same. I know the pressures I put on myself, and I understand why that is. I hope to learn your reasoning someday… The bottom line is that we fought, and we shared something that day that very few people understand. The hundred thousand people that watched us that day don't understand it because they don't get to. They don't know what it's like to risk everything in that pit, and they never will. It's not about the winner or the loser. It's about being willing to step in there."

It was the first time Xavier heard it expressed like that, but he didn't disagree. If he was being honest, he was happy Declan was here.

"You let them go, didn't you?" Xavier asked as Declan was still staring up at the sky.

Declan turned around. "Beg your pardon?"

"You said the father and daughter got away. You wouldn't allow that to happen."

Declan dropped his head and smiled. "They weren't our mission." He made his way to his horse. "Let's get Wiggins and Aaron prepped for travel back to Helmburough."

Xavier looked down at the two lifeless officers. His mind wandered back to his brother, a thought he hoped would eventually fade sooner rather than later. But no matter what he did or how hard he tried to push the thoughts away, Caldwell kept creeping in without welcome.

What have I done?

FORTY-TWO
THE SILENT ONE VI

It was dawn when the continuous banging on the front door shook the guest room floor. Isla awoke with Leo at full attention. Isla placed her hand on him and felt his growl. The fact that she could hear something at such a distance from the far end of the house gave her pause.

Against her better judgment, she decided to investigate.

She held her palm out, signaling Leo to stay on the bed. Her beloved hound showed his disappointment as he rested his chin on the comforter and shot her a dissatisfied glance with his human-like eyes.

Slowly, she slid the door open and prayed there wasn't a creak in the hinge that brought any excessive noise to draw attention. Staying close to the wall, Isla crept through the hallway to the top of the staircase overlooking the foyer. With her back against one of the other guest rooms, she extended her neck to glance at the entryway, at the origin of the vibrations and noise.

Oliver was in irons and was being placed under arrest. Livian, still in her nightgown, passionately protested.

But the greencoats and the officer in charge were not hearing her plea.

Oliver gave little resistance. There was nothing he could do against five men with bayonets inches from his person.

Livian stepped forward, getting into the face of one of the soldiers. She was met with a pistol to the forehead from the officer. Isla recognized the man as one of the governor's guards. The man whose face appeared a melted mess. He carried a sword on one hip and a combat hammer on the other. It was a weapon she didn't see often.

The soldiers grabbed Oliver by the hair and forced him out the front door. The officer kept his pistol on Livian's forehead even after securing her husband. The man took his off hand to play with her hair and pull her closer. He then closed his eyes and smelled her from neck to forehead, where his pistol remained. He whispered something into her ear, smiled crookedly, and took his leave.

Isla waited before making her presence known. Livian was already up the stairs wearing a frantic and sweat-filled face.

"What's wrong?" Isla signed.

"They've taken Oliver on suspicion of treason!" Livian ran her fingers through her hair, trying to wipe away the sliminess the governor's man left behind. "It's the same they did to your mother and your siblings."

"What are you going to do?"

Livian placed her hand on the railing, exhaling a long, drawn breath. "I don't know, Isla."

All Isla could think to do was hug her. All of this was her fault. She alone was causing their family a lot of stress and anxiety. They'd done everything for her and never made her feel like a burden for even a second.

Something had to change. The teetering on the edge of contentment faded away.

It had been a while since she'd seen Sadollah or thought about her lasting words. But after this, she now knew who her enemies were, and she was going to defeat them.

Once night came, Isla took her usual exit strategy out the side door on the opposite end of the house, farthest away from the master bedroom. To avoid any rousing recollection of her or Leo, Isla wore one of Livian's heavy hooded coats. Leo's haircut gave him a much sleeker look and slimmer frame. Though he was still large in stature, he didn't even look like the same hound. His yellowish eyes never shone bigger or brighter after cutting his bangs.

Livian remained locked in her bedroom and had been crying for several hours. The tears hadn't ceased ever since Yula frantically informed them that Oliver had been placed in the market stockades upon seeing him on her daily errands.

She said that Molten City locals were not happy and were currently protesting his arrest and demanding answers. Everyone had discovered that Oliver was arrested for treason without cause and was put on display like a common street criminal.

Perhaps the doctor was the wrong man to falsely accuse, seeing as Oliver Emerson was one of the most liked and respected, if not the most respectable, person in Roguewave Province.

Isla closed in on the market and was met with a massive crowd of people huddled around the square.

There's no way that's a coincidence.

The markets hadn't been this busy since before the pirate raid. While commerce was beginning to return, many businesses hadn't recovered from their losses or need for repair.

As suspected, the crowd that appeared hostile was packed in tight around the stockades where Oliver, disheveled and tired, remained bound by his neck and hands.

Usually, victims in the stockade were ridiculed, sometimes

even pelted with rotting fruit and fish or whatever citizens had on them. That wasn't the case this evening.

Nothing was being thrown at Oliver. And although Isla couldn't make anything out specific that was being yelled, it didn't appear to be condemning him, rather the system that placed him there.

She kept her head down and fought through the dense crowd closer to the stockades to get a better look, with Leo following close behind. It took a few minutes to fight her way to the front. She didn't want to expose herself at the front and have any eyes focused on her, especially now having Leo with her. Isla ensured a buffer of around three people in front of her while assuring her view wasn't obscured.

She noticed one of the stockade guards, who was different from the greencoats, had a key ring dangling from his side. The fear of the encroaching hostile crowd clearly played with his nerves as his eyes darted around to all the angry citizens gathered against him. Usually, stockade guards were there to ward off kids that got too close to prisoners.

I'm going to get those keys somehow. Oliver has no business being in that contraption.

An intense showdown was taking place between a rotund Roguewavian and a greencoat. Even with the soldier using the body of his rifle to keep the citizen back, the large man's frame left the soldier in shadow.

Isla gave the Roguewavian a shove and drove her shoulder into his meaty back, and the situation grew more intense as first contact between the soldiers and citizens activated the dormant streets. Greencoats rushed to the aid of their man, while citizens did the same for their own, and a massive brawl brewed.

Her and Leo weaved away. Two soldiers ran in her direction to join the resistance, paying her no mind. Isla took her coat, pulled it tight, and stumbled around, acting like a sickened beggar. She wedged between them while their focus was on the conflict.

Whatever transpired next for the two men, they would have to face it without their pistols, for Isla had picked them off their belts. She glanced down at Leo and gave him a wink. The way his long tongue dangled out the side of his agape mouth made it appear like he was smiling.

The stockade guard remained behind Oliver. His knees shook as the pushing and shoving escalated. The door behind him was an entrance into the Northwood Trading Company that housed local lumber. Before she made her way around the corner of the building, she took the stolen pistols and fired them into the air.

Chaos erupted.

Everyone, citizen and soldier alike, ran in different directions. The greencoats were outnumbered by about twenty to one. The ones present were quickly consumed by the mob.

Isla and Leo popped into another side door of the building. The only light came from the small slits in the wood foundation. Leo led her as if he knew where to go with his superior canine sight. The inside was empty. Leo escorted Isla to the door where the guard was on the other side. The dog took a stance, signaling he was at the ready for any command.

She placed her hand on the door handle and gently slid it open with her shoulder. The guard still shook and was far too preoccupied with the riot in front of him to watch his back. Isla pointed at the guard's belt and motioned with her head for her hound to react. Leo pounced forward, clenched down on the guard's belt, and yanked him back into the building.

No human I know could've been that fast.

Before the guard realized what was happening to him, Isla had clubbed him with one of the pistols, knocking him unconscious. She removed his key ring and signaled Leo to stay.

Isla adjusted her hood once more and made her way to the stockade as the chaos raged. The violence ramped up as the greencoats and citizens were in full combat. Punching, grappling, and choking were taking place ten feet from Oliver's dangling head.

Isla swung around to the front and lifted his head up. His eyes widened upon seeing her.

"I'm going to get you out," she signed while testing out the many different keys on the lock.

He waved to her with his restricted movement. As she looked at him, he mouthed, "I'll be all right. Thank you so much, but this isn't the way to do things." Upon reading his lips, his words brought Isla pause. "If you free me, and I escape, what happens next? Then, I am a fugitive. That cannot be."

Isla didn't know what he wanted her to do now. This whole time she only thought about freeing him. The consequences of what came after hadn't crossed her mind.

The gunshots to the north of the market square were loud enough for her to turn her head. Reinforcements had arrived to help police the situation. In the middle of all of them, walking very composed with his remaining hand behind his back while his men subdued rowdy citizens, was Governor Cassel, along with his two officers. He seemed rather amused as he made his way through the street of parted conflict.

It didn't take long for the situation to die down as he closed in on the stockade, for the locals weren't equipped with muskets.

Another wave pulled her attention away from Governor Cassel and back to Oliver. "I have had a lot of time to think and discover a solution to our circumstances. I know what to do." He enunciated every word so she could comprehend. Although she appreciated his effort, it wasn't necessary because she had gotten very good at reading lips. "Get somewhere safe. I'll be fine."

She didn't share his confidence and wondered if he was thinking clearly. Oliver was one of the most intelligent men she'd ever known, so she decided to trust and obey his request.

"Isla, you need to go n—" Oliver's eyes jetted off. His surprise replayed as Livian appeared. "Honey, take Isla and get out of here!"

Livian trusted her husband more than anyone in the world and never second-guessed him. She took Isla by the hand and surveyed the dying chaos. Isla took the initiative and pulled Livian into the lumber building.

Her mentor and surrogate mother was very concerned upon seeing the unconscious guard on the ground. Livian signed aggressively. "What are you doing? This is not smart. It's dangerous. Reckless!"

Isla returned the anger. "It's dangerous for me everywhere!" She waved the keys in front of Livian's face. "I almost freed him, but he denied me. He said he'd be a fugitive."

"He's right!"

Isla had never seen Livian so angry.

She took a few deep breaths and signed, "How did you know I was here?"

"Contrary to what you might think, I used to sneak out at night. I know you liked to do it as well, way more often than I'd like, but I'm not your mother. That being said, I figured tonight would be one of those occasions where you would wander."

Isla loved her. The guilt of being a burden got to her, but their exchange was cut short as Livian's attention shifted outside. She shut the door and escorted Isla to a small window with a view of the square.

Isla tugged on Livian's shirt and signed, "What's going on?"

Not only could she not hear, but the window was only

viewable for one. However, Livian relayed the events going on outside.

Her hands moved in rapid succession. "The governor and his men have got control of the situation. He's about to address the citizens near Oliver."

"What's he saying?" Isla signed.

Livian held up her index finger, signaling that she was waiting for something. *"Roguewavians, I am sorry for the confusion, but Doctor Emerson here is accused of treason by housing a fugitive!"* She paused, her eyes fluttered back and forth. "The crowd is still restless. They demand evidence to be shown against Oliver, or else they want him freed. Cassel is about to speak again."

Livian put her finger up and went on signing for the governor: *"I understand your concerns. I really do. Perhaps you're right. Maybe it was premature of me to arrest Doctor Emerson, but I hope you understand my caution. For I was called here to repair the city, the bay, and replace Governor Tytus! A series of objectives that are not easy! Also, when I am acting governor, I will have my respect!"*

"The citizens are claiming they didn't vote for him, so they shouldn't abide by his command. Governor Cassel doesn't seem pleased."

Then her hands stopped altogether. It took another tug from Isla for Livian to continue. And without breaking her gaze from the market, she signed, "He's got keys himself. Cassel looks like he's going to release Oliver... He's doing it. He's unlocking the stockade."

Isla went cheek to cheek with Livian and saw the upper half of the stockade swing open. She couldn't hear them, but she watched as the crowd clapped and cheered. There was a long stare between Oliver and Cassel. There didn't seem to be any love lost between them. No words were being spoken, but the crowd was anxious, including Cassel, who appeared on edge that Oliver was stepping up to address everyone.

"What's he doing?" Isla signed.

Livian signed, *"Friends, brothers, sisters, fellow Roguewavians. I have lived here my whole life. I have served this place as an instructor and a loyal public servant for over fifteen years. I know all your names and faces... which is why, when I was forced out of my home earlier today and placed in confinement over mere suspicion, I was angry. I am enraged, just like all of you are. What happened to our foundational laws, where the people elect whom to run their province, not have one elected for them? Governor Cassel does not govern us. He can't! For he does not know us or our province!"*

Oliver pulled a letter from his pocket. Cassel was fuming, but there was nothing he could do. Oliver had the floor and, from the looks of it, the way the people cheered at his every word. He had the power.

"There was no evidence against me that I have done anything to deserve what happened to me here today. However, it just so happens that I do have evidence that condemns our governor and the people of the Assembly that placed him here. This letter, signed by Governor Andrew Cassel, is a confidential finance record on where our tax dollars are being spent post-raid. It says here that half of our money — our hard-earned, provincial money here in Roguewave — is not being spent on the reconstruction of the market and fort as we were promised. No! Instead, Governor Cassel was placed here so he could make sure that our money was being transported to Helmburough to further fund the construction of the Sea Bridge."

Isla returned to see the crowd's aghast reactions, and they didn't disappoint. Livian seemed surprised. This must have been a new discovery because Oliver made sure to tell her everything. By the look on Cassel's face, it appeared he had been caught red-handed and publicly at that.

Oliver handed the letter to a few of the citizens to look at it with their own eyes. *"Unfortunately, citizens, this is not the worst of their crimes! Surely you all have not forgotten about the great Mathias Battier. I know some of you have reservations about him because he married a clan woman. However, let us not forget that he was once the Savior of the Bay when the East Flame Tower was sundered. Now, we were led to believe that pirates and clan folk were responsible for such an attack, but we were wrong. It was the Assembly who secretly sanctioned the act of terrorism."*

Every mouth was agape. Perhaps if this was coming from an ordinary citizen, it would all sound like a weak conspiracy, but coming from Doctor Emerson, it transcended truth. It was like everyone's eyes were being opened for the first time.

"I have in my possession a series of letters and a journal kept by none other than Mathias Battier that I discovered in Governor Tytus' office. These documents illustrate in detail all of former Grand Captain Battier's suspicions of the Assembly that led to the concrete discovery of their treason! He provides proof that the pirates and the clan folk had nothing to do with the attack. Rather, it was a covert operation set forth by the Assembly themselves to invade the southern territories to claim their resources and spread provincial ways!"

Livian's hands shook with the weight of her husband's accusations.

"You see, our new governor here had no idea I had knowledge of such things. I didn't until recently a man came to me to confess such acts—"

"All right! I think these people have heard enough of this nonsense!" Cassel stepped forward, but the crowd heckled him.

"Citizens, this is unacceptable! We should not let this stand! We decide what happens here. Our province decides where our money goes! We elect our own officials! With that, as of now, I am putting my name out there to become properly elected as the next Governor of Roguewave! I love this place and our people too much to let it further fall into nothing but poverty!"

"That's it! I will not let further talk from a turncoat renegade proceed. I was being kind when I released you. I now know that I was too forgiving. Lieutenant, take Doctor Emerson into custody. I shall summon Judge Barnes to determine his fate."

People froze and whipped their heads around. A plump, balding man emerged from the crowd.

"Who's that?" Isla asked with a tug on Livian's sleeve.

Livian's eyes were wide. "That's Governor Tytus."

FORTY-THREE
RED SAND I

Jameson had his reservations about the mission. However, his trust in his captain took precedence. Tytus hardly spoke a word to him the entire voyage back to Roguewave. The former governor kept to himself like an abandoned child. Jameson let him stew in his thoughts, for deep down, he believed that the captain had convinced Tytus of the Assembly's ways.

If Tytus had reservations or resisted Lockett's mission for him, he would have voiced his objection or attempted to convince Jameson not to take him back to Roguewave. It wasn't until they came upon a large gathering of citizens that Tytus voiced his opinions.

"I concur with everything Doctor Emerson has said!"

To the large gathering of Roguewavians, Tytus' presence was grossly unexpected.

Jameson used his broad shoulders to cut through the mob. He made it near the front but decided to stay back as he was an enemy of the Unified Provinces — and a well-known one, at that.

Tytus seemed to bask in the metaphorical light during his

address. He stood shoulder to shoulder next to Emerson, who was as surprised by his presence as everyone else in the crowd.

Their revelation paled in comparison to the newly-appointed Governor Cassel. His head remained at a tilt as he stared a hole through Tytus. His personal guard's movements stuttered as he awaited command. It was evident to Jameson that the lieutenant wanted to subdue the situation by force, but that ship had sailed.

"I know this whole demonstration is quite irregular and frustrating to witness, but everything the good doctor said here is true," Tytus spoke, pulling a handkerchief from his breast pocket and wiping his sweaty forehead. "I know most of you citizens have no love for me. Perhaps I am at fault for some of our economic struggles and lack of political power. I have been… lazy… idle for matters at hand. I sought my own happiness and significance. I now know that had the opposite effect. I must confess that I have stifled growth, stolen your money, lied to you all… and withheld mountains of information. To confess to you all that I have done in specifics would take hours… days… Things that will come to light in time."

There were boos from the crowd and calls for his death.

"I understand your hatred! Your emotions are well-warranted. But hear me now. Captain Marstellar Lockett captured me the day of the Molten Raid. That much is true. However, perhaps everything else you've been told about that day was a fabrication. The pirates did not plan the casualties. It was intended to be a secret operation in which only I was taken. Their plans had to be altered due to the presence of Grand Commander Cross and the mobilization of Assembly forces. If anyone would have told me a month ago that pirates would attain the moral high ground in this, I would have never believed it."

People cared very little about what he had to say after the mention of Captain Lockett. The boos and shouts only intensified to drown out his words. Oliver had been standing next to him with narrowed eyes, and it was he, by an act of respect or mere curiosity, that held up his hands and helped in silencing the crowd once more.

"Thank you, Doctor Emerson," Tytus said. They shared a glance. It appeared that the encouragement from Oliver kept him solid and provided him with enough constitution to continue. "Again, to believe me is your choice. I just ask that you please listen to what I have to say, and perhaps we can grow from this!"

"You put us here!"

"You won't let us grow!"

"Hang 'em both!"

The isolated shouts didn't carry enough weight, and Tytus powered through them. "It's a shame, really. My post is vacated, and not only am I replaced so quickly, but they also didn't bother leaving it up to the people of Roguewave. No, they brought in some Assembly pawn. One that would sooner wipe their five asses before challenging their dominion over our province."

He edged closer to the audience. Their undivided attention fueled his address. "I was too proud and naïve to understand the vision of Mathias Battier when he came to me with his concerns. All I can do now is admit that I am flawed and apologize. I was put in power as a political ploy. Nothing more. My family cared very little for me and very little for Roguewave, so they sent me away to lead this place. And I was only here to usher in whatever they wanted. If I recall correctly, in this stack of letters, with Assembly seals, there was an exchange between Grand Overseer Kearse and my father."

Tytus removed the stack of tightly pressed paper and displayed it for all to see, especially the acting governor, who whispered to his lieutenant. His message was then relayed to more soldiers below his rank, as he never left his master's side.

Tytus offered the papers to Oliver. The doctor's hands

trembled and went back and forth before he committed to them.

"I think we ought to get those letters to the printing press, don't you agree?" Tytus asked for all to hear. Any doubt of or reservations from the crowd no longer existed, as they were in full support of Oliver, Tytus, and their mission "Everyone needs to know what is transpiring in those tall buildings far away that govern their way of life. For in those letters, you'll find a sentence from our Grand Forerunner Lowden that declares he could 'care less if that province was put under the waves like its namesake. The best that could be done for it is to make it a channel to mass-produce undesirable goods.'"

The Cannon Fire Plot thickens. It's been a long road, but we are finally gaining traction.

Tytus had grown so fond of the attention that he shook hands with the crowd in the first couple of rows, making near-endless proclamations about how the Assembly would answer for all they had done.

As his momentum began to diminish, Oliver stepped back into the fray. "Let us not forget the great man who formulated these plans! A man who sought a better world with the opportunity for all to thrive and prosper. Let us not forget who sundered the East Flame Tow—"

A shocking clap made the mob drop low and cover their ears. People shrieked, and the shuffling crowd went into a panicked scramble as that gunshot ripped through the head of former governor Tytus.

Oliver stood petrified as blood and brain matter were spattered across his face and clothes.

The frantic citizens went in all directions as they tried to escape, and Jameson was sloshed around like a buoy in a tempest. He was forced to grapple and throw men that were trampling over women and children in their cowardice and fear.

To the untrained ear or those uninitiated with battle, the

origin of the shot would be unknown, but Jameson clocked that the gun fired at their back near the top of the governor's office. In the chaos, it was difficult to get a steady visual, but while holding men at bay, he saw movement from a window on the far end of the building on the top floor. The shadow, roughly a hundred yards away, drove his ramrod down the barrel of the rifle to ready another shot.

Jameson's head whipped back to Doctor Emerson, who was without a doubt the recipient. Cassel and the Assembly would want nothing more than to rid those against them. All this commotion and revelation could easily be dealt with if there was a little bit of damage control.

"Doctor! Doctor Emerson! Oliver!" Jameson tried everything to get Oliver's attention on his way to him as he fought the crowd. His yells fell on deaf ears, and Oliver did his best to aid Tytus, but nothing could be done.

A boulder of a man stampeded towards Jameson as he chucked a pair of women aside, and a child bounced off his frame and was driven into the crowd to be trampled.

As the lumbering man grew nearer, Jameson drove his boot into the man's knee, hyperextending it. The earth shook as he hit the ground, but with his dislocated knee and his overweight body, he wasn't getting up anytime soon.

Jameson forced his way to Oliver as chaos raged behind him. A woman and a young girl emerged from the lumber building to embrace the doctor.

Isla Battier?

However, a group of soldiers, ten and counting, including Cassel's lieutenant, were heading towards them. The soldiers noticed Jameson being the only one taking a position against them in the opening.

A seasoned vet, whose green coat had seen many years, squinted at him. "I'll be damned… It's Red Sand."

His delay rubbed off on his fellow soldiers as they failed to engage, aside from one.

A youthful greencoat of perhaps low wit and combat experience charged Jameson with his bayonet far out in front of him.

The vet attempted to call him back: "Rylee, no!"

Jameson grabbed the end of the rifle, ripped it from the greencoat's hands, and swung it like a club into his torso. He twirled it into a firing position like he'd practiced a million times before.

His movements in combat were second nature. Many traveling men, pirates, and sailors alike spoke many different languages. While that was true for him, a very slim few were as fluent in the language of combat as Jameson Roke.

The line of greencoats clenched and feared the potential of being the recipient of the shot. However, the rifle scanned past them and took aim at the window on the top floor of the provincial offices. He could just make out the silhouette of Tytus' shooter, but that was enough.

He pulled the trigger, and the musket traveled far.

The pause worried him.

Then, a rifle fell from the window, and a now-lifeless soldier dangled halfway out the frame.

Jameson's prized helm sabre with a gold guard and echo oak handle sang when unsheathed. It sang a song that whispered a chorus of cries from the lives extinguished by the blade.

The vet attempted to establish a firing line with the dozen or so troops around him, but their disorientation was too much to handle.

Should have fired when you had the chance.

Jameson burst into the fray, engaging all of them at once, choosing his target by who was readiest to fight. He slew the vet first, who parried his initial strike, but not the follow-up slash across the throat. He grabbed a handful of his hair, yanked back, and sprayed the blood into a pair of his companions' eyes. Those with sight stood very little chance against him; those with none stood zero.

Some greencoats attempted to get by him for a chance at Oliver, but that was their final decision. He fired his pistol from his hip into a soldier's spine while evading enemy stabs and slashes.

The bulk of his attention returned to the fight at hand as swords and bayonets whipped all around him. He was surrounded, but it was moments like these that separated him from others. In the madness of battle, he kept calm.

He spun out of the kill zone, driving the edge of his blade across the torso of a soldier along the way. The move freed him from his disadvantageous position and killed another adversary.

They were now angled in such a way that they had to fight around each other and take turns getting to him. He cut them down one by one, almost using the same move on each of them: a simple block and arm drag followed by a slash or stab to the side of the neck.

By the time he was done, all that remained was a line of horizontal bodies in a pool of each other's blood in the dirt. Jameson found himself between the provincial soldiers and rambunctious loyalists to Doctor Emerson. Both sides were strong in number as a stalemate had been reached until Cassel's lieutenant stepped out from the comfort of his crew.

"Lieutenant… Lieutenant… Lieutenant Sauloman, get back!" Cassel commanded. "The fighting must cease for now!"

Sauloman ignored his governor. "If it isn't the famed Jameson 'Red Sand' Roke. I see your reputation is well-earned. I tend to believe that legends and notoriety often get exaggerated. That doesn't appear to be the case with you, but I could be wrong."

Jameson raised a single brow. "You want to find out?"

"Lieutenant, this is insubordination! You are *not* to engage!"

The city grew quiet. Oliver clutched his wife and the Battier girl as he ushered them away from Tytus' body.

"So, now you're a pirate under the command of Marstellar Lockett," Sauloman said, spitting in Roke's direction. What a journey you must have been on. I have probably killed over three hundred pirates in my life. Most of which were turncoats like yourself." The lieutenant drew his blade and removed his coat for more dexterity. "I would love to add you, Mr. Roke, to my list of slain pirates. Perhaps I'll put your sword or your skull on display."

Sauloman leaned forward and charged, keeping the tip of his blade pointed but tucked in close to his body.

Jameson waited… waited… waited… and pivoted off the center line at the last moment, barely tapping the edge of his opponent's blade to throw him off balance with the forward momentum. The lieutenant stumbled past him as Jameson swung down, slicing into the man's spine.

Sauloman halted, arched his back, and screamed into the night sky.

Jameson's next slash ran along the back of his knees, effectively cutting the tendons in his legs. Jameson ended Sauloman's misery by taking the end of his blade and driving it down behind the lieutenant's clavicle to the pommel.

The gasps only grew louder as Jameson removed the sword. Blood shot high from the wound, adding to the scarlet pool around him.

The city market and thoroughfare fell to a hush. No more soldiers engaged Jameson, even ones with rifles. The governor no longer wanted to address the people, for they were done listening to him. All eyes were on Jameson, who casually cleaned his blade and walked back toward Oliver Emerson.

"Perhaps you can retake the floor, Doctor?"

Oliver stepped forward. Jameson made eye contact with

the youngest Battier girl and nodded to acknowledge Isla before addressing Livian: "Can you inform her that I won't let anything happen to her? I promise."

Livian relayed the message, but it didn't appear necessary, for the girl seemed to read his lips.

"She believes you," Livian replied.

He looked into her eyes as she keyed in on his mouth. "Eddison is safe. You will be together again soon."

She kept her composure, but tears spilled down her cheeks regardless. He squeezed her shoulder and nodded once more, hoping it would comfort her at the very least.

"Ladies and gentlemen," Oliver said, climbing the steps of the stockade to attain some order. "This cannot stand! We, the people of Roguewave, should have the authority to decide what happens here, not some group of overseers far off! We elect our officials! Not this pawn!" Cheers sounded from all around with Oliver's unsubtle point at Cassel. "If reparations cannot be found by way of financial compensation and a new, *elected* official, I motion that drastic measures take place! I love this place and this community too much to let it further fall into poverty and ruin! Prepare for the fight to come, my citizens! For our secession is on the horizon!"

FORTY-FOUR
SHARKEYES VII

They traveled west into the heart of the vast Skiatation Mountains. She followed the resistance of Trezbe warriors on narrow trails. So narrow that, in some areas, it was only passable by a width of two horses. Her grandmother, Eralia, was still recovering. While Avery rode next to her aunt, Eralia slept in one of the wagons, getting her much-needed rest.

"You know, I always wanted to hate your father," Ianthia said unprompted.

"Excuse me?" Avery replied.

"Thought he was just another colonizer attempting to come to take our land and force us into submission. I didn't know him well, but he certainly wasn't that. I was with Adelaide when we first met him as he wore his pristine emerald coat and oddly-shaped hat that looked to have never seen the sun. Their attire was horrid for this climate, but they wore it, nevertheless. Anyway, I saw the way he looked at her, and I saw the way she returned his gaze. Whatever they shared was instant."

Avery just nodded. The jagged rocks on both sides of her ascended to the sun. Even in this heat, the summits were caked in snow.

"Have you been to the top?" Avery asked.

Ianthia smiled. "I have."

A cold but welcome breeze cut through the pass. The sensation of the heat being lifted for the first time was fantastic. Avery tilted her chin in the air and basked in the cool air.

"It's part of a ceremony to travel to the top of the highest of the Skiatation Mountains, the tallest being Mount Calibre."

"What's the ritual?"

"Let me ask you something, Avery. If you were to have anything in life, aside from being together with your family again, what would it be?"

All I want is my family together. I want my mother and father. I want my brothers and sister.

"I see the way you wear those tre-axes around your waist," Ianthia said. "They look as if they belong there. So, I'll ask you again. What do you desire most in this world?"

Avery thought about it as she looked back to see the rows and rows of Trezbe people following behind them. They rotated on and off horseback to give weary legs a break. There was no selfishness or hate among them. Everyone was in it together.

"I want no limitations," Avery said. The smile on her aunt's face remained. "I want to live as I want, not the way someone else tells me."

"Well, then you're in welcome company, Avery. I believe if you asked any of the Trezbe people what they wanted, they would reply with something similar. However, they may add something more."

"What do you mean?"

There was a pause. The horse hooves clicked as the sand filtered away, and the hard surface of the mountain's base made its presence known.

"These people – my people have had everything taken from them for reasons we don't even know. I shouldn't have to tell you what that feeling is like." Avery nodded and squeezed her fists over and over. "If you were given the option to address those who cast your family out, how would you respond?"

Avery had introspected enough to know she had been through a lot in a short period of time, and she contemplated the question and thought about her persecutors, who were the same in the only two homes she had ever had. Anger was all she felt.

"I would respond violently," Avery answered.

Ianthia nodded. "Good."

"Can you show me?"

"Show you what?"

"How to beat them?"

Ianthia dipped her head. "I can show you. But you must find what lies ahead. The Keewaul awaits you."

The snowfall from the mountain formed a steady creek that flowed through the adolescent camp. Ianthia's resistance made use of the many caves on the interior of the mountains. Small campfires smoldered at the cave mouths where wounded warriors mended their wounds.

The arrival of the returning Trezbe people seemed to rejuvenate the camp. Family members, young and old, found each other once more. Tears of happiness and joy followed longing hugs.

The focus shifted to Avery as she walked in Ianthia's shadow. There were countless double-takes by the clan of the mountains.

"What are they staring at?" Avery's question fell on deaf ears.

A man wearing the hide of a lion draped over his head and shoulders emerged from a large tent. The mane was thick and tapered down his spine. The paws acted as pauldrons as the clawed thrashers stuck out sharp and primal. Tre-axes dangled from his side, like everyone else. However, this man had an additional pair of sharpened tusks that were forged into knives from the lion's elongated canines.

He approached Ianthia. There was tension in the air between the two of them that Avery picked up on.

He placed a single hand on Ianthia's arm. "Are you okay?" he asked.

Her aunt's prowess made her one of the most intimidating people Avery had come across. But the woman she looked upon gave way to his comfort ever so slightly. "We lost sixteen," she replied.

His face fell, but his focus remained on Ianthia. He kept her gaze for a few moments more until he looked at Avery, noticing her for the first time even though she was only a foot away.

Ianthia cleared her throat. "This is my niece, Avery— Adelaide's eldest daughter."

He placed his hand over his heart with a closed fist and bowed. "It is nice to meet you for the first time. I will say you bear a resemblance to your mother, as well as Ianthia."

"Thank you," she replied, having heard that enough times already.

"Avery, this is Lozi," Ianthia said. "My soon-to-be."

Soon-to-be?

"What's that mean?" Avery asked.

"He will be my husband."

"Does that mean he'll be the tarquin now?" Avery watched Ianthia's eyes soften and her cheeks flush. "I-I'm sorry. I didn't mean to speak so abruptly."

"It's all right, Avery," Ianthia said.

"What happened to Tarquin Alexious?" Lozi asked with wide eyes. "Ianthia, what happened to your father?"

Night in the camp was cold. Avery hated it. She glanced straight up at the summit of Mount Calibre, which was shrouded in clouds.

She opened the flap into her grandmother's tent, and there Eralia lay, weakened but awake. "Hello, dear," she said with renewed enthusiasm upon seeing Avery.

"Hello, Grandmother. How are you feeling?"

"I'm a little weak, but that's not new to an old woman like me. I must say, though-" She hacked out a cough that rattled her frame. "I must say that slaying Colbe made me feel young again." She smiled and stared at the animal skin above her head that made up the tent. "Alexious would've said that the world is better without a man like Lieutenant Colbe in it."

Avery smiled. "I think he's right."

Sadness came over her, and Earlia took notice. "What's wrong, dear?"

"I'm sorry about Grandfather. And I'm sorry for not saying that sooner. I-I was just…"

"Angry?" Eralia finished her sentence.

Although she didn't want to admit that her reasoning was that simple, she did, nevertheless.

"It's okay, Avery," her grandmother said. "Alexious was a good and righteous man who deserved to be our leader. He lived a life that was full and gave me two sensational daughters. Without him, I wouldn't have gotten you. I loved him. I will never move on from him. I shall never allow a day to go by where I don't thank him for being mine. But if we Trezbes are going to adapt and drive out our oppressors, we must do so quickly, for we don't have the luxury to mourn, for that too has been taken from us. Don't you see, Avery? The more they choose violence against us, the more they drive us away, and the more they reveal themselves for what they are.

What they are is evil. And our uprising against them is justified."

Avery thought about her grandmother's words and didn't find herself disagreeing with any of them.

"Grandmother, can I ask you something?"

"Of course, dear," Eralia said.

"Did Mother ever climb to the top of Mount Calibre?" she asked with her gaze returning to the summit.

Eralia cocked her head to the side and looked off as if she was trying to remember. It took her a moment. "No, she left with Mathias before she was able to."

Avery nodded. "Aunt Ianthia told me of a Trezbe ritual that takes place at the top of the mountain. A ritual Trezbe warriors take for a reason she wouldn't tell me."

"She can't tell you," Eralia said.

"Why not?" Avery replied, frustrated.

"Because whatever awaits you at the top of the mountain is unique to you and you alone. It could offer you wisdom, answers, abilities, or nothing at all, but it's yours."

The curiosity overwhelmed her. "I'm going to make the climb."

Eralia just nodded, and silence remained between them. Avery awaited her grandmother's reply.

"Are you expecting me to talk you out of it?" Eralia said with a smile. "Avery, after everything you've been through, I'm never going to command you to do anything. I'll give you my thoughts and advice, however worthy they are. In the end, here, you are free, and you can do what you desire. Just don't forget who's attempting to take that away from you."

I never will.

Avery stood at the base of Mount Calibre. The ascent would be made alone, and that didn't bother her. She was used to relying on herself by now. A path, narrow and seldom traversed, ran up the mountain. One foot in front of the other was the only way to climb. There was no cheating the mountain, for it would always remain tall and unchanged.

Ianthia offered no secrets for reaching the summit. There weren't any. The only way to find something within herself was to keep going through the pain and the fatigue, to keep climbing.

"Are you sure you want to do this?" Ianthia asked her.

There was never a second thought. "Yes," Avery replied.

The hundreds of Trezbe people stayed near the caves, giving Avery her distance and respect for the journey ahead, but watching, nevertheless.

"Are you afraid?" Ianthia asked, tightening her braids.

"Should I be?"

Ianthia cracked her neck and shoulders. "This is your vision quest. Whatever is up there, good, evil, something in between, it lies in wait for you."

Avery looked back at the Trezbe warriors, including her grandmother and Lozi, who all had their dominant hand over their hearts, paying their respects for her journey.

Ianthia threw a sack of food and waterskin over Avery's shoulder. "The higher you get, the colder it will be. Take this as well." She removed her blue robes that were the color of the sky on a clear day with no worry. Patterns and a variety of colors were sewn onto its soft texture. At night, many of the Trezbe people wore their robes.

"Thank you," Avery said, running her hand along the fabric. It was a satisfying feeling, rubbing it continuously. A warmth and comfort came over her as if she was touching the history and memories of Trezbe culture.

"Don't eat the snow," her aunt instructed. "Wait until it melts in your waterskin before consuming it. It's safer for you that way."

Ianthia didn't explain why that was the case, but Avery intended to listen to her either way.

Ianthia grabbed her behind the neck. "You look so much like my sister."

"That means I look like you," Avery pointed out.

Ianthia laughed. "Yes, that's true."

Avery smiled. But her gaze shifted to the mountain, for her journey was about to begin.

~

If she'd known the trek up the mountain would take weeks, she'd have had second thoughts. Without knowing all the details, she committed herself to see it through.

One step at a time.

~

By the eighth day, her rations had significantly diminished. The arrangement of local nuts and berries all but disappeared. She started to crave the dry goat meat saved for last. But the nourishment of the small portions left her wanting. The only saving grace was that the more she ate and drank, the lighter her baggage became. But the air grew thicker, and her breathing was labored.

The summit was within her grasp but looks could be deceiving on the mountain. Avery didn't know if the rest of her journey would only be a few hours or days.

She took a break on a rock and decided to put to practice some of her aunt's advice. Avery crammed some of the crunchy snow into her waterskin and shook it hard in an attempt to accelerate the melting process. Since arriving in Autera, she had lost some muscle in her legs. However, after this journey, she might have recovered what she lost.

On the tenth day, her spirit was beginning to wilt. Not break, but wilt. Her travel time slowed, but she kept moving.

One step at a time.

She did her best not to admit she might have been in over her head on this journey. However, she took the stance that if others had done this, she could very well see it through to the end.

I am Avery Battier.

The bottoms of her feet were blistered and bloodied. She wrapped them as best she could, but the sweat inside her boots dampened the bandages and didn't help matters as they made her skin soft. So much skin on her heels and ankles peeled off, leaving what lay beneath exposed.

But Avery was forced to persevere.

She had stared at the ground for so long, taking her one step at a time, that she didn't realize the ground had begun to level. The summit was blanketed white. Avery looked out, circling the horizon, and all she saw were the tops of the surrounding mountains poking out of the clouds. The wind whipped a cold breeze so hard it felt like she was constantly being splashed with ice-cold water. Snow drifted off the mountainside and flew all around her, a forever blizzard.

She had to cover her face with the robe gifted by Ianthia so that she could see ahead of her. Creeping through the white veil of twirling snow were two torches planted in the ground, unwavering by the harsh gusts of winds. Nothing else resided on the summit aside from the torches.

There has to be more.

She stood there, waiting for something to happen.

Why in the bloody hell would you need torches up here?

Avery stood in the cold, wondering what to do. The only heat to comfort her was derived from her anger. *All of this for nothing. What if I am to find nothing? What if this bloody mountain can't even offer me anything? Or answer my questions?*

Bones and skin and heart brittle, Avery dropped to her knees and screamed. Her initial roar was long and deep. The countless ones that followed were not as impactful, but she kept doing it as if the yelling would make it all disappear. It didn't.

In her state of malnourishment, even on her knees, she became lightheaded. Avery fell forward, and luckily, she was able to catch herself before being forced to eat the snow for the first time.

"Father, Mother, I miss you both so much." Her fingers stung from the icy snow. She didn't even realize she uttered her words out loud until she thought about it. She was used to being on her own, but now, Avery just wanted to be with her family.

She heard the puffing sound of an igniting flame next to her. The twin torches lit, wavering blue flames illuminated the grayness of the summit.

The winds of the blizzard died all at once, and a voice in her mind said, *"Step forward, Avery Battier. Come into the light."*

Avery rose out of fear or obedience to this voice she didn't even know. "Who are you?" she replied aloud.

"I am nothing. I am everything. I am here with you now. And I am not."

"I don't know what that means."

The voice did not reply.

"How do you know my name?" she asked.

"You want everyone to know your name."

Avery grew frustrated. "I don't care if people know my name or not."

"You wish to command vast forces. You wish the people that follow you to know you as a friend and as family. You desire your enemies to know you as their pending destruction. Avery Battier, I know."

More heat exhaled through her nostrils, for this voice, no matter how hard she wanted to deny it, was correct.

"How can I achieve what I want?" she asked.

"How did you scale this mountain? Was it not one step at a time? A vast journey lies ahead of you. One of loss and triumph. However, it's all up to you whether you prevail or fail."

"I made this journey so I can prevail. Have I wasted my time?"

"Perhaps. It's not my decision to see you victorious. It's yours. I alone cannot make you succeed."

Then, the snow swirled around her, confining her in a cylinder of white. But it wasn't cold. It was rather warm and comforting.

"I can show a glimpse of what waits ahead of you. But first, remove your tre-axes. They are not needed here. Throw them into the snow."

The last thing Avery wanted to do was surrender her weapons, even if it was only to a voice. But, as the presence made her feel safe and content, she felt less afraid about parting with the axes. She removed them from her belt and tossed them through the blizzard.

The snow closed in on her, and the isolated storm made her feel like she was floating. Her mind drifted. She struggled to keep her eyes open. Visions came to her, revealing themselves as if they were taking place in front of her.

She saw her father, stoic, brave, and emotionless as he stood with one foot planted atop the railing of a small raft as he faced off against the entire Unified Provincial Navy. His undersized boat swayed to and fro from the ocean waves. The gunports of the armada opened, and thousands of cannons were aimed in his direction. They all fired and found their mark, and her father, with his wavy auburn hair, ceased to exist.

A new vision manifested about her mother. A space in a void, with the absence of light. Giants surrounded her as she clung to the lifeless body of a shrouded person Avery did not recognize. Her mother's dangling head eventually rose and revealed her pale face. Avery watched her mouth growl like a predator and revealed her sharp canines with blood trickling down.

The dark dissipated, and a hue of blue overpowered the space. Avery was transported to the turret of a vast and ancient castle, like one of the many ruined castles across the Unified Provinces but restored to its former glory. Only the surrounding landscape of this castle was black and surrounded by an endless forest of mangled and jagged trees. At the top, alone, was her youngest brother Eddie. He was covering his eyes and crying out in pain, but no sound left his mouth. His flesh dissolved from his body, revealing the bones underneath his skin. Eddie clenched his fist, uncovered his eyes, and screamed a horrid scream that would keep Avery awake at night for the next few days. His eyes flickered with a green and black flame that almost distracted her from his skeletal frame.

A ghost-like mass whipped past her, and Avery was no longer in a new location or a castle. She was back in Roguewave, walking the streets of the markets, watching greencoats hide behind fruit stands, in stores, and in the bay. They were all actively running from something that terrified them. She watched as a specter hunted down the soldiers in their hiding places and killed every last one of them. The ghost floated above the ground, satisfied with its work, and Avery looked at its face and saw Isla's features taking form.

A cannon went off from deep in Molten Bay. Avery was transported to the deck of a Grand Ship. She looked out over the water and was now a part of the armada that fired upon her father. From this perspective, she saw his raft afloat half a mile away.

"Fire!" a familiar voice yelled.

On the main deck, she saw her eldest brother Xavier commanding this endless fleet. The cannons fired, and her father was wiped from existence. Xavier wore an emotionless face as he walked down the steps and made his way to the quarterdeck, where four prisoners with face covers stood. They were bound with two cannonballs chained to their feet. Xavier signaled one of his men to remove the bags over their heads, and Avery recognized all their faces. It was Caldwell and his three best friends, Emil, Fili, and Maynard.

Xavier gave a follow-up signal, and Caldwell's friends, one after the other, were shoved backward, over the railing into the ocean, presumably to sink to the bottom. They stopped when they got to Caldwell. Xavier waved his men away. He stepped close, face to face with Caldwell.

"Goodbye, brother," Xavier said before kicking him backward himself.

Avery yelled, but no one heard her. Then the visions faded altogether, and she was back on the summit on her knees, breathing heavily.

"I-I don't understand," Avery said.

"It's hard to interpret or comprehend what is unknown."

"That didn't tell me anything. I have no answers or guidance on what to do next."

"You don't? If that's true, don't bother reaching for your axes, then. Let them be covered forever by the snow and move on from this place. You know what must be done. You're still putting the pieces together, but you know, and you know how to do it."

Avery stood there, thinking about her family. The blizzard was gone. The cold was gone. It was simply her and her thoughts. For several minutes she stood still with snow covering her boots.

"I know what must be done," she said eventually.

"What must be done?"

"Horror will further befall my family if something isn't done. Horror will befall the clans if something isn't done. I will make sure something is done."

"What will that be?"

"Unite all the clans and people that call the Assembly enemies. And through blizzards, tempests, tornados, raging wildfires, armies, or even monsters, I will find a way back to my family and bring us all together again. And I will destroy the Assembly—its members, its buildings, its monuments. It will all come crumbling to the ground. The forces I'll build and unite will make it so."

There wasn't an immediate reply. Avery had a vast array of emotions flow through her, but the one that she felt more than the others was satisfaction. She didn't question her purpose.

"Good."

A jolt of determination flowed through her, and she went to retrieve her axes.

"No," the voice told her.

"What do you mean?" Avery asked. "I have to get my weapons."

"So, reach out and take them."

Avery was confused and continued to walk forward as they were about thirty feet away. She didn't realize she had tossed them that far.

"No," the voice said again. *"Reach out. Take them."*

Avery extended her arms, opened her hands, and without much thought at all, her inherited axes leaped from the snow, flew through the air, and landed perfectly in her palm. Power flowed through her, and she smiled.

FORTY-FIVE
THE WIDOW VIII

Not a single good night of rest had found her since the raid on Molten Bay. Adelaide found herself waking to the images of her children dying from waves crashing down on them. Regret and sadness of the unknown impacted her soul as she remembered leaving Eddie behind. She often wondered how foolish she could be by sending him off with pirates. If it hadn't been for her husband's assurance that many pirates were not the vile creatures the papers made them out to be, she would have never done such a thing.

Whimpering awoke her. The sound merged between dream and reality. It was a phenomenon she was familiar with, as her children – Eddie, in particular – woke her and her husband many nights due to a bad dream.

Adelaide peeled the covers off her and lit a candle on the nightstand beside her bed. She felt guilty that she was able to sleep in a comfortable bed while her children most likely were not.

She crept down the long hallway with her candle in hand. The flame was enough to light up the wood floor and show the details of the paintings lining the walls. With each step, the whimpering got louder. Two doors down from her room were one of the parlors that seemed to go unused most of the time.

The door was cracked open. Had it been closed, the crying probably wouldn't have awakened her. There was a slight creak in the hinge as she peeked in at Charlotte curled in a ball on the lounge sofa, crying into her elbow. The ray of yellowish moonlight shone on her back and cast her large shadow on the opposite wall.

Even with the sound of the door, Adelaide appeared to go unnoticed. She contemplated going back to her room and leaving Charlotte to herself, but given the circumstances, it didn't seem right.

"Charlotte?" Adelaide asked.

A few sniffles followed as the lady of the estate wiped her nose and eyes. Then, she turned and tucked her head away from Adelaide.

"Is everything all right?" Adelaide probed.

Another sniffle. "Oh… peachy." Charlotte used a handkerchief to blow her nose. "Did you need something?"

"No, I just heard crying is all. Thought I'd see if I could help."

"Help? Why would you help anyone here? Especially me?" Charlotte said, but there was none of the usual bite to her words. "I own you. I'm the last person you should want to help."

Adelaide moved on. "My youngest, Eddison, used to sneak into my room at night and crawl into my bed. He used to tiptoe and gently lift the covers so I wouldn't hear him. Because he was afraid that if I caught him, I would send him back to his room with his brothers."

"Did you ever? Send him back to his room?" Charlotte asked while stretching her neck and rolling her shoulders.

"When my husband was home, Mathias would get up and escort him back and sit on the edge of the bed until he fell asleep. He was a patient man…" Adelaide daydreamed about her husband for a moment. Perhaps it was the grogginess of the middle of the night that made it so easy to fade away. "However, when he was away on duty, and Eddison would sneak into the room, I always knew he was there. But I would let him stay anyway."

"Why?"

"Because he needed someone there. And so did I."

Adelaide placed the candle on the tea table next to the sofa as she sat on the end by Charlotte's feet. Gently, she took the lady's hands and held them both.

Charlotte raised her head, and her purple face was revealed. Her left eye was practically sealed shut from her puffed brow.

Adelaide knew the culprit, but she asked anyway. "Did Barton do this to you?"

Charlotte nodded.

"Why?"

Charlotte whispered when she talked. It seemed she was afraid. "He's an angry man. The fact of the matter is I can't have children. And I think he believes that's somehow going to change."

Adelaide rubbed her fingers across the back of Charlotte's knuckles and said, "I'm sorry."

"I think it's a blessing in disguise. I wouldn't want to bring a child into this world with him by my side. If he'd do this to me, he'd do it to them as well."

"Why don't you leave? Leave him and this place behind."

Charlotte scoffed. "I can't leave this place. I can only leave if he gets rid of me."

They sat there for around half an hour. Adelaide held her hands the entire time.

"Did Mathias ever raise a hand to you?" Charlotte whispered in the quiet.

"No," Adelaide replied. "Never. Men who do such things are not true men. And those are my husband's words."

Charlotte smiled. "He was a good man. I still hate you for stealing him from me."

There was some truth in her sarcastic comment. But Adelaide didn't hold it against her. She understood.

"How much time does your husband put into the estate?" Adelaide asked.

"Beg your pardon?"

"The day-to-day operation – how much is he involved?"

Charlotte cocked her head. "Less and less every day. He mostly just leaves the work to Groundskeeper Ulrick now so he can travel to duels and tournaments around the country."

Adelaide nodded as she contemplated a great many things.

"What are you thinking?" Charlotte asked.

"I'm not sure yet."

Adelaide was too new on the estate to have everyone follow her lead on the plan she concocted. It would take time to convince her fellow laborers. She hoped Christoph would be her secret weapon. He knew everybody, and everybody knew him. There wasn't a soul on the estate that didn't like him, including the estate guards.

Christoph showed reservations about her potential plan as he reminded Adelaide that Barton had saved his life. That small piece of trivia only added to the dilemma.

Adelaide was in the process of cleaning the master bedroom as dusk approached.

There was a crash from downstairs.

She made her way to the staircase to see what had happened.

Standing in the foyer was Barton. He had dropped a glass from the bar. Thousands of tiny shards were scattered across the floor. He paid no attention and was already filling another one with dark alcohol. As he stood, he teetered and couldn't stand up straight.

How much has he had to drink already?

"Charlotte!" he yelled. "Charlotte! Charl—"

Barton took another drink. The foyer bar was a small alcove that housed a variety of bottles in front of Lord Hannah's face. Every type of alcohol anyone should need was there. And Barton was taking advantage of it.

"Where are ya! Come here imm-ediately, at once, now!" he said, slurring his words.

"Can I help you, Lord Hannah?" Adelaide asked.

He cranked his neck back and looked at her with droopy eyes. "Fetch my wife for me."

"She's resting, sir," Adelaide lied. "The fall she had took a lot out of her."

"Ah, yes. The fall." Barton took another drink. He looked at the label on the bottle for a long while before saying, "Go wake her up, or she'll *fall* again."

She stared daggers at him, for they both knew what he meant.

"Yes, honey?" Charlotte said, rounding the corner from the parlor.

Barton finally broke his gaze with Adelaide. "Where have you been?" he demanded, flaring his nostrils.

Her eye looked better. Charlotte had informed Adelaide that she could at least see out of it again. "I've been helping the ladies finalize dinner preparations."

Barton grabbed her dress and pulled her in close. His face became a dark shade of red. "Don't you lie to me!"

Charlotte turned her face away from him as if she couldn't stand the sight of her husband. "I'm not lying, honey, I swear."

Adelaide could almost see the steam rise off his drunken head and shoulders. "She's telling the truth, Lord Hannah," she piped in.

Barton let Charlotte go and focused his attention on Adelaide, marching towards her. "I will not have you lie for her after all the strings I pulled to get you here. You would be rotting away in Colwerth Prison, eating a slice of bread and a handful of flavorless beans if it weren't for me." He pointed to Charlotte. "She may have wanted you here, but make no mistake, it was only so she could belittle the woman that stole her husband!"

Charlotte slumped. Her slouched posture would only cause her more pain before too long. She had lost the strength to manage her abusive husband.

"Isn't it ironic, Battier, that all Charlotte wanted was a family with your husband? All the while, Mathias chose you and had five children, who I'm sure are beautiful. And yet, she can't even give me one! No children to carry on my name! How cruel is that? Fifty thousand gold I had to shell out for you to make this woman I call *wife* happy. Yet, she cannot do the same for me."

Charlotte reached out for his arm. "Honey, I am so, so—"

Her apology was cut short by a backhand that knocked her down. She began to weep as she covered her face.

Barton finished off the glass he was still holding, put it on the table, and stood over Charlotte. He grabbed her dress and hoisted her off the ground.

"Give me a son!" Barton roared in her face. It was so loud that his vocal cords were straining. "Give me a son!"

He went to slap her again, but Adelaide would not let that stand. She hooked his arm and tossed him backward over her hip.

In his drunken state, it took a moment to find his footing. However, he had the advantage of having a sword, dagger, and pistol on his hip.

Adelaide rushed to the noblewoman. "Charlotte, run and go get Christoph. Tell him it must be now!"

"What has to be now?" Charlotte asked as Adelaide helped her to her feet.

"Just tell him!"

Barton charged. He ducked his head and ran Adelaide into the alcove. Glass shattered on her back, and she could feel the slices in her skin.

She brought her elbow down on the back of his neck. Barton pulled away, stumbling while he did. He removed his sword and swung wildly. All Adelaide could do was evade, even with the shards of glass protruding from her tricep. She ducked when he swung high. She pivoted when he went for a thrust. Her head was spinning with what to do. For now, she was just keeping her distance.

With the commotion, Adelaide was worried the estate guards were going to show up and detain her, possibly leaving her open for Barton to kill her immediately.

He went for an arching swing, and she slid to the side, dodging it. She clasped her hands together and slammed them down on his wrist and disarmed him. Adelaide went for his sheathed dagger across his back, but his offhand punched her face and knocked her backward.

He charged at her once more, but she closed the distance on him, scissored his legs, and used his momentum to propel him forward into the wall. His face smashed into the door trim, and he left a bloody stain behind as his nose busted.

Adelaide was still rusty when it came to combat because she failed to realize that his disarmed sword was at his feet. Barton blew blood out his nostrils, picked up his sword, and started swinging again.

As Adelaide stayed at the end of his sword, she rushed to the alcove and grabbed one of the broken liquor bottles. It wasn't much, but its sharp edges could come in handy if Barton got closer, and that was what she was counting on.

Either foolishly or drunkenly, Barton went for another thrust. Adelaide slid again, just a bit, to let the blade pass under her arm. As she locked both of his arms in place, between her bicep and torso, she stabbed him in the shoulder with the broken bottle. His face reddened like a beet.

She reached for his dagger once more. At the same time, he pushed her away.

Her grip found purchase on the handle and removed it from the sheath. Barton's push rotated her, so as she turned to face him, he was already taking aim with his pistol.

Adelaide had no choice. She couldn't cover the distance in time, and if she did, it would only give him a better shot.

In a last-ditch effort, she spun the dagger in her hand and grasped it by the blade tip. Barton had his shot ready, and Adelaide had her throw. She reared back and followed through. The blade rotated as it left her fingertips.

The booming sound of the gun went off, and pain bloomed in her arm.

She fell back against the wall, covering her wound. But she got the better of the exchange.

Barton's dagger was embedded in his heart as smoke filled the room.

She didn't notice the chaos until she walked out the front door. It had begun. Her plan was working.

The slaves outnumbered the estate guards ten to one. A battle was taking place, and her side was winning. It was rakes, shovels, and scythes versus swords and guns.

A few of the laborers fell to the gunfire. But there were too many of them, and the guards were not a cohesive fighting unit, merely hired hands. They were scattered, easy targets for the slaves.

A fire seemed to have ignited in the northwestern wheat field. Adelaide had no idea how it started, but they needed it extinguished. She ran for it. The pounding of horse hooves rumbled behind her. An estate guard rode toward her with his bayonet ready to drive through her back.

The guard closed in, and she had nowhere to go, nowhere to hide or duck behind. If it wasn't for a last-second shot that saw the guard tumble off his horse, that would've been it for her.

Adelaide turned to look where the shot had come from and saw smoke leaving the end of Christoph's rifle with Charlotte at his side.

Adelaide was overwhelmed with thanks she wanted to shower him with, but there was no time.

"We have to get the fire out!" she told him.

He turned his head, noticing it for the first time. He whistled to a few nearby laborers of unknown origin standing over the bodies of a pair of guards they killed.

"To the fields!" Christoph ordered.

Those men gathered more people to assist in putting out the fire.

Christoph approached, reloading his rifle. "Are you all right, darlin'?" he asked.

"Is it done?" Charlotte asked. Her question seemed the more important of the two.

Adelaide didn't know how to answer, so she just nodded, unsure what sort of reaction she was going to get.

Only one tear fell from Charlotte. That was all the emotion she seemed to want to give the man she called husband. She wiped it away and returned Adelaide's nod. She didn't say thank you or offer any gratitude, but that didn't bother Adelaide. *Perhaps the wound is too fresh.* Besides, Adelaide was used to having the thankless job of being a mother, anyway.

Something caught Christoph's eye. Adelaide turned to see a wagon of at least two guards riding as fast as they could away from the estate. They were at least a hundred yards away and only getting farther.

"Where is the next closest estate?" Adelaide asked.

"Uh, uh, the Woodes Estate," Charlotte replied. "To the south."

"That's where they're most likely going," Christoph said.

Adelaide turned to her albino friend. "If they get to the next estate, they'll tell what happened here. We also need to control that fire or neighboring scouts will be dispatched here."

Christoph moved past her. "I understand. I'll see to it, boss. Commander? Captain? Do I call you one of those now?" he asked with a smile.

"Adelaide's fine."

"Not very formal, but all right. I'll take a few men to pursue. You get that arm looked at, understand?"

"Very well," Adelaide said. "Good luck, river runner."

Christoph ran and mounted a nearby horse. He rode off, chasing down the wagon and commanding others to follow him.

The fields turned into violent crashing waves of blazing red and orange. The heat from the fire was constricting, but as her lungs swelled, the endorphins of victory and epiphany rushed through her.

Like the fire they started, the laborers engulfed their estate overlords, wielding agriculture tools and stolen weapons. The battlefield stretched across the vast acreage in all directions. Isolated skirmishes peppered the plains that swayed profoundly in the laborer's favor.

Smoke continued to rise along with the hands of victory. Their wages were so minimal that the prospect of now having none did not deter their enthusiasm. They hugged one another and shed tears of freedom, even if only temporarily. Their contracts were broken, and their wilted spirit found new hope.

Two hands grasped her arm.

"Let's get this wrapped up," Charlotte said.

It was the first time Adelaide had looked at her wound and saw the blood that covered her entire arm. The shot Barton hit her with appeared only to be a grazing blow, which was the best-case scenario other than not getting hit at all.

Charlotte grabbed her hand and clenched it tight.

"You might not want to go into the house anytime soon," Adelaide said to her so she wouldn't see her now late husband with a dagger in his heart.

Charlotte nodded.

"What do you plan on doing next?"

Charlotte looked around. Her mind was thinking, but Adelaide had no idea what it might be. "I plan on seeing whatever you have through." Charlotte gave a reluctant smile. "Even if I haven't concluded whether I like you or not."

"I do not try to win people over. I am what I am."

Charlotte didn't reply. She covered Adelaide's wound with her hand and walked her to one of the side entrances of the estate. To get there, they would have to walk past the front entrance where Barton lay. And as they did, Adelaide watched as Charlotte kept her eyes forward and never looked back.

My plan… My husband wanted revolution. I shall carry it out in his name.

The name of Battier.

ABOUT THE AUTHOR

C.J. Caughman is an author from Tulsa, Oklahoma, who has been obsessed with storytelling since childhood. As an avid consumer of books, movies, and television, it took him a long time to realize crafting narratives was his passion. He began cultivating his enthusiasm for writing at the University of Central Oklahoma, where he graduated with a degree in English-Creative Writing. In college, he focused on writing short stories, screenplays, and eventually novels. Several of his short stories went on to receive publication in various literary magazines. C.J. was a quarterfinalist in the 2019 Final Draft Big Break Contest and is a proud member of the Cherokee Nation Tribe and their Cherokee Nation Film Office.

TO THE READER

Dear Readers,

Thank you from the bottom of my heart for purchasing and reading my novel. Your support means the world to me and is the driving force that allows me to continue the Battiers' story. I hope you enjoyed the journey as much as I loved creating it.

If you found yourself immersed in the world of the Battiers, I would be incredibly grateful if you could take a moment to leave a review on Amazon. Your feedback not only helps other readers discover the book but also inspires and motivates me to keep writing.

Thank you once again for your support and for being a part of this adventure. Your encouragement is what makes this journey possible.

Warmest regards,

C.J.